A DIFFERENT MAN

by

Mary Yungeberg

Mary Y ☺
Have fun with
the continuing
story!

First published in USA in 2017 by
Mary Yungeberg

Nicholas Guilak cover photo by Bjoern Kommerell
Cover design by Mirna Gilman, BooksGoSocial
nicholasguilak.com and BooksGoSocial.com

ISBN-10: 1987553209
ISBN-13: 97-81987553208

ACKNOWLEDGEMENTS

First, I must express my heartfelt thanks to Nicholas Guilak. Your continuing support of this project is much appreciated. No one could better portray Rowan Milani on the cover of my thrillers. In addition, your insight and analysis always improves the story.

Brian Schell, you are an editor extraordinaire. I love your wit, patience, and ability to see the larger plot points as well as the finer details of a story. For anyone who needs an editor, I cannot recommend Brian highly enough. He may be reached at www.brianschell.com.

Thank you Janet McGregor for your sharp-as-a-tack proofreading abilities and your encouragement. Never fear, we will arrange that ride in the Mustang with the top down.

Huge thanks to Arnie Miller for my author image. Check out his work at amlenscreations.daportfolio.com.

While researching *Consummate Betrayal, Unholy Retribution* and *A Different Man,* I have made many wonderful friends in the military, counter-terrorism and law enforcement communities. I treasure each and every one of you and am beyond grateful for your generous assistance.

To my husband Ernie – thanks again, honey. Your support means everything. To my family and many friends who continually offer enthusiastic encouragement – thanks so much. You all probably have no idea how much you mean to me.

A DIFFERENT MAN

There is no grief like the grief that does not speak.

--Henry Wadsworth Longfellow

CHAPTER ONE

Mid-May
Tora Prison, Cairo, Egypt

Rowan Milani prowled the two-by-two-meter cell. He rubbed his nose and eyes, desperate to escape the raw sewage stench, but it lay like low fog over everything in Tora, residing deep in his sinuses and burning in his eyes. He bent over and coughed, deep, hard, and painful, then peered at the narrow, barred grate embedded in the solid steel door, wiping at the grime while his helpless rage boiled to the surface.

He clung to the rage, because he had nothing else. They'd taken everything he stood for, everyone he loved. But goddamn it, the Egyptians, the Brotherhood, and Muusa Shemal couldn't take his rage. Exhausted, he staggered to the narrow cement slab against the wall and collapsed. How long had it been since his tormentor had come for him? While he tried to remember, unable to sort one day from another, the cell door creaked open, admitting two guards.

They wore drab olive-green military uniforms and sported red berets with matching armbands. They carried pistols and clubs strapped to their bodies. One of them spoke. "Get up."

He obeyed, and they forced a black hood over his head. Beneath the hood, he groaned as they wrenched his hands behind his back and secured them with handcuffs. The guards took him from his cell and dragged him between them, along corridors and up stairways, until he was gasping for air and drenched in nervous sweat. He staggered along, semi-conscious, until they shoved him into a chair and yanked the hood from his head.

Painful daylight radiated through a window pockmarked with dirt and smashed flies. A pudgy man sat across from him at a battered metal desk, wearing a desert-camouflage military hat and a matching uniform with gold insignias adorning the shoulder boards. He had a hardened, no-nonsense face and cruel brown eyes. "I am the warden of Tora Prison. The Brotherhood coward Shemal has abandoned you to my care. What shall I do with you?"

While his eyes watered and he tried to catch his breath, he wondered if he could speak, or if the man even expected an answer. The Egyptians could do whatever the hell they wanted with him, and all he could do was take it. And suffer. He could always suffer. The warden continued staring at him as though he expected a reply. He mouthed an answer, but his dried-out tongue and throat refused to cooperate. He tried again. "Let me go." The words came out in a barely audible croak.

The warden sneered, "You murdered a well-known doctor who treated you humanely in the hospital. Freedom is not an option."

"Then execute me," he whispered. His weak voice humiliated him, but God how he wished the man and his guards would do what he asked.

The warden gestured at the guards who stood at attention against the wall. "He wishes to die. Shall we accommodate his request?" The guards smirked and chuckled, and the warden turned his hard gaze back to him. "You do not deserve an honorable death. You will serve a life sentence for your crime. But you will serve this sentence in Al-Aqrab, where you belong."

He didn't try to answer. The warden frowned at him for a moment, then addressed the guards. "Take him to the *Scorpion.* He will remain there until death takes him."

The guards hoisted him to his feet and shoved the hood over his head. He wobbled blindly between them, terrified at what they might do. They led him away, holding him upright when he tripped, dragging him when his legs gave out. A door slammed, and he felt the tantalizing brush of warm air on his arms. Then he heard electronic beeping and the screech of metal on concrete. Cold, dead air replaced the warmth. They dragged him along hallways and around corners in what felt like an endless maze.

The guards jerked him to a stop, turned his body, and gave him a shove. He landed hard, unable to breathe for panicked seconds. Their quick fingers removed the cuffs, pulled the hood from his head, and shoved him onto his back. While he stared up at them, dragging in wheezing breaths, the shorter guard leered at him and spat on the floor. "This is *Al-Aqrab,* the *Scorpion*. Here, you will die." The two guards left him in the tiny cell.

He lay on the floor, hoping for some semblance of strength to return so he could sit up. While he stared at the fracture lines crisscrossing the ceiling, he tried to make sense of the warden's comments about Shemal. The Muslim Brotherhood must have been ousted from power in Egypt. He'd heard bits and pieces of conversation between the guards who didn't know he understood Arabic.

The warden knew who he belonged to, though. That Muusa Shemal had vanished did not surprise him. Naturally, he would return to the security of the United States, where the Brotherhood was esteemed, welcomed into the highest echelons of power. While he suffered, the man who'd orchestrated the destruction of his life remained safe, honored by the country that called him a traitor.

Mid-June
Al-Aqrab Prison, Cairo, Egypt

While Rowan squinted up at the single bulb dangling from the ceiling it winked off. "Oh God, not again." He hollered into the darkness, "Turn on the fucking light." Prison officials turned the lights off in the windowless cells of the *Scorpion* at random. In the dark, the ants and roaches went wild. They crawled on him from everywhere while he huddled on the hard slab, scratching and slapping them away.

His heart pounded in the bug-infested blackness. How long would they leave him in the dark this time? He took rasping breaths and rubbed his eyes with shaky fingers, blinking and straining to see. What if they forgot about him?

While he waited for the onslaught of insects, the light came on, and a key scraped in the door. Two guards entered. The tall one, with eyes that seemed to bulge, held a mud-encrusted metal bucket. The short, stocky man, with an empty spot where one of his front teeth belonged, carried a bowl. The tall guard spoke. "You will eat now."

They dumped soup into the bowl and shoved it into his hands. He kept his head bent, his eyes on the floor. Making eye contact with the guards gave them the only invitation they needed to use their clubs. They left, and he caught a whiff of the soup's rancid smell.

His stomach heaved. "The rats and cockroaches can have this shit." He flung the bowl as hard as he could. It bounced off the wall and clattered across the floor, coming to rest at his feet. Slimy liquid dripped down the wall.

The cell door banged open, and the guards rushed in. They grabbed his arms and jerked him to his feet. Manic outrage registered in the tall guard's bulging eyes. The shorter guard gave him a resounding slap across the face. They spun him around and slammed him against the wall. A coarse rope tightened around his wrists. He felt hot breath on his cheek and gagged at the rank odor. "Stupid, dog-shit American."

They marched him from the cell, down the dimly lit hallway. He pulled back, dragging his feet, desperate to stop them. "No, no, I'll eat. Whatever you want. No, please, not this. Not again."

The guards stopped walking. While the tall guard grinned and held onto him, the shorter guard wielded his club. The pain exploded, excruciating, with each methodical thwack hitting his back and legs. He tried to twist away, but the guard held onto him. The heavy blows kept coming, until he fell, curled on his side and lay still on the cement.

The two men forced him to his feet and continued to the room he dreaded. They flung him face-down in the dirt. While his body shook, the guards tied his wrists and ankles together behind his back with thick ropes. Hard fingers dug into his hair and yanked his head up. He could make out the stocky guard squatting next to him. "Now, you will learn."

The guard released his hair, and his head flopped in the filth. He inhaled, choking and coughing. He heard the guards grunting, the sound of the rope stretching. How much more could his joints take before they pulled apart? How long before his vertebrae shattered? What would they do with him when he couldn't walk? He coughed and spat dirt from his mouth. "No, please, please don't..."

The guards ignored his mumbled entreaty. He groaned as his body rose and hung suspended above the dirt floor, swaying gently back and forth. Burning, tearing pain engulfed him, setting his brain on fire, sweeping away his thought processes. He couldn't stop moaning, his dry mouth and shaking lips couldn't form the words to beg them to stop. His unprotected belly convulsed as the guards took turns kicking him.

They let his body drop to the floor for precious seconds. The rope creaked as it stretched again, the guards grunted, and the agony overtook him. He lost track of how many times he heard the rope straining, the guards muttering, before the ringing that started in his ears grew to a roar, and welcoming darkness took him away.

Agonizing consciousness returned, and he heard the guards' muttered profanities, felt his body bumping and scraping along the hallway. They dragged him between them to his cell and dumped him on the floor. The tall guard nudged his cheek with the heavy club. "Next time, you will eat." The guards left, slamming the door and locking it.

He lay on the floor and took slow breaths. He heard screaming, accompanied by shouting and cursing in Arabic. An echoing gunshot cut short the scream and he shivered. When he couldn't endure the cement any longer, he rolled to his side and pushed himself upright, groaning at the fiery pain enveloping his body.

He sat on the dirty floor and tried to think. Sometimes, in the relentless swirl of agony and terror, he lost himself. "Rowan Milani. My name is Rowan Milani." He licked dry lips and tried to swallow, while a hard lump in his throat caught him off-guard. Hot tears filled his eyes and overflowed, coursing through the dirt on his cheeks. "I used to be one hell of an FBI Special Agent. I used to be a man."

His thoughts drew him down a familiar path. Over and over, his mind played the well-worn litany. How had it come to this? And why? His fragile grip on reality demanded he give an account. *An honest answer, Rowan. No more of your lies.* Defiant, he muttered to himself, "I'm not answering anything." But he didn't have to, because he knew how *and* why.

If only he'd listened to his friends and colleagues, to the woman who loved him. But no, he'd been stubborn; certain he'd never be caught. He was too clever; hell, he was invincible, right? He'd been consumed, blinded by his righteous hatred and his unquenchable thirst for justice. Or had he just wanted revenge? He didn't know anymore. Shemal and the Brotherhood owned responsibility for *how* he'd ended up dying slowly in the *Scorpion*, didn't they? He wasn't sure of that anymore either.

Those other reasons, revealing *why,* kept clamoring for attention, accusing him. He couldn't face them. And why should he? What difference did it make? He tottered to his feet and limped to the cement slab. None of it mattered anymore. If he could find a way to kill himself, he'd do it before Shemal and the Brotherhood could take credit for that, too.

He covered his face with his hands when *she* appeared in his mind's eye, walking toward him, smiling while her dark red hair swirled around her shoulders. Her eyes begged him to stay. Her voice, so desperate, whispered through his mind. *Rowan, all I want is to be with you. I don't care where. I'd hide with you for the rest of my life.* He cringed, remembering. She'd loved him so much.

In the end though, she'd never truly understood his terrible pain and rage; how he could kill with no remorse. She'd never truly understood *him.* They'd argued. He'd never forget her words, cutting him to the quick. *You're a monster.*

She tried to take it back; told him she didn't mean it, but he couldn't let it go. He'd been a jerk, his strong suit, and sent her away. And now, he wanted and *needed* to tell her how much he loved her and how damn sorry he was. But he'd waited too long, the way he always did, and the opportunity for apology, forgiveness, and a second chance was gone. He curled on his side facing the wall and closed his eyes. *"Oh God, Danielle, I'm sorry. I'm so sorry."*

Seattle, WA

Danielle Stratton sat on the front steps of the residence she finally felt comfortable calling home. She'd grown up in Seattle and loved the city, but never dreamed she'd be starting over again in her hometown. When the life she'd chosen fell apart, she came back, spent a month with her parents, and then launched a new existence as bravely as she could. After a month at Boeing as a receptionist, she'd answered an ad for manager of a local coffee bistro repositioning itself as new and high concept, to compete with Seattle's coffee giants. The idea resonated, she could relate, and she'd gotten the job.

Small-Batch-Love Coffee imported sustainably produced organic coffee beans from around the world. Located on a busy side street, within walking distance of her new home, the bistro occupied her mind from 6 a.m. to nearly 8 p.m. almost every day. Exhaustion and red wine finished the task each night and dulled the permanent ache in her heart.

Give yourself time to get past it, her well-meaning parents told her. But they didn't understand. The only man she would ever love had been killed in the most gruesome manner imaginable, and she would never *get past* the simple, brutal truth. She missed him in ways she could never explain. Remembering his touch, the secret smile in his lips when they kissed, and the undisguised desire in his eyes still had the power to leave her breathless. And then the inevitable grief set in as the memories sent her to the finality of their last goodbye.

A whine, followed by the swipe of a coarse tongue on her cheek ended her sad introspection. Her constant companion woofed, and warm breath exploded against her face. "Thanks, Leo. I needed that." She patted the 150-pound Rottweiler's broad head and stood up. She'd taken a rare day off and didn't plan to waste it reliving things she couldn't change. The sun warmed her and the tree-lined street beckoned. "Are you getting antsy? Me too. As soon as Tom gets here, we'll head for the park." Leo's ears perked up at the word *park*. The Rottweiler loved chasing Frisbees.

A couple told her one morning over coffee that they were moving to London and couldn't take their Rottie. She'd been ecstatic, and Leo became her best friend. He walked her to work every morning and spent the day napping in her office, mingling with customers or lying on the settee in the bay window at the front of the bistro.

The distinctive rumble of a Harley-Davidson motorcycle had Leo on his feet, tail stub doing double-time. Tom Hanford roared up the street on his Wide Glide, parked the cherry red and chrome motorcycle in the driveway, and pulled off his helmet. Six feet tall, Tom looked buff in a brown leather bomber jacket over a white t-shirt with *Boeing 787 Project* stenciled in blue.

His faded jeans molded his body in a way her employees called sexy. She'd heard them whisper, *he has a nice ass.* He had a nice face, too. Handsome, for sure, with sandy brown hair and intelligent hazel eyes. Not that she cared. She hoped he'd figured out she wasn't interested in anything more than friendship.

Tom spoke in his low, calm voice. "Hello Dani." He pointed at another helmet, strapped to the luggage rack behind the passenger backrest. "After we're done making sure Leo gets his exercise, I thought maybe we could take a cruise. We could hit those coffee shops you mentioned last week. It's a perfect day for the scooter and we can check out your competition at the same time."

"That sounds like fun. Are you sure you won't be bored?"

He grinned. "Absolutely not. Maybe afterwards we can grab some dinner."

"Maybe. Well, sure."

"I know this great place down on the wharf. It's kind of a hole-in-the-wall, but the seafood's the best in town."

She returned his easy smile, but it felt artificial. "All right. I'm game."

Later That Afternoon

The sun slanted in the window, and Danielle realized she'd lost track of time. Her stomach and cheeks hurt from laughing. They'd found a welcoming atmosphere in the last coffee shop, complete with a fireplace and an eclectic seating area. From the moment they'd slid into overstuffed armchairs, Tom had regaled her with tales of growing up the only boy, swimming in a sea of estrogen with two older sisters and a twin sister, Christina. He'd shared with her how close they were, meeting as often as possible for lunch or dinner as their schedules allowed.

Danielle finished her coffee and smiled at Tom still sipping his. "How's the French roast treating you? Not a fan? You've only had one cup."

Tom replied. "The coffee's great, but after three cups at three different shops, I'm over my limit, and I'd like to get a few hours of sleep tonight. I take it you're an only child?"

"I am. My parents have always been supportive, but they're retired now and traveling quite a bit of the time. I always wished for a sister. You know, someone to share my secrets with. Thanks for this afternoon, by the way. I haven't had this much fun in a long time."

"You're welcome. Now it's your turn. Tell me more. We've covered everything I can think of about my family and my career. I've learned more coffee trivia than I'll ever be able to retain."

She'd give anything to avoid this part of their conversation. "Gosh, let me see. You know I grew up here. At some point, I figured out I wasn't into college. I've always been fascinated by planes, jets especially. That's why I took a job with Legacy Airlines at SEA-TAC. Eventually, I worked my way into management. For the last five years, I ran Legacy's line station operation in Sioux Falls, South Dakota."

Tom said, "That must have been tough, coming from here."

"It was all right. The winters suck, though."

"Oh man, I bet they do. So, how'd you end up back home again?"

She shrugged. "I guess after years of stressing about on-time departures, baggage service, and all the rest, I'd had enough. My background is kinda boring."

"Aw come on, I don't call what you've done *boring*. You've probably traveled more places than most people do in a lifetime."

She plunked the empty cup down on the tiny square table between them. "Probably. Shall we go? I'm starving."

Late Evening

Tom sat in bed, still wired from the extra cups of coffee, perusing the Internet with his iPad. He'd dropped Danielle off and cruised home on the Harley, thinking about the palpable aura of sadness around the woman he found so gorgeous, he did a double-take every time he saw her. He'd never forget the day she showed up at Boeing with her long legs and nice breasts packaged in a black suit with a tight jacket, slim skirt, and three-inch heels. Her direct blue eyes radiated intelligence, but he'd just wanted to get his hands on her, dig his fingers into her thick, burgundy-red hair and kiss her.

He wasn't an idiot, though, and he'd listened to his father's admonition about taking things relaxed and easy with a woman. He'd taken the concept to a new level with Danielle. But that was all right. She felt special, and he was a patient man. He'd been surprised and pleased when she agreed to spend the afternoon and evening with him.

The few times before when they'd met up for coffee or a drink, she never offered much about herself. He wasn't satisfied with the sketchy background she'd given him this time, either. On a whim, he googled her name. Surprised when the page filled, he clicked on the top line, the one that read: **FBI releases Danielle Stratton after Rowan Milani surrenders.** "What the hell," he muttered and started reading. When he finished the article, he stared at the screen. "Holy shit." How in God's name had she gotten tangled up with the man described as America's most-wanted home-grown terrorist?

The article told how Milani had been arrested and injured in a violent encounter with federal agents in South Dakota. He'd disappeared from a Sioux Falls hospital bed, prompting the FBI to detain his girlfriend, Danielle. Milani later surrendered in exchange for her freedom, then somehow escaped from

Quantico's brig. Danielle was thought to be with him, first on the island of Kauai, and later in San Francisco. She'd eventually been absolved of any criminal connection to Milani, who'd been captured again.

He'd been reported officially dead after a video of his beheading by Islamic radicals in an Egyptian prison appeared on YouTube the previous winter. What in the world had Danielle seen in a man like Milani? How would he bring it up? *Hey Dani, I creeped you online. How 'bout that Milani guy?* No, he'd keep what he'd learned to himself.

She needed to know she could trust him. One thing for sure, her involvement with Milani had hurt her. Guys like that, who used women, especially a woman like Danielle, ticked him off big-time.

Mid-July
Washington, DC
Former CIA agent David Harandi paused at the door of the nondescript café, situated on a dilapidated street on DC's southeast side. He'd come early, conducting his own surveillance, opting for cab service instead of driving his Mercedes to the seedy neighborhood. A bell tinkled above the door as he stepped from the humid morning into the café. The pervasive aroma of old grease hit him head-on. Three men, the only patrons at the counter, didn't look at him as he strolled by. A lanky waitress in a Pink Floyd t-shirt and jeans stared, coffee sloshing in the glass pot she gripped in one hand. He angled his head toward four booths across the back wall, and she nodded.

He kept walking, the soles of his shoes sticking ever-so-slightly on the ancient linoleum. He settled into the corner booth and looked at his Rolex: 9:55 a.m. With five minutes to kill before meeting CIA agents Seth Hancock and Lucien Talbot, he ordered a cup of coffee. He grimaced when he sipped the bitter liquid and wished he'd ordered iced tea instead.

He checked his watch again, wondering what could be urgent and covert enough for the two agents to request a meeting off the beaten DC path. He'd only met Hancock and Talbot once, when Rowan Milani had been renditioned from Quantico's brig to Tora prison over his strenuous, and in the end, ineffectual objections. Watching the two agents haul his detainee from the cell had been the beginning of his understanding of the truth about his old friend.

His ties to Milani went deep. His parents immigrated to the US from Iran with his uncle Sa-id and Rowan's father. When his parents died in a car crash, Sa-id became his guardian. He'd spent childhood summers with Milani and his family in Carpinteria, California, a small city fifteen minutes from Santa Barbara, down Highway 101 South.

His uncle had remained a close friend of the Milani family until his murder a year and a half earlier. But over the past dozen years or so, especially after 9/11, he'd lost touch with Milani. While his friend pursued a career as an FBI Special Agent, he operated covertly for the CIA in the Middle East. Leaving the agency after 9/11's tenth anniversary, he'd built a steadily growing security consulting business and rather enjoyed his peaceful retirement from covert operations.

He'd been asked to find and bring Milani into federal custody by the President, via Special Presidential Advisor Patricia Hennessey. He'd only agreed to go after Milani because he couldn't believe the man he'd known since boyhood would betray his country. And also because of his one-time relationship with Patricia, proving even he could be a fool. Looking back, he wished he'd told his erstwhile lover to stick it and let someone else bring Milani into federal custody.

An irritated glance at his watch showed Hancock and Talbot five minutes late. Despite the overload of incriminating evidence, ugly circumstances, and the pile of dead bodies, he now knew

Milani had not been a traitor. He wouldn't call his old friend a pure-hearted hero, but he had not betrayed the United States. A meeting with one of one of Milani's colleagues revealed the truth, but the knowledge had come too late.

Muusa Shemal, a prominent leader of the Council of American-Islamic Relations in Washington, DC, an influential member of the Muslim Brotherhood and an internationally respected surgeon, had provided evidence of Milani's so-called treason. The President and the entire intelligence community never questioned Shemal's proof and went after Milani with ruthless zeal. But it no longer mattered. Milani was dead.

The tinkling bell above the door interrupted his thoughts, and he looked up. Two big men wearing dark blue polo shirts and jeans stepped inside. He raised a hand. Stocky, black-haired Hancock gave him a barely discernible nod and headed his way. Talbot lumbered behind Hancock, his spiked blond hair, broad-muscled body, and bullish look making him seem larger than life in the small café.

The two men slid into the booth across from him, their shoulders touching. The waitress appeared, and both men answered her offer of coffee with a terse "yes" and waved away the plastic menus. She filled their cups and refilled his before he could place his hand over the cup.

He forced himself to swallow more coffee and met Hancock's close-set blue eyes. "I was surprised at your request to meet. What's going on?"

Hancock cast a quick glance around them before answering. "Milani is still alive. The Egyptian army moved him to Al-Aqrab a couple months ago."

Stunned, he sat silent for a moment, then took a couple deep breaths. *"Al-Aqrab?* A couple *months* ago? Why have you been sitting on this? That facility is reserved for the worst of the worst. If you're sure he is alive, we've got to find a way to get him out of there, immediately."

Hancock responded. "We've kept tabs on him and coordinated things with our Cairo Station Chief and Ambassador Givens. They contacted the prison warden and the Interior Minister. Believe it or not, the Egyptians agreed to release him. We think they said yes mostly to screw over Shemal and the Brotherhood. Between the four of them, they worked up an agreement of release both Presidents can sign off on."

Harandi tapped his fingers on the table. "As fluid as the situation is in Egypt, we need to move before any one of them changes their mind. We should have acted as soon as you found out he was alive. I can't believe this. Al-Aqrab is notorious for harsh torture. I have to ask one more time: *Why would you wait on this?"*

Hancock hooked a thick forefinger in the coffee cup and raised it. "The timetable wasn't up to us. Our Station Chief informed us this morning that Givens and the Interior Minister finished their paperwork and would each forward their agreement to both Presidents today. Can you light a fire under Whitman's ass?"

He nodded. "I'll request an emergency meeting with him as soon as we're done. How soon can you be ready to leave?"

Talbot replied while Hancock swallowed coffee and made a face. "Director Abramson approved a jet. It's fueled and standing by at Quantico. It's a twelve-hour flight, give or take."

An idea came to Harandi while he looked at the big blond. "We may need additional backup. I think I can arrange it."

Talbot tore open packets of sugar and dumped them into his coffee. "Such as?"

Harandi continued. "I know a couple guys. Bad-ass operators. Nerves of steel and accustomed to black ops."

Hancock smacked his coffee cup on the table. "You need to know one more thing."

"Yes? Make it quick, so I can get going."

Hancock glanced at Talbot, then fixed him with a wary gaze. "We figured out Milani is innocent."

Harandi stared. "I see. How did you come to this revelation?"

Talbot replied, "To start with, we don't get why Milani never *told us* he was innocent."

He couldn't resist a jab. "Well, perhaps if you hadn't beaten him unconscious, he may have. But never mind. I'm glad you've come to the same conclusion I reached. I'm curious though. Why are you telling me this now? Feeling guilty about the $250,000 blood-money payment you each accepted from Shemal?"

Hancock said, "Somebody needs to know the whole story. We need to cover our asses."

Talbot retorted. "We love this country. Taking Milani out meant doing our part to protect it. But watching Shemal taunt him and go after him with that dagger of his, and Milani talking back, calling Shemal a coward, never admitting a damn thing, got us to wondering."

Hancock added, "Next thing you know, we overheard Shemal telling Milani he's punishing him for all the holy warriors he took out. We looked at each other and said, *what the fuck?"*

Talbot continued. "We've been shitting ourselves ever since we figured it out. First, we damn near killed a guy who is on our side, and then we handed him to the real enemy. How did you know about the payment?"

Harandi took a last, reluctant swallow of coffee, tasted grounds, and set the cup on the scarred table. "How I know about the money is part of my job. You could always give it to charity, by the way. Have you talked to your boss about this?"

Hancock replied. "Come on, we aren't idiots. We told Abramson it'd be advantageous to bring Milani back, before the Egyptian government decided to shit on the agency and the President by bringing him out in public with some trumped-up story."

The two men wearied him. "Sounds like you've got your asses covered. We need to move on this. I'll make sure Whitman signs off with Egypt's President. I'd like to leave right away, before conditions in Egypt deteriorate further."

Hancock replied. "All we need is your go-ahead from Whitman, and we'll be on our way."

Harandi slid out of the booth and stood up. "I'll meet you at the airfield at 3 p.m." He started to pull his wallet from his pants pocket and changed his mind. "Thanks for the coffee." He headed out of the café, thinking about the phone calls he needed to make. Then he'd explain to the President how his administration would benefit from Milani's return. Whitman loved buying into all manner of political bullshit. And that's exactly what he'd feed him. He flagged a cab and jumped in.

Rural Maryland

CIA Director Oscar Abramson walked the length of his study and stood at the bay windows, observing the large yard and the brick walkway leading to his wife's gazebo and gardens. The two of them had purchased the house and accompanying two acres in a secluded area between Potomac and Rockville, Maryland years earlier.

He turned away from the windows, dabbed at the perspiration on his forehead with a handkerchief, and removed his black suit jacket. He placed it carefully over the back of his leather executive chair before seating himself behind his desk. He'd returned home where he preferred to work, usually accomplishing more than in his busy office at CIA Headquarters. But not today.

He contemplated the array of files, notes, and papers strewn across the desk top. They comprised the numerous tasks demanding his attention. Instead, he must ignore the important work of the agency he guided and focus on a problem, a situation; a man whose destruction he'd helped facilitate from far behind the scenes, with careful and meticulous planning. This man stubbornly refused to go away; refused to die quietly so that the holy cause he'd chosen to devote his life and career to could flourish unhindered.

He stroked the beard he kept clipped and dyed black to hide its reddish streaks, an embarrassing reminder of his mother's despicable heritage. Long ago he'd rejected both her Irish Catholicism and his father's Judaism. He'd grown up an only child in the long-established Jewish community of Pikersville, Maryland, a powerless victim of their contentious marriage. Stories about brave Bedouins and their Arabian horses, Egyptian Pharaohs, and the great pyramids offered childish escape from his parents' vitriol. Visiting the land of his dreams became the desire of his heart.

After graduating in 1982 from Harvard's Kennedy School of Government with a Master of Public Administration degree, he'd followed his heart and entered a world far removed from Pikersville. He studied for two years at the American University in Cairo and became fluent in Arabic. He immersed himself in the study of Islam. Fascinated by its integral role in Egypt's political and cultural history, he began to see the world through a uniquely Middle Eastern prism.

He met Muusa Shemal, a young Islamic scholar. His new friend nurtured his changing perspective and helped strengthen and solidify his commitment to the principles of his burgeoning faith. Islam's purity soothed his bitter anger toward the phoniness so evident in the religions he'd been forced to succumb to as a child.

His disdain for the hypocrisy inherent in western culture grew strong as he observed firsthand in Egypt the results of the heavy-handed meddling of politicians from Britain, Europe, and the US. He mourned over the stark footprint left by the CIA, stretching from Iran to the Sinai. The arrogant tactics of the West forever changed the lives of millions of innocent people. He understood their rage and hatred toward a cadre of indifferent western masters.

His search for a meaningful way to mold and impact the policies of his ignorant country led him to join the agency bearing responsibility for many of the wrongs. In becoming a part of the CIA, he saw an opportunity to correct its cataclysmic intervention. Patient determination and strategic preparation over the course of the last twenty-five years had paid off. Starting as an analyst, he'd eventually advanced to Station Chief in Cairo, a position he'd treasured for five years.

After 9/11, he left his post in Egypt and returned to the US to head a CIA counter-terror team focused exclusively on the threat from up-and-coming Islamic groups. His efforts to steer his team toward the truth about why Islam's freedom fighters directed their fury at the US was met with interest by a few, but most of the others stonewalled his efforts and refused to believe America's foreign policy bore any responsibility. After a frustrating eighteen months, he determined to focus his energy on achieving the pinnacle of power. As director of the massive agency for the past three years, he wielded influence in ways he'd been unable to in his former roles.

Over the years, he and Muusa remained close. Their friendship grew to include collaboration on a goal held dear by all adherents to fundamental Islam. The Muslim Brotherhood's intent to transform America into the new Caliphate, begun decades earlier, had never faltered. He supported their vital, secret jihad, but Rowan Milani still threatened everything they'd accomplished, as well as their continuing plans.

The door chimes resonated throughout the home. He left his study and hurried to the front of the house. As he reached the foyer, he stopped to catch his breath, glimpsing his visitor's familiar bulk through the frosted panes. He opened the double doors and greeted his friend with a kiss on each cheek. "As-salaam alaykum."

Shemal returned the greeting and murmured his response. "Wa `alaykum salaam. It is good to see you, my friend."

He made a cursory check of the black-top drive leading to the gated and fenced residence. Nothing looked amiss, and he ushered his friend inside. In the privacy of his study, they would be protected by the finest technology available. Their conversation would be shielded from penetration by any curious or malevolent cyber-snoopers.

He led his friend to the study and gestured toward the comfortable grouping of sofas and overstuffed chairs at the end opposite his desk. "Sit, please, and make yourself comfortable. We have much to discuss."

The stocky Egyptian lounged on the sofa, one creased pant leg crossed over the other, above black patent-leather shoes. Shemal's suit, combined with his perfectly coifed, thick black hair and neatly trimmed beard gave him an urbane air. "I was troubled by your call. Upon leaving Cairo, the warden assured me that Milani would not only remain in Tora, but be transferred to Al-Aqrab."

He sat down on a chair adjacent to the sofa. "The agents I assigned to handle Milani discovered he was still alive. Their misguided loyalty to this country and the CIA caused them to divert from their purpose."

Shemal fussed with the crease in his pant leg. "Your clumsy handlers are the root of our problem. They have proven their ineptitude more times than I care to contemplate."

His friend's analysis grated. "You are correct. But need I remind you that we could not afford to involve more agents after the fiasco in Sioux Falls? Besides, the backgrounds and mindset of those two ensured they would be easily led."

"And so, they have been led again, in returning Milani to this country, alive and once more able to threaten our goals."

Weary of their sparring, he said, "If, as I preferred, you had ended Milani's life while you had unfettered access to him in Tora, this entire affair would be a memory. However, I concede the point is moot. May we move on to a more productive conversation?"

Shemal replied. "As you wish. What would you like to discuss?"

"Our efforts must not be derailed by this man and his surrogates. Milani has a network of support we have yet to identify, besides Ralph Johnston and Chad Cantor."

"True, although Cantor is imprisoned, and Johnston remains in hiding."

"Yes, but there are the others, who spirited him away from Sioux Falls in my agency's sixty-five-million-dollar aircraft, which remains missing to this day. We do not know who ushered him out of Quantico's brig and into the ether, along with everyone closely associated with him."

Shemal countered. "While I share your concern, Milani's colleagues were unable to prevent his eventual capture and rendition to Tora. They cannot prevent his incarceration now, and surely they are not bold enough to attempt another escape."

He saw an opportunity to drive home his point. "We surely do not know, after all this time, exactly *what* his colleagues can or cannot do, or how many there are, or where they are. Even now, they could be watching us. For all we know, they may have followed you here."

Shemal scoffed. "You have become too paranoid. My driver takes care to ensure we are never followed. However, if you wish to take that tack, a larger concern is the Mafia kingpin Giacopino. It is thanks to my interrogation of Milani that we are aware of his responsibility for the bombing of the House of Allah in Houston and Al-Azhar mosque."

"Under duress, Milani may have lied to you. We have no proof of Giacopino's involvement in either of those bombings or in anything concerning Milani."

Shemal replied. "My interrogation techniques are designed to extract facts. I saw the naked truth in Milani's miserable face. I heard it in his voice."

"You must keep in mind Milani's ability to prevaricate. May I remind you of one other thing?"

"Yes, of course."

"With Milani back in the country, we must leave nothing to chance. I will meet this week with the new director of the FBI. I will encourage her to pursue immediate action against Milani. If she chooses to interrogate him, we have no control over what he may tell her or what she may believe."

Shemal replied. "Understood. It is imperative that the CIA remains involved in the proceedings against Milani. That responsibility falls on your shoulders, my friend."

"Unfortunately the CIA has no prosecutorial authority. However, I will remind her of the importance of interagency cooperation between the CIA and FBI, especially concerning Milani."

Shemal stood up. "Excellent. Allah will guide our path forward. Keep me informed as to your progress with the new director."

"I will keep you apprised of every development." After seeing his friend out, Abramson returned to his study. Somehow, he must ensure the final destruction of Rowan Milani. Only then could he rest, certain that the Brotherhood's grand plan for the United States would continue its march toward completion unimpeded.

Washington, DC

Reclining in the air-conditioned comfort of his limousine, Shemal pondered the conversation with his friend. Although their interactions sometimes tasked his patience, he trusted his friend's abilities, as well as his commitment to the Brotherhood and their cause. Above all, he rejoiced at the possibility of fitting recompense for Milani's brazen murder of his precious Marta.

The limousine pulled into the half-circle drive in front of the three-story brick structure housing CAIR headquarters in Washington, DC. From the heart of the beast, he headed the Brotherhood's multi-faceted plans to bring the mighty United States to its knees. However, the peace that usually enveloped him inside the well-appointed confines of his private office remained out of reach.

He hated Rowan Milani for many reasons, but the man's seeming ability to thwart death and once again jeopardize their plans enraged him. Could a man be more like a Jinn? Milani and his surrogates embodied the existential threat to *everything* the Brotherhood had striven to achieve in the United States. Familiar bands of pain tightened around his chest. He took shallow breaths and strolled among the heavy, dark wood furnishings, trying to calm his racing heart.

He picked up his copy of the Qur'an and thought about his father. He had many fond memories of the gray-bearded man caressing his own worn copy with work-stained hands. They would sit for hours while his father thumbed through its inspired pages, teaching and exhorting him. He could still hear the gruff voice. *To serve Allah well, my son, you must pursue jihad. It is your duty to resist the infidels wherever you find them.* His father was no scholar, but he possessed a deep understanding of jihad.

Allah blessed his family, and his father sent him, the first-born son, to Al-Azhar University. He excelled in his studies of Islamic law and theology. The Brotherhood took notice and recruited him into their ranks. He murmured the cherished words, the credo he embraced with every fiber of his being. *"Allah is our objective.*

The Prophet is our leader. Qur'an is our law. Jihad is our way. Dying in the way of Allah is our highest hope."

After graduating from Al-Azhar, the Brothers provided for his attendance at Oxford. He studied hard in the Nuffield Department of Surgical Science. Over the preceding twenty-plus years, he'd become an accomplished vascular surgeon. As his reputation grew, he received invitations to lecture and teach in the UK and eventually the US. The infidels in both countries would never know how his education and practice provided perfect cover for his ongoing efforts in the holy jihad against the West.

He settled into his favorite chair and switched on a lamp. "Aziza, my precious, where have you gotten to?" The long-haired, black cat unwound itself from the adjacent chair, stretched and meowed before leaping to his lap. "Ah, here you are." He gazed into the feline's luminous green eyes. Marta had given him a kitten four years earlier, before he'd lost himself in the search for the Jinn destroying his and the Brothers jihad plans.

The cat purred and kneaded his lap with sharp claws. His habibti's scintillating words weaved their way through his tormented mind. *This sweet pussy is my gift to you. I want her to remind you of me.* Then she'd laughed and tossed back her thick, black hair while capturing his gaze with her sly green eyes. How he'd loved her eyes. They glowed with raw, sensual promise, and left him lusting, even now, for her supple body. She'd willingly given herself to him, and used her prowess to satisfy his every desire.

His fists clenched in powerless rage and he stabbed at his eyes, rubbing viciously, unable to shut out the other vision of his precious habibti, when he'd accompanied Detective Matthews to the morgue in Houston, to identify her body. Milani had slaughtered her, and on *that* day he'd made a secret vow. No, he would never tell Oscar, or any of the Brothers of his intent. No matter how long it took, he would make sure Milani experienced the same loss.

He and Oscar made sure that Milani suffered. They'd taken away the despicable man's career, his reputation, and his carefully hidden blood money, paid by the vile American government. Milani would never harm their holy jihad again. But he'd wanted the arrogant man to *bleed.* Each time Milani's blood ran bright red from his dagger's cut gave him exquisite pleasure. Yet even now, the memory of Milani's mocking eyes, his smirk, and his blasphemous words left him shaking. *Fuck you. Fuck Allah.*

In his own way, Milani had defeated him. No matter how many times he'd cut with his dagger, Milani remained unbowed. He'd failed to humble the man before Allah. That singular failure drove him relentlessly. He would succeed. Milani *must* suffer the loss of his woman. He would see to it. Then and *only* then would he end the miserable man's existence.

Aziza settled on his lap, her loud purring a welcome distraction from his anguished thoughts. He stroked the silky fur and took slow breaths. The tightness and pain in his chest lessened. Allah would guide him on this final quest.

Harandi observed his boss, President Gilford Whitman. Tall and fit, with black hair turning silver at the temples, Whitman wore the presidency well and seemed utterly at home with the power of the office. He'd often thought that Whitman epitomized the word *presidential* to the point of cliché.

Seated in a green-and-gold striped armchair in front of the fireplace in the Oval Office, the President gazed at him through narrowed eyes. "You're quite sure Milani is alive? The call from Ambassador Givens surprised me. I'd hoped it was a mistake. Frankly, I'm put off by the subterfuge involved. Why wouldn't the Egyptian President call me himself, as soon as he knew Milani was alive?"

"Sir, think about it this way. Your administration backed the former president and supported the Muslim Brotherhood's role in the election process. This president is in office as a result of the ouster of the Brotherhood from power. Besides which, I'm sure Milani was not a priority for either president, considering the chaos in the country."

Whitman rose gracefully from the chair and paused to nab an Empire apple, of the McIntosh variety, hand-delivered to the Oval Office every week from his favorite Virginia orchard. He kept a bowl of the apples on the polished coffee table between the gold-patterned brocade sofas. "You've got a point. Our relationship has been rocky at best, non-communicative at worst. However, I'm surprised the Egyptians are willing to release him, and I'm inclined to tell them to keep him."

"With the Muslim Brotherhood out of power, the military and the current government may not want to bother with him. Believe me, leaving Milani to the Egyptians is the last thing you want to do."

Whitman paced the office, as he often did while they talked, tossing the apple from one hand to the other, gazing out the windows and then swinging around to challenge. "How so? Milani has been a major liability to my presidency since this whole thing started. Sometimes it's advantageous to let things lie."

Ready with the bullshit, he affected an earnest tone. "Sir, you need to think about the politics of the situation first. Bringing Milani home to face trial for the murder of Director Ainsley will certainly be a triumph for your administration. It showcases for the entire country the lengths your administration will go to in order to seek justice."

The President finished his trek around the office and returned to the armchair. "If I remember correctly, when we watched the video of Milani's altercation with Director Ainsley, you were of the opinion he'd been forced to defend himself, much as you would have in a similar situation."

He tread carefully. "Yes, sir, you're correct. However, we both know the killing of the top law-enforcement leader in the country must be properly adjudicated. My opinion is secondary to my concern for you and your administration."

"Your concern is noted and appreciated. I had only hoped we were done with Milani."

"Believe me sir, I know how you feel. However, another upside to bringing Milani back here alive is to prevent the Egyptians from executing him. Can you imagine the uproar, or how damning it would be if a news organization such as FOX got ahold of that kind of information?"

Whitman polished the apple on his suit pants. "I hadn't considered that."

"No matter the truth, your opposition would ensure that the entire matter was portrayed as you neglecting an American citizen, leaving him behind, resulting in his death. It would be spun endlessly in the 24/7 news cycle in the most negative way possible."

Whitman grimaced. "You're right, except Milani is no *citizen.* I surely don't need to remind you of his status as an enemy combatant."

He tried to gauge where Whitman was going with the conversation. "No, of course not, sir. But I'd hoped, since you now know Milani is innocent of the treason charges, you may consider rescinding that status."

The President held up the apple and inspected it. "I've considered your claims of his innocence, but upon further reflection, I'm somewhat reluctant to take the word of this associate of Milani's with whom you spoke. At any rate, I am not inclined to rescind his status as an enemy combatant."

He found himself increasingly alarmed at Whitman's tendency to vacillate on important issues they'd discussed, and *he thought,* settled. "Sir, we have the evidence of money deposited into Patricia and Rodney's bank accounts."

"Yes, but neither of them are alive. They can't be questioned."

"Understood, of course. With proper interrogation, I believe we can determine Milani's innocence with more certainty. One other corollary benefit is that your administration will retain its reputation for protecting the homeland and bringing a dangerous man to justice."

The President responded. "Your input is excellent as usual. I'll sign off on his return, with one exception. I want Milani incarcerated in the Administrative Maximum Facility in Florence, Colorado. I'm not naïve enough to place him in any facility which his cohorts could possibly breach. Besides, as an enemy combatant awaiting trial, it's where he belongs."

He heard dismissal in the President's tone and stood up. "I concur with your decision. Would you like me to make the arrangements with the Marshals Service? And do you prefer that the transfer to Colorado happen immediately, or would you prefer a brief stopover in DC?"

Whitman stood up. "I'll contact the Marshals Service, and I'll speak with the warden at ADX Florence. I do not want Milani to step foot inside another facility. He'll be transferred from one jet to the other on the tarmac. If I'd had more notice, the Marshals Service could have flown to Cairo and retrieved him."

"All right, sir. Am I to understand you'll permit me to continue interrogating Milani in Colorado?"

The President waved his hand in an impatient gesture. "Yes, your interrogation may continue. Set it up. And one last thing. Bring Milani back without mishap. I don't want to find out he's killed anyone else before he's locked up on American soil. Can you accomplish that for me, Mr. Harandi?"

He headed for the door. “Consider it done, sir. We’ll leave within the hour. I’ll keep you posted.”

On the way to the airfield, he rehashed the conversation in his mind. Although Whitman had surprised him with the decision to send Milani to Colorado, it made sense. It also allowed him to escape the suffocating advisory role he’d been pressed into after the assassination of Special Presidential Advisor Hennessey. The President had come to depend on him almost exclusively, and he’d give damn near anything to end his participation in Whitman’s inner circle.

A Different Man

CHAPTER TWO

FBI Headquarters, Washington, DC

FBI Director Leigh Berenger, the first woman ever to head the nation's premier law enforcement organization, pulled the phone away from her ear, resisted the urge to sling it across the room, and instead gently replaced the receiver. David Harandi's hurried message about his quick meeting with the President; the brief explanation of his plan to bring Rowan Milani, the man everyone thought dead, back to the US without her input left her deeply angered.

If she'd been kept in the loop and allowed to participate, she would know when Harandi expected to return with the resurrected special-agent-turned-terrorist, so her staff could arrange a press conference, which she could use to show leadership and launch her plan to rebuild the Bureau's image. Milani owned responsibility for tarnishing the FBI in a major way. Knowing he was alive, with his return imminent, she intended to push for his prosecution to the fullest extent the law allowed.

Instead, she'd been left out of the decision-making process, for the first and last time. Decades of experience had taught her when the good old boys club needed to be halted, and she didn't give a damn if its leader was the President. She grabbed the phone and punched the contact she wanted. "FBI Director Berenger here. Connect me to the President, please."

Whitman sounded distracted. "Good afternoon, Leigh. Everything copacetic?"

"Good afternoon, Mr. President. I was surprised and disturbed to learn Rowan Milani is alive and being returned to the US."

"I was as well. Once he's on US soil, I've made arrangements for his incarceration at ADX Florence."

Her irritation flared at one more decision taken from her. "Excellent. I will initiate preparations for interrogation to commence as soon as he's processed."

"That won't be necessary. I've tasked Mr. Harandi with continuing his interrogation."

She set aside her growing anger. "I've examined the transcripts of Mr. Harandi's interrogation of Milani. His efforts produced zero results. The Bureau has a notable track record using a different approach than typically applied by CIA agents, particularly with regard to enhanced interrogation techniques."

"What do you have in mind?"

"Since Milani is a former agent, I would prefer to keep his interrogation in-house. I'll assign my best interrogator to work with him."

"All right. Proceed however you'd like. Keep me informed."

"Thank you, Mr. President and rest assured, I will keep you informed." She ended the call and strode to the windows overlooking the street two stories below. She could practically feel the humidity through the glass. In his brief message, Harandi said he wanted to meet with her as soon as he returned and had forwarded an Intel brief by courier to her office. She'd been surprised to see it concerned Muusa Shemal. Instead of indulging her anger any further, she'd read the brief.

When the opportunity presented itself, she'd let Whitman know how she felt about being left out. She'd quickly discovered that artifice and secrecy appeared to be the President's MO. Her former boss, Rodney Ainsley, had worked directly with Whitman regarding Milani, completely bypassing the Attorney General, who happened to be his boss and now hers.

As deputy director, after Ainsley's death, she'd stepped into the directorship, expecting to hold the position temporarily. Whitman made her succession a permanent appointment, and she'd been approved by the Senate. Afterwards, meeting privately with Whitman, he'd shrugged away her questions about bypassing the AG. He'd also told her how much he admired her strength and commitment to integrity. In Washington's political-speak, she knew he meant since Ainsley created and oversaw a botched mess, he needed someone completely different, like a woman, to take over.

She'd been the perfect choice. Raised in New York City, naturally rebellious and highly intelligent, she found creative ways to circumvent her parents' no-nonsense rules. At sixteen, she'd been where she wasn't supposed to be and witnessed a drug deal gone awry. The experience of cooperating with the prosecutor who'd needed her testimony created a budding interest in the law.

She stayed in the city she loved, attending Columbia University as an undergrad and while earning her Juris Doctor. The FBI recruited her during law school in part because of her proficiency with Russian and Spanish, along with basic competency in Arabic and Farsi. Her career with the Bureau started in 1986 at 26 Federal Plaza in lower Manhattan.

Living and working in the shadow of the Twin Towers, she did well. After the 1993 attack on the World Trade Center, she joined the New York Joint Terrorism Task Force. The missed connections, mistakes, and intelligence failures contributing to 9/11 affected her profoundly. Not a day passed that she didn't think of friends and colleagues whose voices had been forever silenced. She'd vowed to make sure their deaths were neither forgotten nor in vain.

She excelled in counter-terrorism assignments and eventually caught the attention of Director Ainsley. She'd never been able to pin down exactly what the FBI Director saw in her, because as committed as she was to transparent integrity, he was equally enthralled with secrets and deals. In a less-than-lucid moment, after a dinner party in his home, they'd chatted over the Maker's Mark bourbon he favored. She'd gotten her only glimpse into why he'd wanted her on his personal team. *Everything you touch turns out well, Leigh. The Bureau and I need your dedication to the truth.*

He'd made her his Chief of Staff, and in an unprecedented move, his Deputy Director. He told her she represented his right hand, his *good hand.* Thinking back, she wondered at the complexity of the man and the nature of the clandestine goings-on he'd been involved in. Milani fit somehow at the center of it, she felt sure, but the details remained a mystery.

She left the windows and returned to her desk. Unease gripped her when she thought about Milani's return to the United States. How did a man like him, who'd suffered a horrific personal loss on 9/11, choose to join forces with the perpetrators of terror he'd spent his career fighting? She'd known of Milani in 2000, when he graduated at the top of his class and got the plum assignment any number of agents lusted after, working with Ralph Johnston as part of his low-profile Anti-Terrorism Task Force.

Respected, if not necessarily liked by his Bureau colleagues, Milani had been one of Johnston's rising stars, along with Special Agent Chad Cantor, another top achiever. The two men had made Johnston's task force one of the most successful in the Bureau, with a reputation for ferreting out and taking down domestic terror cells.

Choosing an interrogator capable of handling a former agent of Milani's stature was imperative, and she'd already made her choice. Special Agent Wilson Foster answered on the first ring in his deep, courteous voice. "Hello, Director Berenger, how may I be of assistance today?"

"Good afternoon, Wilson. How are things progressing with Mr. Cantor?"

"Things are going well. He's willing to share his cell phone technology and hacking capabilities with us. I've coordinated with officials at County for use of a classroom. Cantor has been teaching his hacking skills to our team. In return for completing four weeks in a row, I've promised him a phone call to his fiancée."

"Excellent. Give Cantor his phone call today and wrap things up with him. I'll assign another agent to follow through with the classes. You are reassigned, effective immediately."

Foster hesitated a moment. "If that's your pleasure ma'am, I'll certainly make the arrangements. May I ask what prompts your decision to reassign me?"

"Rowan Milani is alive. The Egyptian government has agreed to transfer his custody to a team en route to Cairo as we speak. He'll be held in solitary confinement at ADX Florence. I'd like you to oversee his detention, and I'm placing you in charge of his interrogation."

"Thank you for the opportunity. While I look forward to it, may I share one concern with you, ma'am?"

"Absolutely, Wilson. Please speak freely."

He hesitated again, then continued. "In my opinion, making a change at this point in Mr. Cantor's interrogation will not be helpful. Acquiring even a modicum of trust took several months, and he is still not convinced of our willingness to deal fairly with him. As an aside, interestingly enough, he has insisted from the outset that Milani was alive."

"I understand your concern. However, you are my first choice to interrogate Milani. He will arrive in Colorado sometime within the next twenty-four to thirty-six hours. I expect your usual best."

"You'll have it ma'am."

She hung up the phone and considered. While Foster made a good point, she was not overly concerned with Cantor. The former special agent had made a laughingstock of the Bureau and the CIA with his hacking ability. The Bureau had plenty of leverage in the form of his pregnant fiancée, Milani's sister Bettina. She'd bet on his cooperation in order to see her again.

Besides, she had another accomplished special agent in mind to work with Cantor.

She grabbed the phone and punched in the number she wanted. Special Agent Jane O'Brien answered immediately. "Director Berenger. How may I help you?"

The eagerness in the young woman's voice always pleased her. "Hello, Jane. I've arranged for you to take over Chad Cantor's interrogation. Special Agent Foster has been reassigned. You will receive a brief today."

"Thank you, ma'am. I will schedule my first interview this week."

"Very well. I'll expect a report after each session." She ended the call and sat for a moment behind her desk, satisfied with the decisions she'd made. Exiting her office and striding through the reception area, she resisted the urge to fling back her carefully styled platinum blonde hair, but allowed herself a private smile. Her smart, navy pinstriped suit with its short jacket, appropriately snug suit pants, and stiletto heels attracted stares from both male and female subordinates.

Her driver jumped out to open her door, and she slid from the humid afternoon into the air-conditioned coolness of the black Suburban. It would take at least an hour to reach her home. As the SUV made its way through heavy city traffic, she immersed herself in the Intel brief on the man responsible for Rowan Milani's spectacular fall from grace.

While the Bureau's sedan made its way through snarled traffic, Foster scanned the notes from his previous session with Chad Cantor. He hadn't been exaggerating to his boss. Gaining any sort of trust with the man who'd been the Bureau's go-to agent for cyber security had been difficult. But he'd persisted, because in Cantor he saw a level of brain power and ingenuity the intelligence community had never fully appreciated.

Foster had been with the Bureau for twenty years, devoting sixteen of those years to perfecting the art of interrogation. He believed in building genuine rapport with his subjects and had been honored to take on the challenge of extracting information from Rowan Milani's closest colleague. Berenger's reassignment to interrogate Milani surprised and pleased him. He'd worked hard to achieve the recognition she'd made apparent in her choice.

He knew his former colleague only by reputation. Over the years, Milani had been variously described as cocky, a smartass, and in the most heartfelt terms as an arrogant jerk. To his knowledge, however, no one had ever questioned Milani's loyalty to the United States.

He'd heard that in the years following 9/11, Milani was often off-grid, sometimes for a month or more at a time. He'd also heard how Ralph Johnston had resolutely stonewalled any attempt at uncovering his special agent's activities, until last year when Milani exploded into the nation's consciousness.

He looked up as the car slowed and turned, arriving at the entrance to the County Jail. Walking toward the imposing doors through the muggy heat, he focused on his final session with the man who'd stymied the country's intelligence community. He hoped his replacement would have a chance to access Cantor's brilliant mind for the country's good.

DC County Jail

Chad Cantor sat on the narrow bed and stared, unseeing, at the drab, gray wall. Since his transfer from Quantico's brig to the section of the County jail reserved for federal prisoners, he'd been in a perpetual fog. He didn't know whether it was day or night and had no clue what day of the week it might be. But he didn't care. He didn't care about anything anymore, except his fiancée and the baby she carried. *Their* baby.

The interrogator assigned by the Bureau had done his job well. He'd known Special Agent Foster was working him, doing all the right things to gain his trust and get information. But he didn't care about that either. For the first time, he understood the darkness, the pain, and the anger driving Rowan. It had been growing in him too, since his final moments with Bettina.

The darkness consumed and poisoned everything inside him. Only anger lived in his heart and mind, toward all the people who'd screwed them over. Bitter anger and the irrational hope that Foster would believe him and want to help him; that he might see his precious fiancée again and one day hold their child. He flopped on his back and covered his eyes with his forearm.

That last day in the brig, before Harandi released Bettina, they'd had a few minutes together. He'd held her close, pressed his hands against her expanding belly, and felt their baby move. Then he'd watched her walk out the door while he sat helpless, cuffed and shackled to a table in the interrogation room. He didn't know where she was going, or who would help her. That's when the darkness took hold, when the emptiness began to gobble up everything inside him.

The disembodied, monotone voice jarred his thoughts. "Stand up and approach the door." He got up and positioned his hands and feet in the opened sliders, gut clenching as the cold metal closed around his wrists and ankles. He would never get used to the awful feel of the cuffs and shackles.

He backed away from the door as it opened. The guards didn't speak or make eye contact, just took hold of his arms and led him to the interrogation room. They shoved him into a metal chair and secured his hands and feet to the table and floor. One guard left and the other remained at the door.

A fan kicked on, creating a cool breeze in the chilly room. He gritted his teeth to keep them from chattering, while goose flesh rose on his arms and legs. At a gentle knock, the guard opened the door, and Foster entered. Chad slumped in the chair and watched him approach the table.

Foster sat down, meeting his sullen stare with the calm demeanor he'd come to expect. "Good afternoon, Chad. Let's get these cuffs off." The agent motioned to the guard, who obliged before stationing himself back at the door. Foster continued, "I've got some news. Rowan Milani is alive. He's being transferred back to the US from Tora within the next twenty-four hours or so."

He rubbed his wrists, always made sore by the cuffs. "I told both you and Harandi that the Egyptians faked the beheading video."

"Yes, you did." Foster leaned forward and spoke quietly. "If given the chance to exonerate yourself once and for all, would you consider coming back? I speak for the Bureau when I say we would like to see you absolved of any connection to Milani and reinstated as a special agent, in addition to being reunited with your fiancée."

"In other words, if I give you Rowan, admit he's a terrorist, and tell you all the secrets, I'll get my life back?"

Foster nodded. "If that's the case, then the simplest answer is yes."

He leaned forward, mirroring Foster's pose. "Listen carefully, Special Agent. If I never see Bettina again, or never see our baby, I still cannot tell you what I know is not the truth. Rowan Milani is innocent. Ralph Johnston is innocent, and I am innocent."

Foster leaned back and replied. "Your loyalty to your friends is admirable. I sincerely hope it is not misplaced."

"After all the information I've given you, after everything I've shared with you and Harandi about who betrayed Rowan and why, the Bureau still won't investigate Shemal. I don't believe it's my loyalty that's misplaced. I don't have anything else to say.

Except to answer your question. I have no interest in rejoining the Bureau. Ever."

The agent dug in his pants pocket and produced a phone. "Certainly, you remember my promise of a phone call to your fiancée after you completed teaching four classes. I'm giving you the call now. I'm expecting you'll honor the agreement we made and continue with the classes?"

He stared at Foster. "Right now?"

The agent held out the phone. "I keep my promises. You have five minutes. I'll wait outside."

He watched Foster leave, motioning for the guard to follow him. When the door closed, he looked at the phone in his damp palm. With trembling fingers, he punched in the number no one could trace. He held his breath and waited. Would she answer from wherever she'd been hidden away? Hot tears stung his eyes when he heard her voice, tentative and sleepy. "Hello?"

He spoke past the painful lump in his throat. "Bettina? Sweetheart, it's me. Are you all right?"

"Chad? Oh God. I'm doing OK. What about you? *Where are you?"*

He hunched over the table. The hope in her voice opened a new wound, deep inside. "I'm in the County Jail in DC. What about, uh, what about our baby?" It took everything he had to keep his voice steady.

"We've still got a month to go. I want it to be now, except that I keep hoping you'll be here, or I'll be with you."

He wiped the tears dripping down his cheeks with a clenched fist. "I'm trying, sweetheart. I'm teaching the Bureau agents my hacking, and I told them they can have everything I know. I won't tell them Rowan is a traitor, so they won't let me go. I'm sorry."

"I know you'll never do that. I'm fine. I'll have our baby, and we'll choose a name together, after you're freed."

Her fierce courage, so much like her brother's, had always bolstered his. "I can't wait." The door opened, admitting Foster and the guard. "Sweetheart, I have to go. Take care of yourself and our baby. I love you. I'll call again, as soon as I can."

Her voice sank to an agonized whisper. "I love you too. I'll take care of everything until we're back together. Goodbye."

He ended the call and laid the phone on the table. He took a long breath and let it out slowly. No way would he let Foster see how hearing her voice had shattered his fragile hold on his emotions. He looked up. "Thank you."

Foster sat down. "You're welcome. It's been my pleasure to work with you, and I appreciate the knowledge you've shared. I've been reassigned. Since this is our last meeting, I want to emphasize how important your cooperation is to your future. My best advice is for you to continue in that vein."

The lingering echo of Bettina's voice whispered in his mind. He needed to get back to the ugly cell and lie down. Then he could hold her voice close in his heart. "I don't have any reason to do anything else."

Foster turned to the guard. "We're finished. Please escort Mr. Cantor back to his cell."

The guard cuffed his wrists and marched him back to the cell. Freed from the restraints, he sat, disconsolate, on the narrow bed. He didn't trust Special Agent Foster any more than he did anyone else affiliated with the government entities holding him prisoner. Would the Bureau bring Rowan to the same facility where he'd been dumped? He'd love to see his best friend. And his father. And Bettina. He covered his face with his hands.

In the sedan, headed home to pack and catch his flight to Colorado, Foster considered his last, difficult encounter with the former special agent. Cantor's face and his demeanor revealed varying facets of emotional upheaval. And yet, when offered a way out of his dilemma, he'd been resolute. Cantor had told him the truth, or he wasn't the Bureau's best interrogator.

What then, did that make Rowan Milani? The country's most misunderstood hero? What about Ralph Johnston? Director Ainsley had vociferously argued that all three men were heinous traitors. He gazed out the window at the sunlight glinting off the rush of traffic. He needed every minute of preparation time before facing Rowan Milani across another interrogation table.

Mt. Olivet Cemetery, Washington, DC

Jack McKenzie sat on a bench in the sun-dappled shade beneath a massive oak tree. He gazed across the narrow, blacktopped road and beyond the manicured grass to his wife's grave. Her marble headstone, one in a long row among many rows, glowed stunning pink in the late afternoon sunlight. The carved angels with their sad, kind faces hugged the slab of marble with chubby hands, their wings swept back. He always fancied them carrying his beloved Anne away, leaving his arms empty and his heart aching.

They had good years together, he and Anne, just not enough of them. Until her ovarian cancer sucker-punched them, he'd been immersed in his career at FOX News, and she'd been a CPA in private practice. They'd met at NYU while he pursued journalism and she studied accounting. She'd been the perfect foil for his gregarious, sometimes brash nature. When his hair thinned, with baldness inevitable, he shaved his head and she approved. When he decided on law school after getting his journalism degree, she cheered him on. He'd been a damn good trial attorney too, in his ten years of private practice.

The journalism bug wouldn't let him go, though. It tickled in the back of his mind, even in the midst of the rat race. One day a FOX News exec called, offering him a job as a consulting attorney and part-time commentator. He'd answered by saying yes, but how about a developing role as investigative reporter as well? The exec agreed, and his career took off in ways he'd never dreamed possible.

When Anne got sick, his FOX News family helped both of them. She died only six months after her diagnosis, and while he wandered in a daze, trying to cope, his colleagues kept him going. From the brass on down, they propped him up, with a shoulder to cry on, or a meal, or you-name-it. In the years since Anne's death opened the bottomless crater in his soul, he'd traveled around the big round ball called Earth several times over, been on every continent, and to the Middle East more times than he cared to count.

His experience made him the perfect guy to help his long-time contact Ralph Johnston when the sky fell on Milani. He'd dug into the drama surrounding the man, determined to find what qualified as the actual *truth*. Roadblocks and brick walls greeted him wherever he started asking questions, whether at the Bureau or the CIA. No one wanted to talk about Milani. No one offered any explanation for the charges against him. Muusa Shemal and CAIR refused his calls.

When the YouTube video of Milani's beheading surfaced, he'd put the project on hold. He'd been delighted to learn, only hours earlier, courtesy of an 'anonymous' call, that he could rev up his investigation again, maybe even garner an interview with Milani himself.

A trio of squirrels in the tree overhead squabbled and scolded, rustling leaves with their shenanigans. He stared at Anne's headstone for another moment, then looked at the notebook on his lap. Over the years, he'd taken up the habit of driving to the cemetery whenever he returned from a trip. He found a certain kind of homecoming, a centering of his soul. He'd wipe bird doo away and sit on the old cement bench beneath the tree near her grave.

He chatted with her during those times, jotting notes on whatever news story or trip his career required. Her smile, the humorous sparkle in her eyes and her raised brows at something outlandish he'd said resided in their *conversations,* in a journal no one else would ever see. He pulled a pen from his shirt pocket and began writing.

Hi Anne,

I've been out of the country on a story. I'm back home now and this thing with Milani has me juiced. The guy is alive, and my source tells me he's innocent. This puts the story on a completely different level. Now it's about the stinking PATRIOT Act and the National Defense Authorization Act and sending an American citizen to Tora prison to be screwed around with by the Egyptians with no due process. I think our intelligence community wanted revenge for how Milani and his friends screwed around with them.

But get this. The CIA is bringing Milani back, and I'm going to be waiting with my camera when their jet lands. I'll inform the world Milani is still alive and back in custody here. And I'm not going to let the President, the intelligence community, or CAIR and the Muslim Brotherhood hide from this story or sweep it under any damn rug. I'm going to break it wide open, and when I get enough facts, I'm going to host a special on FOX and make everything public.

Sweet Lord Jesus, this could be the effing story of the century. I have to tell you, kiddo, Milani is an unpredictable, dangerous man, and I get the feeling he's a take-no-prisoners warrior, too. I need to talk to him if I'm going to get at the whole truth. He may not want to talk to me, but it'll be one hell of an interesting interview. I love you Anne. See you next time.

Dubai, United Arab Emirates

Michael Cristo tapped restless fingers on the table, leaving damp prints on the polished surface. The Army Ranger in his heart craved action, but the sniper in his head held him back. So far. Asal Tehrani sat next to him and reached up to brush thick black hair off his forehead. Her slow smile dispelled some of his angst, but it flooded back when he thought about the critical twenty-four hours they faced.

Waiting when a situation required action pissed him off. Sitting in a luxury apartment in the Burj Khalifa, first thinking Rowan was dead, and then knowing he'd been suffering in Tora, pissed him off. Accustomed to traipsing around the world in clandestine service to his country, confining himself to the apartment and Dubai, with its two-million-plus population pissed him off. Hell, everything pissed him off.

Asal calmed his mind and helped him think things through. He'd long ago given up trying to figure out what he'd do without her. She knew things; stuff he could never figure out. Always serene and methodical, she manned up and handled a rifle, sub-machine gun, or pistol better than most men. Right now, he craved her serenity most of all.

He'd give anything for one carefree day as a kid on his parents' twenty-thousand-plus acre South Dakota ranch, crawling through valleys and tearing across ridge tops on a four-wheeler with his rifle. He could still smell the prairie grass and pine, and hear the crack of his rifle echo across the hills while he hunted coyotes or prairie dogs. *My early sniper kills*, he used to joke with Rowan. But now, thanks to the FBI, he sat in Dubai in a sissy apartment with those options off the table, probably forever.

Harandi's surprising call a few hours earlier, telling them Rowan was indeed alive, brought him to the long dining room table at 9 p.m. to meet with Ralph Johnston and Johnny Giacopino. Whether he knew it or not, Harandi had sent them a golden opportunity to snag Rowan out of Shemal's and the government's hands. "Third time's the charm," he muttered. If he had anything to say about it, this would be the last time.

Asal massaged his shoulders. "Are you all right, Mikey? Your shoulders are hard as rock."

"Yeah honey." He liked to call her *honey,* because it was the Farsi translation of her name. "I'm just thinking about this crap. You know, a year ago, Rowan was recuperating on the ranch. I had visions of hiding him in South Dakota until we could sort the whole mess out and prove his innocence."

"I know. But you need to remember, you are not responsible for Rowan's choices."

"No, but I should have done more to influence him or make him consider a better way to get things done."

She gave his shoulders a final squeeze. "You are not thinking straight tonight. Rowan has always done exactly what he wants. You know that's true. Are you still kicking yourself over Chad?"

Michael twisted his shoulders, wished she'd keep rubbing them. He missed his tall, blond-haired friend with the quirky thought processes, easygoing grin, and genius-level intelligence. Holding everything together while they followed Rowan's bloody trail around the country had cemented their friendship. "I let Chad down."

"Chad knew the risks. I'm sure he doesn't blame you. Carrying this load of responsibility and guilt is unnecessary. You did everything you could."

"But maybe I could have distracted those SWAT agents for Chad and Bettina. Or maybe I could have met up with Rowan in Houston and told him to forget those two guys following him. I just fucked up. Oh hell, I can't take it anymore. What's keeping Ralph and Johnny?"

"Maybe they're talking to Rowan's parents and Bettina. I'm sure they're ecstatic and relieved."

"You're probably right. I didn't think about that." It blew his mind when he considered the group of people brought together by their connection to Rowan, sharing Johnny's two Dubai apartments. The Don had become a major ally, facilitating their exit from the US to prevent the government from using them as levers against Rowan.

Ralph and Johnny tromped into the room and slid into matching chairs across the dark wood table. Stocky but fit, with thick iron-gray hair, seventy-five-year-old Johnny had damn near twenty years on Ralph, but you'd never know it. The Don wore an aura of robust energy, clothing him as neatly as the charcoal gray pinstriped Italian suit and silver-striped silk tie draped around his neck. Johnny operated his Mafia empire on a global scale and dealt in oil, minerals and other, less respectable commodities like firearms and explosives.

Wearing a faded black FBI t-shirt and cargo shorts, Ralph's hard-muscled frame stretched several inches past six feet. Michael looked at the craggy face and watchful blue eyes and wondered for maybe the one-hundredth time how his friends had put up with the hard-assed former SEAL. Known for exercising an iron-clad commitment to the rule of law, Ralph had given up his career, reputation, and pension in support of Rowan.

He wondered what Rowan would think of his law-and-order boss collaborating with Mr. Mafia. With any luck, before the next twenty-four hours had passed, he'd be able to ask him. The thought cheered him, and he sat up straighter in the chair.

Johnny puffed on a cigar, gazing at him with a crafty smile on his tanned face. They'd called the Don away from a business meeting fifty floors above the apartment, to act on the phone call from Harandi. Michael looked past Johnny and Ralph to the reflection of the dining room in the floor-to-ceiling windows. The early evening sky beyond the windows created the perfect backdrop for the surreal scene.

Ralph cleared his throat and scowled. "I don't like this set-up. I don't trust Whitman. For all we know, he and Harandi have cooked this up as a way to nab us. But if we can ensure Rowan's safe transport out of Tora, I'm on board with it."

Michael met Ralph's uneasy stare. "Anything is possible, but I'm not interested in helping them transport Rowan back to DC. This is our opportunity to surprise Harandi and those two goons and bring Rowan here." His right leg couldn't stop bouncing. Asal placed her hand on his knee, and he took a deep breath, willing his body to calm down.

Ralph countered. "Whoa. Slow down, son. Much as I'd like to snatch Rowan out of their hands, if we attempt that, we *will* end up in custody."

Johnny spoke up. "We need to focus on one goal at a time. I've got a plan in place. Once it plays out, Rowan will have a permanent 'get out of jail free card'."

He stabbed a finger first at the Don, then Ralph. "You think we should help them haul Rowan off again, and you're afraid of getting caught. Fuck me. I never thought I'd see the day. We'll never have an opportunity like this again. We need to act on it."

Ralph argued back. "It's not fear; it's common sense. You tell me, smart guy, how we're supposed to hold off the Egyptian military when all Harandi needs to do is ask them for help. A fat lot of good we'll do Rowan from cells in Tora or DC."

He opened his mouth, felt Asal's hand tighten on his knee, and made his point. "We're betraying Rowan to the three assholes who put him in Tora in the first place. To top it off, we're acting like a bunch of pussies. If it was one of us, Rowan would do whatever it took to get us out."

Johnny puffed on the cigar, then held it aloft between his thumb and forefinger. Fragrant smoke created a haze around the table. "Here's the deal, and you can take it or leave it. We're gonna make sure Rowan gets on the CIA's jet and headed back to safety in the good ole USA. Then I'm going to put my plan in motion." The Don pointed the glowing end of the fat cigar at his chest. "You in or not?"

Anger burned all the way to his scalp. He glared first at Johnny's implacable face, then at Ralph's arctic stare. "Honestly?

No. I'm not on board. I know Rowan, and he will never, ever forgive us. And he damn sure won't forget."

Asal stirred next to him. "Gentlemen, may I suggest we continue this discussion during the flight? The more time we give ourselves to analyze the situation on the ground, the better prepared we'll be to help ensure Rowan's safe transport."

Ralph nodded curtly. "The more we can plan the better, because the last thing we want to do is go off half-cocked and get into a mess in Cairo. Nobody wants to see Rowan free and clear of this crap worse than I do, but we're going to do it the right way."

Michael faced Asal. "You're OK with this? You'd willingly hand Rowan off to Harandi and those CIA thugs who almost killed him?"

She took hold of both his hands. "No, I'm not OK with any of this. But you're thinking with your heart. Your guilt and pain are blinding you, and your perspective is off. I know you can't see it, but we risk Rowan's life by attempting a rescue. And in the future, we may need Harandi's trust."

The Don waved his hand, scattering ash across the pristine table top. "She's right. As soon as we're underway, I'll enlighten you about my plan. You'll see its merits."

Ralph's gaze softened. "Trust me, son. This leaves me with a bad taste too. But Asal's got it right."

He squeezed her hands and pulled away. "All right. Let's move. I'll listen to your plan. If I can't stomach it, I'll do what I know is right."

CHAPTER THREE

The Next Day
Al-Aqrab Prison, Cairo, Egypt
Rowan sat hunched over on the narrow cement slab. His heartrate skyrocketed when he heard the key in the cell door. His dry-mouthed fear turned to shock when CIA agent Hancock sidled through the narrow entry. The agent glared at him with the pig-like eyes he'd seen in too many nightmares. Agent Talbot followed, turning sideways to insert his broad-shouldered body into the cell.

They stood next to each other, and Hancock gestured with a sheaf of papers. "Come on, let's go."

Talbot held up hand cuffs and leg irons. "Stand up, Milani. You're going home today."

He didn't move. *"Going home?* What does that mean? Why now? And why with you two?" Talbot grabbed him by his wounded left arm and wrenched him to his feet. Sliced open by a holy warrior he'd killed before his capture, the sutures ripped out while he'd endured months of mistreatment, it had never healed. He gasped at the pain and staggered.

Talbot grunted and held him up, pushed him against the wall and pulled both arms behind his back. The cold metal clicked closed around his wrists and his arm throbbed. He leaned against the wall, grateful for its support, while the agent attached the leg irons around his ankles.

Talbot led him, half-supporting him, to the door where Hancock waited. They paused to tug a black hood over his head. He heard Hancock's voice close to his ear. "Not everyone is in favor of you leaving today. Don't try any of your stupid shit, or you might end up staying."

The suffocating blackness amplified his ragged breaths as the agents marched him out of the cell. They took him down the hallway and around corners, letting him trip and stumble through raised doorways in what felt like an endless trek. He heard the grating sound of a metal door opening and felt warm air on his arms. The agents jerked on his arms, half-dragging him while the leg irons scraped his ankles. He heard the electronic beeping sound he remembered, accompanied by metal grinding and shrieking.

Loud voices argued in Arabic. *"Stop. Who is under the hood? Close the gate. No one has permission to leave Al-Aqrab today. Stop and remove the hood."* Hancock argued back in Arabic, something about the warden, the Interior Minister, and a special agreement.

He heard the distinct pop-pop of shots fired. Bullets thudded into metal close by. Vehicle doors creaked open and urgent hands halfway tossed and shoved him into a seat. He heard a voice he recognized, yelling in English. "Let's go. We need to get the hell out of here."

The vehicle doors slammed, and another voice he knew surprised him. "Fuck me. Put this bitch in gear before they fire that RPG." He slammed backward against the seat as the vehicle squealed its tires and roared off. How could Ralph and Mike be in Cairo, taking him from Tora? Why would they team up with the two CIA bastards who'd helped put him there?

He swayed back and forth as the vehicle swerved and honked, alternately accelerating and slowing. No one spoke and the total darkness inside the hood kept his body tensed for action he couldn't take. The vehicle screeched to a stop, sending him lurching forward. Doors opened, rough hands yanked him out, and the sound of jet engines let him know they'd made it to an airfield.

They pulled him along what seemed like a mile of painful steps. His bare feet burned on hot cement. The roar of jet engines grew louder, and beneath the hood, he caught the acrid scent of burning jet fuel. He heard Ralph barking commands and Mike swearing. The rough hands jerked him up. He tripped on something hard and sharp.

Talbot bellowed in his ear. "You need to board the jet." His foot found a narrow metal stair, and he took tentative steps. The two men cursed as they lifted and guided him. He took deep, heaving breaths, sucking the fabric of the hood into his mouth.

The engines' roar diminished, and he felt carpet beneath his feet. Shoved down into a seat, he sat awkwardly, the cuffs digging into his wrists. Blood slicked his ankles, scraped raw by the leg irons. The hood lifted, and he squinted in bright, artificial light.

His ex-friend Harandi stood in front of him. "Rowan, it's good to see you. Agent Talbot, get the damn cuffs and leg irons off and buckle him in. I've got to take care of a few things up front, and then we've got to get out of here, and fast."

He gritted his teeth when the agent thrust him forward and fumbled with a key, releasing his hands. Pulling his arms forward took all his strength. Talbot buckled the seat belt around him and unlocked the loathsome shackles from his ankles.

He watched as Ralph tromped down the aisle of the aircraft, looking over his shoulder. "You can kiss my ass, Harandi. I'm going to see for myself that he's all right, and then I'll be on my way. You know what else? *You're welcome.*"

Talbot spoke. "Make it quick, Johnston, before we decide to haul you back with him."

Ralph looked every bit the SEAL in camo fatigues and a Kevlar vest. "I'd like to see you try." His former boss knelt beside his seat. "God almighty, Rowan. Mike and I, we're not happy about this. I'm sorry we have to leave you with these jerks. But help is on the way. You remember that."

He swallowed and coughed, managed a hoarse whisper. "OK."

Ralph shook his head, then stood and headed back up the aircraft aisle. Rowan heard the aircraft door thud shut and felt the jet shudder into motion. Trying to escape the pain everywhere in his body, he closed his eyes and concentrated on the engine noise. The whine became a rumble as the aircraft rolled along the taxiway.

The rumble turned to a roar, and he felt the jet wobble as they sped along the tarmac. The aircraft lifted and climbed fast, pushing him against the seat. His breathing slowed, and his tensed shoulders slumped. Whatever happened to him now didn't matter.

A gentle tap on his shoulder brought instant panic. He blinked and tried to orient himself. He stared at the man seated across from him; the old friend he'd come to despise, with his college-boy Oxford shirts, khaki pants, and Ivy League goatee.

Harandi eyed scribbled notes on a legal pad and said, "First things first. I know you're innocent. I've done everything I can to convince Whitman, but he's always considering other angles." Harandi stroked his goatee. "For what it's worth, Whitman tried to get you back. Things spun so rapidly out of control, we lost the opportunity. After the beheading video circulated, we no longer tried."

The lame excuses had him breathing hard, clenching his hands into useless fists. "You're sorry? What beheading video? There must have been one hell of a political upheaval for me to be sitting on this jet, because I know Whitman doesn't give a shit whether I live or die."

Harandi replied. "A group of Islamists posted a video on YouTube. They faked your beheading. You're here now because Hancock and Talbot found out you were still alive and being held in Al-Aqrab. I told Whitman we needed to bring you back before the Egyptians decided to actually kill you. And sure, you're partly right. I told him it was politically advantageous to bring you home."

He read the sincerity in Harandi's face, but couldn't resist a sneer. "Of course you did." He thought about the guards and shuddered. "Thank you."

"I'm afraid there's more. Whitman intends to see you prosecuted for Ainsley's murder, and he's made arrangements for your pretrial detention at ADX Florence, in Colorado. Even with the evidence I've presented, Whitman won't rescind your status as an enemy combatant. I'm sorry, Rowan. I wish we could go back and start over."

"OK."

"That's all you have to say?"

He raised his hands and winced. "What do you want me to say? It's not like I have a choice about where I'm headed. And just so you know, there isn't one goddamned thing you can say or do that will *ever* make me willing to accept an apology from you, or *start over*, whatever that means."

Harandi jotted more notes, then slapped the pen down. "Look, I get it. You hate me. I can't change that. But understand something. I want to help you. I'd go back and do everything differently, if I could. Wouldn't you?"

His adversary's last comment struck home. He wilted in the seat, feeling faint, while his mind rambled back. Lying on the cold cement, he'd wished with all his heart that he could go back and be a different man. He remembered the figure kneeling beside him in the filthy cell. He heard the kindness in the whispered voice. *Redemption is yours, if you choose it.* God, he'd wanted to believe that. But it had been nothing more than an illusion, concocted by his desperate mind.

David snapped fingers in front of his face. "Hey, come on back. I know you've been through hell. I can't change that. About all I can do is offer you a sandwich and some coffee. But you're out of Tora now, and you won't ever go back there."

Gathering his fragmented thoughts seemed impossible. His mouth watered, and his stomach rumbled at the mention of a sandwich. “You know what? I’m done. I can’t fight anymore. I’ll take whatever I’ve got coming. I killed that dumb fuck Ainsley, and I’d do it again. Nothing is going to change that.”

“Well, this is a first. Can I tell Whitman you’ll cooperate to the best of your ability with your interrogator?”

“Sure. I’ll say whatever you want to hear.”

“Not to me you won’t. Whitman called while we were en route. Apparently, the new director of the FBI felt the need to throw her weight around. She’s assigning her own interrogator.”

“She?” Panic stricken, he said, “It’s not Hennessey, is it? Whitman wouldn’t be that stupid, would he?”

“No. Her name is Leigh Berenger. But that reminds me of something I’ve wanted to ask you. Someone who knows their way around a sniper rifle shot Patricia. That doesn’t ring a bell, does it?”

“Someone shot her? Is she dead?”

“Yes. She took a classic sniper hit behind her left ear. Law enforcement has no leads.”

He shifted in the seat, remembering the godawful agony the bitch had inflicted on him with her pointy-toed shoes. “Huh. Where did it happen?”

“They found her at Ainsley’s grave site with some crazy letter stuffed in her jacket pocket. The letter listed the names of Mexican cartel members and claimed they were working for you.”

Plenty of men could make the shot Harandi described, but he only knew one man who’d want to. “How would I know who killed her? And Mexican cartel members? None of this makes sense to me.”

Harandi gave him a shrewd look. “Law enforcement is completely stumped. I’m sorry you can’t shed any light on the case.”

He'd have given anything to be a part of the op that took her out. He slouched lower in the seat. "Me too."

Harandi stood up. "I'll grab you a sandwich and some coffee. I've got some pain meds too. Sorry you can't wash off the stink, but that'll have to wait."

"OK." The thought of sparring with a clever Bureau interrogator, of balancing when to lie and when to tell the truth only magnified the hopelessness he couldn't escape.

FBI Headquarters, Washington, DC

Harandi yawned while FBI Director Berenger sat behind her desk, scowling at him. He wondered what he'd done to earn her disapproval and wished he'd waited to meet with her until after he'd slept. In the thirty-plus hours since he'd left DC for Cairo, he'd dozed when he had the opportunity, but sleep hadn't been an option. Berenger insisted he honor the *commitment* he'd made in his phone message. "Good evening, Director. At least I think it's still evening. It's not midnight yet, is it?"

"No, Mr. Harandi. It's five minutes past ten. What's the status of my detainee? How would you rate his mental and physical condition?"

Her tone irritated him, but responding in kind wouldn't get him anywhere. Thankfully, she'd opted for subdued lighting, and they faced each other in the glow of lamplight. "Milani's mental acuity is surprisingly intact. He's physically weak, which is to be expected after spending months in Tora, and he needs medical attention for several issues." He paused to rub his bloodshot eyes. "I'll prepare a report for you, as soon as I've had some sleep."

Berenger gave him no quarter. "I would appreciate your report as soon as possible, preferably on my desk by 8 a.m. I need to give his interrogator every possible advantage."

He wasn't in the mood to be pushed around by a bureaucrat he didn't answer to. "Director, I'll give your report my due diligence, and you'll have it sometime tomorrow. Also, I'd like to give your interrogator a few pointers."

"My special agent is quite capable of conducting an interrogation, Mr. Harandi. The Bureau has a track record of success utilizing time-honored techniques, unlike the questionable methods you and other CIA agents used with Milani."

For reasons he couldn't fathom, she seemed determined to insult him. He stifled yet another yawn and hoped he could avoid a pissing match. "The Bureau may certainly employ whatever techniques you choose, Director. I only meant to offer tips specific to dealing with Milani. I know him very well."

"Thank you, Mr. Harandi. As you can see, your report is germane to my ability to proceed, which is why I'd appreciate it first thing in the morning."

A pissing match appeared to be what she wanted. "I respect your wishes, ma'am. However, I've crossed more time zones than I can count in just over a day, and I'm not accustomed to that any more. My report will suffer, and I want to give it my best effort."

Berenger regarded him with raised brows. "Yet you managed to conduct an initial interview with Milani and assess him accurately before meeting with me, or sleeping. Just have your report on my desk by 8 a.m."

She'd managed to push too far. He stood up. "I conducted an interview on the flight back so that I could meet with you as a courtesy, to ensure you're informed. And while Milani may be under your purview, I am not. I work for the President. You'll have your report after I get some sleep. Good night."

She folded her hands on her desk. "Sit down, Mr. Harandi. Since you mention your desire to keep me informed, I have a question for you. Why has this entire affair in Cairo been initiated and accomplished by the CIA in cooperation with our embassy, without the FBI's Legal Attaché even being notified Milani was alive, let alone allowed to handle his return?"

He sat down, as the source of her attitude dawned in his enervated mind. "Yesterday morning, the two CIA agents assigned to handle Milani during his incarceration in Tora informed me he was alive. They'd already made arrangements via the CIA's Station Chief, in cooperation with Ambassador Givens and Egypt's Interior Minister, to return him to the United States. Knowing the volatility of the situation in Egypt, my *only* concern was getting Milani out as soon as possible. Honestly, there was no intent on my part to leave you or the Bureau out of the process."

Berenger replied. "And yet, that is exactly the result. Here's another mystery I'd like to solve. Why were CIA agents involved in the first apprehension of Milani in South Dakota? The CIA has no arrest authority."

"My involvement came later, at the explicit request of the President. Director Ainsley worked quite closely with the President, Patricia Hennessey, and Muusa Shemal. Involving CIA agents was certainly not my decision."

"Interestingly enough, the people most capable of answering my questions are no longer alive."

He replied. "Have you brought these concerns to the President?"

Berenger gave him a rueful smile. "What do you think, Mr. Harandi?"

"My guess would be, no."

"You would be correct. So many things about this entire debacle trouble me. However, my instincts tell me to keep my concerns to myself."

"And yet, here you are, in what qualifies as close to the middle of the night, discussing them with, of all people, a former member of the damned CIA."

"Right you are. For some reason, I trust you."

Surprised, he spoke without thinking. "But you don't trust Whitman, do you?"

"Let's just say, I prefer to have all the facts before going to the boss."

Her response jogged his memory. "Have you read the Intel brief I sent on Shemal?"

"I have. The information in the brief stunned me. Are you confident the intelligence you've gathered is accurate?"

He gave Berenger a weary nod. "I've independently verified everything Milani's people told me. If I'd listened to Milani at the outset, we'd be looking at a different set of circumstances."

Her look turned skeptical. "Milani still needs to be held accountable for Ainsley's murder, among a slew of others."

"Oh, I agree. He's earned everything he faces. But he's not a traitor. He has been effectively portrayed as one, which is why I wanted you to read about Shemal's activities."

Berenger replied. "Although your report casts aspersions on Shemal's evidence, it does not necessarily absolve Milani, at least not in my mind. I intend to conduct an exhaustive investigation to determine once and for all if we're dealing with a traitorous double agent."

Desperately tired, he wished he'd quit remembering pertinent things so he could end the conversation and get some sleep. "You'll be interested in the flash drive Milani used to record information on his assigned targets. My contact in the Houston PD provided me with the copy he made."

"Care to explain why we're in possession of a copy instead of the original flash drive?"

Of course, she'd want to know every detail. "Through questioning Milani's sister at the beginning of this mess, I discovered its existence. My Houston contact found it in the evidence gathered when Milani was apprehended. He personally handed it to Director Ainsley, but first made a copy, in the hope it might help his murder investigation."

"While I appreciate your attention to detail, I'd still like to know why we're dealing with a copy and not the original drive."

He rubbed the back of his neck and couldn't stifle one more yawn. "Right. Sorry. Ainsley was not in possession of the drive when his effects were searched. Nor was it found among Hennessey's things after she was killed."

She leaned back, massaged her forehead and observed him. "The more I learn, the more I simply cannot believe the abundance of treachery and disinformation on every level. This is beyond disturbing to me."

"Agreed. Now, put yourself in Milani, Cantor, and Johnston's shoes for a few days, and let me know your thoughts."

"You present an interesting proposition. I'll take everything you've said about Milani under advisement. Thank you for your diligence. And for meeting with me."

He stood up and held out his hand. "I'm sorry we seemed to get off on the wrong foot tonight. It's my pleasure to meet with you and now if you don't mind, I need some rest."

She stood and gave him a solid handshake. "Our footing is fine, Mr. Harandi. I'll look forward to your report and please, feel free to share anything you deem relevant as we go forward with this fiasco."

"I'll do everything I can to help you. Good night." He exited her office and left the Bureau's deserted headquarters. The oven-like heat and humidity lingered, enhancing his weariness. He couldn't wait to hit the sack.

Early Morning, The Next Day
Administrative Maximum Facility (ADX) Florence, CO

Rowan watched the guards file out of his cell. The solid steel door closed firmly and locked with a loud clunk. Finally alone, he stood in the middle of the cell, taking in the cold sterility of the white walls, the molded concrete bed, stool and tiny table, and the sink/toilet unit, all crammed into the seven-by-twelve foot space.

He rubbed his gritty eyes and heaved a sigh. The flight from Cairo to DC had been endless and miserable. Harandi and the two CIA thugs handed him off to the US Marshals Service on the tarmac when they landed in DC. Two hard-faced, stoic agents had helped him board another jet. They'd buckled him into a seat and ignored him for the three-and-a-half hours it had taken to fly to Pueblo, Colorado, where they transferred him to a van and drove another hour to the Supermax.

It had been daylight, sometime in the afternoon he guessed, when they'd taken off from Cairo. They'd arrived in DC just after sunset. The clock in the underground entrance at ADX Florence read 1 a.m. when they unloaded him from the van. He'd stood, exhausted to the point of stupor while the two Marshals exchanged paperwork with scowling prison guards. The guards' complaints about his arrival time and the stench of Tora clinging to him were met with shrugs and the lead Marshals' only comment: "Our job is delivery. He's your problem, not ours."

The disgusted men stripped the dirty prison uniform off his body and made him shower, then shaved his beard, cut his hair and deloused his scalp. He'd tried to follow their barked orders, but the unrelenting pain and exhaustion slowed his responses, made him clumsy. Their indifferent shoving and prodding humiliated him, bringing his always-simmering rage to the surface, but he didn't fight back. He shuddered, remembering the Tasers and clubs they carried, along with their pistols.

A taciturn doctor had stared at the purple and yellow bruises marring his weakened body, raising bushy brows at the numerous scars from Shemal's dagger. The doctor muttered over his injured arm and sutured the wound for what he hoped to God was the last time. He'd somehow endured those additional hours of in-processing and pulled on a scratchy orange jumpsuit in the final act that made him an official ADX Florence prisoner. And now, goddamn it, he'd had enough.

Punching the flat pillow into some semblance of shape, he lowered his pain-racked body to the thin foam mattress atop the concrete slab. He closed his eyes, wishing he could slow his mind and fall asleep. But his jumbled thoughts fell one over the other. Soon the guards would come, like they always did. His heart pounded. Sweat dampened his palms and arm pits. They'd use their clubs, if he resisted, and drag him to the dark torture room. The agony wouldn't stop until he passed out.

He opened his eyes and stared at the ceiling, squinting at the bright light panel. He sat up and let his feet stretch to the floor. What the hell was wrong with him? They wouldn't come because he wasn't in Tora. The two guards who took such pleasure in stringing him up couldn't hurt him anymore.

A loud buzzer interrupted his panicked thoughts. After a few seconds, he heard it again, then the cell door swung open. He watched, dry-mouthed and breathing hard, as three guards crowded inside. They'd come after all, like he'd known they would.

They stood in front of him, and one of them spoke. "When you hear the buzzer, stand up and face the wall with your hands behind your head, fingers laced together. Do it now."

His heart rate spiked and beads of sweat popped on his forehead. "I can't."

The guard scowled. "What do you mean, you *can't?* Stand up and put your hands behind your head. *Right now.*"

He stood up and turned to the wall. His abused, injured shoulders wouldn't allow his arms to lift his hands high enough to comply with the order. He put his hands behind his back and clenched his jaws, waiting for the blows he knew were coming. He heard quick footsteps. Strong hands grabbed his arms and wrenched them up. His knees buckled and he groaned.

The guards swore, hoisted him to his feet, and cuffed his hands behind his back. They turned him around. His shoulders burned, and hot pain streaked down his arms. He stood, head bowed. Waves of nausea rolled through his gut while the guards shackled his ankles. The same guard jerked a thumb toward the door. "C'mon, let's go."

They walked him to an interrogation room and left him seated on a sturdy chair with his hands secured to a metal table and his swollen feet shackled to an eye-bolt in the floor. One guard remained, standing in front of the door. The room had the same sterile white walls as his cell and felt cold, like every other interrogation room he'd ever been in. Sweat soaked his chest and back. The jumpsuit clung to his skin. He shivered and bent over to wipe his always-running nose on his hand.

He looked up when the guard turned and opened the door, admitting a man with brown hair, wearing a short-sleeved shirt and jeans. The man carried a miniscule spiral notebook and ambled to the table, pulled out the opposite chair, and sat down. His new interrogator laid the notebook on the table, pulled a pen from his shirt pocket, and gazed at him with sober brown eyes. "Hello Rowan. I'm Wilson Foster. I'm not sure we've met before, but I'm with the Bureau."

He sniffed and bent low to wipe his nose again. Engulfed in a fog of exhaustion and pain, he'd never be able to think coherently about how to respond to a series of questions. His interrogator must know. Maybe that was part of the guy's plan. He stared at the unremarkable face and grasped at a wisp of a memory, something he and Ralph had discussed about the Bureau's star interrogator, sent to Afghanistan, Iraq, and Gitmo on numerous occasions to gather intelligence from terrorists.

Foster opened the notebook and clicked the top of the pen. "I wanted to meet you and clarify a few things."

He already felt outmaneuvered by the nondescript man. "Like what?"

Foster gave him a brief smile and laid down the pen. "You must know your reputation precedes you."

He raised a brow. "What part?"

"That's a good question. Let's just say I've tried to do my homework and learn as much as possible about every aspect of your career."

"I see."

"I confess, though, what I'm lacking is your perspective. Gaining your insight is one of the things I'd like to accomplish here."

Unreasoning, bitter anger flared and he glared at Foster. "Why?"

"We want your side of the story."

The cold steel restraints pressed against his wrists and ankles. Hopelessness overwhelmed him, but he couldn't shake the anger. Foster had to know that his only options were lifetime incarceration or the death penalty. "You're too late."

Foster's eyes flicked over him. The agent tucked the pen and notebook in his shirt pocket. "We'd better postpone our first talk for a bit. Right now, I think you need pain medication and something to eat. I'll have the lights in your cell dimmed so you can get some sleep. I might even be able to arrange for a better mattress on that miserable excuse for a bed."

Acts of kindness from an interrogator always came with the expectation of reciprocation. He didn't want to give in or accept anything from Foster that would give the interrogator leverage, but he wasn't sure he even had the strength to stand up or walk back to his cell under his own power. He couldn't maintain the anger, and it trickled away, leaving only the monumental exhaustion. "OK."

Foster shoved back the chair, stood up, and turned to the guard at the door. "We're finished for now."

The guards helped him back to his cell and left him, hunched over on the edge of the concrete bed. A few minutes later, the door opened again, admitting the same three guards. While one remained watchfully at the door, the second set a paper plate with two sandwiches and a container of milk on the small table. The third gave him two small, round pink pills and a plastic cup of water. "Take these right now." He obeyed while the guard observed. The three men left, closing the door securely.

After the lock clunked into place, he pushed off the bed and limped to the table. If he sat down on the molded concrete stool, he'd never be able to stand up again. He grabbed the sandwiches and ignored the milk. How could Foster know how much he liked peanut butter and grape jelly on plain white bread? He sat on the edge of the slab and gobbled the sandwiches, licking jelly from his fingers when he'd finished. He could have eaten two or maybe three more.

A huge yawn overtook him, and he covered his mouth with his fist. He needed to lie down. While he tried to get situated, the lights overhead dimmed almost to darkness. He lay flat on his back with a meager blanket covering all but his feet, conscious of the utter stillness in the cell. No screams or echoing gunshots permeated the walls. The narrow, barred window had been covered, leaving him with no idea whether it was day or night.

Creeping numbness replaced the burning pain in his shoulders, back, and hips. He closed his eyes as his body's overstressed muscles relaxed, free from excruciating pain for the first time in longer than he could remember. The cell felt like a refuge. Shemal couldn't touch him here. The Brotherhood couldn't get their hands on him. No one could hurt him. His thoughts slowed and he drifted into peaceful darkness.

Dubai, UAE

Clifton Cantor reclined on a sofa in Angelo Blevins' private study on the backside of their Dubai apartment. At a lanky six-foot-four, with blond hair and bright blue eyes, he didn't blend into the local population of Dubai the way most of the others could. Consequently, he spent the majority of his time in the apartment.

That wasn't necessarily a bad thing. He'd had plenty of time for the introspection he needed. His entire life had been not just disrupted, but completely destroyed by the vindictive actions of President Gilford Whitman, a man he'd called friend for upwards of thirty years.

He contemplated Angelo, sprawled comfortably on a chair adjacent to the sofa. The psychiatrist had tied his gray hair back in a ponytail and gazed at him over wire-rimmed glasses.

Angelo sat up straight, signaling the formal beginning of the sessions he'd come to appreciate. "Why don't you tell me what's on your mind, Clifton? You know I don't have many answers, but I'm always willing to listen."

Recent thoughts had created a depth of sadness he was suddenly anxious to be rid of. "You know, both Natalie and I were always proud of Chad. He was a handful in a different way than most people think. His insatiable curiosity, combined with his intelligence made it incredibly difficult for us to manage him positively. His expertise with computer and cell phone technology is breathtaking."

Angelo replied. "We've all benefited from his skills. Tell me more. How did the two of you harness that combination of curiosity and brainpower?"

"Well, he did so many hair-raising things early on, with his hacking ability, that we thought it only prudent to work with the authorities instead of letting his antics reach the level of criminality. Natalie loved the challenge. When she succumbed to Alzheimer's, Chad lost his greatest advocate, and I lost the best partner I could ever have." He stopped talking. Why did the loss of his wife's beautiful mind to Alzheimer's, after so many years, choose this moment to devastate him?

Angelo's gentle voice prodded him. "Life's losses have a way of catching us off-guard, often when we're overwhelmed. Please continue, if you feel up to it."

"I'm very happy Natalie isn't here now, to see what has happened to our son. My heart aches every day when I see pregnant Bettina carrying our first grandchild. It's an ugly state of affairs, but in the midst of it, I'm grateful to David Harandi for facilitating Bettina's release and for enabling us to leave the country without Whitman knowing."

"I know you trusted President Whitman. It must have been surreal to find yourself entrapped and detained. Have you been able to deal with that?"

He paused, sickened by the recollection. "The stress, fear, and realization of physical helplessness defies my understanding or description. After what I experienced for a matter of days, I can't imagine how Rowan has survived all the things that have happened to him over the past year and a half. He must be one incredibly tough human being, both mentally and physically."

"I'd have to agree about Rowan. I understand your helplessness and terror, having dealt with my own issues after being held a prisoner of war by the Viet Cong. The things that happened to me are what ultimately led to my becoming a therapist." Angelo shrugged. "But that's ancient history. What about you, now?"

He met the psychiatrist's compassionate gaze. "I vowed to never, ever trust a politician or anyone in our government again. I am not entirely sure what game Whitman is playing, but I do know his overarching commitment is to his administration and his legacy. He is first, foremost, and always a political animal. He has no morality other than that. He willingly destroyed everything I've built over the years as far as my reputation and business."

Angelo whistled softly. "I had no idea."

"Chad used to admonish me over and over that the government should never be completely trusted, although I'm certain he didn't envision *this* scenario. At any rate, I listened to my son. I stashed money in a set of accounts spread around the globe for the day I hoped would never come. But, it did come, didn't it?"

"Yes, it did, my friend. For all of us."

He continued. "After arriving in the UAE, I accessed each of those accounts and liquidated over $10 Million in US currency. Whitman and his henchmen will never know. The money has been safely reinvested. Bettina and my grandchild will be provided for no matter what happens to either Chad or myself in this debacle."

"What a blessing," Angelo murmured.

"Yes, I agree. So you see, I shouldn't complain. I'm not exactly destitute."

Angelo replied. "Positive action helps every time. In my opinion, it's the best way to get the last word, or as you put it, stick it to those who've caused unbearable pain. As I said before, we've all benefited from Chad's foresight and intelligence. It's a shame our government, specifically the FBI, has not utilized his abilities on behalf of the country."

"I'm heartsick over what our government has done to Chad. David Harandi was closed-mouthed about what is really going on, although I believe he's on our side. He even mentioned leaving and coming to join us."

Angelo looked thoughtful. "David Harandi has played a pivotal role in this entire situation. If not for him, Rowan may not ever have been apprehended. The fact that David helped Bettina and you, does give him a certain amount of credibility."

"David is a consummate professional. He certainly set me up. I never saw the smack down coming. I didn't even get a whiff of it when Whitman asked me to come to the Oval Office. David orchestrated the entire thing."

Angelo replied. "We've all been taken by surprise in one way or another throughout this whole mess. Rowan was the master of misleading and confounding me. Quite often, I fight despair, wondering if I'd been smarter, less trusting that he was telling me the truth, would I have been able to prevent him from taking the path he chose. I wonder if he'd be free if I'd been more astute."

The psychiatrist's words surprised him. He'd always appeared resolutely positive, cheery even. "Rowan has always been a wild card. Chad used to tell me stories. Rowan would defy Ralph, do things his way, and come up with results that earned him and his bosses all kinds of accolades. I'm sorry I've never met him."

Angelo said, "I'm grateful to have known Rowan. My only regret is that I never broke through his tough exterior. Ralph told me not to beat myself up. He told me Rowan had lied his way around the globe for the better part of ten years. I'm not sure Rowan has ever truly been *himself* with anyone."

"Maybe with Danielle?"

"Possibly. Although, I believe his honesty with Danielle is the root cause of his eventual rejection of their relationship. Being himself has caused Rowan great pain, which I must acknowledge, is a monumental understatement."

"You're right about that, Angelo."

The psychiatrist replied. "We could spend hours discussing the things we regret. However, I believe our responsibility both individually and collectively, is to find a way to rebuild our lives and make them purposeful and satisfying."

"Well said, my friend. I couldn't agree more."

Washington, DC

Special Agent O'Brien tapped her foot to Celtic Thunder's spirited tune *Whiskey in the Jar* playing full blast on her iPhone earbuds. The music helped her concentrate. She looked up from her spot in the back seat of the sedan Director Berenger had sent for her. While they sat in traffic, headed to DC's County Jail, she reflected on the goals she'd worked so hard to accomplish, all of which combined to give her the most important assignment of her career.

Her background included sixteen years with the Bureau, ten of them as an FBI interrogator specializing in counter terrorism. She'd traveled to Iraq and Afghanistan to interview terror suspects. A few months earlier, she'd celebrated her thirty-eighth birthday at Gitmo, while on assignment to interrogate a high-value terror suspect.

She'd become known among her fellow agents as an invaluable team member, gifted with the ability to empathize. Getting into another person's head and heart came easy for her because she genuinely cared, not just for results, but for the people she interrogated. She couldn't *not* see them as fellow human beings, albeit on differing sides. Her barely tamed, naturally curly red hair and five-foot, two-inch height seemed to take even the most hardened jihadist off his or her game.

The sedan pulled into the jail's parking lot. She closed the file folder she'd been scanning, making final mental notes about the man she was about to meet. She'd studied everything she could unearth about the former special agent and his activities. She exited the car and strode toward the entrance through the muggy heat. No way would she let her boss down.

DC County Jail

Chad paced back and forth, counting the steps, three in each direction. Ever since his brief conversation with Bettina, he'd been unable to think of anything else. How long before he earned his freedom? Or even another phone call? He'd done everything Foster asked. No other agent had appeared. He pounded his fist into the opposite palm. Damn the Bureau. He needed to be with his family.

His family. The words took his breath away. How long had it been since they'd talked? Did he have a son or daughter? Frustrated, he pounded on the door, then swung around and glared at the narrow, uncomfortable bed. How long had it been since he'd been able to stretch out and sleep? His legs hung over the edge by a foot or more, forcing him to curl on his side.

The intercom buzzed, and the voice he hated spoke. "Approach the door." The sliders opened. He obeyed because he didn't have a choice. The cold metal closed around his wrists and ankles, and he shuffled back.

The guards escorted him to the same chilly interrogation room and shoved him into the metal chair. One guard remained inside the door, and the other left. This time, the guard opened the door to a petite woman. She wore a tailored black suit jacket and matching skirt with high heels, FBI credentials prominently displayed on the lanyard draped around her neck.

She held a notebook and file folder, which she laid on the table before perching on the chair opposite his. She stared at him with determined green eyes. "Mr. Cantor, I've been looking forward to meeting with you. I'm Special Agent O'Brien. Director Berenger assigned me to take over for Agent Foster."

He eyed the woman. She was pretty, in an Irish-pixie sort of way. "I don't have anything more to say to you or anyone else. I've done everything Foster wanted. It's time for the Bureau to do something for me."

"You must understand you're not in the position to make any kind of demands. You've breached our national security protocols, undermined the FBI's ability to protect itself with your hacking ability, and humiliated the country's entire intelligence community in the process. Also, if I understand correctly, you've developed some quite advanced cell phone technology. What do you have to say for yourself?"

"You must have Foster's notes. I don't know why I have to keep repeating myself, but here you are, asking the same damn useless questions. I did what was necessary to protect my friend and colleague, a *real* American hero, from the *real* traitors in our government who betrayed him and wanted to silence him. I'd do it again, if necessary, even though it cost me everything that matters."

O'Brien fingered strands of her unruly hair and watched him, long enough to make him shift uncomfortably in the metal chair cramping his six-foot five-inch frame. When she finally spoke, the intensity in her voice wasn't what he expected. "According to my notes of your conversations with both Harandi and Foster, a money trail exists that proves who the real traitors are, as you said. Will you help me out with that?"

Nonplussed, he could only stare at her and wonder whether she was sincere, or simply pulling his chain. She stared back at him. He didn't know if he could trust her, but she looked like she wanted an answer. "If you give me access to my laptop, I'll show you where all the money came from, where it went, and who accepted it."

"I'll make your laptop available. We'll set up in the same classroom where you've been teaching our agents." O'Brien stood up. "We're going to access that information today. I'll be back with your laptop. The guards will move you to the classroom shortly."

She left, and he heaved a gusty sigh. Would someone in the Bureau believe him and act on his evidence? The guards took him to the same room where he'd been teaching the IT agents his hacking skills. They left him restrained, but free to wander the windowless, locked room. His notes from the last training session were still faintly visible on the blackboard, even though they'd been erased. He made his way to the back of the room, with its neatly arranged tables and chairs and surveyed the podium where he stood to teach.

It felt good to move around, even though the shackles above his ankles necessitated short steps. While he moved among the tables and chairs, he thought about how much he enjoyed teaching, even under the stressful circumstances. The Bureau's IT agents, some he'd met previously, were enthused to learn from a master hacker, and he took the honor to heart.

He didn't teach them everything, but they would never know what he'd left out. No one besides Rowan and Mike would ever know. He'd built a backdoor into *all* of the Bureau's security. It was his own personal access into anything he wanted to see. If he and Rowan ever regained their freedom, he'd always know what the Bureau was doing, as well as every other agency in the realm of national security.

He slouched into a chair at the front of the room. Special Agent O'Brien had a quality about her that made him want to trust her. But could he? Or did she plan to jack him around? Was she on Shemal's payroll, too? He didn't have a choice but to show her the evidence he'd accumulated of the money funding Rowan's betrayal.

The door opened, and O'Brien entered with his laptop. She placed it on the table in front of him and tapped it with her forefinger. "Get to work and show me the money trails, the bank accounts, emails, you name it. None of our Bureau experts have been able to access anything. Your laptop is the same as the last time you used it."

His heart thudded while she spoke. An unexpected flood of memories hit him, and he closed his eyes. "Oh shit." He'd been sweaty and covered with dust after digging through boxes, retrieving and packing the important things at the Kauai estate. Pregnant Bettina needed to use the bathroom before they headed to the airport. He'd gone back inside to hustle her along and retrieve one last item, his laptop. He shuddered and opened his eyes.

O'Brien stood in front of the table, frowning. "Is everything all right? You can access what we need, correct?"

"Of course. Just let me get this baby fired up." Without thinking he tried to crack his knuckles. The cuffs stopped him. "Ouch."

O'Brien said, "Deal with it. Your Second-Degree Black Belt skills are well-known. I'm not taking the cuffs off."

"That's all right. Did you want to pull up a chair and observe? You want to make sure I don't try anything untoward, right? No telling the mayhem I could create from right here in DC County Jail."

She twirled her hand in an exaggerated gesture. "The cameras have you covered. Besides, I know you don't want to jeopardize our trust."

"You're right. Any chance of getting some coffee?"

"Of course. I'll get a whole carafe of coffee for you."

"Thanks. I'll get started though, if it's all right with you?"

O'Brien gave him thumbs up. "Absolutely. I'll be right back."

He watched her leave and opened the file revealing Ainsley's banking records as well as those of the President's special advisor Patricia Hennessey and CIA Agents Capello, Talbot, and Hancock. A brisk knock put the guard in motion.

O'Brien entered with a white carafe of coffee and one ceramic cup. "Coffee as promised." She poured and set the cup within his reach before grabbing a chair and planting it next to his. "Let's get started. I'm anxious to see proof of the claims you've made."

He sipped the coffee. "I never made *claims.* These transactions are real. Harandi knows and so does Whitman."

She laid a scrap of paper on the table. "We want the proof from your laptop. Send everything to this printer, would you? Director Berenger wants to see everything right away."

Three hours later, he hit 'send' for the last time. He'd be willing to bet he'd never feel his ass again. He blinked dry eyes and looked at O'Brien. She'd refilled the carafe for him, and he'd lost track of how many cups of coffee he'd slurped. "We're done. That's every bit of information I have on the principal players. If you want to continue our conversation, I need to use a bathroom first."

O'Brien had been sitting with one leg tucked beneath her. She stretched, yawned, and patted her mouth. "I think we're good. I'm sure this information will prove invaluable. However, don't touch your laptop again. Slide it to the center of the table, please." She stood up and smiled when he complied. "Thank you, Mr. Cantor."

"Uh, sure, it's my pleasure. I can't wait to see what Director Berenger does with this information. I hope it helps Rowan and me get out of here."

O'Brien spoke earnestly. "I know things seem to move slowly. Our investigation is ongoing, and I want you to know your cooperation is appreciated at the highest level. We'll talk again after your information has been analyzed."

"I've done everything you've asked. I've done everything Foster wanted. Ask Berenger when the Bureau plans to reciprocate, will you?"

O'Brien gazed at him with her green eyes. "I will."

CHAPTER FOUR

Seattle, WA

Danielle pulled her hair back in a ponytail and flipped on the TV while she waited for Tom. She'd let him talk her into another ride on his Harley. Her assistant manager at the coffee bistro had begged for more management experience, giving her another opportunity for a carefree afternoon. She enjoyed Tom's easygoing personality more than she wanted to admit, and he seemed content with their relationship as friends.

Well, she'd noticed a few things. He liked to help her with a soft touch on her elbow or a quick hand on her back, but otherwise he kept his distance and didn't push her for anything more. His friendship eased the aching loneliness and the crushing guilt she so often couldn't escape. Why did she feel guilty for enjoying herself? And why should she be alone and lonely? Rowan had insisted she move on with her life.

She perched on the edge of the sofa and glanced at the TV. An excited anchor narrated a breaking news story. While she watched, a video played of a private jet landing in early twilight. It came to a stop under a blaze of lights.

The background seemed familiar. She'd seen a similar video somewhere, sometime before. The breaking news banner piqued her interest. ***A Suspected Terrorist Returns to the US.*** The anchor's first words sent paralyzing shock sizzling through her body.

"Anonymous sources have informed FOX News that former FBI Special Agent Rowan Milani, the terror suspect presumed dead at the hands of radical Egyptian forces, is alive. The CIA returned Milani to the United States, and our very own International Investigative Reporter Jack McKenzie recorded this exclusive video of his arrival. The US Marshals Service took custody of Milani upon his arrival and transported him to

Colorado's Supermax prison, known as ADX Florence, where he is currently detained, pending further action."

The anchor droned on, but she didn't hear any more. She couldn't look away from the images on screen. Black Suburbans, gleaming in the artificial light, pulled up in front of the jet as the aircraft door opened. Soldiers with rifles seemed to be everywhere. A uniformed man exited one of the vehicles and trotted to the stairs to raise the railings. The doorbell rang and Leo woofed, but she couldn't stop watching. "Come in, it's unlocked."

She heard Tom. "Leo, how are ya, big buddy? Dani? Are you ready?"

A man she'd never seen before descended the steps and waited. She held her breath when the camera panned a close-up of the doorway. A big man stepped out first, and then Rowan appeared. Shadows obscured his features, but she'd recognize his form anywhere. His thick black hair scraped his shoulders, and his beard had grown long. She unconsciously touched the side of her face. He'd often told her how much he hated wearing a beard.

Another man stepped out and grabbed his arm. She watched while Rowan made his way down the air stairs. His hands were cuffed to a chain around his waist and leg irons made his limping steps short and awkward. The overhead lights illuminated his face, and the camera tightened in for a brief close-up. His gaunt face showed only exhaustion. A thin scar lined one cheekbone above his ragged beard. "Oh Rowan," she whispered.

Tom laid a gentle hand on her shoulder from behind the sofa. "Are you all right?"

She raised her shoulders and let them fall, not sure how to answer, or even if she could. The three men wasted no time hustling Rowan into the back seat of one of the Suburbans. They closed the door, and he was gone. She couldn't stop staring at the TV.

Tom sat beside her. "Do you want to talk about it?"

She turned slowly and looked at him. "What?"

"We don't have to go out on the scooter. Do you want to hang out here? I'm great company, you know. I don't say much, and I can even bring you some wine."

"Um, no, I don't think we should stay here."

He touched her arm. "You're shaking. Pale. How about I bring you a glass of wine? Maybe the Bolgheri, whatsit called? You know, the bottle you told me you're hoarding."

"Oh no." She covered her face with her hands as memories she'd tried so hard to leave behind overtook her. Rowan, with his sexy smile, pouring her a glass of what became their special wine. She'd never forget the first time they made love, and afterward, laying with her head on his chest, listening to his slow, steady heartbeat. She could still feel the strong warmth of his arms wrapped around her. She could still taste his skin and smell the tang of his aftershave.

Tom reappeared next to her. "Here. I brought you some water. Take a sip. I think you need it."

She stared at the glass of water, then looked at Tom. "Did you open the bottle of wine?"

She couldn't miss the kindness in his eyes. "No. Not without your express permission. Besides, I think you need some water first."

Relieved, she huddled on the sofa and sipped the water while he sat beside her. Leo lay in front of them, head on his paws. The TV screen was black. Thank goodness. "You don't have to stay. I'm all right. I mean, I saw someone, but it doesn't matter."

"I think it does matter. Dani, you're tough and capable, but sometimes handling things alone isn't good. And it isn't necessary." Tom leaned back and draped his arm across the top of the sofa behind her. "You don't have to talk, but if you want to, I'm a great listener."

She didn't miss the subtle, maybe even sub-conscious invitation of his arm on the sofa. But she didn't want or need Tom. The man whose touch she ached for remained as far out of reach as if he were dead. Knowing he'd been alive only increased her heart-wrenching sadness. What had the monsters in Tora prison done to him? She shivered, thinking about his desolate face. Tom eased her back until she was leaning against him with his arm around her. She scrunched her body away from him. "I can't, I'm sorry."

Tom pulled her close. "Hey, I get it. Let me be a friend. I understand someone else has your heart. Why don't you tell me about him?"

She twisted around to look at him. "He's not a terrorist." She searched his face. "Are you sure you want to hear about him?"

Tom nodded. "Let me get you another glass of water. Then you can tell me everything."

FBI Headquarters, Washington, DC

Berenger sat at her desk with her hands folded tightly together in front of her. She noticed the white in her knuckles and told herself to dial back her anger. David Harandi faced her with a look she'd classify as purposeful innocence. She gave him a hard stare. "Earlier today I was treated to FOX News' exclusive coverage of Milani's return to the US."

Harandi remained poker-faced, with the hint of a question in his response. "Oh? Great."

"Indeed, everything about it was great. The video was great. Milani looked just great, too. And it was great hearing he'd been returned to the US in the custody of the CIA. And although I love surprises, it would be *super great* if you would tell me what exactly I should expect next."

"Excuse me, Director. I'm not sure what you mean."

"Stop, Mr. Harandi. You may have fooled our enemies in the Middle East, but this particular covert operation has your fingerprints all over it." She tilted her head. "Still not sure what I mean?"

He stroked his goatee for a moment, then heaved a sigh. "Do you want the story or just an apology?"

She leaned back and crossed her arms. "I love stories more than surprises and even more than apologies, especially if the truth is involved."

He spread his hands wide. "I've always told you the truth. On some level, you must realize that, or we wouldn't be chatting again."

She scowled. "Except for the parts you leave out. The story, Mr. Harandi."

"Yes ma'am. Jack McKenzie is a long-time media contact of Ralph Johnston's. Last winter, Johnston contacted him, asking if he'd look into the people most invested in seeing Milani destroyed."

"Interesting. Why didn't Johnston reach out to any of his colleagues?"

"My guess is he wasn't sure who he could trust. Anyway, McKenzie poked around and couldn't find anyone who'd talk. After the video surfaced showing Milani being killed, he didn't pursue it any further."

She looked away from Harandi for a moment, gazing out the windows along one wall of her office, working to get a firm handle on her frustration. "How did you come into contact with McKenzie?"

"His contact information came into my possession this spring."

"I understand your reticence, to a point. But I'd appreciate the specifics."

Harandi met her gaze as she turned from the windows. "In that case, I'd appreciate knowing I'm not going to end up in a cell in County because you've conducted a warrantless search of my townhouse. Or, that you're not going to use the PATRIOT Act to detain me."

"Similar to the methods used with Clifton Cantor, of which you were an integral part?"

A dull flush spread upward from his neck before stalling in his cheeks. "Correct."

"Mr. Harandi, it seems you have placed yourself in charge of your very own investigation, which at best runs parallel to the one I intend to conduct. At worst, it runs at cross purposes."

"Director, let me state most emphatically that I have no interest in causing problems for your investigation."

She leaned forward again, intent on cracking the façade he insisted on presenting. "You already have. Tell me what you're up to."

Harandi's shoulders slumped. "From the outset, I wanted to see justice done. That's why I took the assignment to bring Rowan into federal custody in the first place. I believed a number of things which turned out to be falsehoods."

"Such as?"

He raised a hand and let it drop. "As the Intel brief showed, Rowan did not murder my uncle. Nor did he funnel money to our enemies. Further, there is no evidence that he embraced violent jihad."

"Continue, please."

"His actions caused me huge embarrassment with the Houston Police Department. Because of that, when I did have him in custody, I cut him no slack. I didn't believe *anything* he said."

"Hence the two sessions of water boarding."

Regret flashed across Harandi's face. "Yes, unfortunately. He never gave me anything, until just before Hennessey had him hauled off."

"You mentioned something at our first meeting which caught my interest. I've thought about it several times. I believe your exact words were, *if I'd listened to Milani at the outset, we'd be looking at a different set of circumstances."*

"That's the truth. I allowed my emotions to take over, because he pissed me off and made me look like a fool."

"And now? Are you looking for redemption, Mr. Harandi?"

"Maybe Milani deserves some kind of redemption."

"That's a novel idea, since at last count he's murdered ten people throughout the course of this odyssey. The last time we met, you agreed he needed to pay for everything he's done."

He shrugged. "I've gone over the evidence presented by his colleague again. I've reviewed my interrogations with Milani and researched the information on his flash drive."

"All of which has led you to conduct your own investigation in concert with, of all people, a FOX News reporter."

Harandi stroked his goatee and appeared unrepentant. "Jack McKenzie is a world-class investigative reporter, regardless of his employer. If Ralph Johnston trusts him, so do I."

"What's your endgame?"

"I'd like to see the truth about Milani become public knowledge and maybe see him regain his freedom."

"That's *never* going to happen."

"Look, if I'd handled things differently, he'd never have been put in the position of defending himself against Ainsley. If Hancock and Talbot hadn't strung him up and beat him nearly to death, he may have been reasonable. For another thing, have you ever observed the digital recordings of the five days he spent in Quantico at the mercy of Sal Capello?"

"I have not. But listen to yourself. You're making excuses for a man who, as far as I can tell, has committed cold-blooded murder. *Ten times."*

"Well, Director, you should look at those recordings and read the transcripts. It might give you a different perspective."

“Poor treatment is no excuse for murder, regardless of the depravity. You know that.”

Harandi continued, undeterred. “We didn’t call it murder when he was eliminating terrorists in other countries. Not to mention, of course, that when we pursue justice instead of face-saving, we allow the claim of self-defense as a viable option.”

She bristled. “In what manner are we talking about *face-saving?* And, if you want to take that line, what about the concept of *reasonable force?* Milani could have stopped short of breaking Ainsley’s neck.”

“You know very well what manner of face-saving we’re talking about. It doesn’t take a genius to connect the dots. Milani and his colleagues caused huge, unforgivable embarrassment to the entire intelligence community, maybe especially to the Bureau. They put an indelible stain on Whitman’s legacy. Tell me you aren’t interested in making him pay.”

He’d damn near read her mind. “Once again you’ve piqued my interest. I’ll watch the recordings and read the transcripts. But I don’t promise anything.”

“You’ve certainly proven yourself capable of making reasoned, intelligent decisions. I’d like you to consider one more thing.”

A headache had begun behind her eyes. She needed to be done with the former agent she’d wanted so badly to chastise. “And what would that be, Mr. Harandi?”

“I’d like to combine forces. Let’s investigate together and see where this goes.”

She shook her head. “No. The last thing I want is a FOX News reporter with any kind of access. I couldn’t do that.”

“Please, Director. Set aside your bias for a moment. McKenzie brings a lot to the table. I think you should meet him and then make the kind of decision you’re known for, instead of entertaining a knee-jerk reaction.”

She wasn't sure if he was playing her, but he'd spoken the truth. Harandi brought a lot to the table too, she realized. But she wouldn't give him the satisfaction of hearing her admit it. "You make a salient point. I'll consider it. Thank you for meeting with me today."

Harandi took her cue and stood up. "I'll arrange a very out-of-the-way meeting with McKenzie. We can air concerns and discuss possible scenarios for cooperation."

Somehow, he'd managed to reel her in. He must have been one hell of an asset for the spy agency. "All right, Mr. Harandi. Set it up."

The Next Day
Dubai, UAE

Johnny Giacopino moved restlessly through his office suite in Burj Khalifa, one-hundred and fifty-four stories above the city of Dubai, coming to a stop at the bar he'd crafted along one wall. He poured a generous serving of eighteen-year, single-malt Macallan scotch and took a hefty draught before continuing his march among the opulent furnishings. His fingers skimmed the butter-soft leather of the sofa as he passed by, and he paused to smile at the Monet original mounted on the wall behind his desk.

He'd appointed his private enclave with treasures from around the world. Better that these particular items remained out of the United States and out of the reach of nosy IRS or FBI agents. His reputation as the most successful Mafia Don in America had been hard won, and his Dubai office offered him the opportunity to enjoy what he'd earned.

Not many people understood him. Most of the world chose to see him as a gangster and a murderer, a liar and a cheat. Oh, it saw him as powerful too, as it should. But he had a heart and believed in justice. Real justice, not the candy-ass shit that passed for the concept in the United States. He wasn't any more crooked, dirtier, or more of a murderer than the politicians running things at home.

He downed more scotch before heading to the floor-to-ceiling windows overlooking the city far below and the Persian Gulf beyond it. He didn't need to justify who he was or how he lived his life. His own code served him well. He had contacts and a network spanning the globe. When he needed something done, it happened, quietly and expeditiously. He liked things that way.

People who did know him called him a family man, too. For nearly fifty years, he'd been married and faithful to one woman. Screwing around with whores or with a mistress on the side had never appealed to him. His wife Eloisa was a one-of-a-kind woman. She'd kept him satisfied for a lot of years and had given him three sons and a daughter. She'd known about his family's business from the get-go. He wouldn't have had it any other way.

He stood brooding, staring out the window at puffy clouds floating below his suite, thinking about Rowan Milani. He'd initially involved himself in the shit-storm surrounding Milani because of his good friend and long-time business associate Clifton Cantor. When the camel turd Shemal hauled Milani off to Tora, and Clifton's son Chad ended up in DC's County Jail as a federal prisoner, he'd decided to make it his mission in life to clear their names with the country and the world.

Part of his plan necessitated the cooperation of former President James Linden, who'd hired Milani as his own personal, presidential assassin. Linden had so far shied away from his efforts to get him to speak up on Milani's behalf. Because of Linden's reluctance, he'd decided to up the ante. He tossed back the rest of his scotch and headed to the bar for more. The intercom beeped, and a disembodied voice spoke. "Sir, Mr. Johnston is here to see you."

"Thank you, Georges. Send him in please." The door buzzed and opened, admitting his newest friend and confidant. "Good afternoon, Ralphie. Allow me to pour you a drink."

Ralph's craggy face lit up. "Scotch is first and foremost on my agenda today. Marion is taking the Milanis out shopping. Bettina decided to tag along at the last minute. Gino and Roberto are escorting them. Getting that entourage organized and out the door is a half days' work."

He poured scotch and handed a full glass to his friend. "Ah, Ralphie, that puts your skills as a special agent-in-charge to good use."

Ralph took a long swallow. "Damn, that's nice. You make a good point, but I'm ready for a diversion. Is Linden arriving soon?"

"He is. Here's to the successful implementation of my plan."

Their glasses clanked together, and Ralph replied. "To complete success."

"You know, Ralphie, it's safe to say you're the first and only fed whose presence is ever going to grace my private domain."

Ralph gazed around the room. "A man needs to enjoy the fruits of his labor. And don't forget, you're speaking to a former fed."

He chuckled. "You're right. Not many people understand me. I believe you do."

"Not too long ago, I'd have been happy as hell to bust your ass. But those days are done and gone. You might say my thinking about following the rule of law to achieve justice has evolved."

He replied. "Rowan reached that conclusion before you did, didn't he?"

Ralph agreed. "He did. All those principles I put so much faith in, the institutions, the people I believed in and spent twenty-five years serving, got corrupted somewhere along the way. And I got played for a fool."

"They're nothin' more than a bunch of fuckin' hypocrites. You sit back and watch today. I called this meet with Linden for the express purpose of achieving justice. I wasn't joking about a get-out-of-jail free card."

"Well, that's something I'm looking forward to."

He watched the continuing progression of clouds floating below the suite. "My plan is fail-safe. You can have faith in that."

The intercom beeped and his assistant spoke. "President Linden is here to see you, sir."

"Thank you, Georges. Please send him in." The door buzzed and opened, admitting James Linden. At five-feet, nine-inches tall, with brown hair gone mostly gray and pale blue eyes, the former Commander-in-Chief appeared unassuming. He wore what had become his trademark cashmere sweater vest, in red this time and a short-sleeved, white button-down shirt with black dress pants.

When the former President spoke, either to a jam-packed auditorium or a small group, the unpretentious manner vanished. His lyrical voice and story-telling ability mesmerized the people. He'd been a two-term leader and charted a bold course after 9/11 with a one-time-only united Congress. His policies and guidance had kept the country safe during his eight-year tenure.

After passing the baton of control to President Whitman, Linden reentered private life and chose not to comment on his successor, other than occasionally wishing him well or agreeing to lend his oratorical skills to charity events. Linden had not weighed in on the situation with Rowan, but he was about to change that. "Good afternoon, Mr. President. You've met Ralph Johnston. May I offer you anything to drink before we have a meet?"

Linden demurred. "Nothing for me. Hello, Ralph. I'm surprised, to say the least, to find you here."

Ralph shook Linden's hand and settled into one of two brown leather arm chairs opposite the sofa. "It's good to see you, Mr. President. I'm only here by the kindness of Mr. Giacopino. He's offered safe haven for those of us involved in the mess surrounding our mutual friend Rowan Milani."

Linden sat on the sofa. "Is that right? I've often agonized over the situation surrounding Milani, whom I trusted, obviously. But his actions caused me to revise my opinion. The evidence of his guilt has proven overwhelming. You and Cantor aided and abetted his crimes. For the life of me, I cannot understand why."

Johnny intervened. "Now, now. Not so fast, Mr. President. We've been friends for a long time. I explained on the phone about the circumstances which brought Rowan and his associates to this unfortunate juncture. Have you ever known me to tell you less than the hard truth?"

Linden regarded him with the pale eyes. "No. Your honesty over the years, and your assistance when the country needed your business acumen were appreciated while I was in office. Those are the main reasons I agreed to meet with you today."

He tossed back more scotch and wiped his mouth. "I'll never lead you astray, Mr. President. Like I told you on the phone, I got into this deal with Rowan in the first place because Clifton Cantor is a long-time business associate and friend. His son Chad is in the middle of this crock of shit, too, as you mentioned."

Linden nodded. "I'm acquainted with Clifton Cantor. He was well-known and respected in Washington before this debacle ensued."

Johnny added, "Here's the thing. When I make up my mind to accomplish something, I don't let anything get in my way."

Linden replied. "As I said, your talents have benefited both our country and the government many times."

He accepted the former President's acknowledgement and strutted to the sofa. "I've met Rowan. He's young and brash, got way too bigga balls for his own good, but I like that. I offered him a job, but he had to go off and do things on his own. If I had to guess, I'd say he's seen the error of his ways by now."

"One would hope so," Linden retorted.

Ralph had remained mute, focused on his glass of scotch. At Linden's comment, he spoke. "Mr. President, Rowan completed many of those ops at your request. You share some level of responsibility."

Linden countered. "Yes, and he performed admirably. But somewhere along the line, he lost his way. The evidence of his wrongdoing appears incontrovertible to me. And none of that is my responsibility."

Ralph blustered. "Can you look me in the face and tell me I gave up my career and reputation for a traitor? God almighty, I thought you knew me better than that."

Johnny said, "Our purpose today is not to assign guilt or create acrimony. Mr. President, I'm asking for your help."

Linden replied, "What can I possibly do to help you?"

Johnny continued. "If memory serves, my assistance to the United States government came in the form of facilitation. Specifically, I arranged the sale of all manner of arms and ammunition to regimes your administration wished to support, behind the scenes."

Ralph muttered, "Bloody hell."

Linden sat back with his fingers steepled together. "Yes. But those deals, made on behalf of your government, have nothing to do with Milani."

He sat down facing Linden. "I think they do, and here's how you're going to help me. You're going to arrange a meet between yourself and President Whitman. You'll call him on the carpet over his lack of support for Rowan and his associates when they coulda' used his help. Then you will instruct him to pardon Rowan, Chad, and Ralph."

Linden snorted. "Why would I do such a thing?"

He leaned forward, so he could catch Linden's direct gaze. "Because Rowan Milani deserves real justice. Besides, I can't see how making my facilitation public, with regard to illicit arms deals and regime backing, can be good for our country's prestige among either our allies or our enemies."

Ralph chimed in. "You know, Mr. President, I think our friends around the world would take exception if they knew how Rowan operated on foreign soil per direct orders from two Presidents. He recorded names, dates, and locations on a flash drive."

Linden's face took on a distinct, rosy tint. "This is nothing short of blackmail. Johnny, your assets in the US have been protected because of your discretion in assisting your country. That protection will end."

He leaned back. "My discretion and assistance didn't buy the protection of my assets. I take care of what is mine. But I'll remember your warning for the future."

Ralph grinned at Linden. "May I pour you a drink now, sir?"

Linden shook his head. "No. I'm not interested in drinking with blackmailers. Johnny, you must consider one other thing. Reversing his stand on Milani's status will damage Whitman's credibility as President. Not only will his administration be permanently maligned, the office of the Presidency will be as well. I'm not about to let you foist this poison on the American people."

Ralph replied. "Whitman made choices throughout this ordeal which he alone is responsible for, and he can live with them. Rowan deserves to have his name and reputation cleared. Chad and I do too, by the way."

Johnny added, "Mr. President, if I don't have your unconditional agreement to my plan before you leave today, you probably won't enjoy tomorrow's headlines."

Linden parried back. "Do you have any concept of the fallout from what you're proposing to do? We'll lose allies. Our standing in the global community will be diminished. The setbacks to our strategic foreign policy will be disastrous. Our national security will most certainly be damaged as well. You can't do this."

He shrugged. "Whether or not the information is publicized is in your hands, Mr. President."

Linden glared. "I can't believe I'm forced to consider this. You must know, even if I agree, Whitman is a different story. I can't promise he'll go along with your blackmail."

He said, "I'm sure a man of your considerable skill will have no trouble conveying the delicacy of the situation to our President. He has more at stake, of course. It's hard to say, really, whether he could even stay in office."

Linden stood up and straightened his red vest. "For the sake of the country, I'll do what you ask. But I promise you, one day there will be an accounting for this."

He shot back. "You'd best not threaten me. It just doesn't sit well. You know what I mean? That aside, thank you for freeing a great patriot. Rowan Milani has paid a heavy price for serving his country in ways you and every other politician I've ever met don't have either the guts or the balls for."

Linden responded. "I'll schedule a meeting with the President next week. You have my personal guarantee of his cooperation. After this, this *coup* is finished, don't ever contact me again. I'll see myself out." The former President left, closing the door quietly behind him.

Johnny turned to Ralph. "Rowan's get-out-of-jail-free card is in the works. Yours and Chad's too."

Ralph lifted his glass. "I'll drink to that."

The Next Day
Leôn, Mexico
Gabriel Hernandez sprawled in a chair on the deck circling the villa where he lived with his wife Sherie and their two children. He stared through a haze of tequila at the fragrant potted flowers scattered around the deck. The flowers, with their splashes of

color, should cheer him, but they did not. He raised his glass to his lips, surprised to find it empty. He reached for the bottle of Don Real on the table next to him and poured again.

He gazed past the deck railing to the sun-browned grass and tossed back another hit. A light breeze rustled the tall trees at the edge of the yard, but the heat prevailed, heavy and oppressive, like the guilt draped around his shoulders. He did not belong here at the villa in Leôn, hiding from his responsibilities to the men he'd sworn allegiance to; men he called brothers in the deepest sense of the word.

He swore no loyalty to Mexico. His parents immigrated to the United States long ago, and he'd been born in San Diego. He'd served as a proud Army Ranger, becoming an accomplished spotter for his sniper brother Michael. After 9/11, he'd chosen to serve his country in a different way with Rowan and Michael. Together, the three of them had protected their country from many bad hombres and conducted more black ops in hostile countries than he could keep track of.

When the Islamists targeted Rowan, everything turned to shit. His brother went loco with the lust for retribution. And he, Gabriel, left the fight, to hide with his family, telling himself it was his duty to keep them safe. Now he knew, from watching news on the satellite TV stations, that Rowan had survived Tora. What would his courageous, loco friend think of him now, slinking around in Mexico, becoming a drunk?

He could see Rowan's face; the raised brow, the smirk. *Come on, amigo,* he'd say. *We gotta do some things.* Heavy emotion clogged his throat. He missed his brother Rowan. Michael too, although his barb-tongued friend often wounded him with the truth. What would Michael say? The answer stared at him from the bottom of the empty glass. *Don't be such a little girl. Stop hiding from yourself and get your shit together.* His brothers knew him well.

His cowardice ate at him, day after endless day. Sherie had been ecstatic over returning to Mexico, bringing their two children, Jamie and Sophia, close to their grandparents. Her family loved them, and they welcomed him, even wanted him to join the family business. Holy Mother of God, they owned and operated a *bus company;* the largest in Mexico, with close ties to the government. The company conducted business with the permission of the cartels, sometimes in collusion with them.

He would never work for a bus company, and he could not condone a business arrangement with either the corrupt government or the barbaric cartels. No, he would never join his father-in-law's company. Besides, he was a warrior. He belonged on the battlefield with his brothers, not wasting his life working for a bus company. Or drinking. He poured more tequila and stared at the amber liquid for a moment, then gulped it down.

The patio door slid open, and Sherie stepped out. He watched her approach, tapping his numbing lips with two fingers, wondering what she would say about his drinking this time. The sexy sway of her hips and the swell of her generous breasts in the sleeveless yellow dress overlaid his morose thoughts with raw desire. He needed her in ways she couldn't seem to understand anymore.

Being with her, making love to her, used to keep him sane. Coming home from an op, after witnessing sometimes unimaginable horrors, he'd regained himself by becoming one with her. Lost in his need, conscious of the slow swelling in his groin, he blinked and tried to sit up straight when he heard the edge in her voice.

"Gabriel, we're ready to go. Jamie and Sophia are waiting. You remember, don't you, about the picnic at the park with Nana and Grampy?"

Guilt warred with resentment while he tried to compose a coherent answer. He did not want to attend a sissy picnic. But his ninôs looked forward to every outing, and he could not let them down. No, he'd go with them. He'd listen to Sherie's father drop hints about joining his shitty bus company. He'd swing and twirl Sophia until she screamed with little girl pleasure. He'd take Jamie on a hike. Yes, he, Gabriel, would do it all, to please everyone, if he could stand up and walk. "Of course, I remember, mi Amor."

"Good. You know how much my father enjoys telling you about the family business. And my mother loves to feed you."

Oh no, it would never do to disappoint her parents. His resentment expanded into hot anger. Why did no one care whether he wanted the obligations suffocating him? Every day it was something more. He managed a twisted smile. "Your mother's food is legendary here in Leôn. Her mole is my favorite, along with her tamales."

The door slid open again and ten-year-old Jamie skipped across the deck. "Papa Bear, are you ready? It's time to go."

His son's child body showed the bare beginnings of the man he would grow into. Jamie was stocky, like him, with the same thick, curling black hair. He loved his son, and yet something inside him resisted the tightening family bonds. That something fostered both the guilt and resentment, which increasing amounts of tequila could not douse. "Yes, Papa is ready. Go and get in the truck with your sister." He needed a moment to see whether or not he could stand up and walk.

"OK Papa, but hurry up." Jamie skittered back across the deck and into the house.

He grasped the arms of the deck chair, pushed himself upright, and took a step, then another. "We'd better not keep them waiting."

Sherie said, "How much tequila have you had before noon? I'm worried about you, Gabriel. You need to do something productive with your time. Besides, I'm sure we need the money."

"A couple shots. You don't need to worry." In four sentences, she'd managed to stomp on every exposed, raw nerve. If he were living his life the way he wanted, no one would question his consumption of tequila. Rowan and Michael had their own poisons. They would drink together. The time of day did not matter.

She persisted. "Please promise me you'll talk to my father today about your place in the company. But wait until after the picnic. I don't want him to smell alcohol on your breath."

"Your father and I will talk as much as he wishes about my future in the company. But mi Amor, you don't need to worry about money either." His offshore account, the one he'd been paid from for the last ten years, set up by Rowan, was no one's business but his. They spent considerably less living in Leôn than they had in San Diego, and the account still held enough money to maintain his family for a year or more.

But Sherie couldn't let it go. She argued with him as they walked from the heat of the deck through the cool stillness of the house to the brand new, expensive Tahoe he'd purchased for her, waiting in the driveway. "How can you say I don't need to worry about your drinking or our finances? Every day you sit out there with your tequila. You don't work. I have to remind you of every family event. If I hadn't said anything, you'd still be out there with your bottle."

Hell yes, he wanted to say. *And I'd be much happier.* But he hadn't been happy in many months. Now he needed to pacify his wife, because his body ached for her. If he pissed her off, she'd cling to her anger, turning her back and huddling on one side of their bed. He'd spend another lonely, frustrated night, staring at the ceiling. He managed to climb into the front passenger seat and waited until she'd climbed into the driver's seat. "Sherie, mi Amor, I'm sorry. I'll talk to your father. Don't worry. We're fine."

She put the SUV in gear. "I don't know, Gabriel. I just don't know."

The lack of trust in her dark eyes stabbed his heart, and the guilt rushed back. As they drove off, childish shrieks and clapping from Jamie and Sophia in the back seat drowned out his reply. He closed his eyes and wished he were anywhere else.

Late Evening
Florence, CO
Foster finished reading and stared into the darkness of his hotel room, beyond the circle of light radiating from the bedside lamp. Director Berenger had sent him new information, which included video and transcripts of Milani's entire saga, along with an Intel brief about Muusa Shemal. She'd also sent the contents of a flash drive, providing details of the terrorists Milani had killed while in the secret employ of the President. He'd been poring over the information since shortly after three o'clock in the afternoon, and his laptop told him it was 11 p.m.

He closed his laptop and gazed at the ceiling tiles outlined by the glow of lamplight. He'd decided to let Milani sit for a few days, let him begin to feel the limits of the eighty-four-square-foot cell and wonder about his future. The utter silence, the white walls, and the claustrophobic, bathroom-sized room did things to most prisoner's minds. Although, after what he'd read and watched, he didn't think Milani was like most prisoners.

After their initial meeting, he'd observed his detainee on a closed-circuit video feed from his office until Milani fell asleep. He'd met with the warden and the prison physician who'd examined Milani. A thicker mattress would be located. Pain meds would be provided regularly. The lights in the cell would dim to near darkness every night at 10 p.m. and remain that way until 7 a.m. the following morning. Everyone involved with Milani's care had been made to understand that *he,* under the auspices of the FBI, made all the decisions regarding this particular prisoner.

After that, he'd grabbed a late lunch and retreated to his quiet room in the tiny Riviera Hotel in Florence. Everything he'd read and seen left him ambivalent, and because of those feelings, restless; unable to sleep. What Milani had endured in Quantico's brig, while in the hands of Capello, amounted to torture. Harandi's methods were similar, although he hadn't had as much time with Milani. Why the CIA operatives had resorted to water boarding baffled him. Was it because they couldn't think outside that particular box? He believed that relationship building, when done correctly, was a much more effective method of obtaining truthful, valuable information from a detainee.

He'd gained a lot of understanding of Milani from the transcripts and the videos. Thinking about it, he shook his head. Milani could have ended his ordeal if he'd given in, on *any* point. But he hadn't, and suffered for it, with Capello especially. Why hadn't he admitted his crimes and stopped the abuse?

Only one reason made sense, and it kept him staring unblinking into the darkness. The stubborn man must be innocent. There could be no more powerful reason for Milani to endure what he'd been subjected to. Milani's friend Cantor had never wavered in his claims of innocence either. Cantor had begged for an investigation of Muusa Shemal, which he'd assumed was nothing more than an attempt to discredit the man. His review of the Intel brief had him rethinking that assumption.

Taken in its entirety, the information from Berenger had him wondering why not one man or woman in the intelligence community had bothered to question any part of the claims against Milani. His hours of study gave him a new perspective on Cantor and Johnston's actions as well. He could understand why they'd gone to the lengths they had to protect their friend.

The hair rose on his arms when he thought about how Sal Capello had died. Milani had posed as Harandi and met the CIA agent in Chicago. Capello ended up dead, his guts spilling out all over himself, on the floor in a room at the O'Hare Hilton. Apparently, Milani had exacted his own version of justice for the brutality he'd endured. After watching the videos of Capello humiliating and torturing Milani, he almost couldn't blame the guy, and that bothered him. *A lot.*

Investigators in Chicago were left scratching their heads, because the room where Capello had been killed was wiped clean. No evidence tying Milani to the murder was ever found, except for video images of a man resembling him. The check-in clerk at the Hilton remembered a handsome man with a goatee, who'd identified himself as FBI agent David Harandi. Of course, Harandi had offered rock-solid proof of his whereabouts in Houston during the time frame of Capello's death and had identified Milani as the man in the grainy images.

Marta Pinella was another example that troubled him. Why had Milani killed her? He planned to ask his detainee that question. Would he get any kind of answer? Would Milani respond to the interrogation methods of the Bureau? After all, Milani had been an agent for over ten years. Could he gain Milani's trust? If he could get inside the man's head, maybe he'd be able to get through to him.

Acting on a quick thought, he grabbed his phone and dialed the number he'd jotted down. A groggy voice answered after several rings. "Hello, Harandi here. Who is this?"

Remembering the two-hour time difference too late, he grimaced. "This is Wilson Foster, FBI. Sorry to disturb you by calling so late. I'm in Colorado studying the info on Rowan Milani. Director Berenger assigned me to interrogate him, and I'd like to discuss his situation, but I can call back in the morning."

Harandi yawned into the phone. "I'm awake now. And actually, I told Director Berenger I'd like to talk to you before you begin the process with Milani."

"She mentioned that. I've studied everything we've got on Milani, but you're the only one who's interrogated him who's still alive or available."

"Milani and I have a history, which in retrospect makes me think I may not have been the best first choice to interrogate him."

"You CIA boys have a different approach. But that's a conversation for a different day. Or night. Talk to me about Milani."

"He's tough, and he's loyal. I water boarded him until he damn near passed out, and he didn't give me squat about his colleagues."

"My experience with him yesterday gave me the same impression. He could barely sit up straight in a chair, but he still had the temerity to question me."

"I'm not surprised. Even after being dragged out of the hellhole in Tora, his mind was sharp. He did however, tell me he doesn't want to fight any more."

"Interesting he'd say that. Do you believe him?"

"In this instance, I believe he's telling the truth. After enduring months in Tora, I think he's got to be finished. I'm honestly surprised he managed to survive. The truly unfortunate thing is that he ended up there in the first place. Your boss isn't quite convinced, but I know he's innocent of the terror-related charges. However, he's created a mess he can't escape, with Ainsley's murder and others."

Thinking about the broken man he'd seen in the interrogation room, Foster found himself inexplicably saddened. "From everything I've read and watched, I'm inclined to agree that he's innocent. It seems to me that if he'd reached out, instead of taking matters into his own hands, he'd have found someone willing to listen."

“I tend to disagree with you. For reasons I haven’t been able to figure out, Ainsley was gung-ho to believe Shemal. He steered the reaction of the entire intelligence community.”

“Well Mr. Harandi, it disturbs me to think the culture in our intelligence community is such that a man like Milani could be destroyed completely without any kind of recourse available. Any final thoughts before I let you get back to sleep?”

“After talking with one of Milani’s colleagues and doing my own research, I’ve learned that something is amiss in our country, and Shemal represents the tip of a large iceberg. His affiliation with CAIR and the Muslim Brotherhood is troubling. If Ainsley were still alive, he would have culpability also. It’s entirely possible that a few of my former colleagues in the CIA deserve scrutiny as well.”

“Is this research included in the Intel brief Director Berenger forwarded to me?

“It’s in addition to the brief. In the morning, I’ll forward the rest of my information to the director.”

“Thank you. I appreciate it. I’ve read the brief on Shemal. He definitely targeted Milani. Again, my apologies for waking you.”

“Before you go, there is one primary thing to remember about Milani.”

“What’s that?”

“He’s an accomplished liar. Keep that in mind when you’re face-to-face. Good luck Special Agent Foster. And good night.”

“Good night.” Foster ended the call and laid the phone on the bedside table. He closed his eyes and pictured Milani, sitting hunched over at the interrogation table. The man had already paid, with his reputation and his body, for things he hadn’t done. He switched off the light and slid down until the pillow cradled his head. Before the penalties for the things Milani *had* done were exacted, he intended to learn the truth. He only hoped the damaged man would help him find it.

CHAPTER FIVE

Early Evening, Three Days Later
Old Town Alexandria, VA

Berenger paused in the shadowed entryway of the elegant restaurant and observed Abramson seated at a corner table. Sconces cast mellow lamplight against the earth-tone walls, helping create the special ambience Brabo was known for. In his requisite dark suit and tie, Abramson looked at home in the chic environment. The request to meet from the aloof director of the spy agency had piqued her interest. Brabo had been a favorite of her former boss, who'd claimed close friendship with Abramson.

That alone made her suspicious of the CIA Director's probable involvement in the Milani debacle. The money trail from Cantor's laptop, however, showed no deposits from Shemal to Abramson.

The maître d' greeted her. "Good evening, Director Berenger. Allow me to escort you to your table."

"Thank you, Percy." They moved into the dining room as Abramson spotted her and nodded.

He stood and then sat down as she arrived at the table. "Good evening, Leigh."

The maître d' seated her and breezed away. "Hello, Oscar." A suit-coated waiter appeared and gave her an expectant smile. "Perrier with a lime twist, please."

The waiter sketched a bow, murmured "Yes ma'am," and left the table.

Abramson sipped from a cup of tea and didn't waste any time in getting to his agenda. "I am looking forward to discussing Milani's return to our custody and how to ensure that he pays the full price for his crimes."

The waiter returned with a tall glass of Perrier, inviting with its gentle fizz and fragrant lime. She declined the menu he flourished. "No, thank you."

Abramson continued. "We must reach an agreement on how to proceed with Milani."

His assumption of inclusion in what she considered none of his agency's business irritated and surprised her. "Oscar, I'm finding myself somewhat confused as to why you and I need to discuss Rowan Milani at all."

Abramson's nostrils flared, ever so slightly. "My agency has suffered because of Milani and his antics. The Bureau was dealt an egregious blow as well, with the murder of Rodney Ainsley. It is past time to see justice served." He took a long swallow of tea and set the cup carefully in its saucer, but his eyes never left hers.

She sipped her Perrier and considered. "I'm curious. What led you to assign CIA agents to apprehend Milani in South Dakota, in direct violation of your agency's jurisdiction? Why wasn't he arrested by FBI agents in a counter-terrorism operation?"

"Rodney asked for my help. He had no inkling of how deep into the Bureau Milani's treason may have spread, and he authorized my agents to pick up Milani, with the intention of delivering him to the brig at Quantico."

"And when he was apprehended for the second time, did my predecessor also agree that rendition to Tora, of all places, was the best way to gain information from Milani?"

"We chose Tora because both Rodney and I wanted to prevent another escape attempt by Milani's colleagues. Besides, Milani had proven himself too skilled and clever for our methods. We felt harsh interrogation would yield faster results."

His callous answers felt too well-rehearsed. She wanted to shake the grip he'd seemed poised to lose at the start of their conversation. "Indeed, he did make a mockery of those methods. In return, I'd have to say, the choice to rendition Milani to Egypt for interrogation by an Egyptian, with CIA handlers in attendance, was most brazen."

His nostrils flared again, wider this time. "The President signed off on the rendition. Milani had been deemed an enemy combatant. As such, interrogation in Tora fit the situation."

"Milani was arrested, detained, and renditioned with no due process. In addition, I've been apprised of new intelligence germane to his case. I intend to conduct an exhaustive investigation."

Abramson responded. "Milani's guilt is well established. He operated with impunity as a double agent and was correctly labeled an enemy combatant. What new intelligence have you uncovered?"

Satisfied she'd rattled him, she decided to offer a couple vague references from the detailed brief on Shemal and gauge his reaction. "Bureau resources have identified a possible financial link between a representative of the Muslim Brotherhood and the intelligence community, which may be tied to Milani's case. We are also, re-opening an unsolved murder case which we believe may be linked as well."

Abramson ranted. "That's outrageous. The Muslim Brotherhood seeks only to further the cause of peaceful Islam. Why would you choose to muddy the waters with unsubstantiated intelligence? Where did this information originate?"

"I do not reveal my sources."

Abramson said, "Did you know several of Milani's colleagues assisted with his return?"

He'd upstaged her. Infuriated by the blush of anger she couldn't hide, she took a drink of the cold Perrier. Harandi would answer for this, as soon as she finished the meeting. She forced her voice to remain even, met his gaze, and lied. "Interesting *you'd* know that."

"Yes, they assisted my agents in Milani's removal from Tora. Unfortunately, the circumstances did not permit my people to return them to the US as well."

"No surprise there. Your agents have earned a certain reputation where Milani and his colleagues are concerned."

Abramson practically sneered. "The day will come when Milani and his cohorts answer for everything."

She'd heard enough. "Other obligations require my presence. You and your agency's participation in Milani's future are no longer needed."

"You're making a mistake. This is not the correct course. You don't have the authority to cut me out of the decision-making process."

She pushed back her chair. "You seem to have forgotten one thing. Milani's custody and interrogation fall under my purview, not yours. I'm not granting the CIA any special privileges."

Abramson sputtered, "You are destroying the inter-agency cooperation Rodney and I spent the last three years cultivating."

Undeterred, she continued. "Do I need to remind you which agency lost Milani three times, including the Tora abduction by a rag-tag group of zealots? Consider yourself fortunate I'm willing to meet and discuss him with you at all. This will be our first and final discussion about Milani. The matter is no longer your concern."

The CIA Director opened his mouth and closed it as deep red flushed his entire face. A vein bulged in his neck. "You'll regret this."

She stood up. "I don't believe I will. Good night, Oscar." She exited the restaurant, barely restraining her anger. Her driver opened the door of the SUV and she climbed in. "Sam, take me back to my office please."

She dug her phone from her bag and punched the correct contact. Harandi sounded out of breath. "Hello, Director Berenger."

"I need to see you in my office. Now." She smacked END and stuffed her phone back in her bag.

FBI Headquarters, Washington, DC

An hour later, Harandi sat scowling at her in a sweat-dampened t-shirt, shorts, and running shoes. "What is it now, Director? How may I help you?"

"How many more times will I be blindsided by something you've chosen to do at your own discretion? How about you fill me in on everything, right now. And I mean *everything.*"

He raised both hands and let them drop. "I have no idea what you're talking about."

She gave him a sarcastic chuckle. "I'm tired of you implementing your dirty work behind my back. Tell me, which of Rowan Milani's esteemed colleagues assisted in his return to the United States?"

"If you don't mind, I'd rather not say."

She tapped the desk top with her forefinger. "You'll tell me, this instant, or I'll have you detained in DC County Jail for as long as I deem necessary."

He stroked his goatee. "Ralph Johnston and two others, whose identities I haven't been able to figure out. One man, one woman."

"I see. How did they know to assist you?"

He shrugged. "I don't know, they just appeared at the airport."

She tapped the numeral "1" on her office phone. "I need security in my office immediately."

A deep voice responded. "Yes ma'am. We're on our way."

Harandi raised both hands. "Whoa. *Damn it.* I talked to one of Milani's colleagues months ago. He provided the bulk of my Intel. We've talked about this. I called him because I know how incompetent Hancock and Talbot are, and I wanted to be sure we got Milani out of Al-Aqrab."

Her office door burst open and bounced against the wall. Two agents, Glock pistols drawn, rushed into the room. The lead agent spoke. "Sir, place your hands behind your head."

Harandi muttered, *"Really?"* and complied. Her agents forced him up and cuffed his hands behind his back, then shoved him down in the chair.

"Thank you. I'll take it from here." The agents clumped out of her office and shut the door. She glared at Harandi. "Now's your chance. Spill your guts. If you prefer not to, I'll have you escorted to County."

Harandi eyed her for a few moments, his mouth clamped shut, brows drawn. He twisted his shoulders, sniffed, and finally spoke. "This isn't funny."

"Humor was most certainly not my intent, Mr. Harandi. I am *damned tired* of your shenanigans."

"I thought you respected due process and the rule of law."

"Ah well, let me enlighten you. I respect honesty. I have no qualms about treating you in the same manner you treated Clifton Cantor. Rowan Milani too, now that I think about it. You're CIA, so there are probably others. Most likely *myriad* others."

"What do you want, Director?"

"The truth, Mr. Harandi. Sooner rather than later, and not an abridged version."

He sniffed again. "Milani managed to give me a name before Hancock and Talbot hauled him out of his Quantico brig cell to rendition him to Tora. He told me to ask Cantor for a number and then make a phone call. So I did, and we arranged a meeting. As I said, he's the man who helped me gain most of the Intel I've shared with you."

"I see. So you *do* know the identity of one of the other two colleagues."

"Not really, no."

"Stop screwing with me. Do you think I'm joking about County?"

"No, ma'am."

"One more smartass comment and you'll know for sure. Keep talking."

Harandi heaved a sigh. "All I know is his first name, which is Michael. I kept the number, and called. The same guy, Michael, answered. I told him when we'd be in Cairo, and he agreed to provide backup. When we disembarked at the airport, Johnston and Michael and the woman were waiting."

"And you have no idea who the woman is, or what Michael's last name might be?"

"I do not."

"Did you attempt to take Johnston into custody?"

"No."

"Why not?"

"He was armed, as were the other two. I didn't push it because not everyone at Tora appreciated the fact that we removed Milani. We needed to get out of Egypt as quickly as possible."

"Any idea where they flew in from?"

He shook his head. "No."

She leaned back and took a deep breath, releasing it slowly as her anger began to lessen. "You know, Mr. Harandi, I believe you're telling me the truth. For once."

"Yes, ma'am."

"What, no cocky remark? You have anything else buried in that sneaky brain of yours? Something that'll blow up in my face when I least expect it? If so, I suggest in the strongest terms possible that you unearth it for me now."

His rounded shoulders suggested defeat. "No, ma'am. Nothing else. I'm quite sure."

"Remember this. If you *ever* lie to me again or put me in a compromised situation, I will find a reason to detain you. Do you understand, Mr. Harandi?"

"Yes, ma'am, I understand."

She flipped open her laptop and pulled up a file. "The name Michael reminds me of something. Several of my agents have been tasked with investigating the Cristo family ranch in South Dakota."

"Why a family ranch in South Dakota, of all places?"

"During the Kauai estate raid, my agents rescued Derek Norris, a former friend of Danielle Stratton's. He provided the Bureau with what I'd hoped would be valuable information. Unfortunately, he was murdered in his home in Sioux Falls, South Dakota, last spring."

"I'm not sure what you're getting at."

"Just a moment. Ah, here it is. Mr. Norris told us about two of Milani's colleagues, Michael and Gabriel."

"You're correct. Rowan admitted they were his colleagues. It's in the transcript of my interrogation of him."

"Yes, I remember. But until now, I didn't realize the connection. Frank and Georgia Cristo have a son, whose name is Michael. He served as a Ranger. The Army says he was a lethal sniper with seventy-six confirmed kills in Afghanistan and Iraq."

Harandi glared at her. "Son of a…"

"What is it, Mr. Harandi?"

Harandi replied, almost more to himself than to her. "A sniper killed Patricia. I asked Milani about it, but he's such a damn good liar. Something told me he knew."

She added, "The crime scene offered no evidence whatsoever. No fingerprints other than Hennessey's, no shell casing, no tire tread or even footprints. Only a somewhat flattened area on the hill top we determined as the origin of the shot that killed her. I investigated myself."

Harandi winced. "Can you call your goons and remove the cuffs? I promise to keep talking."

"You sit tight. I'm quite sure you'll survive a few more minutes. According to Army records, Cristo paired up with a talented spotter. Care to guess *his* name?"

"Don't tell me. Gabriel?"

"Correct. Army records tell us Gabriel Hernandez is his name. We've been unable to find any record of either man after they left the Army."

"No surprise there. You know, Director, it makes sense. If they worked with Milani on his secret ops, there'd be no record of them, anywhere. It's probably an oversight that their Army records still exist."

She gazed at him sitting across from her, hunched over, sweating, and hid a smile. He deserved the discomfort. "Correct again. What about the colleague who helped you infiltrate the jihadi chat rooms? Suppose she's the woman with Johnston and Cristo in Cairo?"

He shrugged. "Could be. Hell, probably. They used some sort of voice changer, although I did notice a certain rhythm to the voice. Honestly, it made me think of my Iranian relatives."

"Did the woman in Cairo look Middle Eastern?"

"She wore a ball cap and had a bandana covering half her face. I remember a black ponytail and a lithe, athletic figure, dressed in some sort of military fatigues."

She hit "1" on her phone. "Come in please." The door opened, admitting her agents. "You may remove the cuffs. Please wait outside. You'll be escorting Mr. Harandi from the premises shortly."

Her agents shoved Harandi forward, released him, and exited the office. He grunted and straightened up, rubbing his wrists. "Thank you."

She didn't intend to let up. "I'm impressed with how a bit of discomfort clears your mind. We've had our most productive conversation to date. Still, your tendency toward duplicity makes me leery of meeting with your FOX News correspondent. Put that on hold for now."

"Oh, ma'am, I wish you'd reconsider. McKenzie is a stand-up guy."

"Unlike you, apparently?"

He scowled. "I apologize for not being completely forthcoming. Old habits die hard. However, we've covered a great deal of ground this evening. You might say we connected some important dots. Will you give me a chance to rehabilitate myself?"

"I'll consider it." She punched "1" again. "You may escort my guest now."

Harandi stood up when her agents entered the office. "Have a nice evening, Director. I hope we'll speak soon."

"We'll see. Enjoy the rest of your evening as well, Mr. Harandi." She waited while her agents escorted him out, his muscular arms firmly in their grasp. When the door closed, she propped her elbows on the desk and rested her head in her hands. What else had the cunning man been up to? She'd give anything to know.

Old Town Alexandria, VA

Abramson picked at the tuna crudo he'd ordered after Berenger's departure. He pushed the plate away. What kind of new evidence did Berenger possess? How had she garnered new intelligence?

Shemal arrived at the table, along with the beaming maître d'. "It's always a pleasure to serve you, Doctor Shemal. Your waiter will be right along. Enjoy your evening."

His friend responded with proper graciousness. "Thank you, Percy. I shall."

Abramson waited until their waiter poured fresh tea and took their orders before sharing his fears. "Our entire plan may be in jeopardy."

Shemal raised his cup of tea and frowned. "Surely the situation is not so dire. Allah is the source of our strength. We must remain calm and have faith."

He dabbed at the sweat on his face with a white linen napkin. "Director Berenger is not an ally. She claims to possess new intelligence involving a financial link between a member of the Muslim Brotherhood and the intelligence community, which she thinks may be tied to Milani's situation."

Shemal replied. "It sounds as though she intended to bait you. How did you respond?"

"I asked why she'd pursue unsubstantiated intelligence and asked where it originated. She would not reveal her sources, which is no surprise."

"This is concerning."

Abramson gazed around the elegant restaurant before focusing on his friend. "She also mentioned re-opening an unsolved murder case, which she believes may be linked to Milani. You know what that means."

Shemal said, "We have come too far in this endeavor to accept defeat at the hands of Milani through the actions of this woman."

"Agreed. However, we must exercise great care in how we choose to move forward. My agents informed me that Ralph Johnston and two other of Milani's colleagues assisted with his return to the US. Harandi must have arranged their participation. Berenger already knew."

"Why did your agents not take the opportunity to apprehend them?"

"Harandi was not amenable to the idea. Milani's colleagues were armed. A skirmish ensued at Al-Aqrab, and they needed to leave quickly."

Shemal snorted. "You've given me a laundry list of excuses my friend."

Abramson concurred. "Indeed. I no longer trust their fealty."

"Your concern is justified. We must ensure that the Brotherhood's goals, *our goals,* are not hindered. We must seek Allah's guidance on how to deal with these issues."

"You are correct, of course. I simply find it maddening to think Milani may yet unravel years of planning and work."

Shemal commiserated. "Only a Jinn could survive as Milani has, but Allah will never allow him to prevail."

Their waiter appeared with his roasted duck and Shemal's chicken roulade. "May I bring anything else?"

Abramson hid his impatience and gave the waiter a brief smile. "No, thank you. This looks delightful."

The waiter nodded. "Enjoy, gentlemen."

He speared a forkful of salade gourmande, although Berenger had succeeded in ruining his appetite. "Because of this unfortunate turn, we must consider one more thing."

Shemal paused, knife and fork in hand. "Yes?"

He spoke with conviction. "I believe it is only prudent for you to return to London until we know more about what Berenger is planning or what information she may possess."

Shemal sliced into the chicken. "This situation has become untenable. I'll return to London as soon as I finalize travel arrangements. You *must* keep me informed. If necessary, I'll make arrangements to stay in Qatar."

"I agree. A wise choice, given the circumstances."

Shemal replied. "I say again, and we must trust this. Allah will not permit Milani to prevail. We shall see him and everyone associated with him brought to defeat. Allahu akbar."

"Allahu akbar," he murmured, wishing he felt as confident as his friend.

Two Days Later
London, UK
Shemal unlocked the door of his London flat and let himself in. He hadn't been in his home since beginning the final push to rendition Milani to Tora. The aroma of lemon furniture polish greeted him. A vase of fresh-cut white roses, apricot dahlias, cow

parsley, and dill adorned the occasional table in the reception area. His housekeeper had done well in preparing for his return.

He left his suitcases and squatted down to release Aziza from her carrier. She meowed and bounded away to explore. Aziza remained as his only connection to Marta and would always accompany him. He made his way to the tiny kitchen and began preparations for tea, then wandered from room to room, opening blinds and trailing an index finger across the end tables, checking for dust.

The teapot whistled and he returned to the kitchen. He poured boiling water over the mixture of black tea and mint, inhaling its refreshing scent. After stirring sugar and milk into his tea, he followed Aziza into the front room and stared out the narrow windows overlooking the steps leading to his flat and the street beyond.

Northwest London, in the center of Cricklewood had not been his choice. But the Brothers had insisted, and he'd purchased the flat five years earlier. He would have preferred a location more accommodating to his tastes, such as Knightsbridge, Mayfair, or Chelsea. Instead he endured the crush of people amid the endless lineup of despicable shops and restaurants, including a McDonald's.

Dismay filled him as he watched a man of medium height, wearing a dark suit and white keffiyeh cross the street. The doorbell buzzed, and he muttered a curse. His masters had wasted no time in sending an ally to chastise him. He hastily set his tea on the table and pulled open the door. "Haji, as-salaam alaykum. It is a pleasure to see you after so many months. Come in, please."

Haji al-Khattab, one of the most influential members of the Brotherhood's Shura Council, and a long-time personal friend, swept into his apartment. "Wa `alaykum salaam, Brother Muusa, it is good to see you as well. Ah, you have made tea? I would like some."

"Of course. Make yourself comfortable while I prepare it for you." He gestured toward the luxurious, black leather sofas crammed into his living area, but his visitor accompanied him to the kitchen.

Haji leaned against the counter and patted his well-groomed beard. "You were wise to make an expeditious departure from the US. Your obsession with Milani has gotten out of hand."

He stared at his Brother, anger rising in his chest. The shrill hiss of the teapot jarred him. "I seek only to obey Allah, blessed be his name."

He poured the steaming water over the tea and worked to hide his true thoughts. The Brotherhood would find a way to circumvent his plans if he revealed the state of his heart and mind. The tea steeped, and he kept Haji engaged in small talk about the things he'd missed while residing in Cairo and the US.

Haji followed him to the front room and perched on one corner of the sofa with his cup of tea. "I come of my own volition to offer counsel. You have angered many in the Guidance Office with your reckless actions."

Surprised by his friend's tone, he responded. *"My actions?* I have always upheld the honor of Allah."

"We have labored long in infidel lands, in the face of moral rot and corruption. You have forgotten the essential nature of our struggle against the West. Patience is our strength. You would do well to internalize this once more, my brother."

His hands trembled. The cup rattled on the saucer and his heart thumped. "I have forgotten *nothing.* Has the Guidance Office *forgotten* the lives taken, the monies lost, and the plans abandoned because of this Jinn, Rowan Milani, who mimics *Malak-al-Maut* with impunity?"

Haji spoke soothingly. "My friend, listen to yourself. Your zeal and impatience threatens the jihad. You have accomplished our goal with Milani. He has been neutralized. His own government will punish him. My advice? Take this opportunity to redeem yourself."

Sweat beaded on his forehead while agonizing bands of pain tightened around his chest. He loosened his tie and took a slow breath. "I will seek redemption and obey my Brothers' exhortation."

Haji finished his tea and stood up. "I will inform our Supreme Guide of your wise choice. He will determine another path for you."

He walked his friend to the door. "I will await a new assignment." He gave his friend a slight bow. "My only goal is to serve Allah in whatever capacity the Supreme Guide deems acceptable."

Haji lingered on the stoop. "Your many skills will not be wasted. Perhaps you will teach at a university here or practice surgery in one of our hospitals. I will speak on your behalf."

He bowed again, lower. "Thank you, my friend," he murmured, and closed the door. He staggered back to the kitchen. Taking careful breaths, he prepared more tea. The agony in his chest subsided as he sipped the strong, comforting brew. He would never abandon his pursuit of Rowan Milani. Allah had entrusted him with a sacred duty. Even the Brotherhood could not supplant Allah's perfect will.

The doorbell buzzed again and he made his way slowly to the front door. Joy replaced his anxiety when he saw his brother, Issa. "As-salaam alaykum. Come in, come in. It has been much too long."

Issa gripped his arms and they exchanged kisses on each other's cheeks. "Wa `alaykum salaam. Your entire family has missed you. It is past time for your return from America."

He ushered his brother inside. "Sit, please. I've just made tea. Would you like some?"

Issa replied. "You know I'd love some, with milk and sugar, same as you. We need to catch up."

They chatted while he fussed with brewing another cup of tea. "How is your family? Rhashida and Khait must be getting big."

Issa sipped his tea and smiled. "Rhashida is thirteen now and was eager to wear the hijab. Khait just turned eleven and loves to copy her older sister. They are good girls, setting an example for others in their school. In Egypt, the girls are choosing modesty at a younger age. I am beyond satisfied that my daughters are doing so here, as well."

He nodded gravely. "Indeed, Allah must be pleased."

"Pleasing Allah is my highest endeavor, as you know. But enough about the girls. What are your plans now that you have returned to London? May we expect that you'll be here for more than a few months?"

He wondered for a moment if the Shura Council had co-opted his brother, along with Haji. But he saw only authentic interest in his brother's eyes. He led Issa back to the living area and settled on one of the sofas. "Yes, I will stay in London for the foreseeable future. And truly, Issa, your daughters maturing faith encourages me. Our efforts are for their benefit, and millions of others like them."

Issa sat across from him. "Yes, of course. My fondest hope is that the culture we leave them is more pure than what we must deal with presently."

"We will not rest until Sharia is enshrined, here and in America."

Issa said, "Unless you have already made a commitment, the London Vascular Institute would very much like to have a surgeon of your caliber on their team. The director reached out to me a month or so ago, asking if you were returning to London anytime soon."

He considered. Talking with his brother cleared his mind and chased away the always present ugliness spawned by Milani.

Perhaps a complete change of direction would do him well, for a time. "I am awaiting an assignment from the Supreme Guide. If he has no objection, I will certainly explore that option."

Issa grinned. "Excellent. I will speak with the director tomorrow. And Muusa, I've already heard whispers from some about your sermons becoming the norm again. You will be present for prayers this Friday?"

Aziza chose that moment to race from the short hallway leading to his bedroom, into the living room. She leaped into his lap and playfully batted his bearded jaw. He stroked her head. "Oh yes, I am looking forward to it."

Issa sipped his tea. "You have a cat? America has changed you, Muusa."

Aziza curled in his lap and commenced loud purring. "She was a gift from someone I treasured."

Issa spoke softly. "From your habibti, perhaps? The woman murdered by Milani?"

His brother's words sent a shaft of pain through his chest. His hand rested on Aziza's back, her purring vibrating against his palm. "Yes."

Issa said, "My heart aches for your loss. Your family stands ready to assist you in exacting Allah's vengeance."

"You must tread carefully in expressing your support. The Supreme Guide wasted no time in castigating me for my zeal in pursuing Milani, with Haji as his messenger."

"You and I are brothers. You know that our conversation will remain between the two of us and Allah. May I offer a suggestion?"

He met Issa's sober gaze. "You know I value your opinions. Please, speak freely."

"I believe wholeheartedly in bringing Allah's justice to the scourge that is Milani. You have worked tirelessly, for *years*. I am certain your mind and spirit will benefit from taking some time to rest and seek Allah's direction for the future."

Much as he chafed at *any* thought of relenting in his pursuit of Milani, he knew Issa spoke the truth. "You are correct. Seeking Allah's guidance is never a mistake."

Hours later, after he and Issa had consumed their fill of tea, and his brother had left, he sat their cups in the sink and returned to his front room. Ready to succumb to jet lag and go to bed, he sat on the sofa and dozed while Aziza lay across his lap. For the first time in over a year, the peace he'd felt only on occasion, began to fill his heart and mind. With Milani incarcerated in the US, he could take his time, and plan wisely.

ADX Florence, CO

Rowan sat on a metal chair in the sterile interrogation room, shifting his weight from one aching hip to the other as much as he could with his feet shackled and anchored to an eye bolt in the floor. The guards had come to his cell at intervals he'd lost track of, with food and pain meds. The pills dulled the pain encompassing his body, but nothing offered complete relief.

He squinted at the lights in the ceiling and bent over to rub his eyes, wondering whether it was day or night and how long he'd been in the prison. He spent the time lying on the hard bed, drifting from wakefulness to sleep, and most of the time he couldn't tell the difference. The door opened, and he sat up straight. Foster entered, followed by a guard carrying a carafe of what smelled like coffee and two cups.

Foster addressed the guard. "Just set it all on the table. Thank you. That will be all. I'll knock when we're finished." The agent carried his tiny notebook and looked as unremarkable as he had the first time they'd met. The guard left, closing and locking the door. Foster held up a handcuff key. "Hello, Rowan. Let's get these cuffs off so you can take a decent drink of coffee."

He held up his hands, but couldn't stop the tremor going through them. Foster unlocked the uncomfortable steel restraints. While he rubbed his wrists, the agent poured the steaming liquid into both cups. He took the cup from Foster, inhaled the aroma and managed not to burn his tongue. "Thank you."

"You're welcome." The agent settled into the chair across the table and sipped his coffee. "Are the pain meds helping? Are you able to sleep?"

He barely hid a sneer. Foster had access to his every moment by way of the cameras in the cell, and he resented having to answer the inane questions. "I'm OK. Yeah, I can sleep."

"Good." The agent opened his notebook before fishing a pen from his shirt pocket. "We can talk over coffee. If you're hungry, I'll ask the guards to bring something in for you."

"Special Agent Foster, let's cut the crap. What do you want? Why are you here?"

Foster looked up from his notebook. "You may not remember our first meeting. I stated that your perspective is what's been missing, and I'd like to hear it."

"Oh. Right. My perspective was the truth, about what was happening to me and why. No one ever listened. Why would you? And why now?"

"For one thing, I'm not a CIA agent committed to a false narrative propagated by Muusa Shemal. I've been tasked by my boss to get at the truth. Period. It seems like the fastest way to do that is by hearing your point of view for myself. Are you willing to cooperate with me?"

The admission of Shemal's culpability, for the first time, from a bona fide federal agent other than Harandi, shocked him. "Yes, I'll cooperate. I've been telling the truth, but like I told you, it's too late."

Foster concentrated on his notebook for a moment, scratching notes across the short lines on the white paper with his pen, and then spoke. "I've read every transcript and watched every video of your interrogations. I've utilized every intelligence avenue available to me in verifying the information on your flash drive. I've spoken with David Harandi and gone over the information he accumulated after talking to one of your colleagues."

"And?"

"It may be too late for you because of certain things that can't be undone, but it's not too late to redeem your reputation or provide some mitigation. If you'll work with me, I'm willing to do my best to see that happen."

He took another sip of coffee and held the foam cup in both hands. "By *certain things* you mean the elimination of jihadists in this country, along with a few traitors, right?"

"I mean the murder of Rodney Ainsley, Sal Capello, and seven people in Houston."

This time, he couldn't hide the sneer. "So much for wanting my perspective. You're just like all the rest."

Foster replied. "Tell me how I'm missing your perspective."

"For God's sake, murder is a misnomer."

Foster scratched more notes. "A *misnomer?* Please explain."

"Three of the men I killed were Iranian nationals. Two were skinny Arabs from Afghanistan. Another was an Egyptian. All of them were here illegally, courtesy of Shemal."

Foster kept writing. "And the others?"

He finished the coffee, turned lukewarm, and gazed at the white carafe, wanting more, knowing he didn't have the strength in his arms or hands to pour it. "There's no proof I killed Capello, although the bastard took money from Shemal. Marta Pinella was Shemal's whore. She collaborated with an enemy of our country. Both her and Capello committed treason."

"David Harandi identified you from images captured by video surveillance at O'Hare and in the Hilton. Getting back to Houston, you slit Ms. Pinella's throat after you shot her several times in the belly."

"She got what she deserved; what any other jihadist would get from me."

Foster stopped writing and stared at him. "In your mind, she was just one more jihadist?"

"Yes. I am not a *murderer.* My extracurricular *job* for the past decade or so has been to *eliminate* people who endanger the security of the United States. On occasion that includes women."

"What about Rodney Ainsley?"

He shook his head, remembering. "The crazy son of a bitch lost it. He wanted to kill me. I defended myself and ended the threat."

"Couldn't you have disabled him without killing him?"

"Did you watch the video recording from my cell?"

"I did."

"What would you have done differently?"

Foster tapped his pen on the notebook and frowned. "It's difficult to judge without being in the situation."

"Exactly."

"But you're saying Ainsley committed treason."

"He was in cahoots with Shemal and the Brotherhood to get rid of me."

"Why?"

He took a ragged breath. "If anyone had taken the time to ask that question a year and a half ago, my life might not be over. But that didn't happen, and so, here we are."

Foster observed him, brows furrowed. "You're saying the *director of the FBI* knowingly betrayed you?"

"For some reason, Ainsley chose to believe I was a traitor. I think a large sum of money had something to do with it. Same for Patricia Hennessey. She hated my guts, and it didn't take more than a whisper from Shemal for her to buy into his lies."

"Why did Hennessey hate you?"

He laughed, short and bitter. "That's a long story and like damn near everything else, it doesn't matter now."

Foster leaned forward, intent. "Tell me why Shemal singled you out. Why did he invest so much in your destruction?"

"Because he figured out I was the one ruining the Brotherhood's plans, killing his jihadists and stopping the money train. And because he knew what else I'd figured out."

Foster gestured with the pen. "Go on."

He stared into the empty cup. Foster noticed and poured more coffee. His mind drifted. The coffee's aroma took him back, reminded him of the life he'd never experience again. God, he missed it.

Foster cleared his throat. "Tell me what you figured out."

He blinked and tried to recapture his wandering thoughts. "What? Oh yeah. Shemal is the Muslim Brotherhood's point man in their secret jihad against the country."

"You know, I talked recently with David Harandi. He alluded to something similar. The Intel he shared with Director Berenger and I tends to corroborate what you're telling me."

"David is nothing more than a CIA tool."

Foster ignored his derision. "Do you have proof of the jihad supposedly taking place?"

He shifted in the chair and couldn't stifle a groan. Sweat popped on his forehead. Irritated with the unending pain and the badgering agent, he snapped. "As an FBI Special Agent involved in counter terrorism, how can you ask me that? Tell me you haven't read *The Project* or *The Memorandum,* whatever you want to call it."

"Are you all right?" At his impatient nod, Foster continued. "Yes, of course I've read it. Again, the Intel from Harandi suggests its motives as well. However, over the years we've seen a moderate face of Islam promoted by CAIR and various other Islamic organizations, and by Shemal, I might add."

"CAIR's blather about moderate Islam is window-dressing, nothing more. CAIR and Shemal prey on useful idiots like Ainsley. Maybe Abramson at CIA, too. The problem is you don't know who to trust in the intelligence community."

"You're certain this plan is ongoing?"

He hunched over, unable to sit up straight any longer. A thin line of sweat made its way down the side of his face, and he swiped at it. "I've been in mosques all over the country and abroad. I've sat in caves and in their camps, listening to their plans. The jihad is ongoing. It's been ongoing for a few decades, and they have no intention of stopping until the United States is an Islamic caliphate. *The* Caliphate."

Foster closed his notebook. "I think you've had enough. We'll talk again soon."

"OK." He couldn't care less if they never spoke again.

CHAPTER SIX

The Next Day
Georgetown, Washington, DC

Berenger watched as Harandi cleared the table in his dining room. She'd requested a private meeting, and he'd surprised her by inviting her to his townhouse for lunch. Perhaps he felt more penitent than she'd thought after their last, confrontational encounter. She knew better than to trust him fully, but he still managed to engender her confidence and that said a lot about Harandi's skillset.

Making a mental note to never forget how adept he must be at deception, she smiled at him as he returned. "Thanks for lunch. After reviewing the information I received from Cantor's laptop, I knew we needed to meet."

Harandi sat down across from her. "You're welcome. I'd like to hear your take on it now that you've had a chance to see everything."

"Frankly, I was first stunned, then angered. I've had to reevaluate my approach to both Milani and Cantor. The transfer of funds from CAIR and Shemal to the director of the FBI, three CIA agents, and the President's closest advisor would be difficult to explain under any circumstances. However, the accompanying emails between all of them are, to say the least, damning."

Harandi replied. "I'm very interested in your new approach. Please continue."

"I'm sickened by the enormity of this situation. When I think about what's happened to Milani, courtesy of our own government, I find it hard to grasp."

Harandi added, "Do you find it easier to understand the actions Milani took, on his own?"

"Yes. But I still don't condone what he did. Too many people are dead."

Harandi grimaced. "We are never going to see eye-to-eye on that."

"You may be correct on that point. Back to the matter at hand. Abramson did not receive any monies from CAIR or Shemal. He exchanged no emails with Shemal or Hennessey. However, I know he's been seen on a few occasions, having lunch or dinner with Shemal, at Brabo."

Harandi said, "I believe it's possible that Abramson has been a behind-the-scenes player from the get-go."

"A few lunch or dinner dates are hardly enough to warrant questioning him, especially since he doesn't know Cantor hacked his records. At this stage of our game, so to speak, I don't want to spook Abramson or make him suspicious."

"I agree. What do we know about a more private connection between Abramson and Shemal? Anything in either of their backgrounds to suggest complicity?"

"That's an excellent question. I'd like to conduct an undercover investigation of both men."

Harandi raised an index finger. "Aha. I concur. We have access to a veteran investigative reporter in Jack McKenzie. Why don't we make use of his talents and bring him into this little cabal of ours?"

"Mr. Harandi, a few discussions about matters of mutual importance does not make us a *cabal.*"

Harandi scoffed. "Semantics aside, McKenzie could discreetly look into both men without raising suspicion. If Abramson or Shemal get any whiff of the Bureau poking around, they'll make it much more difficult to unearth information."

"Damn it. I may have inadvertently put Abramson on alert."

"What happened?"

"I met with Abramson last week, at his request. He became quite agitated when I told him the CIA would have no further access to Milani. In order to gauge his reaction, I made purposely vague reference to a Muslim Brotherhood connection in Milani's situation, as well as my intent to reopen an unsolved murder case for a possible connection. I found his reaction unusual, over the top."

Harandi replied, "All the more reason to bring McKenzie on board. Let him do the legwork he excels at and keep the Bureau out of it."

Damned if he hadn't snagged her again. "Leaving the Bureau out of this at present would be my preference. All right, Mr. Harandi. Somewhat against my better judgment, I'll meet with McKenzie. May we conduct our business here?"

"Yes ma'am, we may. You won't regret this, I promise. McKenzie is a consummate professional."

She fixed Harandi with a hard stare. "Let me remind you. Any sleight of hand by you, in regard to any part of our collaboration, and I will respond with the full authority of my position. Understood?"

"Yes, I understand."

"Good. Here's another twist to this mess. Whitman completely bypassed the Attorney General, my boss. He's kept this whole matter strictly in-house. Need to know, don't you know, and I'm doing the same thing by keeping the Attorney General out of the loop."

"And once again, you're hesitant to take this information to Whitman because you aren't sure you trust him."

"Correct. The President's closest advisor took money and worked closely with a foreign national in the person of Shemal, to rendition an American citizen, Whitman's declaration of enemy combatant status notwithstanding, to Tora prison with no due process. What does that say about Whitman? Or his administration? How much of this does he know?"

"I knew Patricia was on a power trip. And for some reason, she hated Milani. But I had no idea of the extent of collaboration between her and the others. Whitman is aware of at least part of the money connection. We discussed it last spring."

"I find his lackluster pursuit of justice troubling."

Harandi replied. "You have no idea. I've watched him go from one end of the spectrum to the other with regard to Milani. Last spring, he appeared ready to investigate Shemal. Now he's demurred, saying he isn't convinced the Intel I received from Milani's colleague is trustworthy."

"Thus, our reasoning for not taking this investigation in its entirety to our joint boss."

"Exactly true."

She said, "Juxtaposing the Intel from Milani's source regarding Shemal, CAIR, and the Brotherhood lends credence to Milani's claim of innocence, as well as his assertions about their unstated goals."

Harandi replied, "What we're dancing around here is the fact that Milani is not a traitor, a domestic terrorist, or a double agent. He was cleverly set up by people eager to *literally* buy into blackballing him."

"Correct again. The question remains: Did Ainsley and Hennessey knowingly betray Milani and the country, or were they genuinely duped by Shemal? And, is Abramson working with Shemal to further the Muslim Brotherhood's goals?"

"This is why we need McKenzie on this. The sooner the better. When would you like this meeting of ours to take place?"

"As you said, the sooner the better. We need to know what's going on in order to proceed in an effective manner. I'm also planning to interview Milani myself."

Harandi gave her a sarcastic chuckle. "Good luck. He's tough to interview."

"Be that as it may, this situation is too crucial to our nation's security and the rule of law. I need to look Milani in the eye, observe his body language, and know for certain he's been telling the truth."

"Of course. What about bringing McKenzie on board?"

"Give him a call. If he's available, I'll clear my schedule for the afternoon. I'd like to make a decision on this as soon as possible."

"I'll call right now."

McKenzie settled into an armchair in Harandi's living room and tried to make a surreptitious assessment of the FBI Director seated on an adjacent love seat. She seemed like some kind of ice goddess to him, with her finely sculpted features, ocean blue eyes, and hair he knew was blonde, but seemed almost to match the silvery sheen she'd polished her nails. Her left ring finger was bare, and he scoured his memory for any news about her personal life.

Harandi, seated on a sofa facing the love seat, started their conversation. "Thank you again, Director Berenger, for agreeing to talk with us. I believe we'll make an effective team."

Berenger turned her speculative gaze his way. "Whether we'll cooperate together remains to be seen. It's nice to meet you Mr. McKenzie, although I didn't much appreciate you upstaging me on Milani's return."

He turned on his most engaging smile. "It's Jack. Please accept my apologies, Director Berenger. My main thrust from the outset has been to bring attention to Milani's situation and allow the American people to learn the truth."

Her eyes narrowed and she crossed her long, nylon clad legs. "I'm not here to collaborate with FOX News."

A glance at Harandi told him he had the ball. Encouraged, he decided to run with it. "Believe me, Director, the unvarnished truth, regardless of where it leads for Milani, the intelligence community, or even the President is my only concern."

Berenger said, "I'm squeamish about meeting with or involving the news media in any circumstance. How do I know the conversation we're having right now won't end up on the 24/7 news cycle?"

"Director, may I remind you, I don't work for the cable version of a supermarket tabloid. My trustworthiness is well known throughout the news industry. Any one of my sources will attest to my integrity. I value my reputation and don't intend to sully it with you."

He noted the miniscule softening of her features. She removed her navy-blue suit jacket and laid it next to her. The sleeveless white silk shell beneath it revealed her toned, bare arms. Even in DC's late afternoon heat and humidity she looked cool; unfazed. "Tell me what you've got in mind, Mr. McKenzie."

He replied. "Ever since Ralph Johnston first contacted me, insisting Milani was innocent, I've tried gaining access to Muusa Shemal, CAIR, and the Muslim Brotherhood. No one will acknowledge my calls. No one lets me in any doors."

Berenger at least looked interested. "CAIR is understandably reluctant to speak with a news organization such as yours. Go on."

"I thought Shemal, as CAIR's representative, would be ecstatic to tout their role in exposing a double agent. Seems to me that would have bolstered their creds in the eyes of everyday Americans."

Berenger replied. "Unless they had something to hide. In that event, they'd shy away from any kind of scrutiny."

He nodded. "Precisely. Abramson brushed me off as well. I kept digging, but then Milani supposedly died. I was thrilled to get the call from David saying he was still alive."

Berenger appraised him with her tantalizing eyes. "My overriding interest is in restoring the image of the Bureau. However, new information about both Shemal and Milani has given me a different frame of reference. *If* we come to an agreement about cooperating on an investigation, I may consider sharing more information with you."

Apparently, he'd scored a few points. He appreciated her tough, no-nonsense approach, but he could hold his own, with ease. "Thank you, Director. You may rest assured any information shared with me will be held in utmost confidence. I *never* reveal my sources."

She replied. "Yes, I understand the importance of your professional integrity, as well as its impact on my decision."

He responded. "We are dealing with a complex set of circumstances. I believe we can all agree that the *truth,* first and foremost, is our common goal. Determining the extent of the Muslim Brotherhood's machination of our intelligence community would be next on my list. Informing the public of the truth and clearing Milani's name, if that is possible, would be my logical conclusion to this process."

Berenger said, "You seem to recognize the important elements of the situation we're facing."

He tried to contain his zeal. She appeared poised to acquiesce, and he couldn't wait to get started. "What else can I say to convince you that a joint investigation is in the Bureau's and the country's best interests?"

Berenger glanced at Harandi, and then leveled her gaze on him. "You can state unequivocally that if I deem it necessary, you will withhold any or all of what we uncover through any kind of joint investigation."

He nodded his acceptance. "Agreed."

Harandi addressed Berenger. "Now that we've established Mr. McKenzie's trustworthiness, would you be inclined to share his possible role in our investigation?"

Berenger nodded. "Yes, I believe so. Mr. McKenzie, I would like to conduct a background investigation of both Muusa Shemal and Oscar Abramson, focused on finding out whether they have a shared past. I would like this investigation to be discreet and thorough, and not affiliated with the Bureau in any way."

He could barely hide his intensifying enthusiasm. "You've described my modus operandi to a T, Director. I'd also like, very much, to see the data and the Intel brief you mentioned."

Berenger's crossed leg moved gently back and forth and the heel of her pump slid from her foot. She let it dangle. "Don't get ahead of yourself, Mr. McKenzie. As I said, at some point, *if* we continue, and *if* I deem it germane, you'll have the opportunity to examine information pertinent to your quest for the truth."

He forced his gaze away from her ankle. "That's good enough for me. I'm committed to the pursuit of the truth in the best interests of the United States and Rowan Milani."

Harandi agreed. "This is a good thing we're doing."

Berenger added, "All right, Mr. McKenzie. I'll take this gamble one step further." She held out her hand.

He grasped her hand in his. The warmth of her touch sent longing tingling through his body. He took a quick breath and met her eyes. "Please, call me Jack."

Late Evening
Camp David

President Whitman regarded James Linden in the mellow lamplight. They sat in matching leather armchairs facing the massive stone fireplace, one of five in the President's cabin. Responding to Linden's urgent request to meet privately, he'd decided to offer the former President a few days at Aspen Lodge. His predecessor had utilized the Catoctin Mountain Park residence more often than he had. It's dark, wood-paneled walls, high-beamed ceilings and heavy furniture created a rustic ambience he didn't care for.

The two of them had enjoyed Maryland's finest crab cakes and sat long into the evening, reminiscing. They'd started on the upper terrace. Camp David's eighteen-hundred-foot elevation made for cooler evenings and as the day waned, they'd moved to the sun room and finally the living room. A bottle of Linden's favorite single-malt scotch sat on the low table in front of them, half gone. Restless, concerned about the former President's obvious reluctance, he proceeded cautiously. "We've covered the usual topics, Jim. To what do I owe this private meeting? What is the national security issue that couldn't wait, which you've put off until nearly midnight?"

Linden drained his glass of scotch, plucked the bottle from the table and poured more. "I'm unhappy about coming to you with this, but I didn't have a choice."

Even in the low light, Whitman read anger in his companion's thinned lips and drawn brows. "I've racked my brain over what information you may be privy to about national security that I wouldn't already know."

Linden replied, his words clipped. "You will pardon Rowan Milani for every terror-related charge, including the death of Rodney Ainsley. You will also pardon Chad Cantor and Ralph Johnston. Milani and Cantor will be released immediately after you address the nation and make their pardons public."

He stared at the former President. "I have no intention of doing any such thing. Milani is culpable for every one of those charges, including Ainsley's death and treason."

Linden drank more scotch and held his glass in both hands. "I'm afraid you will do exactly what I've said. You have one month, no longer, to prepare and then make your announcement. You will allow Milani and Cantor to walk out of their respective facilities as free men."

"You care to tell me *why* I would do this? You know I'd lose the confidence of the entire country. A reversal of this nature would undermine my administration beyond repair. It would also give my detractors on the other side of the aisle ammunition for years to come. Good God, I could write the attack ads myself."

"You will do what I'm asking, Gil. If you don't, the consequences will be even more catastrophic."

He downed the rest of his scotch and sloshed another generous serving into his glass. "I'm hard-pressed to understand what could be worse than the fallout of the course you're proposing."

"Try this. Every regime you or I have backed with secret, illicit arms deals, as in weapons we've provided under the table, becomes public knowledge, to the entire world."

"No one knows the details of those transactions except you and me."

"And the facilitator of our private foreign policy. He knows the details and will share them with the world if you refuse to acquiesce."

He stared at the amber booze and gulped more. "I don't intend to be bullied by an illicit arms dealer." He glared at Linden. *"Damn it.* Johnny Giacopino is behind this, isn't he?"

"He is. And he's not bluffing. Can you imagine the reaction of our allies? Arming and advising a less-than-desirable government, enabling said government to best one of our allies in order to prevent that ally from gaining too much power or economic strength, is not something either of us needs made public. We both did it more than a couple times, Gil."

"Agreed, and yes, I know how many times. But there must be a way to counter this threat. What if I promise to execute both Milani and Cantor if he proceeds?"

Linden spoke earnestly. "You need to understand something. *It's over.* Giacopino wields influence with other governments on a global level. He's not some piss ant trying to bully you."

"Here's what he needs to understand. I'm the goddamn President of the United States of America. Compared to me, he is a *piss ant.* We have the resources to crush his Mafia empire."

"Gil, you're talking out your ass and you know it. Whether you or I like it, Giacopino, along with his father and grandfather before him, have facilitated, greased rails, whatever the hell you want to call it, enabling this country to achieve certain goals which could never have been accomplished otherwise."

"I don't care what he or his crooked ancestors have done. I won't be told what to do by a criminal."

Linden replied. "Listen to me. If Milani and Cantor and Johnston aren't pardoned in a month, a shit storm will overtake your presidency. My best guess is you and your administration won't survive."

He tipped his head back and finished the scotch. He stared at the empty glass, felt the alcohol taking hold. "What about the shit storm coming if I do what Giacopino is demanding?"

"You're the master of the spin, Gil, and I'll help you. We'll make a big deal of me speaking publicly for the first time about what an asset Milani has been in our country's fight against terrorism. I'll stand right beside you when you make the announcement, if you want me to."

He ground his teeth. Hot anger combined with too much booze spread heat from his chest upward. He hefted the whiskey glass and threw it as hard as he could at the fireplace. The glass hit the stone face just below the presidential seal at its center and shattered, sending shards of glass in a fine shower across the hearth and into the carpet. "I knew I should have left the son of a bitch to rot in Tora. I should have sent all three of them there when I had the chance."

Linden replied. "Make your public pardons, set Milani free, and let certain people know how much you'd pay them to take him out in a couple years. Lull him into a false sense of security, and he'll never see it coming. In a couple of years, Giacopino won't be able to blame you for anything that happens to Milani."

He nodded in the semi-darkness. "I can live with that."

Two Days Later
Washington, DC

Whitman stood at the big south windows behind his desk in the Oval Office, gazing at the summer day unfolding before him. The weatherman had promised mid-nineties ahead of a thunderstorm. A round of golf before the rain would suit him. Instead, he'd initiate the charade of pardoning Milani.

Finding it difficult to square the cold, black anger he felt with the bright heat of the day, he left the windows and sat at his desk, perusing the notes he'd jotted in preparation for his deception. He leaned back and stared at the presidential seal on the domed ceiling. For more than thirty years he'd pursued the goal and dream of the presidency, starting in the Commonwealth of Virginia's General Assembly. His athletic stature and dark-haired good looks made him an irresistible candidate. The charm he poured into his campaigns became his trademark.

Behind-the-scenes gladiators of the political world took notice of the intelligent, college-educated business owner with a soaring vision for America. He shared their far-reaching goals and they asked him to run for the US Senate. They promised financial backing, and more important than the promise, they actually delivered. His career catapulted him into the national spotlight, and he'd made productive use of their support. Thirty-odd years down the road, he'd reached the apex and approached his sixtieth birthday in robust good health. His graying temples added gravitas to the persona he'd cultivated.

The only bump in the road had been the Rowan Milani affair. But he would never allow Milani to hinder his administration and his plans for the country. Many of his policies needed nurturing to become fully developed and implemented. His legacy depended on another eight years of governance with his VP at the helm. In addition, much depended on the trust of the people. If he lost that, he'd never finish what he'd started all those years ago in Virginia.

His foes had created a wedge issue out of the havoc and embarrassment Milani and his cohorts had caused. He'd needed to spend more political capital than he'd planned to rebuild his administration's image. Patricia's murder left him without an advisor, and he missed her savvy, unfailing assessment of the political landscape. If he could add her murder to the charges against Milani, he would.

After Patricia's death, he'd relied more than he'd wanted to on David Harandi. The man had risen to the challenge and done his job. But Harandi's heart was not in the fray. For him, truth was set in concrete. When he'd tried to explain that in politics, perception equaled truth, the man had been vehement in his disagreement. Harandi had been much more concerned with the CIA's abuse of Milani and had been appalled at Milani's incarceration in Tora Prison.

He'd approved the rendition of Milani to Egypt, and he'd do it again. Though he'd never admitted it to anyone besides Patricia, he'd wanted Milani out of the country to avoid another embarrassing rescue by cohorts who seemed able to operate with impunity. The report of Milani's death ended the incident, and he'd been glad. Now he owned the problem. For the last time.

After further reflection, he'd begun to question Harandi's outspoken belief in Milani's innocence. Harandi's information came from Milani's sources, which made it suspect in his mind. In addition, his advisor's past connection with Milani through his family created niggling doubts he couldn't ignore. Harandi had been vocal in his condemnation of Muusa Shemal as a trustworthy representative of the Muslim community and portrayed him as a wolf preying on clueless sheep.

However, his interactions with Shemal had been nothing but professional and congenial. As a leading member of CAIR and of the Muslim Brotherhood in the US, Shemal had worked closely with Rodney Ainsley to foster tolerance and inclusion of the Muslim population. Ainsley had overseen a complete overhaul of FBI training manuals and procedures in dealing with mosques and the Muslim population, with his blessing. An entire rewrite had eliminated inflammatory language that could be construed as discriminatory toward Islam.

And then along came Milani with his claims that CAIR and Shemal were part and parcel of a long-standing plan of the Muslim Brotherhood to topple western civilization. Of course, he knew about the *Memorandum*. But his experience, and that of others whom he trusted, led him to believe it no longer applied to the role of either CAIR or the Muslim Brotherhood within the United States.

He stood up and paced the office. He'd been forced to continue the relationship with Milani that his predecessor had started in the uncertain months following 9/11. Linden had chosen Milani as the country's de facto assassin; their ultra-secret weapon in the wearisome war on terror. He'd violated both domestic and international laws and sent the man, and presumably a team of Milani's choosing, into numerous arenas, both domestic and foreign, to eliminate jihadists. Milani had operated off the radar of the entire intelligence community, at the sole discretion and direction of first Linden and then him.

He'd violated the same laws as his predecessor, because the clandestine program worked. Milani had been ferocious in his pursuit of terrorists and vastly successful. A variety of terror plots, both domestic and foreign-born, had been quashed before they could be implemented. Sometimes, operating on foreign soil, Milani got close to the jihadists and returned to the United States with detailed plans of attacks, along with coordinates of terror camps. Drones completed the destruction of human and physical targets.

But had Milani provided bogus information? Had the country's drones destroyed inconsequential personnel and benign targets? The truth, when it came to Milani, remained elusive. Or was it simply a matter of perception? He returned to his desk and sat down. None of that mattered any longer. In a short time, Milani and his cohorts would be free. His angry reverie ended with a brisk knock. A Secret Service agent opened the door. "Mr. President, your visitors have arrived."

He stood up. "Thank you. Send them in."

"Yes sir." The agent retreated. David Harandi entered the Oval Office, followed by Abramson and Berenger.

He gestured at the brocade sofas and chairs. "Make yourselves comfortable." He chose one of the chairs and waited while Abramson chose the chair adjacent to his. "Good afternoon, Oscar. Thanks for making time to meet."

"I'm at your service anytime, Mr. President," Abramson intoned.

Harandi chose one sofa and Berenger the other. Whitman surveyed the group he'd ordered to meet him in the Oval Office *post haste.* He made eye contact with each one, then began. "The matter I'm about to discuss goes no further. Understood?" He waited until each one nodded. "After much thought, I've reached a decision regarding Rowan Milani and his colleagues Ralph Johnston and Chad Cantor."

Abramson fidgeted, Berenger gave him a cool stare, and Harandi relaxed, hands in his lap. They were all so predictable.

Abramson spoke first. "Finally. Proceeding with their prosecution is in the best interests of all of us." Abramson looked at the others and added, "And for the country, of course."

Berenger's lips began to curl. She looked like she wanted to spit on Abramson. Not in the mood for a squabble between his intelligence chiefs, he raised a hand. "Believe me, I understand your predilection, Oscar. However, after consulting with former President Linden and considering every feasible ramification, not to mention intended as well as *unintended* political consequences, I've decided to pardon all three men for every terrorism-related charge. In addition, I will pardon Milani for Rodney Ainsley's death."

Abramson's eyes widened. "Mr. President, this is unconscionable; I can't condone or support this course of action."

Berenger gave him a crisp nod. "I support you, Mr. President and will plan accordingly."

He returned her nod. "Thank you, Leigh." He leaned forward and gave Abramson his most practiced presidential glare. "Oscar, *you will* publicly and privately, in every communique, support this decision one-hundred percent. Do I make myself clear?"

Abramson stammered on. "Sir, you must reconsider. This is a disastrous course for everyone concerned. I simply cannot endorse this."

He stood up and gestured to the door. "Understood. I expect a letter of resignation on my desk this afternoon. Please be specific with the reasons behind your precipitous decision to leave your directorship at the agency. Your presence is no longer required. I'll see you out."

Abramson blushed strawberry red and sputtered. "No. I can't— that will not be necessary, Mr. President. My apologies. I will support your decision. One-hundred percent."

He observed Abramson. The groveling man had earned dismissal with his silly attempt at insurrection, and forcing the issue would give him immense satisfaction. However, in this instance, indulging himself would only create another firestorm, and the one he faced was plenty. "Thank you, Oscar." He returned to his chair and addressed Harandi. "David, we haven't heard your input."

Harandi stroked his goatee and said, "And regarding the seven people Milani allegedly killed in Houston?"

Linden hadn't mentioned Houston. Irritated, he fired back. "Houston's not part of the deal. The state of Texas will decide his fate regarding those murders."

Harandi's rejoinder came fast. "And what *deal* is that?"

"David, as you know, I am not required to inform any of you regarding the details of my decision."

Harandi replied. "Understood, sir. My first concern is always for the political fallout of any course of action. If you believe you've covered those bases, then you most certainly have my full support. I'll assist you with this in any way possible."

How Harandi maintained his dignity, while still managing to kiss his ass amazed him. "Thank you, David. I plan to address the nation from the Rose Garden in exactly one month. You three will stand behind me in a show of solidarity. President Linden will join me at the podium as well. We will both speak, and I will announce the pardons. Milani and Cantor will be released following my announcement."

Berenger replied. "Sir, will you accept questions from the press?"

He shook his head. "No. I want to make this as short and sweet as possible."

Harandi spoke up. "Sir, you may want to reconsider. Avoiding questions will only beg more questions. If you entertain a limited number of questions, I believe you'll do more to quell the naysayers."

Anxious to wrap things up, he stood. He needed to get started on the announcement, which would be, for him, the same as perjuring himself. "All right, I'll consider taking a few questions. I'll make sure each of you has a copy of my announcement within a week. Respond as necessary with any questions or comments."

The CIA chief rocketed off the chair and strode to the door. "Thank you, Mr. President."

Berenger lagged behind, watched Abramson leave, then spoke. "I chose not to speak in front of Oscar, sir. Are you convinced this is your only choice? If so, I meant what I said. I fully support you. In the interim, I would like to proceed with my ongoing projects, if you are in agreement."

"Yes, Leigh, this is my final decision regarding the entire matter of Milani and his colleagues. What projects are you referring to?"

"Special Agent Foster has been interrogating Milani. I'd like to see the process continue. If Milani knows he's being pardoned, he may stop talking. I'm planning to interview him as well."

"Milani doesn't need to know anything. His custody will be transferred to Houston anyway."

Berenger said, "Mr. Cantor is cooperating with Special Agent O'Brien. I'd like to see her work continue."

"Yes, please carry on. Gain as much information as possible. Delay informing Cantor of my pardon. In fact, don't tell him anything until after my announcement."

Berenger replied. "Thank you, sir. We will proceed." She left the Oval Office.

Harandi looked like he wanted more of an explanation, but his advisor would have to accept that none was forthcoming. "David, thank you for your input. You made excellent points, as usual."

"You're welcome sir. I know you requested that we keep your announcement in-house. Would it be problematic for me to notify Detective Matthews in Houston of your plan?"

"Most certainly not. Coordinate with Berenger and Foster as well. Make the arrangements to transfer Milani's custody the moment I announce his pardon."

"Yes sir. I'll take care of the matter."

After Harandi left, he sat behind his desk and heaved a sigh. He'd live up to the blackmail agreement he'd been forced to accept. But he'd look forward to the day he got a call or even read in a damned newspaper about Rowan Milani's death. The man could be eliminated in a Texas prison more easily than if he were incarcerated at ADX Florence. One way or another, he'd make sure Milani paid for every sin committed against his administration and his legacy.

CIA Headquarters, Langley, VA

Abramson entered his office, barely acknowledging his secretary. "No calls, please." He shut the door and locked it before seating himself behind his desk. He produced keys from the pocket of his suit pants and unlocked the bottom desk drawer with shaking fingers. From beneath a false bottom, he pulled one of the dozen or so burner phones he kept on hand for private calls.

He dialed the international connection, his still-trembling fingers necessitating three tries. "Stupid, piece of *shit* phone." Finally getting the numbers strung together correctly, he yanked a white handkerchief from his suit pocket and dabbed at the droplets of sweat on his brow.

He tugged on his tie with thick fingers until it came undone. Shemal answered after six rings. "Hello my friend. What is it that could not wait? You are aware of the time difference?"

"I just left a meeting with Whitman. Milani and his associates will be pardoned in exactly one month for all the terrorism charges. Cantor and Johnston will be freed. However, Milani will not be pardoned for the murders he committed in Houston. He will be transferred to Texas."

Shemal replied, his tone brusque. "Once more, the Jinn escapes my grasp. But at last, some measure of justice will be served. Milani will pay for the murder of my habibti and the others."

"Yes, of course, but don't you understand? It's one more opportunity for Milani to speak. His cohorts will be free. Do not presume their silence. My concern extends to what they may decide to pursue next."

"Oscar, get hold of yourself. We must seek Allah's direction in this matter. Above all we must not act rashly."

"Certainly we must seek Allah in this matter. But you don't seem to appreciate the delicacy of my situation. It is vital to our continuing success that my role is not discovered. The pardon of Cantor and Johnston puts that in jeopardy."

"We have both taken great care to ensure that your involvement will never be discovered. We must be patient and act only after we have considered every option."

"As you wish." He ended the call and threw the phone back in the drawer.

Georgetown, Washington, DC

Harandi rubbed his temples and gazed at Berenger. "What do you think happened this afternoon?" They were on his deck, behind the privacy fence enclosing his tiny yard, seated at the glass-topped table he kept pristinely clean. A light breeze stirred the humidity and lifted the edges of the striped umbrella above them.

Berenger shrugged. "Offhand, I'd say someone gave Whitman a direct order. I cannot begin to imagine who is in a position to do that, but, I'd give darn near anything to know. Thank you for agreeing to meet with me away from my office."

He had an idea of who'd put the screws to Whitman, but for now, he'd keep his thoughts to himself. "You're welcome. Did you notice how quickly Whitman shut me down when I asked what *deal* he was referring to?"

"Yes. He clearly has no intention of revealing anything."

"No, and none of this makes any difference for Milani. I believe our investigation needs to go on, and I hope you think so as well."

Berenger replied. "Abramson's reaction alone is reason enough to continue our investigation. He's on shaky ground. You're right about Milani. He'll get what he's earned."

Her comments irked him. "Milani's going to end up in the hands of a vengeful Houston District Attorney who's quite likely still fuming from the missed opportunity to prosecute him, thanks to me."

"Vengeful? I'd say the DA in Houston is well within his rights to prosecute Milani to the fullest extent allowed by Texas law."

"Then if I may, why are you still planning to interview Milani yourself?"

"Whitman's decision doesn't change my interest in the truth, as you keep alluding to."

"It seems to me you've already reached a decision about the truth regarding Milani. Why bother with a personal interview?"

Berenger continued. "Honestly? I want to see Milani for myself. I need to observe his body language. Foster's reports indicate he's in a lot of pain. I believe, as the head of the Bureau, I need to interview him and make my own judgment, much as I trust Foster."

He chuckled. "Interesting. You're taking the philosophy of *relationship building* to a new level."

"As I stated, in my role as FBI Director, I believe it is incumbent upon me to form my own judgments regarding Milani and the entire situation surrounding him."

He knew when to let it go. "All right. Would you mind if I touch base with Foster? Whitman asked if I'd coordinate Rowan's transfer with him and the Houston Police Department."

"I have no objection to you contacting Foster. Go ahead and make the arrangements. I'll fill him in on the details of Whitman's decision tomorrow."

"I'll take care of everything concerning the transfer. You know, with Rowan headed to Houston, I believe my usefulness to Whitman is ending. Can't say I'm sorry about that."

Berenger stood up, smoothing her skirt and picking up the blazer she'd shed while they sat outside. "You've been in Whitman's orbit for a while now. Time to let someone else deal with those pressures."

"You've got that right. Have a good night, Director."

He saw her out and wandered into his living room, mulling over his next step. Once he made a certain phone call, he'd have done all he could to help his former friend. Would it matter? Because regardless of Milani's explanation for the Houston killings, homicide detective Kyle Matthews was never going to buy it.

Matthews had collaborated with him, and their joint-op helped lead to Milani's arrest. While working toward that end, Matthews had run across Milani and nearly been killed. After giving him a severe concussion, skull fracture, broken nose, and a ruptured quadriceps tendon, for his own unexplained reasons Milani let the detective live.

Over the course of their joint venture, Matthews had become a good friend. But on this hot, humid afternoon, he'd betray their friendship. He pulled his phone from his shirt pocket and called. His friend picked up on the second ring. "David, to what do I owe the pleasure?"

He slumped down on the sofa and propped his feet on the coffee table. "Hello Kyle. How's Houston's finest Irish cowboy detective getting along?"

"Well now, Mr. DC, we're doin' damn fine. How about yourself?"

The repartee that usually made him smile caused a painful prick of conscience this time. "Been a long day here, my friend. I wish it was over. How are Erin and the boys?"

He pictured the rangy detective sitting with his lizard-skin boots parked on his desk and heard simple happiness in the Texas drawl. "Erin and the rug rats are great. Guess what else? I'm officially done with rehab as of this week. So, tell me, why is your long day not winding down? Does it concern my nemesis?"

"Doesn't everything I do concern your nemesis? I've got some information for you, which won't be made public for a month. President Whitman has done an about-face. He has chosen to pardon Milani and his two colleagues for the terrorism-related charges. Milani will be released from ADX Florence immediately after Whitman makes his announcement."

"Are you telling me Milani gets to skate on *everything?* Listen, I'm gonna inform my captain as soon as we hang up. We've got a gung-ho DA, and he'll jump on this. We'll prosecute that SOB for each and every one of the murders he committed in my city. You tell Whitman we'll take him off your hands and save his administration the embarrassment of releasing him."

His friend reacted exactly as he'd expected. "As you know, Milani swears the people he killed in Houston were all jihadists, and he was doing his job, as ordained and approved by the President, to eliminate terrorists here and abroad."

Matthews boasted. "I've got a bloody knife and two pistols covered with Milani's prints sitting in our evidence lockup, not to mention his bloody clothes. Ballistics show that the gun used to shoot Pinella and shred the limo was his 9mm Glock. She was no terrorist. He had no need to murder her."

"I know, my friend. I know."

"I've researched the others he killed. He's right, as far as them being here unlawfully, but no evidence exists tying them to terrorism, other than the fact they were all connected to the House of Allah, where Shemal taught and presided, or hung out or whatever the hell he did there."

Harandi half-listened, unable to stop thinking about the stupid choices his former friend had made. They would come back to bite him in the ass, no matter how he tried to help him. "Whitman is already on board with sending Milani to Houston. I'll put things in motion from my end."

"Thanks. But hey, now that you're done with Milani, you should think about taking a vacation down here. We'll show you an old-fashioned Texas good time."

"I'll definitely consider it. Tell your lovely wife hello, and that I'm looking forward to seeing her sometime soon. Take good care Kyle."

"You do the same, and thanks again for the heads up."

After ending the call, he stared at his phone for a long moment before laying it on the sofa. Now for the betrayal. He dug his wallet out of his back pocket and extracted a slip of paper Clifton Cantor had given him months earlier. *If you need quick access to a safe location, tell this person that I told you to call.* He considered his next move. He hadn't lied about putting things in motion.

If Matthews and the hardnosed DA in Houston ever got a whiff of what he was about to do, quick access to a safe location would be preferable to incarceration in Texas, never mind a vacation. He grabbed his phone and punched in the number. Someone fumbled on the other end and then a sleepy, gravelly voice answered. "Hello."

Surprised at the simple greeting, he returned it. "Hello."

"Tell me who's calling so we can either continue our conversation or hang up. Capisce?"

"This is David Harandi. I'm calling on Rowan Milani's behalf. Are you willing to hear me out?"

"I'm still on the damn phone, aren't I?"

The remark confirmed his thoughts about who'd given Whitman his marching orders. "Thank you, sir. As I'm sure you know, Rowan will be released soon. However, I've got a problem in Houston and I'm hoping you can help me."

The gravelly voice replied. "Keep talking."

Woodley Park, Washington, DC

Berenger stood outside the door to Jack McKenzie's home. She'd kept telling herself they were professionals, collaborating on a serious, important investigation. Dinner together seemed appropriate, or at least not inappropriate, but now she wasn't sure.

Reminding herself that as the director of the FBI, she didn't owe anyone an explanation, she rang the doorbell and waited.

McKenzie opened the door looking relaxed and comfortable in a white polo shirt, Chinos, and leather boat shoes. "Hello Director Berenger. Come in, before you expire in this heat."

She stepped into the welcoming coolness and wished she'd stopped at home to change from the severe black business suit that felt almost like armor. "Thank you. It's beastly today." While her eyes adjusted, she managed a brief glance around the dark wood foyer as McKenzie guided her down a dimly lit hallway into an open kitchen-family room. She blinked at the contrast from the dark hallway and fell instantly in love with the subtle, chardonnay-painted walls, brilliant white cabinets, and warm, gray-brown granite countertops.

McKenzie pulled out a tall, padded chair for her at one end of the L-shaped bar where he'd already poured a glass of pinot grigio. "Chilled appropriately for you on this momentous day."

The wine slid across her palate, tangy and bright with a hint of lemon. "My, this is excellent. Tell me, what makes this a momentous day?"

McKenzie gestured to the island in the center of the kitchen. "I will enlighten you while I swill a beer and get working on our repast."

She sipped more wine and hooked her purse on the chair's back. "I'm listening."

He dug in the fridge, emerging with his arms full of groceries, plus a Shock Top Lemon Shandy. After dumping the pile of food on the island, he popped the top on the beer and took a hefty swallow. He covered a belch with his fist. "Pardon me, please. Here goes. Anytime I get the opportunity to prepare dinner for, and I hope you don't take offense, a beautiful woman who is also head of our country's premier law enforcement agency, and my lead on an important investigation involving our national security, I call it a momentous occasion."

She drank more wine, wanting to unwind and lose the harsh demeanor she felt her position demanded. His irrepressible grin dared her to tease him and for once, she wanted to enjoy some harmless banter and hoped she could pull it off. "Goodness, how long did it take you to memorize your speech? You didn't even pause to catch your breath. I'm not offended, by the way. And I'd have to agree, dining with a world-class investigative reporter who works for the most irritating network in the business is momentous for me as well."

He raised his bottle of beer. "Well said. Although I could take exception to the irritating bit, if I were so inclined, which I'm not."

"Good. I'm glad." The crisp wine flowed easily, relaxing her. She took another appreciative swallow and decided she was too warm. McKenzie helped her out of the linen jacket and refilled her glass. "Thank you. It's been a long day. A long few months, when I think about it."

He began chopping, dicing and cubing. "Do tell, about your day and the months, if you'd like."

While he prepped, she chatted, ending with words she wanted to recall as soon as they fell out of her mouth. "I had a meeting with the President today. His topic surprised me." She paused, feeling the heat reddening her cheeks. "And I honestly can't say more."

McKenzie shoved his ingredients into a large wooden bowl and added a pair of tongs. He grabbed plates and laid out silverware and napkins. "Of course, you know, as an investigative reporter, especially for that most irritating of networks, you've commandeered my complete attention."

Mortified at her utterly out-of-character comments, she clutched the wine glass and forced a nonchalance she didn't feel. "Mm, I didn't consider your nose for news. It's not generally my nature to provoke or tantalize. I shouldn't have said anything. My apologies."

"Nonsense. You should be able to share your day with your partner; I mean, with a friend, or a colleague."

She looked on, surprised to see him blushing bright red, right up to the crown of his head. What had happened? And then she knew. He'd called her *partner.* They were, but he'd clearly had an entirely different context in mind. Something fluttered inside, and she felt the warmth rising from her neck, while her cheeks burned for the second time. "You're absolutely right. In about a month, give or take a few days, I'll give you the exclusive."

He served her what looked like a delectable salad. "I'll hold you to that, Leigh. Oh, I am sorry. I don't mean to presume a more casual relationship. You are the director of the FBI, and I'm grateful for your willingness to share dinner with me. But, uh, is it all right if I call you Leigh?"

She poured vinaigrette over the salad and decided to take whatever he'd inadvertently started a tiny step further. "Of course, Jack. It's absolutely all right. And don't worry, you'll get your exclusive."

He grinned. "I can't wait."

After dinner, he ushered her into the cozy family room off the kitchen. While FOX News murmured in the background on his unbelievably huge, curved-screen TV, she drank more wine, and he had another Shandy. Comfortable at opposite ends of a cushy sofa, they veered from shoptalk to sharing their backgrounds. She learned about Anne, and how he'd dealt with losing her.

She told him about her unsuccessful foray into marriage. Three glasses into the luscious wine, feeling carefree for the first time in months, she realized she liked him, a lot. A reluctant glance at her watch told her she needed to cut the enjoyable evening short. "I should be heading home." She punched an app on her phone and stood up.

He escorted her to the door, but didn't open it. Instead he turned to face her. "I'm sure your service is waiting."

Feeling whimsical, she rolled her eyes. "Oh yes, they're out there, wondering what we're doing."

"Thought so. That's why I want to do this before I open the door." He leaned close and kissed her, his lips brushing hers, then stepped back. "How was that?"

The soft warmth of his lips and the avid readiness in his eyes dampened her palms. "I liked it."

"Me too." He put his arms around her and kissed her again. This time, she let her arms go around him and pressed her lips to his with an eagerness that surprised her. He responded, pulling her close while his mouth seemed to devour hers.

When he pulled away, she wanted more. He grasped her hands in his. She tasted the Shandy, and *him.* "Thank you for the evening. For dinner. For everything. I better go."

McKenzie squeezed her hands and pecked her cheek. "Yes, you better. Everything was my pleasure. Have a good night, Leigh."

Later, lying in bed, she drifted to sleep smiling to herself, thinking about his lips and his hands, wondering how long she'd have to wait before she could be alone with him again.

CHAPTER SEVEN

The Next Day, 6:00 p.m.
Dubai, UAE

Johnny mulled over the phone call from David Harandi. He hadn't considered the murder charges brought against Rowan by the state of Texas. Those charges made the game more interesting, but he didn't mind. Winning mattered. Nothing else. And he would win. He checked the time and punched a contact on his iPhone. After a few rings, a man answered. "Hello."

"Good morning Judge Caito. Congratulations on your election to the 177th District Court of the state of Texas."

"Thank you very much. I appreciated your assistance. What's your pleasure this morning?"

"Your DA in Houston is busy preparing a high-profile case against my guy, Rowan Milani. I'm sending a crew down there, and I'm gonna need you and your crew to help them out."

"I've already heard about that case. A grand jury is being impaneled virtually as we speak. What do you need?"

"I need the shit-pile of evidence against Milani to become non-existent. I need the entire chain of evidence to become fucking extinct. After his attorney asks to see the evidence that doesn't exist, I need the case dismissed in an expeditious manner. And I need Milani released in the same kind of manner."

"Chain of evidence. Hmm. Do you have anyone with hacking ability?"

"I do."

"All right, I'll put your guy with mine. He's someone I trust. My contacts inside the department can work with your crew. What kind of timeline are we looking at?"

"Milani will arrive in your jail a month from now. Once this is finished, clean-up needs to be thorough. No loose ends with looser tongues."

"I'll take care of it. Anything else?"

"A limo sitting in the sheriff's impound lot needs to go south of the border with an expendable driver and mode of transport."

"Consider it done."

"Thank you. Usual fee acceptable?"

"Well, I am enjoying my election to the 177th District Court of my fine state."

"I intended that as a gift. This is a big project."

"My friend, you are a prince. The usual fee will suffice, along with dinner at your restaurant sometime in the not too distant future."

"My pleasure, Judge. Let me know when you'll be in my city, and I'll lay out the red carpet."

"I look forward to it. Take care. See you soon."

Johnny's best crew, Roberto and Gino, filed into his office and sat in chairs facing his desk. He opened the cherry wood humidor with his initials engraved in flowing script on the top and chose a Cohiba Robusto Cameroon. He snapped the lid shut and clipped the end off of the cigar. Gino produced a lighter and reached toward him. He grunted his thanks and puffed, enjoying the beginnings of a cloud of aromatic smoke.

He pondered the two men facing him. His nephew Gino had squirmed his way out of his younger brother's wife twenty-seven years earlier. He'd seen potential in the kid almost from the get-go, and Gino had never disappointed. The kid drove him around in the Town Car at home in Chicago and all the time he listened, seeming to know by instinct how to keep a low, barely noticeable profile.

Later, they'd sit in his private office in the back of his restaurant and chat. Gino had insights even he didn't think of, and he'd come to depend on the kid's perspective. He wouldn't let Gino know, at least not for a few more years. Until then, he had the best damn driver in Chicago. And once his plan had been initiated, they'd all be headed back there.

Gino didn't know the meaning of fear, either, which made him the perfect pal for the stocky man seated beside him. Gino and Roberto's looks were a study in opposites, something he found entertaining. Where Gino had inherited his father's crop of wavy black hair and his mother's snoozy eyes, Roberto didn't possess one solitary hair on his bumpy head. He did have memorable blue eyes, though. On occasion, he'd seen them glint with a certain kind of malevolence guaranteed to put piss in a mark's pants.

He waved through the expanding haze. "I've got a job for you boys. Together."

Roberto leaned back and folded massive hands in his lap. "What you got in mind, Boss?"

"How'd you two like to exchange Dubai for Houston?"

Gino cracked his knuckles and leaned forward. "You need me to drive you around Houston, Boss?"

He flicked ash off the tip of the cigar into an ornate, carved stone ashtray an Arab Sheikh's young son had given him. "You'll be picking up Vinnie at Ellington and driving him around town. When Milani is released, you'll take Vinnie and him from the lock-up to the airport, but we'll get to that later. Here's the thing. I need you to retrieve and destroy every single piece of evidence against Milani from the Houston PD's evidence storage facility. Except for his guns and knife. I wanna surprise the hell out of him and give 'em back to him."

Roberto said, "You got a crew in Houston with a few cop friends?"

"You and Gino will be my crew in Houston, along with Tony, who'll meet you there." His second son, Antonio, managed his cyber-security. The kid, now forty, had become a hacker as a teenager. Understanding the benefits of those skills to his organization, he'd encouraged and financed his son's penchant for cyber-crime. Tony had learned from some of the best. "I got a friend in the city, and he's got a crew of his own, including some cops on the string. They'll cooperate. The PD built a big fancy warehouse, and it holds damn near everything under one roof. A forensic lab affiliated with Methodist Hospital houses the DNA evidence."

Roberto asked, "You got a list of everything we need to retrieve?"

He nodded. "You'll have a list. The biggest obstacle is the limo Milani offed that broad in and then shot up with his 9mm. It's in the Harris County Sheriff's impound lot. My friend will make sure you have access to its location, along with a semi to transport everything. Once you get the limo and the rest of the evidence out of Houston, it all needs to head south of the border. Capisce?"

Roberto gave him a slow smile. "We'll take care of everything, Boss."

Gino said, "When do we leave?"

"You'll leave first thing tomorrow morning. Keep me apprised of your progress."

The two men stood up. Roberto spoke first. "Will do, Boss."

Gino added, "No problem, Boss."

"One last thing. My friend and his crew will take care of cleanup. You get in and out. After you finish, lay low. Milani will be shipped to Houston in a month. After that, it could be a month or more before he's released. When I tell you to head for the lock-up, you haul ass and pick him up. I'll see you in Chicago when it's all said and done." He watched them file out of his office while he puffed more on the cigar.

He considered the man who'd play the public role in Houston. Vincent Black had been in his employ since shortly after graduating from the University of Chicago's Law School. Black had grown up with his sons, playing in the same neighborhood, marinating in the same business culture. Of course, he'd made sure to keep their personal connection obscured. A few years back, after he'd added Texas oil interests to his global empire, he'd wanted a smart advocate to protect those interests and his employees.

Vinnie had performed magnificently in every situation, in addition to establishing his own criminal law practice. The man possessed natural acting skill and knew how to read people better than damn near anyone he knew. He hit the contact number. A robust voice with a Chicago accent answered right away. "Hello Boss. What do you need?"

"Vinnie, how are you enjoying Texas life?"

"Best move I ever could have made. Austin is a beautiful city."

"Your work has been appreciated over the last fifteen years. How's your lovely Melanie? Still allocating your resources responsibly?"

"Hell, she allocates everything I make."

He chuckled. "Good for her. You been acquainting yourself with Rowan Milani and his situation?"

"Yeah, Boss. Interesting as hell, although he's been jerked around by a bunch of pricks."

He tapped ash into the ceramic ash tray. "That's about to end, and you're my star player. I'm going to need you in Houston in a month. Milani will be detained in the Harris County Jail. I'll send you the particulars."

"I'm looking forward to this."

"I'm counting on you to manage these cowboys in your usual fashion. One especially; his name is Kyle Matthews. He's the homicide detective who helped apprehend Milani."

The confidence came through, from seven thousand miles away. "Don't you worry, Boss. I'll introduce him to the Chicago version of the Two-Step."

"Do your homework on this guy. He's got a hard-on for Milani."

"Got it, Boss. Don't worry."

"You take care, Vinnie."

He ended the call and drew deep on the cigar, listening to the crackle of the tobacco, watching the burning leaves at the tip turn to embers. Things would fall into place in the way he intended. Satisfied with everything he'd put in motion, he made one final call. Ralph answered right away. "Johnny, what can I do for you?"

"Join me for a smoke in my office, would ya? I got an idea bouncing around, and I wanna get your take."

"Be right there." While he waited for Ralph, he strolled to the windows comprising one curving wall of the room. A cloudless sky provided him with a view of a hodgepodge of buildings crammed together far below, the city stretching to a strip of white sand and the Persian Gulf beyond. He'd taken this trip not planning on staying in Dubai for more than a couple weeks. Much as he enjoyed the city and its locale, he looked forward to dining in his own restaurant, and taking Eloisa to the theater.

Georges' voice crackled over the intercom. "Sir, Mr. Ralph is here."

"Send him in." The door buzzed and Ralph entered. He left the window and gestured expansively. "Grab a cigar. I'm in a mood to celebrate. Everything is fixed for Milani, but I'm in sore need of your assistance in organizing the return of the whole bunch of us to Chicago."

"God almighty, that's the best news I've heard in a long time."

They settled into their usual spots, him in one corner of the sofa, and Ralph in the adjacent leather chair. He took a long puff on his cigar. "Here's to the final chapter. I got a few thoughts about Rowan, an' I wanna run 'em by you because as far as I can tell, you're the closest thing he's ever had to a real father."

Ralph frowned. “Aw hell, Khalil’s a good father. I know he loves his son. Both he and Janice have suffered through this ordeal.”

“I agree, Khalil is a good and decent man. He’s quiet and kind. You might say that puts him at a disadvantage with a son like Rowan. On the other hand, Janice is like a battering ram, which is why I got her to drinking whiskey. She needed a chill pill.”

Ralph concurred. “That’s for damn sure. Then you have Rowan. He’s headstrong, smarter than both his parents put together, and stubborn as a mule. Brave as hell too. That combination is probably what’s kept him alive.”

“Which brings me to my dilemma. I’ve been thinking about the woman he gave it all up for. The redhead. I know they parted ways when Rowan went off on his own to screw things up.”

“Rowan can be one hell of a pain in the ass. But I know he cared for Danielle, and let me tell you, she loved him, pure and simple. What’s your dilemma?”

“If you think he still cares for her, I’d bring her to Chicago. Do you think she’d be up for it?”

Ralph puffed on his cigar for a long moment. “If it was me, I’d wait on that, although it’s a nice idea. Rowan is a proud man, and from what I saw on the airplane that day, he’s lost a lot of himself. If he feels like he’s less than the man he always was, he is *not* going to want her to see him.”

“What about our resident shrink? He’s got an in with Rowan, doesn’t he?”

Ralph gave him a rueful smile. “We always thought so. But the last time Angelo tried reaching out to Rowan, it didn’t go so well.”

“The shrink doesn’t seem like the type to give up. When Rowan gets to Chicago, I’ll set up a meet. First with me, then the shrink. Somebody’s got to knock some sense into him.”

Ralph held the cigar between his fingers and his smile faded. "That's been tried, more than a few times now. How about we get a bead on him after he's been released and give him a few days to get his head wrapped around being free? Once I have a chance to talk to him, I'll have a better idea of how to proceed. I'll talk to Angelo in the meantime and get his thoughts."

"We'll have a meet with Rowan together. I'm serious about this stuff. He's got a bright future."

"I used to think so, but I gotta tell you, my experience with both Rowan and the forces aligned against him make me less than optimistic about his prospects for starting over."

He'd keep his plans for Rowan's future to himself, for now. "Aw come on, Ralphie. We gotta think positive. We're on a roll."

Houston, TX

The Honorable Judge Samuel Caito laid his phone on his lap and stretched out in the lounge chair next to the pool. The weatherman had promised a hot one, and even at 8 a.m. the humidity caused his shirt to stick damply to his back. He sipped his orange juice, inhaled the scent of chlorine, and shaded his eyes against the sun sparkling on the water. The call from his friend and family benefactor made him glad he'd blocked off the morning for personal business. Making the necessary arrangements for this latest collaboration would take some time and careful planning.

He remembered the day twenty-five years earlier, when he'd reached out to Johnny Giacopino. Two years out of Stanford's Law School, he'd left California for Texas, because the young woman he'd fallen in love with in college was from Houston. His parents, originally from Chicago, had moved the family to Los Angeles in 1970. His father had developed a thriving import-export company, and he'd grown up in upper-middle-class comfort.

He'd been a pup, hard at work in the DA's office in Houston when his father called, panic-stricken. A Korean gang had been harassing his father for months, offering payoffs and bribes in return for using his business for their smuggling enterprise. His father had continually refused, but the gang leader escalated the bullying with a visit to their home, threatening violence or worse. He'd racked his brain for ways to help his parents before their problem became a tragedy.

He remembered his father's stories from Sunday afternoon drives around Chicago, especially the tales about a man who shared their Italian ethnicity, but not his father's unmovable moral code of an honest day's work for an honest day's pay. Escaping the pervasive influence of the mob had been one of the reasons his father had moved the family to southern California.

Desperate to help his father, he made a phone call. Johnny had listened intently to his explanation and asked pertinent questions. He told the Don he'd do anything to help his father's business survive and to keep his family safe. Johnny had taken care of the problem, and he'd never told his grateful parents how he'd helped them.

He'd sold out to the Mafia Don, but he'd never regretted it. Over the years, he'd lost track of their various collusions. Johnny had connections in Texas which had proven useful. The powerful man became a good friend, almost a surrogate father. He'd eventually realized that he had more in common with the Don than he did with his own father.

He finished the juice and made his way into the cool interior of his fifteen-thousand-square-foot brick home, to his spacious office. The bottom drawer of his desk held a supply of alternative smart phones, each equipped with a voice changer app. He chose one and dialed. The voice on the other end was subdued. "Yeah."

"Ed, I need you and Juan to pick up details on a new assignment this evening at the usual spot."

"Our shift runs until seven. We can be there by half-past."

"The information will be waiting." He ended the call and smiled. A few years earlier, he'd contemplated adding to the small, trustworthy stable of Houston police officers he'd recruited to work dually for him and the department. His research revealed a short list of Houston's finest who'd occasionally crossed the line in their interactions with the public. The department's efficient inner machine hid most of those officer indiscretions.

Further careful probing exposed which of the officers lived beyond their means and were heavily in debt. Two men, Juan Morales and Ed Nelson, fit his ideal profile. Remaining nameless, he'd contacted the men and offered them a life-changing financial opportunity in exchange for their ability to work within the system to achieve his goals. Both had expressed initial reticence, but capitulated when he'd tossed out dollar amounts.

He recruited in pairs and neither Morales nor Nelson or any of the other officers on the string knew who they worked for. Everything from contact to assignment completion and pay took place anonymously. Should one of the officers decide the opportunity he'd afforded wasn't enough, no amount of investigation would implicate his meticulously compartmentalized organization. He'd made it clear from the beginning how things would end if any one of the men's conscience got the better of his common sense. After witnessing a cartel version of interrogation and justice, his operatives remained loyal and quiet.

His next call went to Mexico. "Good morning, Luis. I am in need of your services."

His friend replied in heavily accented English. "Of course. What do you require?"

"A disposable semi-truck and driver."

"Your timing is perfect. One of my workers has become an annoyance; a whiner. I am no longer certain of the depth of loyalty he holds to my enterprise. He is ripe for plucking by the Federales on either side of the border."

"I'm surprised you haven't taken care of this problem yourself, Luis."

The shrug came through in his compatriot's voice. "Unfortunately for me, he is my wife's cousin. If you are able to eliminate this problem and keep my hands clean, I will consider it a favor of great magnitude. No charge for the semi; it's an old truck, long past its prime. Let me know when and where you need it. I will inform the worthless one of his final job."

"Excellent. I'll be in touch. Have a nice day, Luis." He made one final call. "Hello, Ben. How's your mother?"

The raspy voice sounded groggy. "Uh, hello, Judge Caito. My mother is doing great. What, uh, what do you want?"

He'd been impressed with the eighteen-year-old hacker who'd ended up in his courtroom after a lengthy cyber chase. The young man possessed unbelievable talent and eluded capture for two years while paying for his mother's impossibly expensive cancer treatment using stolen credit card information. He exercised the authority and discretion of his judgeship to keep Ben out of prison, paid for his mother's treatment, and took the young man under his wing. That was four years ago. "I need your considerable skill on a project. Why don't you come over in about an hour, and I'll fill you in on the details."

Ben cleared his throat and sounded more awake. "I'll be there, sir."

He ended the call and considered. To society in general, Ben presented the façade of a lazy stoner. His blond hair stuck out in tufts, and he was certain Ben never gave combing it a thought. He'd never seen the young man in anything but a t-shirt and jeans or shorts. The t-shirts always sported faded logos of rock bands whose names he didn't recognize. Ben remained awkward and socially inept, seeming to prefer the life he'd stumbled into.

But he knew better than anyone that Ben was no loser. His high school records had shown a kid with genius-level intelligence who could have had a free ride to any university he wanted. Instead, Ben had chosen to take care of his mother in the best way he knew how. He couldn't help but admire that, especially after the steps he'd taken to help his father.

Because of his genuine affection for the young man, he'd nurtured his talent and provided opportunities Ben couldn't access on his own. Consequently, the kid could hack into virtually anything. And he'd made sure the compensation more than matched the risk in every job. He'd also decided, practically from the outset, that he'd protect Ben if one of those jobs ever went south.

He and his wife Vicki had decided against having children as their mutual careers took off and other things filled their lives. Even so, a certain emptiness plagued him. There were no school functions to attend, and the big house often seemed too quiet. Doing things for Ben and interacting with him dispelled some of the emptiness. Oftentimes, he wished he could share his thoughts with Vicki, or let her meet Ben, but she knew nothing of his secret doings. He wouldn't have invited Ben to the house if she hadn't been on a business trip for the marketing firm she owned.

Occasionally, it occurred to him that he'd left himself vulnerable in a huge way if Ben ever chose to betray him. But he'd taken steps to minimize his risk and besides, he took extraordinary care to ensure nothing went wrong with the double-dealings he devised and oversaw.

Satisfied for the moment that he'd put the correct elements into motion, he stashed the phone in the drawer and chose another. Now he'd use his connections to find out who the DA intended to assign to what had quickly become a high-profile case. After that, he'd refresh his memory on the man for whom the entire apparatus of deceit had been put in motion.

ADX Florence, CO

Foster strode down the hallway toward the interrogation room, mulling over the calls he'd just taken, first from Director Berenger and then David Harandi. For all practical purposes, he had no reason to pursue further interrogation of Milani, but his boss wanted him to continue. The entire situation felt distasteful to him, on more than one level. He reached the interrogation room and nodded at the guard. Entering the room, he thought his detainee looked more alert than at their earlier meeting. "Hello, Rowan."

Foster removed the cuffs. Rowan gazed at him with a neutral expression and rubbed his wrists. A thin line of sweat made its way down the side of his face. "Why are we still doing this?"

"I'm interested in hearing what you've got to say, and so is my boss. Would you like some coffee?"

"No. What I say doesn't make any difference. We both know that."

"Our investigation is ongoing. You sure you don't want some coffee?"

Rowan appeared to be in pain. "I don't want any goddamned coffee. And I don't want to answer any more questions."

"You led me to understand that you wanted to cooperate. Why not take the opportunity to tell your side of things? You have nothing to lose, as you've pointed out."

Rowan shifted his weight and winced. "It's not like I can get up and walk away, right? You win, Special Agent Foster. Ask your questions."

"Are the guards giving you pain meds on a regular basis? You seem to be uncomfortable."

Rowan glowered at him. "Just ask your questions."

"All right. Why don't you tell me why and how you got involved in Linden's pilot assassin program?"

"This seems so useless, but OK. About a year after 9/11, President Linden let it be known in certain circles that he was looking for someone interested in a unique approach to fighting the jihadists. Someone with firearms and knife skills; someone who could blend in. It was personal for me. I wanted to kill every one of those bastards, so I responded. That's how it started."

He jotted a few notes. "How did the President contact you? You obviously didn't work alone. Did you pick your own team? How did it work?"

"I chose my own team. I wasn't the only one who responded to the President, and a few of the others clicked with me. But when it got going, I was the only one he contacted. I'm sure the White House logs won't show I was ever there, but I met with Linden and Whitman regularly. I got paid in two offshore accounts. Both my team and I got reimbursed through those two accounts."

"Did the President give you assignments? Were you out of the country frequently?"

"Linden had his daily intelligence reports and sometimes we responded to those. I developed contacts in mosques and other places around the country, posing as a disenfranchised Iranian-American, wanting to join the jihad. That became an effective cover in and out of the country."

"Interesting. How did you balance black ops with your career at the Bureau?"

Rowan shrugged. "I made it work."

"That's an understatement if I've ever heard one. You were quite an asset to the Bureau. Everyone knows about the accomplishments of Ralph Johnston's Anti-Terrorism Task Force."

"We all did our jobs."

"Ralph must have covered for you at times."

Rowan wiped at the sweat making its way into the stubble on his jaws and stared at his hands. When he looked up, Foster saw only sadness in the dark eyes. "I told Ralph he could put up with me being gone, or I'd resign. He gave up everything for me. I hope he's all right."

Irresolute, he badly wanted to tell Milani that his former boss would be more than all right. Instead, he followed a hunch he'd gotten reading the transcript of Harandi's first attempt at interrogating Milani. "Did Ralph flee to Dubai from the compound on Kauai?"

"How would I know? When the Bureau hit Kauai, I was in Houston."

"We'll get back to that in a minute. Weren't you also in San Francisco?"

"Nope. I haven't been to my house in San Francisco in a couple years."

"According to a transcript I read, you told Harandi that Ralph was in Dubai. Were you lying then, or now?"

Milani's hands clenched into fists and he smirked. "You're the Bureau's hot-shot interrogator. You tell me."

"My gut tells me you told Harandi the truth and now you're screwing with me."

"Congratulations, Special Agent."

A detail from one of the myriad reports he'd read pricked his memory. "The San Francisco house was empty when our agents arrived, but I think you know as well as I do who was there."

Right in front of him, Milani shut down. "I'm done talking."

He must have struck a nerve. Curious, he decided to keep probing. "Danielle Stratton's fingerprints were found in the house, along with yours and others which were never identified."

"I'd like to go back to my cell now."

"I know Ms. Stratton was important to you. The last record the Bureau has is from a debriefing she gave two agents in Seattle when she relocated there from an unknown location. We also have proof, from your phone, of a call made to her, moments before you were apprehended."

Rowan slumped in the chair. "I said, *I'm done talking.*"

Somehow, he'd lost the connection. Whatever had happened with Danielle Stratton had affected Milani, deeply and adversely. "I'll get the guards." He shoved back the chair and left his detainee sitting hunched over at the table.

Rowan waited while the guards removed the restraints and left the cell. He sat on the edge of the concrete bed, hating the stark white walls, the closed-in space, and the steel bars. The lock clunked into place, and he shivered while images, sensations, and the memories he desperately needed to forget flooded his mind. Foster's mention of Danielle had sliced into his heart with all the viciousness of Shemal's dagger.

He stared unseeing at the blank wall and gave up. She invaded his mind with the sound of her voice, the strawberry scent of her hair, and its luxurious feel between his fingers. Reliving how her body responded to his left him groaning. She'd loved him passionately and he'd never appreciated her, until much too late.

He stretched out on the thin mattress and closed his eyes. He'd give anything for a bottle of single barrel Jack and his .45 Glock. The whiskey numbed the agony inside his mind and heart like nothing else ever had. He'd drink until he couldn't feel anything and then, by God, he'd end his wasted life.

Mid-Afternoon, Orcas Island, WA

Danielle gazed at the waves rolling and sparkling in the afternoon sun. Tom's idea to spend the day on Orcas Island was a godsend. She hadn't been to any of the San Juan Islands since she'd taken on management duties with Legacy Airlines, years earlier. Coming back felt good, almost like a homecoming. The events of the past two weeks had enhanced her sense of being at home, of being where she belonged.

Knowing Rowan was alive, yet forever out of reach, had touched her in a place beyond her grief. A place of finality. She knew he'd tell her, if he could, to *move on.* She'd repeated the mantra to herself for months and now, she was ready to not only listen, but act. More than anything, she wanted to feel settled. Her new career satisfied her. She loved the Pacific Northwest and Seattle, her true hometown, in particular.

She tipped her head back, enjoying the warmth of the afternoon sun. They'd decided on lunch and wine at the West Sound Café. Their square table on the wood-railed deck offered a perfect view of the harbor. She took a sip of wine and caught Tom watching her. He'd become a good friend and sometimes she wondered why he stuck around. Because although she needed to move on with her life, the thought of loving anyone besides Rowan felt foreign, utterly disloyal, and *wrong.* Her heart would never want anyone else, and she had accepted that.

Tom poured more wine into her glass. "My parents have a place here, on Orcas."

"Does your family spend a lot of time there?"

"My sisters and Mom and I spent summers there while we were growing up. My dad is a real estate investor, has been for his entire forty-year career. You'd love it, Dani." He gestured with one hand. "It's above West Sound, right on the water, with a couple acres. Sometime we'll bring the scooter over and check it out."

She sipped her wine. "I'd like that."

"You seem sad today. I was hoping this would be a fun diversion."

"And you were right. I love it here. It's been way too long. I'm just, you know, trying to process a few things."

"You want to talk about him some more?"

She twisted the stem of the wine glass. "I don't want to bore you with my issues."

Tom emptied the bottle into his glass and flagged the waiter. "Another bottle, please." He stretched long legs and replied. "We've got all afternoon, the evening, you name it. Nowhere to go, just chillin'."

She took a fortifying swallow of pinot noir. "Well, here goes then. I find myself thinking about how, on some dark level, Rowan must have known how things were going to turn out."

"Seriously? As in, his eventual capture?"

She nodded. "He found a reason to push me away. It's taken me a long time to figure that out, but I get it now."

"What do you mean?"

She stared at a couple seagulls, floating in lazy circles over the water. How long would regret weight her heart? "We had a fight. I said some things. We both did."

Tom gave her a lopsided smile. "Those things happen in any relationship."

"We couldn't seem to stop, and I called him a monster."

"Ouch. I bet he didn't take that too well."

"I could tell right away I'd hurt him. He walked away from the conversation and a couple days later he left. I never got to see him again."

"You're saying he used the fight as an opportunity to let you go, or push you away?"

She finished the wine and let him refill her glass. The slow numbing suited her mood. "Yep. But at the same time, he took care of me. I know he still loved me."

"What kind of man does that to the woman he truly loves?"

"The kind of man who knows that what he's doing isn't going to end well."

"Look, I believe you, and I know you love him, but you gotta admit, and this seems like a whopper of an understatement to me, most people would find his way of doing things unorthodox at least; more likely unacceptable. Can I ask you something?"

"Sure. Anything."

He gazed steadily at her. "Why do you think you were attracted to someone like him? He's obviously a dangerous man. He's killed probably dozens of terrorists and a few other people who maybe just got in his way."

His words took her back to the cold, snowy night at the airport in Sioux Falls and the first time she'd seen Rowan. Aching, heart-wrenching longing swept through her. "Um, I'm not sure I can explain. I saw him, and that was it. I knew, somehow, that he was special."

"Are you up for one more question?"

She took another swallow of wine, surprised to see she'd emptied the glass and nodded her assent when Tom held up the bottle. "I think so. Why stop now?"

He chuckled. "With the questions or the wine?"

"Definitely don't stop with the wine. We'll see about the questions."

He poured more wine in both their glasses before he spoke. "How do you see yourself moving forward?"

"You know, I'm ready to belong somewhere. I love my bistro, and I enjoy managing the crazy bunch of kids who work for me. I want to take a deep breath and know I'm at home."

"Good for you. You know, I get that you love Rowan, but I have to tell you, I'm not a fan of his, and here's why. I can't see how a man could ever purposely hurt you. Or willingly walk away."

Painful tears sprang into her eyes. "You don't understand. He didn't want to walk away. He didn't ask for all the horrible things that happened to him. But he had to deal with them."

Tom leaned forward and replied, his voice gentle. "I'm sorry. The last thing I want to do is hurt you even more."

"I'll always love him," she whispered. Telling herself to buck up, she sniffed and sat up straight. "But like I said, I'm ready to be home, in Seattle."

Tom drank more wine and sat back. “I’m glad. And Dani, you can count on me, always. Don’t forget that.”

She thought he seemed happy. Content, even. “Thank you. I won’t forget.”

CHAPTER EIGHT

The Next Evening
Houston, TX
Roberto peeled six sweat-dampened twenties from the wad of cash in his pants pocket and paid the Yellow Cab taxi driver. He followed Gino across the cement parking lot, dodging weed-laden cracks, to the apartment building where Tony Giacopino waited. The Boss's son had rented a three-bedroom apartment in South Houston. He yawned and stared through gritty eyes at the building, a two-story brick structure painted in garish orange and yellow with bright blue trim. The place looked ready to audition as a whore house.

If they were lucky, the interior would be better than the exterior, or at least have functioning air conditioning. At just after 8 p.m., the expiring daylight glowed orange, gold, and pink between apartment buildings and trees across the street. Even at dusk in what he thought of as the concrete city, the heat had nowhere to go. The taxi driver told them the temp had hit ninety-eight degrees that afternoon, and the heat index had topped out at 114.

He trudged alongside Gino with his suitcase bumping along behind him on the sidewalk, around the corner to the backside of the building. They stopped at the blue door with a metal number eight attached at eye level, bleeding rust down the center of the door. He wiped at the sweat beading on his forehead while Gino knocked.

Tony opened the door and waved them inside. "Welcome to Texas, boys." They dragged their suitcases into dank coolness.

He stood in the middle of the dingy living room and propped his sunglasses on the crown of his head. The place smelled like a swamp, and the A/C sounded like a lawn mower. A cracked leather sofa in what used to be bright orange sagged in one corner, bracketed by two mismatched arm chairs. Heavy brown-and-orange drapes covered a picture window. The carpet felt spongy under his shoes, and he didn't think he'd want to walk barefoot across it.

While his eyes adjusted to the dim light, he frowned at Johnny's still-youthful-looking son. "How'd you find this dump?"

Tony shoved black hair off his forehead and answered with his typical boyish grin. "Dad said, *keep a low profile. No fancy digs. Get the damn job done right, pronto.* Nobody's gonna give a shit about us in this place, right?"

Roberto nodded. "I gotta say, you're right about that."

Tony gestured to the laptop on the rectangular dinner table in the kitchen/dining area. "I've got everything we need to get his latest project done exactly how he wants."

Gino chimed in. "Yeah, we were discussing this *project* of his on the flight. Which, by the way, took seventeen hours. What's your take on what the Boss sees in Rowan Milani? I thought the guy was kind of a prick when we met him in Chicago last winter."

Tony shrugged. "He's got something big in mind, but he hasn't let me in on it. I know once he springs Cantor, he wants him to teach me his stuff. As far as Milani is concerned, beats me. But hey, the guy's got an Italian side, ya know?"

Roberto said, "Milani's a good shit. Devious as hell, though."

Gino punched him on the shoulder. "You figured that out in Key West, huh?"

"Don't remind me. Tony, are we getting started first thing in the morning or what? Fill me in quick, cuz I'm jetlagged and ready to hit the sack."

Tony replied. "The Houston crew will contact us first thing in the morning. You two will meet with them somewhere else. They'll explain their setup."

So far, he wasn't crazy about what he was hearing. "What's up with meeting them ahead of time? I don't trust who I don't know, and I don't know these cops from Adam."

Tony said, "You two have to work out with them how it'll go down with the physical evidence. They know the layout of the evidence warehouse, which you need to study."

He countered. "We coulda studied the layout on our own. What about uniforms? The coppers got them too?"

Tony continued with his patient explanations. "Your Houston PD uniforms and IDs are stashed in my closet. The Boss arranged that with his friend. The hacker is coming over tonight. We'll work on penetrating the PD's server. Once we're in, I'll eliminate the digital footprint of the evidence. Destroying the actual paper trail and disposing of the physical evidence is up to you two and the cops."

Gino cracked thick knuckles. "No problem."

He glared at Gino, then turned to Tony. "You're bringing someone else who we don't know, *here,* to our secure location?"

Tony parked his lanky frame on the sofa. "The Boss cleared it with his friend. Evidently this hacker kid is solid."

Tony's glib assurances didn't set well. "I got no beef with you, but this whole fix could just as easy go south on us as not. We gotta be extra careful and make sure this job goes down the way it's supposed to. And be ready to clip those cops if need be."

Tony agreed. "That's what the Boss is counting on."

He gave Gino and Tony a once over. "We won't be disappointing him, that's for damn sure. How long you think it'll take to crack the server?"

Tony gave him thumbs up. "It's child's play. A couple hours, max. We get in, set everything up so we can take care of business when we're ready to move. After, we'll cover our tracks and get out."

He stifled another yawn and didn't comment on Tony's optimism. "Where are we bunking?"

Tony pointed. "I'm in the first room, on the right. Pick either of the other two."

"All right. I'll see you two in the morning." He left Gino and Tony sitting on the ancient furniture and ambled to the bedroom at the end of the hall. Undressed, except for his t-shirt and drawers, on his back in the lumpy bed, he stared at the ceiling. This was by far the most complex assignment he'd taken on for Johnny Giacopino. Too many things hung in the balance and had to go right the first time in order to see Milani walk out of the Harris County Jail a free man. And those things made him uneasy.

Taken together, they'd probably interfere with his sleep as much as the springs creaking and poking him through the old mattress. He trusted Gino and Tony with his life, but what about the Houston PD crew and the hacker? What kind of hold did the Boss's friend, whoever *he* was, have on them? It better be damn good, or the entire deal could blow sky high. His shoulder itched, then his calf. "Shit. Bed bugs," he muttered.

While he scratched first his shoulder and then his leg, he wondered, was Milani worth their two months' worth of screwing around? He'd never seen the Boss shell out this kind of capital before on behalf of one person. He hoped Milani had the good sense to appreciate it, because there'd be all kinds of hell to pay if he didn't.

The Next Day

Roberto pulled on his jeans, left his shirt untucked, and headed down the dim hallway. He'd slipped on his shoes, not willing to put his bare feet on the carpet. Stepping into the grimy shower had been enough. He'd slept better than he'd thought he would though, after forcing himself to quit thinking about bed bugs. He rounded the corner into the living area and caught the aroma of coffee. A man he'd never seen before stretched out on the sofa, wearing a t-shirt and shorts. He couldn't believe it, but the guy was barefoot. Shaggy blond hair covered his eyes, and reddish stubble surrounded his open mouth. The man snored gently with every breath.

Tony sat prone at the table, head in his arms. Gino turned, holding a cup of coffee, and whispered, "I wonder how far they got?"

"Let's find out." Not in the mood for dinking around, he gave Tony's shoulder a quick shake. "Wake up. It's morning. We got work to do."

Tony sat up and stared, bleary-eyed. "Huh? What time is it?"

"6:30 a.m., Central Time. When will the cops contact us?"

Tony rubbed his eyes and groaned. "Eight o'clock. We cracked the server at five-thirty. Oh man, I gotta get some sleep." The dark head drooped.

He gave Tony another shake. "Hey, don't you have to hurry up and finish?"

Tony's head jerked up. "Today, after I sleep for a few hours, we'll get back at it. This is going to take some time."

His uneasiness of the previous night returned. "I thought you said it was child's play. And what about the guy on the sofa? We need him anymore?"

Tony said, "Uh-huh, that's Ben. He's a genius, and he's going to be here for the duration. He'll remotely control the video surveillance at the forensic lab," he yawed, "ya know…at Methodist Hospital. I'll be taking care of everything to do with the Property Room, and the impound lot."

Gino replied, "You mean, when we're in there?"

Tony nodded. "Can we talk about this later? I can't stay awake."

Irritated, Roberto gripped Tony's shoulder and squeezed. "No. We'll talk about it now. Gino, get your cousin a cup of Joe, so he can pep up a little bit."

Tony slipped out of his grasp. "Ouch. Give me a break. Everything's under control. After you meet with the cops, I'll input your IDs into their system. You'll have access when you need to get in. They're bringing schematics of the warehouse to the meet, so you can study the layout. You'll know where everything is before you step foot inside."

Gino sat a steaming cup of coffee in front of Tony. "Here ya go."

Tony shoved back his chair. "I don't want any coffee. I need to get some sleep. Look, Bobbie, we're getting a good start on what the Boss wants, and we'll accomplish everything we need to, on the necessary timetable. You can trust me on that."

He met Tony's earnest, bloodshot eyes. "All right. Go get some sleep."

Tony said, "I'll be ready to hit it hard at noon. Ben, too. You don't gotta worry about him. Dad's friend handpicked him to help us."

He gazed at the hacker, who'd turned toward the back of the sofa, his face buried in a faded, grungy orange-and-green accent pillow. "I don't trust anybody I don't know."

Tony gave him a dismissive wave as he headed down the hall. "If Dad trusts his friend, and his friend trusts Ben, then so do I. See ya in a few hours."

"Hey, one more thing. Where's the keys for the Impala? And what's the name of the guy I'm meeting who's going to drive the semi across the border into Mexico?"

Tony muttered, "Silverware drawer. Miguel Sanchez." The bedroom door closed.

He turned to Gino. "The Boss wants me to take care of the semi and the driver. I'll work with you on the inside to begin with. Once we got our hands on the physical evidence, I'll make sure it gets loaded in the semi while you finish up with the coppers. Then we'll head south to Laredo and cross into Mexico. You OK with following me down there and helping finishing things up?"

Gino gulped coffee. "No problem."

"All right. Afterward, we need to check in with Tony, so we know the digital evidence is gone and that we aren't parading around on any cameras."

"No problem."

He picked up the cup of coffee Tony didn't want and blew on it before taking a cautious swallow. He peered at Gino over the edge of the cup. "There damn well better not be any problems."

An hour later, Roberto sat with Gino in the uncomfortable front seat of the Impala outside the apartment building. He figured it must already be at least 90 degrees in the sunny, concrete parking lot, but they couldn't talk privately inside the apartment. The hacker woke up and annoyed him by sitting hunched over his laptop at the table, munching and slurping through endless bowls of Captain Crunch.

He'd kept his mouth shut because Tony said the kid knew his way around the cyber stuff they needed to accomplish in order to spring Milani. Maybe his sense that something wasn't quite right, that he was missing a crucial element somewhere just beyond his reach, was due to his preference for simpler jobs with fewer moving parts.

His phone rang, jangling his stretched taut nerves. "Hello. Who's this?"

"We're ready to meet with the information you need. Do you have the address?"

"I got the address. We're on our way." He hit END and nodded at Gino. "We're good to go. Let's get this over with."

He marveled at Gino as they cruised through a decaying and mostly abandoned industrial area in South Houston. His partner possessed excellent instincts when it came to less-than-clear directions. No wonder the Boss depended on Gino's driving in Chicago. Scouting the street signs, thinking faster than he'd thought the younger man capable of, Gino had driven through Houston's traffic and the insanity of its street layout with one hand on the wheel, laid back and relaxed like they were heading out on a picnic.

Scanning the block as the car rolled along, he caught a glimpse of what he hoped was their destination. A sagging chain link fence, half-obscured by tall grass, weeds, and scrub trees surrounded a dilapidated group of sheds and a warehouse. Two men waited at an open metal gate. He pointed. "I think that's it."

Gino grunted and swung the car around the corner, through the gate and to an abrupt halt. "Those must be the dirty cops."

"I'm guessing you're right. Keep your eyes open."

"No problem."

If he heard *no problem* one more time, he'd have to stop himself from backhanding his partner. *Problem* was the number one word for this job, any way he looked at it and he'd voice his concerns to the Boss later, in a private phone call. "Don't take your sunglasses or cap off unless absolutely necessary."

"No problem."

He gritted his teeth and waited while Gino exited the car, then followed. The two men approached the car, feet crunching on the graveled lot. He felt exposed, naked. The cap and sunglasses did nothing for his sense of security. Out in the open, they were vulnerable to any kind of ambush the crooked cops might have hatched. *If* these were the cops sent by the Boss's friend and not some government goons who'd set them up for screwing around with the Milani deal.

The two men faced them. Both wore nondescript shirts and jeans. One was a Hispanic guy with a buzz cut and a gut that hung over his belt. The other, a pasty white guy, had a balding head and blue eyes that darted back and forth. He couldn't believe they hadn't bothered to disguise themselves, and the fact added to his expanding list of things that didn't seem right.

The white guy carried a couple of rolled-up papers tied with string which he assumed were the prints of the layout of the PD's Property Room. Whichever cop he'd talked to the day before had complained about needing the actual printed paper and wanted an email address so he could send digital copies. How stupid did the guy think they were? He gestured at the papers. "Is this what we need?"

The Hispanic cop spoke up. "Yes. We'll take a look inside. We've got an office over here."

The two cops trudged across the lot. He trailed along behind Gino, on edge, sweating and miserable. He had heat rash where no man should ever have any kind of rash. Who knew if he'd even be able to extricate his 1911 from its holster if he needed to? Sweat saturated the holster and his entire body. His paranoia increased when he stepped into the oven-like stillness of the warehouse. He took off his sunglasses, only because otherwise he'd be blind as a bat, and tried not to sneeze in the overpowering odor of diesel fuel and dirt. Cracks in the walls and a few holes in the ceiling sent shafts of sunlight into the gloom, but the light didn't reach the corners.

Inside the poorest excuse for an office he'd ever seen, the four of them huddled on rickety chairs around a card table. Over the course of a couple hours in the hot, still room, while he and Gino sweated, the cops took turns making dotted lines and circles on the drawings with a red marker, showing them where each necessary piece of evidence resided in the monstrous building. They used a blue marker to denote surveillance camera locations. He guessed they didn't know about the hacker who'd be controlling the cameras and deleting footage of them after the fact.

By the time they finished, all he could think about was talcum powder, a shower, and getting back to a northern climate. He jerked his chair away from the table, scraping marks on the filthy concrete. "Are the two of you authorized to enter the Property Room on any given day? In other words, if I call you in three days and say we're ready, will you be available?"

The white cop with the non-stop eyes focused momentarily on his Hispanic counterpart, then briefly on him. "We'll make sure we're both available when you need us. We'll generate the paperwork you need beforehand and date it accordingly."

Gino leaned back and mopped sweat off his face with a white handkerchief. "We need a police van to haul everything. That gonna be a problem?"

He sighed and did a poor-ass job of suppressing a snort, when the Hispanic cop said, "No problem."

Gino frowned at him. "You got anything else you wanna cover here?"

He stood up. "No. I think we're good." He gestured at the two cops. "We'll be in touch using the same phone number unless either of you says different right now." The Boss had said not to worry about burner phones for the cops. Supposedly, the friend took care of those details. Knowing that didn't comfort him in the least.

Both men shook their heads, and the Hispanic answered again. "The phone number you have is valid. We'll be ready when you call."

They left the two men staring after them as they drove away. He spoke over the A/C running full blast. "What's your take on those two?"

Gino kept his eyes on the road while he talked. "They seem timid to me. Kinda like they know they gotta do what they're told. Maybe scared is more like it. Why, what do you think?"

"I think you're right. They're scared shitless to make a mistake. I don't think they'll give us any trouble during the job. It's afterwards I'm concerned about."

Gino glanced at him, then bore down on the accelerator as they entered a busy eight-lane. "You think they'll rat on us?"

"I think it's fifty/fifty they do something stupid. My gut says something isn't quite right, and I'm calling the Boss."

The Next Day
DC County Jail

Agent O'Brien entered the interrogation room. Chad Cantor waited, hunched over the table. His height must make sitting secured to the table and floor uncomfortable, and she wished she dared remove the restraints. But she wouldn't. His obvious emotional distress raised red flags. She noted the dark circles beneath his eyes and the hopelessness in his downturned mouth as she slid into the chair across from him. "Good morning, Mr. Cantor."

He raised his head and gave her an empty-eyed stare. "Morning."

Persisting in extracting Intel when she'd prefer to inform him of his imminent release taxed her abilities as an interrogator more than she'd ever admit. "Would you like a cup of coffee to get the juices flowing?"

He responded in a flat, dispassionate voice. "No thank you."

The old adage about *still waters* told her to remain cautious. "Well then, let's get started. I've got questions about emails between Muusa Shemal and the two CIA agents who apprehended Rowan Milani the first time, in South Dakota."

"What do you want to know?"

"I'm curious, because this communication came in mid-January, requesting delivery of a certain *package.* A week later, both agents received another email, informing them that $10,000 apiece payment would be forthcoming for receipt of said package."

He frowned. "You don't know about that?"

"No. Help me out, would you? $10,000 was deposited in each of their accounts, but Milani wasn't apprehended until the first week in March."

"Sa-id Harandi was one of Rowan's informants. He worked at CAIR's DC headquarters. Somehow Shemal or one of his buddies at CAIR intercepted info Sa-id was sending to Rowan. Shemal had those two jerks pick him up. Shemal tortured him until Sa-id gave him Rowan's name. That's what started this whole mess. Jesus, how could you *not know that?"*

She replied. "David Harandi shared the Intel from one of Milani's as-yet-unidentified colleagues, which provided proof that Shemal murdered Sa-id. We did not, however, know he'd used the services of Talbot and Hancock in that effort."

Anger glowed in Cantor's eyes, and he straightened up in the chair. "Has Shemal been arrested and charged? Is he in a cell down the hall or maybe next door?"

"We're working to reopen the murder case with DCPD, but no physical evidence exists. We can't arrest and charge someone based on a screenshot from a questionable source, no matter how damning."

"I don't see why not. Rowan and Ralph and I were charged on the word of Shemal. No one ever asked for his evidence."

"I can't go back in time and correct the unfortunate errors committed by our intelligence community. I'm working hard to get as much information as possible so we can mitigate the effect of those errors and correct the situation on your behalf. I hope you'll continue cooperating with me."

Cantor stared at her. *"Unfortunate errors? Mitigate their effect?* I've done everything in my power to cooperate, and I haven't seen any *mitigation.* For all I know, I'll spend the rest of my life in this shithole."

"The information you've given me this morning helps us bring those agents one step closer to accountability. Your input won't go unnoticed."

He sneered. "They should have been made accountable for damn near beating Rowan to death a year and a half ago."

She replied. "I understand your frustration. But we need your help. Now that Milani is in US custody, we'd like to learn how a few things were accomplished, as well as bring closure to some remaining mysteries. Your answers may bring about the mitigation I'd like you to benefit from."

"Agent O'Brien, you don't know squat about my frustration. And I don't have much hope for any kind of break. But let's get it over with. What kind of questions do you have?"

"Thank you. First of all, we've learned that the CIA's missing Gulfstream G650 is possibly in operation with a fraudulent tail number assigned to ownership by a bogus corporation. What can you tell me about that?"

Cantor stared past her for a moment and then gave her a puzzled frown. "I'm afraid I can't help you. I don't know anything about tail numbers on jets, or even how to go about creating one. Don't tail numbers have some sort of significance?"

"The tail number functions like a license plate and registration number. And according to our information, you created a new tail number for that aircraft."

Cantor shook his head. "Your information is wrong. What else is the Bureau trying to figure out?"

She persisted, even though she knew he was lying. "Milani assembled a team to assist him in conducting black ops on behalf of the US. We're looking for names."

He shook his head again. "Rowan kept all that stuff to himself. We were pretty pissed off about it, too. Ralph and I couldn't help him like we wanted to in Sioux Falls because he wouldn't tell us anything. Next thing we knew, he was gone."

"Mr. Cantor, please. I'm going to share something with you, which I usually wouldn't consider. But I want to see you get the best deal possible."

He slumped in the chair. "You and I both know the Bureau has no intention of giving me anything unless I betray Rowan. Foster tried that, didn't you know?"

"I understand your loyalty to your friend. But you need to know this. You won't hurt Milani by helping us, because he's not going anywhere. He's killed too many people. You, on the other hand, have an opportunity to rejoin your fiancée if you cooperate."

Cantor gave her a look of utter despair. "I told Foster and now I'll tell you. If I never see Bettina again, or never see our baby, I still cannot tell you what I know is not the truth. Rowan Milani is innocent. Ralph Johnston is innocent, and I am innocent. From here on out you can take your cooperation and stick it up your ass."

"I'm not going to quit on you, or the mess you're embroiled in. The Bureau won't either. Don't quit on yourself." She paused, hoping he'd relent, but he stared at his hands and didn't say anything. "I'll get the guards."

Houston, TX

Roberto left the 610 Loop at Exit 24A and pointed the Impala toward Love's Travel Stop. He'd been instructed, in broken English, to meet his contact there. The man who'd drive the semi with the limo and all the evidence stashed inside said he'd be in a blue Dodge Dakota pick-up. He pulled into the truck stop and surveyed the activity. Vehicles maneuvered to and from the gas pumps. Semis and motorhomes jockeyed for position, and men, women, and kids milled around everywhere.

He'd already decided he'd take Chicago at its worst over Houston and the surrounding metro area on its best day. So far, he'd counted three blue pick-ups, but they weren't Dakotas. He drove through the parking lot, dodging vehicles and people. He adjusted the ball cap he wasn't used to wearing and peered over his sunglasses as he cruised around the back side. A rusted, blue Dakota sat practically obscured between a straight truck and an RV. "It figures," he muttered.

A Hispanic man in a sleeveless denim work shirt and dirty jeans climbed out of the driver's side door as he pulled up. He rolled down his window and spoke into the wall of heat. "Miguel Sanchez?"

The man smiled. "Si."

He jerked his thumb toward the passenger side of the Impala. "Get in."

Sanchez darted around the car and climbed in. "Good morning Señor. We will see the semi now? It's close, on Banner Drive."

He put the car in park and left it running. The A/C barely kept up to his standards, and he didn't want to give the heat any advantage. He unbuckled his seat belt and silently cursed the corduroy-like cloth beneath him that made it nearly impossible to turn and face his passenger. "No, we will not see the semi now. I need to know where to meet you when we're ready to use the semi. Also, I need to give you a phone. We'll use it from now on. I'll call you. Comprende?"

Sanchez' head bobbed up and down, reminding him of the bobble head dog in the back window of his mother's old Buick. "Si, si, you meet me here. You call and I be here, now." The wiry man snapped his fingers and grinned, his face creasing into myriad wrinkles.

He reached in the back seat for the burner phone and held it out. "Good. Take this and don't lose it. I'll be calling sometime in the next few days or maybe a week."

The bobble head began again. "Si, I wait. You call. We go."

"You got it. Now you go."

Sanchez opened the door. "So long, Señor. See you soon."

"Right." He watched the man clamber into the pick-up, crank it up, and drive off. Where did Johnny find these people? Was a cartel involved? His job included getting rid of both the semi and its expendable driver, and he had definite instructions on where and how. But he couldn't shake the uneasiness niggling in the back of his mind.

One misstep or a less-than-loyal tattletale, and Milani's story would end in Texas. It bothered him to think he could be a part of something like that. Every job he'd done for the Boss had been clean and quick. Except for the last one, in Key West. He'd felt a certain kinship with Milani and made the mistake of trusting him. No one had ever fooled him like that before. He put the car in gear and navigated his way out of the busy truck stop and back to the 610. It would never happen again. Especially not this time.

The Next Day

Judge Caito dozed by the pool in his lounge chair. The striped umbrella protecting him from the sun hung limp in the oppressive heat of mid-afternoon. He should go inside, but he liked to sit and sweat after swimming. It helped him sort through things and clarified his thoughts. The ringtone reserved for the one man whose call he never ignored startled him. He raised his sunglasses to his forehead and plucked the phone from the table. "Hello, Boss. To what do I owe the pleasure?"

The booming, energetic voice always made him smile. "Good afternoon Judge. I spoke last evening with my crew in your fine city. My main guy expressed some concern with your people."

"I see. What kind of concern?"

"Seems like your boys are extra jumpy. My guy thinks they can't be trusted to keep things to themselves once the job is done. I trust my guy. His gut is reliable."

"Interesting. I'll take care of it."

Johnny's voice turned businesslike. "Permanently?"

"Yes. You need confirmation?"

"I'd call it a favor."

"I'll let you know."

"Thank you, Judge. Enjoy the rest of your day."

"You do the same." He squinted at the sun-sparkled water, inhaled humid, chlorine-scented air, and tapped the contact he wanted on his phone.

His friend answered right away. "Hola. Why aren't you taking a siesta, my friend?"

"Good afternoon, Luis. For some of us, the work never ceases."

"You need to move to Mexico. What can I do for you today?"

"I've got a paying job if you're interested. I need help with cleanup."

"Of course. How many and when?"

"Two. I'll let you know when and where. How much?"

"Fill me in on the details."

He slid his sunglasses back down. "I'll send what you need to the secure email address. It has to look like some kind of robbery, or a drug deal gone bad. You choose after you get the details."

Luis chuckled. "Too easy, my friend. Don't worry about it. I'll bill you."

"Thank you. I'll be in touch."

"Don't let those gringos work you too hard."

"I won't, Luis." He ended the call and headed for the diving board at the deep end of the pool. One more quick dip, and he'd be ready to take Vicki out for dinner. Then he'd have to begin the process of recruiting new police officers.

Three Days Later

Tony sat hunched over his laptop at the dinner table, tapped into the server controlling the system of cameras at the Houston PD Property Room. Once his crew finished there, he'd switch to the PD's impound lot. Ben sprawled on the sofa with his bare feet on the coffee table, laptop appropriately on his lap. His fellow hacker would manipulate the erasure of every digital footprint of the stored evidence at the Property Room, the impound lot, and the forensic lab. He'd also make sure no video surveillance existed at Methodist Hospital for a full twenty-four hours. The two of them had discussed a few different scenarios and decided it only made sense to disable the entire hospital. That way a suspicious investigator couldn't confirm the forensic lab had been targeted.

He rubbed his burning eyes and yawned. Bright fissures of sunlight leaked into the living room around the edges of the drapes covering the picture window. Discarded burger wrappers, tiny white Chinese food containers, and pizza boxes littered every open table and counter space. Cleaning up after themselves comprised the least of their worries. Keeping their tracks covered, disabling the PD's cyber-security, and monitoring any probes into their work had kept him and Ben awake, damn near 24/7 for the past three days.

They'd traded off, taking turns napping, but he drank so much coffee during the day and Coke at night that he'd get to twitching and couldn't sleep anyway. Ben didn't have his problem. The kid drank a couple Red Bulls every morning and continued with a Mega Monster or some such crap in the afternoon, and still nodded off with no problem. He swore there must be something wrong with a guy like that. But it was none of his business as long as Ben did his job and so far, he'd been great to work with.

Preparations on their end were complete. Once he got the text from Gino, their part of the actual job would commence. He hiked his shoulders up and twisted around, but the tension didn't quit. His father erected tough standards, and he'd always met them. He wasn't about to fail this time. He excelled at his chosen profession, but he couldn't escape the far-reaching ramifications of this job.

He'd thought about it from every angle, and he couldn't figure out what exactly had inspired his old man to take on two Presidents and the entire Texas legal system. What made Rowan Milani so damn special? If he was being totally honest, the all-out push for the guy made him kind of jealous. His phone dinged, and he grabbed it. Gino's text read: *We're there.*

He cracked his knuckles and stretched. "Hey Ben, it's on. You good?"

Ben raised his head. Reddish stubble covered his cheeks, matching the guy's bloodshot blue eyes. "Yeah man, I'm ready for this shit to get real."

"Good, because as of now, the shit is as real as it's gonna get."

CHAPTER NINE

Roberto resisted the urge to squirm in the uncomfortable police uniform. Sweating, itching, cursing under his breath at the abominable rash he couldn't get rid of, he walked from the police van toward the entrance of the 59,000-square-foot building looming at least two stories tall in front of him. Bold black lettering graced the side of the behemoth and identified it as the *Houston Police Department Property Room*. The descriptor gave a whole new meaning to the word *room*. He thought it looked like a giant, grayish cement block.

Gino grunted alongside him, looking as ridiculous as he felt in a tan shirt and dark blue uniform pants, with a black leather belt cutting into his stocky frame. His usually upbeat companion had complained bitterly about the polished black shoes pinching his feet. For his part, he'd insisted on authentic HPD ball caps, and they'd spent an hour the night before battering the caps into shape. They needed to look as natural as a Chicago crew could, impersonating Houston cops. He eyed the two dirty cops trudging along in front of them. "Look sharp."

Gino nodded. "No problem."

He heaved a sigh while one of the cops keyed the entrance code and gestured them through the heavy metal door. They cleared the first hurdle, presenting their IDs to the officer on duty. The two cops had chattered like a couple of nervous monkeys on the way over, telling them how they didn't need to worry about anyone hassling them. Duty assignment in the Property Room meant a cop was unfit for field duty or had fucked up somehow. A bunch of disgruntled cops wouldn't give a shit about them carting off evidence for another trial. Besides, they were understaffed and overworked, checking in thousands of pieces of evidence every month.

Once they passed the check-in area, he stopped and tried to square the layout of the mega-room with the schematics they'd studied. He'd spent a fair amount of time online looking at images of the building's interior. The images he'd seen didn't do justice to the sheer vastness. Sections branched off down hallways too long for him to see the opposite end.

He gazed upward at one of the sections, at cardboard boxes marked with bright orange tags, stacked five levels high. Another hallway held what looked like two-by-two-foot blue tubs stacked in levels just like the boxes, damn near reaching the ceiling. Everything sat on a specialized mobile shelving system that moved on rails. He'd never seen anything like it.

Movement down one of the hallways caught his attention. A police officer walked along, dragging a set of mobile stair steps. After consulting a paper, the officer climbed the staircase. While he observed the police officer retrieving a box of evidence, he ran through the mental list he'd memorized. Somewhere down one of the endless corridors Milani's pistols and knife waited.

The Boss had been emphatic about him keeping track of those weapons. He poked thick fingers inside his shirt collar and tugged. No way would he disappoint the Boss. Tense muscles in his neck and shoulders, combined with the tight ball cap, gave him a headache he didn't need either. Time to get the show on the road and get the hell out of the nest of cops.

The Hispanic cop angled his head toward Gino. "You come with me."

It figured he'd be stuck with the pasty Anglo and his psychotic eyes. He tapped the side of his head. "Gino, you got your list up there?"

Gino winked. "No problem. I'm good to go."

He gritted his teeth and didn't answer. The kid needed to learn some new words. And after this job, he needed a vacation that didn't include Gino.

The Anglo cop spoke, his voice low. "We'll meet back here when we're finished. Juan, text me with your progress. Shouldn't take longer than a few hours unless we run into a snafu."

He glared at the cop. "There ain't gonna be no *snafu.* We're gonna get what we came for and mosey on out of here. Period."

The guy ducked his head and stammered. "Uh right, sure, I know. I'm just sayin,' see, because we got a rep here of things getting misplaced or just flat disappearing."

Juan spoke up. "Shut up, Ed. Let's go and get what we came for, like he said."

"All right, all right," Ed mumbled and shuffled off.

He followed, reluctant to split up with Gino and wishing like hell he could calm his nerves. Fluorescent lighting kept the entire place brighter than he liked. Tony and the hacker better be doing their jobs because he didn't need to appear in some video surveillance recording lit up like a damn Christmas tree.

Three-and-a-half painstaking hours later, he slumped in the front passenger seat of the van and pulled off the ball cap. His bald head had leaked enough sweat to soak the inner band clear through to the brim. The evidence they'd collected, ranging from Milani's bloody clothing, the clothes from each of the suckers the guy had offed on his rampage, a pile of shoes, a shitload of 9mm shell casings, two Glock pistols and a badass Karambit, lay securely packed in the rear of the van.

Locating the evidence in the gigantic warehouse had proven tedious, but none of it had gone missing. Checking it out and hauling it to the van kept him on edge and sweating, apparently for nothing more than his own paranoia, because none of the other cops in the building seemed interested or concerned. They'd given cursory, bored glances to the release forms provided by the two dirty cops and waved them on.

While the nervous Anglo cop drove, he turned to the back seat and addressed Gino. "You ready for part two?" He waited for the predictable words.

Gino cracked thick knuckles and surprised him. "We go to the forensic lab affiliated with Methodist Hospital. We check out the rest of the stash of evidence. DNA and whatnot."

"You got it. Ed and me will pick up the semi and head for the impound lot for the limo. You two," he gestured at Gino and Juan, "meet us back at the warehouse. We'll get there as quick as we can."

Gino gave him an off-hand salute. "Righto."

Maybe the kid had read his mind. "Stay in touch."

Gino gave him thumbs up. "No problem."

He swung his muscular bulk around to face the front and didn't answer. The Anglo cop hunched over the steering wheel with a white-knuckle death grip. The guy's constant, frazzled state wore on his own nerves. Did he know something they didn't? Were they walking into some kind of trap?

He couldn't shake the heebie-jeebies about the whole job. The Boss had some balls, pulling off what amounted to a major heist, from the cops no less, and right beneath their noses. That reminded him of one last thing he didn't trust the dirty cops to do. "You remember about getting rid of the paper trail, right?"

Ed gave him a sideways glance. "Uh huh. We'll take care of it."

The answer didn't exactly fill him with confidence. "And when will you do that?"

The cop turned his way again. "Right away, soon as we're done loading up. We'll take care of everything in the Property Room and the impound lot. And uh, at the lab. Right away."

He eyed the pasty cop one more time, cranked up the A/C, and then focused his grim stare on the crazy ass traffic in front of them. "You better be damn sure of that." He hunkered down in the seat. They'd be walking a nerve-wracking tight rope until he and Gino finished the job. He wished the Boss would have let him take care of cleanup because he didn't trust the two cops. His gut told him that given half a chance, the cops would screw them over, either out of stupidity or sheer, cowardly malice.

Somewhere South and West of Nuevo Laredo, Mexico
Roberto grimaced as the semi bounced along through a string of potholes. Miguel ground the gears, cussed in Spanish, and wiped sweat from his brow with a gloved hand. The stale air in the dusty cab stank like tamales. Miguel had brought dinner along in a plastic sack and offered to share, which he'd declined. They'd stopped for a few precious minutes at a truck stop in Laredo before crossing the border, and he'd grabbed a couple burgers and two large coffees. He yawned and started on the second container of the bitter, oily coffee.

This had to be the longest day in the history of jobs he'd undertaken. They'd started at 6 a.m. and after thirteen-and-a-half hours, they still weren't finished. Miguel met him and Ed at the truck stop, and they'd retrieved the semi. He'd waited for something to go wrong at the Houston PD impound lot, but again, Ed had the necessary paperwork, and the cops on duty there had the same attitude as those at the Property Room. And although Milani had shot the hell out of the interior with his 9mm, the Caddy was still drivable. Ed ran it up the ramp and into the trailer.

Gino and Juan recovered everything from the Methodist Hospital forensic lab without a hitch and met them at the warehouse. They'd parked the semi inside and transferred every single piece of evidence into the trailer, along with ten five-gallon cans of gasoline. Miguel had tarps and tie-downs ready to cover everything and insisted there'd be *no hay problema* at the border crossing in Laredo.

The wiry Mexican hadn't lied. They'd cruised out of Houston on I-10 and connected onto I-35 South, getting off once on a county road to swap Texas plates for Mexican plates. At the checkpoint, the guards conversed in English and Spanish with Miguel, who'd remained at ease, which made sense if he was used to working both sides of the border. Once in Nuevo Laredo on the Mexican side, they got on Highway 1 and headed south and west.

Thirty-some miles into the countryside they turned east onto a secondary road that he guessed could only be classified that way in Mexico. The truck lurched and he spilled coffee on his pants. "Son of a bitch. Are we getting close to the drop-off point?" According to the Boss's instructions, Miguel knew exactly where to go. The only thing the Mexican didn't know was that he wouldn't be leaving.

"Si, we are almost there. Only a few more miles."

"It's about time." In the side mirror, he saw the bouncing headlights of the Impala glimmering through the billowing dust thrown up by the semi. The day had started out sunny and stayed that way. At dusk, the temperature hung in there at ninety degrees. His phone told him the temp in Laredo had topped off at a hundred-and-two degrees while they were passing through. Once they'd finished the damnable job, he'd never step foot in Texas again.

Miguel spoke up. "This is our turn off. Two more miles, Señor."

"Good." He gulped more of the awful coffee. His wits needed sharpening before putting the final touches on the destruction of the evidence implicating Milani. The truck careened around the corner, and he hung onto the seat. They headed down a steep hill on a dirt trail. Miguel downshifted, damn near sending him through the windshield. The truck shook while the gears roared and the engine revved. He hoped they'd make it to the bottom without losing control.

The day held enough light for him to tell they were driving into a ravine. Dark hills rose on either side. Whoever helped plan this part of the job had known exactly what kind of location they needed for the gigantic bonfire it'd take to eliminate everything in the trailer. A series of ruts caught the front tires in deep grooves, and he bounced off the seat. The foam coffee container flew out of his hand, the plastic lid popped off, and coffee splattered across the dash. Miguel gave him a quick glance. "Sorry, Señor."

"Just keep this rig on the road." He gritted his teeth and hung on as they continued to bounce and shake their way further into the ravine. In the wobbling illumination from the headlights he saw the poor excuse for a road level out and end. Miguel brought the truck to a grinding halt, the air brakes' explosive hiss punctuating the end of their journey.

He sat in the stillness, trying to regain his bearings. The quiet diesel rumble continued, and he looked at Miguel. "Shut this piece of shit down. We need to finish up and head back."

"Si, si. What you say, Señor." The motor shuddered to silence.

"Let's go. We're out of daylight down here." He waited until Miguel opened the driver's side door and climbed out, then opened the passenger door. He saw Gino. "Park the Impala with the lights shining on the ass end of the trailer so we can see what we're doing."

For once, Gino didn't talk, just spun on his heel and headed for the car. Miguel had a flashlight and had already cranked open the rear doors. The interior lighting sucked, but he could see enough to find the gas cans they'd hidden behind the false front of the trailer compartment, along with Milani's weapons and their pistols. By some stroke of luck or a miracle, nothing had come loose or spilled out during the wild ride down the ravine.

Thirty minutes later, he stood at the rear of the trailer and mopped even more sweat from his head. They'd stashed Milani's weapons in a cleverly hidden metal box in the trunk of the

Impala. He and Miguel had emptied all ten gas cans and the entire trailer compartment reeked of fuel. The fumes alone had his lungs burning. He'd sat nine of the cans on the ground and left one at the front of the trailer on purpose.

He jumped to the ground. Miguel and Gino stood waiting, silhouetted by the Impala's headlights. Insects buzzed in the headlights, creating fluttering shadows. He waited a beat, then spoke. "Damn it, I forgot a gas can up in the front of the trailer. Miguel, grab that for me, would you, por favor?"

"Si, Señor, I get it for you." Miguel climbed back into the trailer and made his way to the front.

Roberto pulled his pistol, screwed on the suppressor, and waited until Miguel picked up the gas can and turned around. The man deserved better than being shot in the back. "Wait right there, Miguel." He took quick aim and fired three .45 rounds into the surprised man's chest. Miguel staggered a few steps and fell face down.

He unscrewed the suppressor and holstered his pistol, wondering what Miguel must have done to piss off his boss. He turned to Gino. "You got the matches?"

Gino nodded. "Yeah, right here. I grabbed 'em out of the glove box when we got here."

"Let's get this miserable show on the road. We still got seven or eight hours of driving ahead of us."

Gino handed him the box of wooden matches. "You finish it off. I'm gonna move the Impala part way up the hill. We don't need to lose our ride."

"That's a good idea." Gino backed the car and made a three-point turn, then headed up the dirt trail. He waited until the car stopped, then pulled a handkerchief from his back pocket and tied it into several knots. He struck a few matches, lit the cloth on fire and tossed it as far as he could into the trailer. He heard the telltale *whoosh* and ducked at the immediate rush of flames.

Gino yelled from up the hill. "You better get back, before it really goes up."

He turned and stumbled in the dark. The crackle of flames grew to a roar, and he hoofed it as fast as he could up the piss-poor excuse for a road until he reached the Impala. Gino sat on the trunk lid watching the fire. "You OK, Bobbie?"

He fought to catch his breath, his voice hoarse. "I'm all right. Come on, let's get the hell out of here. This ain't over until we're back in the US of A."

Houston, TX

Ed pounded the steering wheel of his Honda. "We gotta do something about this. We're so jammed up, I can't believe it." He turned to Juan, seated in the passenger seat, holding a sheaf of papers. They'd collected the paper work trail as instructed and returned to the warehouse to change clothes and hide the police van for the night.

Juan gave him a wide-eyed stare. "I know, I know. But what can we do?"

He rubbed a shaky hand over his face. "I'm not sure. Those guys we're dealing with, they scare the shit out of me. But we gotta do something. This whole Milani deal is like the effing crime of the century down here. If the brass finds out what we did, they'll crucify us. We'll do hard time, or worse."

Juan perked up. "Hey, what about the detective involved with the case? What if we went to him? Maybe he'd help us."

He stared into the darkness in the parking lot outside the warehouse. "You might be onto something there. What was his name?"

Juan scratched his protruding belly. "Huh, lemme see. I think it was Matthews. Yeah, Kyle Matthews."

"You think we should call him? He wouldn't be in on it, would he? From what I hear, he's one of the good ones."

Juan said, "That guy, Milani, he damn near killed Matthews. Don't you remember? It was in all the papers."

"You're right. I'm gonna dial him up. If he'll meet us, we can fill him in on what's going down."

Juan's head bobbed up and down, illuminated by the street light outside the gate. "Do it."

He punched in the number for the Homicide Department, listened for the correct extension, and entered it. After a couple rings, a deep Texas drawl answered. "This is Detective Matthews. How may I help you?"

Dry-mouthed, unsure how to proceed, not wanting to spill everything on the phone, he hesitated, then responded in a croaking whisper. "Detective, this is Officer Ed Nelson. We, uh my friend and I, Officer Juan Morales, we have some information for you."

"What is this regarding, Officer Nelson?"

"It's about a case you were on, but I, uh, not on the phone. I can't, uh we want to meet in person. But, it's important. You want to see what we got."

"All right, I'll bite. Meet me at my office. I'll be here until nine o'clock tonight."

He checked his watch. "We'll be there." He ended the call and heaved a sigh. "He'll talk to us at the precinct tonight. We still have time to hit the drop box, where we're supposed to leave these papers."

Juan cursed in Spanish. "No, what are you thinking? We have to leave the damn papers. Why did you give him our names? What if that *demon* who owns us finds out? You know what he told us. You know what we saw."

He ran a hand through his sparse hair. "I don't know, it just seemed like he needed to know who we are. We can make copies at the CVS across the street from the drop-off. No one will know but us. You aren't thinking of wimping out on me, are you?"

"No, no, I'd never do that. Come on then, let's get going and get it over with. We need to be there in less than an hour."

Ed put the car in gear and headed out of the parking lot. They weaved through traffic and headed toward the Fourth Ward and the CVS Pharmacy on Main. The man who told them what to do had directed them to Main Street Square Station. He'd instructed them to leave the paper trail they'd collected in a folder beneath one of the benches in the area near the reflection pool the trains ran through.

They parked in the ramp down the street and headed for CVS. A homeless guy lugging a huge plastic bag full of belongings stood by the glass doors and asked for change. Ed reached in his pants pocket and dumped a handful of coins into the man's grungy hand, trying to look past the creased, filthy face and stringy gray hair. Juan followed him inside, and they trudged across the dirty, carpeted front end of the store to the photo shop and copy machine.

Nervous, belatedly wondering if someone might be watching them, he dug for quarters in his pocket. "Shit, Juan, you got any change? I gave mine to the homeless dude outside."

Juan checked his pockets. "Uh, I don't know man. Why didn't you think of that before you gave that bum your money? Just give me a minute, I'll get some change."

He pulled a single quarter from his pants pocket. "I'll get started. Hurry up." He placed the release form from the Property Room on the glass and closed the copier lid.

He spun around at the crash of breaking glass and loud voices. Three men with black masks covering their faces, two armed with pistols, the other with an AK-47 stood at the counter yelling, "Get on the floor. Get down. Everybody, get down right now."

He raised the copier lid, scrabbled for the release form as the lid dropped, and hit the floor. He skittered around the backside of the copier and fumbled for his Smith & Wesson .40 holstered beneath his t-shirt. Juan screamed, "No, please, no."

The staccato bang-bang-bang of the rifle left his ears ringing. Pistol in hand, he snuck a glance around the side of the copier. A brutal kick in the gut caught him by surprise, and his pistol flew out of his hands. He curled on his side, clutching his belly. A foot stomped his shoulder and wrenched him over, flat on his back. The man with the AK-47 stood over him and aimed the gun at his chest. He saw the flash, heard the three-round burst and felt the instantaneous thud of the bullets entering his chest. Next came excruciating pain and then nothing.

Detective Kyle Matthews glanced one last time at his phone. 9:30 p.m. He grabbed his hat and briefcase and stood up. The cops evidently weren't coming, and he wasn't in the mood to wait or call them back. He'd promised Erin and the boys that he'd quit the evening work. Somehow, he got caught up in the cases he worked and ended up breaking that promise. Not like he was committed or anything. Like a dog with a bone, Erin always said, and with a smile too, but he wondered sometimes how she held up.

He shoved the hat on his head and headed out of the squad room. A few detectives were still working. One of his friends snagged him as he walked by. "Kyle, did you hear?"

He hovered at the cubicle entrance, anxious to head home. "Hear what?"

"Two off-duty cops were murdered tonight. At the CVS in the Fourth Ward, down on Main Street. Looks like the work of one of the damn cartels. Bunch of prescription drugs were taken. I guess they were in the wrong place at the wrong time."

"You got names?"

"Just a sec. Here ya go. Juan Morales and Ed Nelson."

Stunned, he stared at the detective. "Damn." Erin would be pissed, and for good reason. His night had just gotten longer.

An hour later, at the crime scene, he showed his badge. A uniformed patrol officer took him past the yellow tape and inside the drug store. The officers' bodies were gone; congealed blood and white tape marking where they'd lost their lives. He always thought the darkened, coagulating blood made a damn sad commentary on the end of someone's life.

No matter how many crimes scenes he attended, it never failed to creep him out on some basic level, thinking of how a victim's life leaked away and pooled on the ground. He always pictured someone trying futilely to scoop it up and put it back in its human container. As if that would bring the person back to life.

He gave himself a mental shake and found the detective who'd caught the case. "I'm Matthews from Homicide. Mind if I take a quick look around? One of these officers called me earlier tonight and wanted to meet with me."

The detective shrugged. "Go ahead. You know the drill, just don't disturb anything."

"Thank you." He wasn't sure what he'd find, but since they'd contacted him, he wanted a look-see. According to the pooling blood and tape, one of the men had been shot next to the copy machine. He pulled a nitrile glove from his pants pocket and pulled it on. He lifted the lid of the copier and frowned. A ragged, crinkled scrap of paper laid askew on the glass surface. He lifted it by one end and turned it over.

His frown deepened when he read *Evidence Release Form.* The rest of the form detailing the evidence released was tantalizingly missing. "Well *shit,"* he muttered. "A fat lot of good this miserable scrap of paper does." He handed it off to the detective on the case, thanked him and headed home. What did those two officers want to show him? He'd never know, thanks to whichever cartel had killed them.

The Next Day

Roberto faced Gino and Tony at the dining table. His eyes felt like they were full of dirt, and the lousy rash itched where he didn't want to scratch in public. Gino yawned and sipped steaming coffee. Tony looked more chipper than he should, but then he hadn't gotten back from Mexico at 3 a.m. and roused out of bed at 8 a.m. He addressed Tony. "We gotta call the Boss, but before I make the call, I wanna know for sure that the job's done."

Tony nodded vigorously. "It's done. Ended. Finito. Ben and I covered our tracks. The kid's amazing. He taught *me* stuff, and I've been in the biz a lot longer than he has."

He took a cautious swallow of coffee before replying. "Great. Can the whiz kid be trusted? That's my concern. He knows where we live, which makes us sitting ducks if he decides to rat us out."

Gino said, "You think we need to move somewhere else?"

Tony jumped back in before he could say anything. "Nah, Ben's golden. Told me how cool it was to be a part of our crew. Plus, the Boss said his friend here vouched for the kid. If he trusts his friend, then I do too."

He'd had the misfortune of observing the consequences of blind loyalty more than once. Something still nagged at him from the back of his mind, but he'd take that up with the Boss privately instead of arguing with Tony. "As long as you're satisfied, we'll take your word. I'm gonna call the Boss now and fill him in. Either of youse can add your two cents while I'm on the phone."

Tony said, "Let's do it."

Gino gave him thumbs-up and thankfully didn't say anything, just kept yawning and drinking coffee.

"All right, here we go." He punched the contact, put his phone on speaker, and laid it on the table.

Johnny answered right away. "Bobbie, how's Houston?"

"Hey Boss, Houston is the shits, but the job is done."

Johnny replied, "Damn, you didn't waste any time."

"We met with the cops right away. Things moved fast once Tony and the hacker penetrated the PD and hospital servers. Those cops seemed spooked, and I didn't want to drag it out over a couple days. On top of that, we didn't have a secure location to leave the evidence sitting overnight."

Johnny added, "That's good thinking and good work. Tony there with you?"

Tony spoke up. "Yeah, I'm here, and we're good. Your friend's hacker did a bang-up job. We got in and out, and he covered our tracks with some new program he developed himself. It's better than anything out there."

Johnny said, "Good. I'll let my friend know. About those cops; they're taken care of. Should be on the local news. They won't be causing any problems."

Relieved to have one less moving part he couldn't control, Roberto replied, "Thanks Boss."

Johnny chuckled. "You've got some well-earned down time until Vinnie arrives. Gino, you up for doing some more driving around Houston?"

Gino's responded. "No problem, Boss. Whatcha got in mind?"

"Vinnie likes a decent hotel. You boys are moving to the Marriot Downtown. Rent a Town Car and take a tour every day; get familiar with the route from the hotel to the lockup, and the route to Ellington. You can switch from cops to businessmen. Capisce?"

Roberto said, "Whatever you want, Boss." It wouldn't hurt his feelings to get out of the crappy apartment. He'd bet the Marriot had a spa, too, and he could get rid of the damn rash.

Johnny continued. "Tony, you can head home. I'd like you to get things ready at the house. We've got quite a crew moving in from Dubai in a few weeks."

Tony said, "I'll fly out in the morning."

Johnny wrapped things up. "You boys take care. I'll see you in Chicago when you bring Milani."

"So long, Boss. I'll stay in touch." Roberto gazed at his two companions. "Let's pack up and get out of this dump. We might as well check in at the Marriot today and pick up the Town Car. Gino, you can practice your Houston driving skills and give Tony a ride to the airport in the morning. I'm spending the rest of today and tomorrow in the spa."

Washington, DC

Harandi strode restlessly along the sidewalk toward the entrance to the White House. He'd made up his mind about certain things and needed to act on them. The plain white envelope in his hand contained his carefully worded resignation for Whitman. The President had agreed to see him within the hour. Once he'd gotten that out of the way, he planned to meet briefly with Berenger. He needed to see Rowan in person, one last time, before he was transferred to Houston and only the FBI Director could give him permission.

Thirty minutes later, he stood outside the door to the Oval Office while the Secret Service agent on duty announced his arrival. He entered and saw Whitman standing next to the windows. The President turned and made his way to the armchair in front of the fireplace. "Hello, David. What's on your mind this afternoon?"

He took his place in the chair adjacent to the President. "Thank you for meeting with me on short notice, sir." He handed Whitman the envelope. "This is my formal resignation. If you've no objection, I'd like to make it effective immediately. As we both know, you deserve an advisor of a much higher caliber than you're ever going to have with me."

Whitman grasped the envelope. "I've been pleased with how you've conducted yourself in a role you were more-or-less thrust into."

"Thank you, sir. It's been a pleasure to serve you, even in my limited capacity."

The President chuckled. "I've always thought you were much more of a politician than you give yourself credit for."

"So you've mentioned, sir. You know I was simply doing my job." One I'm sick to death of, he wanted to add. "Will you honor my request for immediate resignation?"

Whitman stood up. "I'll honor your request, with a few conditions."

He stood and faced the President. He needed total freedom from the poison of DC and had no intention of allowing Whitman to keep him hooked. "Sir?"

"I'd like you to stand with the others on the day I officially pardon Milani, Cantor, and Johnston. In addition, I would like you to brief your replacement at some point. Lastly, I would appreciate it if you would entertain an occasional inquiry from me. I've often benefited from your perspective as a true Washington outsider."

He could already feel the hooks settling into his psyche. One didn't overtly say no to the President. However, no one could force him to own a cell phone. He mustered his best faux congeniality and held out his hand. "Absolutely sir. It would be my pleasure to do all of the things you mentioned."

The President shook his hand. "Thank you. All the best to you, David."

"Thank you, sir. Take care."

Whitman ushered him out of the Oval Office for what he hoped would be the last time.

An hour later he sat across from Berenger in her office. "I just met with Whitman and made my exit official."

"You resigned? Good for you. Where does this leave our ad hoc investigation?"

"I have no intention of abandoning the work we're doing. In fact, I have a request directly related to our investigation."

"Let's hear it, Mr. Harandi."

"I'd like very much to see Milani before he's transferred to Houston."

Berenger pursed her lips. "I see. Is this part and parcel of your need for redemption?"

"It could be. We both know what's going to happen in Houston. Seven counts of capital murder puts Milani on death row. We grew up together, and for better or worse, he's the closest thing I have to family. In addition, I'd like one final opportunity to question him."

"I'll approve a visit, or interview, since he's going to be out of our hands in a matter of days. I'm curious though. What makes you think he'll be willing to answer your questions now?"

"Tora may have adjusted his attitude. I'm not sure he will talk, but I'd like to give it a shot."

"Fair enough. However, I've scheduled my interview with Milani for later this week. Let's give agent Foster another interview with him after I've been there. Then I'll set a time for you to make the trip."

"Thank you, ma'am. I appreciate it, very much."

Berenger gave him a glimmer of a smile. "You're welcome, Mr. Harandi."

CHAPTER TEN

Three Days Later
ADX Florence, CO

Rowan stared at Foster. The agent sat across from him at the table in the interrogation room, next to an empty chair. He couldn't imagine who else might want to *interview* him. Foster laid his tiny notebook on the table. "Good afternoon, Rowan."

Foster hadn't offered to remove the cuffs, which had become a ritual between them, along with the offer of coffee, also absent. He didn't care about the coffee. He needed to return to the tiny cell and lie down. The pain meds administered earlier by the guards weren't working. Sitting in the hard metal chair, unable to move around, enhanced the agony throughout his body. "What's going on, Agent Foster?"

"You've got a special visitor."

The guard opened the door, admitting a tall, slender woman. She wore a navy-blue suit jacket over a white silk blouse and narrow skirt. She stalked to the table and stood in front of him, hands on hips. "Hello, Mr. Milani. I'm FBI Director Berenger."

Irritated by the eager aggression in her eyes and stance, he raised a brow. "Should I be impressed?"

She didn't take his bait. Instead she sat down across from him, in the empty chair next to Foster. "I wanted to meet you in person and learn the truth."

He knew now, why Foster hadn't removed the cuffs. He met her expectant gaze and didn't say anything.

Foster tucked the notebook back into his shirt pocket. "I'm going to leave you two for now. If you'd like, I'll bring some coffee later."

He smirked at Foster. "You sure it's safe to leave your new boss alone in here with me? You know I don't have a good track record in that department."

Foster grimaced. "Rowan, please. Director Berenger traveled here because the Intel we've gathered sheds new light on your situation. Cooperating with her is in your best interests."

Berenger asserted her authority. "That will be all, Agent Foster. Coffee sounds good, later. I'm ready to get started, and I'm not concerned for my safety."

Foster shoved back his chair and stood up. "I'll check back in thirty minutes."

After Foster left, Berenger tilted her head and studied him. "You've had a tough go of it. Tora is no joke."

Like she gave a shit. He didn't answer.

She frowned at him. "I inherited the mess involving you, Cantor, and Johnston after you killed Rodney Ainsley. And yes, I watched the video. I know you were defending yourself."

Did she expect him to thank her? His shoulders burned. Pain traveled in zigzagging waves from his lower back and hips all the way down his legs. Frustrated with his helplessness and the never-ending misery, he glared at her and didn't respond.

Berenger turned in her chair and crossed one long leg over the other. "I can see you're in pain. However, I expect you to answer me when I address you. This interview can be relatively short and productive, or it can be long and uncomfortable. It's up to you."

She had him by the balls, and they both knew it. "OK," he muttered.

"Thank you. Let's proceed. When I learned you were alive and returning to US custody, I decided to make an example of you and rebuild the Bureau's reputation, which you helped to diminish."

Her words galvanized his pain-blunted mind. "You're kidding, right? Rodney Ainsley is responsible for diminishing the Bureau's precious reputation, not me."

"I agree, in part. Thanks to David Harandi, we fully investigated the contents of your flash drive and confirmed the veracity of the kills you've made on behalf of the United States.

The Intel your colleague Chad Cantor shared with us clearly shows how you were set up and who benefited from it."

"Then why am I still sitting here? And before you say it, spare me the lies about your ongoing investigation."

She sat up straight and uncrossed her legs. "Whether you like it or not, our investigation *is* ongoing, and it's the reason I'm here, meeting with you personally."

He slouched in the chair. Sweat dripped down the sides of his face. The scratchy prison jumpsuit clung to his body. "I don't give a rat's ass about your *ongoing investigation* because you and I both know it won't change anything. I'm done talking, to you *and* Foster."

"No, you're not done. Not by a long shot." She pointed a vehement forefinger at him. "You're going to sit right here at this table until I say we're done, and *I* don't give a *rat's ass* how long it takes. You got that, Mr. Milani?"

He saw confident victory her eyes and heard the steel in her voice. "Yeah, I get it. Continue your investigation. I'm your captive audience."

Berenger had the audacity to smirk. "Right you are. First, tell me about Sa-id."

Her mention of the man tortured and murdered because of their friendship blindsided him. "Why the hell do you want to talk about Sa-id?"

"I ask the questions. You answer them. You must know the drill by now."

Stark grief overwhelmed him, followed by unreasoning anger. He stared at the steel cuffs biting into his wrists. By God, he'd enjoy ending her power trip. "What does Sa-id's death have to do with your investigation?"

Her nails rapped on the table in triple time. "Let me repeat. I ask, you answer. I'm waiting, Mr. Milani."

Hating her, he spoke because he didn't have a choice. "Sa-id was a long-time family friend and a good man. Sometime after 9/11, he told me he wanted to serve the country that had rescued him from the tyranny of his homeland. His words."

"Why did he choose CAIR, or did you make the choice?"

"We talked, and I told him what CAIR was up to. He applied for a job at their DC headquarters, as a Computer Security Specialist. He had access to private documents, money transfers, you name it."

"How long did he funnel Intel to you?"

"Seven or eight years. I lose track of time. Especially now."

"Did you have any inkling he'd been compromised?"

"No. I didn't know he'd been murdered until more than six months after the fact."

"I'm sorry to say, Shemal informed Patricia Hennessey, the President, and David Harandi that you killed Sa-id."

He squinted when the sweat making its way down his forehead leached into the corners of his eyes, blurring his vision and stinging. He clenched his fists. *"You're sorry? I didn't kill Sa-id."*

"Take it easy. We know Shemal killed him. I simply wanted to understand the connection between the two of you. Let's move on to the six men you killed in Houston."

The longer he sat, the more the burning, stabbing pain in his shoulders and hips intensified. He couldn't understand what she wanted from him; he couldn't hold onto the rage, and he couldn't think. "What?"

Berenger frowned at him. "The men in Houston. You killed four of them at the House of Allah and two others in Discovery Park. You've stated that all six were here illegally, pursuing jihad against the US."

He tried to shift his weight and couldn't stifle a groan. "Why are you asking questions I've already answered?"

She tapped a silver-lacquered nail on the table. “I need clarification only you can give. We verified your claim that they were here illegally. How did you determine their intentions?”

He sneered. “I was an FBI agent for more than twelve years, on an anti-terrorism task force. I’ve spent the last decade hunting terrorists for our country. I know a jihadist when I see one.”

“You need to be more specific, Mr. Milani.”

“All right. This is what I’ve already told Foster. I met two of the men before, one in Afghanistan, one in Iran. Shemal’s limo driver was an Egyptian national. Another was an inexperienced sidekick of the Afghani. Two were guards, armed and protecting the mosque. Trust me, none of them were interested in becoming upstanding American citizens.”

“Thank you. Now, regarding Ms. Pinella.”

He couldn’t sit up straight in the metal chair. “I told Foster why I eliminated her.”

“I’ve read Agent Foster’s transcript of your reasons for killing her. I don’t understand her connection to Shemal or why she’d have a vendetta against you and Ms. Stratton. However, let’s leave that for now.”

“OK.”

“When the CIA removed you from Tora prison, Ralph Johnston and two of your extracurricular colleagues assisted them.”

He let his surprise show and hoped his shock remained hidden. “Huh. That’s news to me.”

“David Harandi informed me, eventually, of Johnston’s assistance, along with Michael Cristo’s. He also mentioned a woman, whom he thought might be Iranian.”

“David is a CIA tool, nothing more. He’s probably lying.”

“Your handlers, Hancock and Talbot, recently confirmed your colleagues’ participation to Director Abramson.”

He shrugged and winced. "Shemal's CIA puppets put a hood over my head. They didn't remove it until we were on board the aircraft. I never saw anyone besides them and Harandi."

"We also discovered the identity of another of your cohorts, Gabriel Hernandez. I'd like the woman's name as well, please."

"The team I chose didn't include a woman."

"So you admit you chose a team to assist in your clandestine activities on the country's behalf."

"If you've read any of your agent's transcripts or watched the digital recordings, you already know Linden started the program and told me to choose a team. I couldn't function alone."

She ignored his assertion. "We've investigated a company called *Business Jet Express.* Apparently, its proprietors, Jerry Reynolds and Bryan DeMuth, were also a part of your team."

She kept striking close to home, and he didn't know where she'd go next. "Like I said, I couldn't function alone."

Her lips curled in a smile he could only read as smug. "Thank you for confirming their involvement. We've learned a lot about your covert organization. As you must know, the country, specifically the CIA, is short one aircraft. The loss of a sixty-five-million dollar Gulfstream G650 is no small matter."

"I can assure you, I did not steal the CIA's jet."

"No, but you've benefited on more than one occasion from its use."

"My team acted when no one else would help me. Why the hell are you sitting here? Why aren't you interrogating Shemal, or Talbot and Hancock?"

Her brows arched. "You've confirmed the involvement of these people in stealing expensive government property. Regarding Shemal and the others, our investigation…"

He interrupted her. "Right, I know, it's *ongoing.* Here's what I don't understand. Even though you know Shemal set me up, your main concern is screwing over innocent people. I'm not going to help you."

Berenger scoffed. "Innocent people? I question that claim. One more issue remains. A highly skilled sniper assassinated Patricia Hennessey. Michael Cristo possesses those skills, as well as, perhaps, the will. Call it desire if you want. Turns out Gabriel Hernandez was his spotter when they served as Rangers."

"I told Harandi and Foster, I don't know anything about how that bitch met her end."

"Yes, they both reported your response. They both believe you know more than you let on. Do you?"

A ripple of fear coursed through his gut. He didn't trust her or what she'd do to him to get answers. "I *do not know* who killed Patricia Hennessey."

"I believe you do. I believe you know where the CIA's jet is hidden. I believe you know where both Cristo and Hernandez are, and I believe you know the identity of the mystery woman Harandi saw in Cairo. I expect you to tell me. Everything. Right now."

He saw the unyielding set of her jaw. "Why would I?"

"In case you haven't figured it out yet, your part in this interview is providing honest answers. I'm waiting."

He shifted in the chair and groaned again. *"I don't know*, on all of the above."

"You're lying. Why won't you help yourself? Give me a reason to help mitigate the mess you've gotten yourself into."

"I'm done answering your questions."

She leaned forward. "Listen to me, Mr. Milani, and make sure you understand. *You're done when I say you're done."*

He leaned forward slowly, got as close to her as the restraints allowed, and heard the quick intake of breath she couldn't hide as her body veered away from his. "Now *you* listen to *me*. These *people* are my friends. You're mistaken if you think I'll give you and the Bureau anything that makes it easy for you to fuck them the way I've been fucked."

Their eyes locked. He glared until she shoved back her chair, stood up and paced around the room. "I knew you were lying."

He'd succeeded in making her uncomfortable. Maybe he'd frightened her. His satisfaction at the realization faded, obliterated by his impotent rage. She'd nailed him again. He stared at her, breathing hard. "You don't know anything."

Berenger returned to the chair. "I know enough."

Something in her tone caught his attention. "You're lying. If you *knew enough*, you'd be conducting headline-making arrests and bolstering the Bureau's reputation. Your investigation hasn't produced anything more than circumstantial evidence about *anything* you've questioned me on, has it?"

Her cheeks turned pink, answering the question for him. "May I remind you, I'm asking the questions here?"

He raised his hands as far as the cuffs and chain allowed. "How could I forget?"

She caught him off-guard by changing the subject. "Do you know who murdered Derek Norris?"

"Murdered him? No, I don't know. I'd like to thank whoever did, though. He was a useless, sniveling moron."

"Mr. Norris provided us with valuable information about your colleagues. He was last seen leaving a bar in Sioux Falls, South Dakota, with a dark-haired woman. The bartender said she had some sort of an accent and was beautiful. Why don't you tell me her name?"

Dismayed, he tried to think through the haze of pain. What the hell had Mike been thinking, to involve Asal? "How would I know who killed that fool? Didn't the crime scene tell your extra-special agents anything?"

"Our crime scene investigation is not germane to our discussion. However, I will tell you, Mr. Milani, I don't believe in coincidence. I do believe in connecting dots that make sense. This woman is wanted for questioning in the murder of Mr. Norris."

"Whoever did the world a favor in offing that waste of flesh must have known what they were doing. Good for them."

She leaped on his comment. "You're telling me more than one person was involved in his murder?"

He tried to shift his weight from one hip to the other and groaned. "I was in Tora, remember? I can't do this anymore. I'm done talking."

Berenger shoved back her chair and stood up. "You've confirmed one more thing for me. You are without doubt the most stubbornly loyal individual I've ever run across."

He sneered. "Glad I could help with that."

"You are also the most arrogant man I've ever met. It's difficult to understand, given your circumstances."

He wilted in the chair. "Not anymore."

She tapped one foot. "Go on, I'm listening."

He raised his head, wishing he'd kept his mouth shut. "At this point in my life, or what's left of it, I guess you could say I'm cynical. But I'm not arrogant."

"I believe that's the first honest answer you've given me, but you need to remember one thing. My investigation into what happened to you, as well as the role you and your cohorts have played since then, will continue until I'm satisfied."

Paralyzing despair overwhelmed him. "I'm not answering anymore questions."

She shook her head. "You can't see the irony, can you?"

"I don't know what you're talking about."

She replied. "As an FBI agent for twelve-plus years, your mission has been to protect the United States from terrorist attacks; to deter foreign espionage threats; to uphold and enforce our criminal laws."

"I don't need your recitation of the FBI Manual. I've done my damnedest to fulfill that mission."

"A lot of people would say you've done your damnedest to sabotage every single thing the Bureau stands for."

"And those same people would say and do anything to stop me from exposing their goal of undermining and destroying the country and benefiting from the process."

A quiet knock interrupted their sparring. The guard opened the door, and Foster entered with a carafe of coffee and three cups on a tray. "Director, are you ready for a break?"

Berenger replied. "We're finished, for now. Coffee sounds good. Guard, remove the cuffs so Mr. Milani can have some coffee."

No way in hell would he sit and drink coffee with her after enduring her grilling. "I don't want any coffee. I'd like to return to my cell."

Foster placed the tray on the table. "Are you sure, Rowan? It's hot and fresh."

He met Foster's gaze, despising the concern in the agent's eyes. He'd never give anyone affiliated with the Bureau another opportunity to force information from the screwed-up mess in his mind. "I'm sure."

Berenger said, "We've had a productive conversation. You've earned a cup of coffee."

"I said, *I don't want your goddamned coffee*. I'd like to return to my cell now, please."

Berenger turned on her heel and gestured to the guard. "Please escort Mr. Milani to his cell. Agent Foster, bring the coffee to your office." She swept through the door. Foster ignored him, picked up the tray and dutifully followed her.

"Good riddance," he muttered as the door closed. God, how he wished he never had to see her again. He only wanted the guards to release him from the miserable chair and take him back to the solitude of the tiny cell.

Foster watched as Berenger sank into the chair facing his desk in the small room that served as his office in ADX Florence. She pointed at the carafe of coffee on the desk. "Please, Wilson."

He poured, and she took a long swallow. She held the cup in both hands and rolled her shoulders. "After interviewing Milani, I have new respect for your abilities. He is the most difficult subject I've ever dealt with."

"He is a unique individual, and you correctly assessed him as loyal to a fault. May I ask a question?"

"Certainly."

He chose his words carefully. "Do you think exchanging his pain medication for a placebo worked to your advantage?"

"Observing his body language *after* he answered questions which inadvertently gave me information, I'm inclined to believe so. If his thought processes weren't impaired by pain, I'm sure he would have evaded answering quite adroitly. What are your thoughts?"

"As you must know, I'm old school. I believe in complete honesty with my detainees, in order to build trust."

"You would not have given Milani the placebo, would you?"

He forced himself to meet her determined gaze. "No, I would not have done that."

Berenger sipped more coffee and frowned. "My analysis is not complete. However, I'm encouraged by what we learned today."

He nodded slowly. "Milani had a tough time throughout the interview. As you correctly noted, he is a stubborn man."

"Instruct the guards to administer the placebo again. I want to see how Milani responds when his prowess at duplicity is completely derailed. We may yet learn the absolute truth."

"Of course, I'll instruct the guards. I do have another question, ma'am."

Berenger poured more coffee and gave him a vigorous nod. "Anything, Wilson. What are you thinking?"

"Are you planning to pursue Milani's cohorts, namely Cristo and Hernandez, along with the proprietors of the business jet company?"

She shrugged. "Although Milani perceived correctly that our evidence is circumstantial, I would very much like to question them."

Curious about her endgame, he continued. "What further information do you hope to extract from Milani? His answers, to Agent Capello, Harandi, me, and now you, have never varied. Besides which, we know he's not a double-agent or home-grown terrorist."

Berenger finished her coffee and set the cup on his desk. "I'd like to gain enough information so that I could move forward with prosecuting his colleagues for stealing the CIA's aircraft. I want to find the mystery woman who murdered Derek Norris, and I'd like to question Cristo and Hernandez about the death of Patricia Hennessey, as well."

"If I may, based on my experience with him, I believe Milani will be more amenable to offering information if he is not in severe pain."

Berenger rubbed the back of her neck. "Your observations are astute, and I appreciate your input. However, I prefer to continue this course. Advise the guards to administer the placebo and let's see how Milani responds tomorrow. I'm ready to head to my hotel and relax."

"What time would you prefer to schedule another interview session?"

Berenger paused at the door. "Early. 8 a.m. I want to catch Milani at his lowest point."

"I'll see you then, Director. Have a good evening."

"Thank you, Wilson. You do the same."

Much as he admired his boss, abiding by her order filled him with a repulsive mixture of guilt and sadness. After she left, he sat at his desk and observed Milani on the closed-circuit monitor.

His detainee sat on the edge of the concrete slab and held his head in his hands, stretched out on the bed for a few minutes, then got up and prowled the small cell. Without the pain meds, he knew Milani wouldn't sleep.

Not in the habit of disobeying a direct order from the director of the FBI, he called the infirmary. A nurse answered. "May I help you?"

"This is agent Foster. Please administer a placebo in place of Mr. Milani's normal dose of pain medication this evening and tomorrow morning."

"I will notify his guards and make sure your orders are followed."

"Thank you." He hung up and switched off the monitor. He couldn't bear to watch Milani suffer needlessly. He'd worked hard to earn the man's trust and respect. Berenger's hard-boiled approach puzzled and concerned him. What prompted her adversarial role with Milani after all the evidence indicting Shemal? He'd expected her to reach out to Milani in a forthcoming manner, or even with an apology.

Her actions undid his careful work and the inroads he'd made. Milani wasn't a stupid man. He'd figure out something was amiss, and he'd know why. How would he handle more interrogation? Would he even be coherent and willing to answer questions? Or would he tell Berenger to stick it? One thing he knew for sure. Milani would never trust or respond to him again.

The Next Day

Rowan sat hunched over the metal table in the interrogation room, eyes closed, jaws clenched against the unremitting pain. Sometime during the interminable night, he realized that the pain meds faithfully administered by the guards were bogus. In his moment of revelation, he decided Berenger would *never* get any more information from him.

At a brisk knock on the door, he opened his eyes and forced his head up. The guard admitted Berenger. She'd ditched the suit and dressed down in a Bureau polo shirt and belted pants. She carried a single cup of coffee. He could smell it and see the steam rising from the cup when she sat down across from him. "Good morning, Mr. Milani. I'm ready to continue our conversation. Did you sleep well?"

"What do you think, Director?"

"I think you must understand how serious I am about learning as much of the truth as possible from you, and that I'll go to whatever lengths I need to in order to facilitate your participation in that endeavor."

He could barely follow her rambling statement, but he caught the part about facilitating his participation. His heart pounded. He couldn't take any more pain. "I've done nothing but tell the truth since this shit storm started in South Dakota." He raised his cuffed hands. "And look where it's gotten me."

"You played a part in that as well, when you proceeded to *eliminate,* as you call it, the people who got in your way."

"You know what, Director? You're right. Guilty as charged. I want to go back to my cell now, if you don't mind."

"Not until you answer my questions."

"I told you, I'm done answering your questions."

"No, you're not. You know more than you're revealing, and I intend to get to the truth, one way or another."

Spasms in his back muscles took his breath away. He tried to stretch but couldn't stop the pain. Sweat beaded on his forehead, slicked his back and chest, and he couldn't suppress a groan. "I need to go back to my cell now."

Berenger took a long swallow of coffee. "I don't care how long it takes to get the answers I want. You're going nowhere until you cooperate."

The spasms in his back continued. Taking shallow breaths hurt like hell. Light-headed, at the end of his endurance, he murmured, "I can't answer any more questions."

"Mr. Milani, we are not finished, and I..."

He interrupted her. "I can't…" His words ended in a moan as he tipped forward and slumped over the table.

He heard the frustration in her voice. "Guards. Take him back to his cell."

Strong hands wrenched his body upright and held onto him. Somehow, he walked between the guards until they reached the cell. They removed the restraints and he staggered to the cement slab, half falling onto the thin mattress. Groans punctuated his ragged breaths while he lay with clenched fists, unable to stop the spasms.

He stared at the ceiling and wondered how long before he'd be back in the hard metal chair, expected to betray the friends who'd helped him. Would she stoop to enhanced interrogation? He squeezed his eyes shut. His body couldn't go through it again. Not after the monsters in Tora. But if they wanted to hurt him, he couldn't stop them, and no one would help him.

The Next Day

Rowan closed his eyes and waited. The cuffs held his hands on the table and the leg irons kept him sitting in the hard metal chair. The pain had receded somewhat, but left him miserable and exhausted. Why had Berenger relented and allowed the guards to give him his pain meds? He heard a brisk knock and opened his eyes.

The guard admitted Berenger, and she sat down across from him. "Are you feeling better this morning?"

"Sure. What now, Director?"

Berenger said, "I wanted to meet with you once more before I leave for Washington. Perhaps an apology is in order."

He raised a brow. “Why start now? You are, after all, conducting an ongoing investigation of monumental importance.”

His sarcasm didn’t seem to bother her. “You are correct, Mr. Milani. And…”

He interrupted her. “You wouldn’t know anything if not for Chad, yet he’s still sitting in County. He deserves something for helping you. Why won’t you let him go?”

“Once again, you seem to forget that I ask the questions and you answer them.”

“Oh, right.”

She observed him for a long moment before replying. “I’m not usually given to harsh treatment. I wanted to interview you without pain medication enhancing your well-known ability to deceive. Perhaps my approach was incorrect, given the level of injury you’ve sustained as well as the level of pain you suffer.”

She sucked at apologies, which didn’t surprise him as much as the fact that she’d offered one.

“Don’t trouble yourself, Director. No one so far has cared whether I’m in pain or how much I suffer.”

“As I started to say before you interrupted me, we have documentation which supports your claim of innocence. I acknowledge that you were, as you have insisted in every single interrogation you’ve endured, *set up* by individuals in our intelligence community operating in tandem with the Muslim Brotherhood.”

“And my reward for telling the truth is a cell in ADX Florence, which I don’t think I’ll be leaving anytime soon.”

“You need to understand something, Mr. Milani. By taking matters into your own hands and dispensing your version of justice, you’ve created a quandary for the Bureau and for me. I cannot sanction murder, no matter your claims of either self-defense or national security.”

“I understand perfectly, Director.” He couldn’t stop his hands from forming fists. He took harsh breaths and glared at her.

Berenger shoved back her chair and stood up. "I need to return to Washington, Mr. Milani. I hope you will continue to cooperate with agent Foster."

The misery he'd endured because of her overbearing power trip ensured he'd never answer another question posed by anyone from the Bureau. "Of course."

"Thank you. Meeting you has been most instructive."

He met her arctic blue eyes and wanted to say *fuck you.* Instead he gave her a faint sneer. "Same here, Director."

CHAPTER ELEVEN

Three Days Later

Rowan stood in the small, barred cage, breathing hard, wiping at the trickle of sweat making its way down the side of his face. In an utterly humiliating act, the guards had started taking him from the cell and depositing him in the barred space. They instructed him, in their barked orders, to exercise, to *move.* For an hour, he walked back and forth, sometimes in circles.

The cell had succeeded in numbing his mind with its white walls and complete silence. But the cage they forced him into each day brought his simmering rage and hatred boiling to the surface. And he could do *nothing* but endure the degradation of being treated like a dangerous animal.

He walked to one end of the nine-by-twelve-foot space and turned. Foster stood outside the enclosure, watching him. The guards waited at the cage door with their handcuffs and shackles. With no option but to obey, he walked to the door. While he stood with jaws clenched, trying to control his breathing, they restrained him and led him to Foster. He glared at the agent and didn't say anything.

Foster took his arm. "Let's go have a talk."

Like he had a fucking choice. "OK."

Foster half turned to look at him. "Would you like some coffee?"

"Sure." He'd rather put a couple .45 slugs in the agent's chest and add one between his eyes to finish the job, but he didn't have a choice about that either.

Once in the interrogation room, Foster sat opposite him, leaned across the table and poured coffee, then unlocked the cuffs. "As you know, our investigation into your situation is ongoing."

"Of course it is."

As usual, Foster retained his equanimity and ignored his comment. "I know we've discussed this before, but I feel compelled to repeat: Everything I've seen has, frankly, been unbelievable to me. You have not received anything approaching equitable treatment, at any juncture."

He studied the interrogator's face, but could find no hint of mendacity. "Unbelievable though it might seem, I know that."

Foster didn't even blink. "Everything you've told me, Berenger, and prior interrogators has been borne out by the information Cantor provided. The leaders of our intelligence community pronounced you guilty on the basis of *one man's* declaration."

The agent's comments didn't do anything to dispel his anger. "I know that, too."

Foster continued. "I can't help but wonder why no one in the intelligence community bothered to check out your assertions or the validity of the serious charges lodged against you."

"Like I told you before, Shemal's money helped convince them. Besides, the rest of the intelligence community was never made privy to anything other than his concocted evidence. I understand now that I never stood a chance. Everything I tried to do was destined to fail."

Foster grimaced. "True on all counts, unfortunately. While I concur with Director Berenger's assessment and can't condone your decision to pursue your own version of justice by stepping outside the law and committing murder, I find myself in a position I didn't expect."

In the midst of another cautious sip of coffee, his rage overflowed and he burned his tongue. "Ouch. Goddamn it, I told you, I didn't commit *murder*. Ridding the country of traitors and people who intend its harm or destruction is not murder."

"I have to tell you, although I didn't expect this, I find myself beginning to agree on that point as well. I'm going to work hard to find some sort of mitigation on that front."

"Good luck. I don't hold out much hope."

The agent leaned across the table with the handcuffs. "I intend to give it my best shot. We're done for today."

"OK." He held out his wrists, unable to stop the bitter, churning anger, while the cold steel clicked closed, leaving him helpless. He didn't believe Foster's proclamation any more than he believed Berenger's.

Two Days Later – Mid-August
Dubai, UAE

Bettina Milani heaved a sigh and looked at her mother, doing her best not to let her disappointment show, or turn into full-blown disgust. Over the past months, missing Chad while their baby grew inside her, she'd felt overwhelmed, drowning in sadness. Despair sometimes left her uninterested in the effort it took to get up and go on every day.

She could have used her mother's support. But Janice had been consumed with her own issues of grief, or maybe guilt. Whatever plagued her mother, she had no room for her daughter. Janice had always been deep into her own problems, but she'd foolishly hoped her pregnancy would make a difference. Even her father Khalil, normally kind and supportive, had been distant when she needed him the most.

The people who'd faithfully encouraged her, tugged her out of bed and drawn her into their daily lives in the Dubai apartment were Chad's father Clifton, Angelo, and Ralph's wife Marion. They'd promised to be her family. Clifton especially, had never let her down. Their relationship had been special from the first time she'd met him, on the trip they'd taken together, fleeing the country.

She'd needed someone, when David released her from the brig, after her final, heartbreaking goodbye to Chad. Walking out of the interrogation cell and leaving him had been one of the most horrible things she'd ever experienced. Clifton had sat for hours on the jet while they flew to Dubai, listening and smiling and asking concerned-but-polite questions about how she was doing. Without him, she wouldn't have been able to function.

Janice interrupted her thoughts. "Oh my, how can I ever recover from this mess?"

She rubbed her protruding belly. "You'll be all right, Mom. At least we know Rowan is alive. He may be in tough shape, but Johnny says he'll take care of him and all of us, too."

"This has been so difficult for your father and me. I wish sometimes that Rowan had never joined the FBI. What if he'd chosen a different career? He could be married to Michelle and raising a family in California. Instead he chose to rebel, to go his own way."

How could her mother remain so firmly stuck in the past? "Well, you know as well as I do, he wanted to get away from everything." *From you,* she bit the inside of her lower lip to keep from blurting.

Janice finished her bourbon and held the glass in both hands, seeming to read her thoughts. "I know. I drove him away. But that was years ago. When we were together, on Kauai, he never knew how much I regretted the things I said, because he would never listen. He never gave your father and me another chance. He rejected us."

"Rowan had a few other things on his mind while we were at the estate. And why would you bring up Michelle? We have to live in the present."

"I just wish things could have been different. Your father and I have been uprooted from our home and our lives. We live like gypsies, depending on the charity of people like Mr. Giacopino."

The whining self-pity in her mother's tone grated. "And you blame Rowan, I'm sure."

"Well, if not for the path Rowan chose, your father and I could be enjoying retirement, our home, and our friends. We might have grandchildren. Now, we can never go home. We can never face our friends. The shame is too much for me to bear sometimes."

Bettina grimaced as a contraction wound its way through her abdomen. Unlike the Braxton-Hicks contractions she'd experienced during the last week, this one hurt. Besides, she couldn't relax when every word her mother spewed made her angry enough to break something. "You have a son who's sacrificed his entire life for his country and you're *ashamed?* You need to rethink a few things."

"Rowan has made it impossible for us to ever conceive of a normal life. We'll always be looked at with suspicion. This is especially difficult for your father. What's to stop the government from deporting him, sending him back to Iran out of spite, because of Rowan's selfish actions?"

Another contraction, stronger than the first, dampened her palms. She gripped her lower abdomen. The low back ache annoying her for the past few days wouldn't let up. She pushed herself upright on the sofa. *"You* should be ashamed of the things you're saying. And if you don't mind, will you please tell Johnny I need to see the doctor he arranged for me? I'm not sure what's going on, but I think *your first grandchild* might be making an appearance before too much longer."

Janice stared, slack-jawed, taking precious seconds to process what she'd said, then blinked and wobbled to her feet. "Oh, dear Lord. Bettina, my darling, are you sure? Oh my, I'll tell him right away." Her mother lurched from the room.

Bettina gasped as another contraction sideswiped her. At thirty-seven weeks, it should be three more weeks before the baby came. She'd held onto the irrational hope of Chad being with her, holding her hand, encouraging her, cheering her as only he could, while they brought their first child into the world. Johnny had explained it was only a matter of time before both Rowan and

Chad were freed. Tears stung her eyes, and another contraction had her squeezing them shut.

The unwanted tears trickled down her cheeks while she tried to breathe. Liquid warmth gushed between her legs and she knew. Their baby was coming, while the man she loved sat alone in a cell, seven thousand miles away. She tried not to moan when another contraction stitched its way across her belly. Damn it, she wasn't ready. She didn't want to do this without Chad. It wasn't fair. He deserved to be present.

She opened her eyes and held onto her belly. God, she hated David Harandi. He could have believed Rowan. He could have believed her, and he could have believed Chad. The stupid shithead could have helped them. He was worse than the devil, and she'd punch him in the face if she ever saw him again. Then she'd spit on him. And after that, she'd claw his eyes out.

She brushed at the tears and tried to take a cleansing breath. Another contraction came fast on the heels of the last one. Maybe Rowan could teach her how to kill with her hands. She'd find David and make him pay.

Clifton rushed through the door and crouched beside her. He smoothed her hair from her face and gripped her hand. "Bettina, sweetie, what's happening?"

The concern in his kind eyes, so like Chad's, had her stupid tears overflowing again. "I'm afraid the baby's coming. Did anyone ask Johnny to call the doctor?"

Angelo appeared in the doorway, ever calm. "Johnny is at a meeting. Your mother called. The doctor is on her way and is bringing a midwife to help. As we agreed, we will avoid the hospital unless absolutely necessary. Are you able to walk? We should get you to your bedroom and settled in before they arrive."

Angelo's quiet authority helped her. She shoved aside her bitter thoughts. Their baby deserved a strong mother. "Yes, I can walk. Let's get this show on the road. Angelo, will you please make sure my camera is set up? Chad can't miss this. And, um, if you don't mind, could you ask Marion to help me? I think a warm bath is what I need."

Clifton and Angelo helped her stand up and walk to the bathroom. Angelo ran the bath water. Clifton kept her hand tightly in his while she tried to relax on the chaise lounge next to the tub. He said, "Marion is at the market with Ralph and Asal. You may be stuck with us. I'm sorry. I'll do whatever you need and be as discreet as possible."

"It's all right. Someday it'll be a funny story to tell Chad."

Angelo ran his hands under the water and adjusted the faucets before turning to give her a frown. "We need to time your contractions. Do you have any idea how far apart they are?"

She shook her head. "No, like an idiot I left my phone in my room. They seem close together, though, and my water broke."

Angelo clamped his mouth shut and turned back to the tub. Clifton waved his phone in front of her. "We can keep track now."

"Oh good. Call Marion, would you? Ahh, here comes another one. Ooh, it's stronger." She focused on Clifton's hand wrapped around hers, crushing her fingers, as the contraction deepened and another sensation took her breath away. "Oh no. I think I need to push. Maybe it's too soon? Where's the damn doctor?"

Clifton's face paled. "Bettina, I think we better forget about the bath. Angelo, let's get her in bed."

The two men hoisted her off the chaise lounge and helped her walk back down the hall. She moaned with another contraction while they positioned her into bed. "Ooh, no. They're too close, or something. Ohh. God." She clutched at the sheets. *"I hate everyone who took Chad away."*

Clifton shoved pillows behind her back so she could sit up. "I know, sweetie, so do I. Every last damn one of them. Now, let's get you out of these clothes."

Angelo disappeared while Clifton peeled off her soaked, ruined shorts and undies. He reappeared with a pile of fluffy white towels and a mixing bowl with water slopping out. The psychiatrist's glasses sat askew on his prominent nose. She battled a sudden, hysterical urge to giggle and remembered. "Angelo, my camera. Please. Chad's got to see everything."

He shoved the box of tissues and book off her bedside table and deposited the bowl of water. He tossed the towels onto a chair. "I'll turn it on right now." Every day she made a video of her pregnancy to show Chad, *someday.* She didn't want him to miss a second of their baby's entrance into the world. Angelo straightened his glasses and fiddled with the camera she'd set up on a tripod. "We're good to go."

Clifton hovered beside her and Angelo stood in the middle of her bedroom. She loved them both, but wondered if they knew anything about babies. Another contraction began and intensified. She panicked. "Where is Johnny's damn doctor?"

Janice leaned against the door jam and gave her a bleary stare. "Bettina, honey, what can I do?"

The last thing she needed was her half-soused mother mucking around, blaming Rowan because Chad wasn't with her. "Find Dad and say some prayers for the baby, OK?"

Janice looked uncertain. "Are you sure? I could sit with you."

Another contraction started. The unbearable urge to push came over her again. "No, Mom, you're drunk. Just go. *Please.*" Her words came out as more of a gasp. Her mother turned and left without another word.

Clifton stroked her hair. "That took courage."

Angelo took her other hand in his. "You told her the truth. Good for you. The doctor should be here soon."

She moaned and gripped their hands. "Ooh, oh God, I don't know if I can wait."

A Week Later
Florence, CO

Harandi shook hands with Special Agent Foster. "Thank you for meeting with me. I'm appreciative of the opportunity to talk with Rowan, as well as get your take on his state of mind."

Foster faced him on the tree-shaded sidewalk in front of the unassuming brick building housing Louie's Place on South Pike's Peak Avenue. "It's nice to meet you, Mr. Harandi. Director Berenger asked me to provide whatever assistance I can. I'm happy to answer any questions you have about Milani, although you know him better than I do."

They entered the cool, semi-darkness of the bar and grabbed a corner table. Country-western music played at a decibel level ensuring privacy. The waitress smacked two frosted mugs of Coors on the table, grinned and winked at Foster, then swept away, her colorfully stitched boots crunching on peanut shells scattered across the painted cement floor. Harandi watched, appreciating her tight jeans, then took a swallow of chilled beer. "You come here often, Special Agent?"

Foster grimaced. "You've interrogated Milani. What do you think?"

"By now I'd be an important consideration in their weekly whiskey order. The waitresses aren't bad either, if she's any example."

"There is that. What's your continuing interest in Milani?"

"Unfortunately, he's the closest thing I have to family. I'd like the opportunity to explain to him why I did what I did. Once he's transferred to Houston, I've got a feeling things will move quickly."

"You mean as far as how they deal with him?"

"Justice is meted out quickly in Texas. They'll be anxious to see him get what he's got coming."

Foster took a long pull on his beer. "There's a certain inevitability about his status, which is a shame."

"I've been outspoken with Berenger regarding the entire debacle, but it's a moot point. I simply want one last chance to redeem myself, or offer my version of an apology for the way I treated a former close friend."

"I've read the transcripts. Milani knew how to push your buttons. I hate to admit this to a spook, but I hit a wall with him myself during one of our sessions."

He couldn't resist the by-play. "How so? The Bureau's interrogation techniques are designed to succeed where harsher methods have failed."

Foster chuckled. "Let's not go down that road."

"Agreed. What happened?"

"He answered my questions willingly enough during each session, until I brought up Danielle Stratton. That's where I hit the wall. Director Berenger didn't get far either."

"Meaning?"

Foster replied, "She made a few classic mistakes, which is easy to do with a man like Milani. She pushed him into a corner, and he told her to stick it, in so many words."

He whistled. "I'd have paid money to see that exchange. In my experience, she doesn't take no for an answer."

"You are correct. Milani is a tough individual, and I worked damn hard on gaining his trust. However, I'm afraid he's been screwed over too many times."

"I'm anxious to clear my conscience. Would you entertain a special request?"

Foster finished his beer and raised the mug. The waitress replaced it with another, its foaming head overflowing and pooling on the varnished table. "What do you mean?"

"The things I want to say to Rowan are of a private, family nature. If you'd consider allowing me to speak to him alone, just me and him, in his cell, I'd be incredibly grateful."

"That's a highly unusual request for a case like this. Especially when you consider he killed Ainsley when he was left alone with him in his cell."

Harandi swallowed more beer and covered a belch with his fist. "I know. But I'm not going to force him to defend himself. And believe me, if we weren't talking about a man who is headed for execution, maybe in part because of my own pride and stubbornness, I wouldn't ask."

Foster said, "Afraid you'll embarrass yourself?"

"You never know. Actually, it's more of an airing of family crap that's no one's business but mine and his. What do you say? Can I have a few private moments?"

"I'll allow you the opportunity to set things right, ask forgiveness, or whatever you need."

He finished his beer. "Thank you. I appreciate it more than you know."

ADX Florence

Rowan lay on the narrow bed and tried to ignore the agony in his body. Back spasms had plagued him ever since his sessions with Berenger. The meds helped, but nothing erased the pain completely. When he couldn't stand the thin mattress any longer, he forced himself upright and swung his feet to the floor.

The closet-sized cell closed around him. The silence alternately howled and whispered through his mind, taunting him. *How many years will you sit here, staring at these walls? You can't stop them from hurting you. You might as well be dead.* God, he must be losing his mind. He covered his face with his hands while his untrustworthy thoughts sheared off, dredging up too many gut-wrenching memories.

He'd been so lonely, for such a long time. Over the years, his fellow agents had misread his awful grief and pain. None of them had known about his engagement to sweet Michelle and his obsession with Ground Zero after losing her. They'd only seen his infamous affinity for Jack Daniel's whiskey.

Ralph had covered for him too many times. He looked up for a moment and pictured his hardnosed boss, shaking a finger in his face. Ralph had chewed his ass as often as he'd covered it, insisting he tow the law-and-order line. He missed Ralph and Chad. Mike and Gabriel, too.

Danielle's face swam into focus, and he closed his eyes. He took deep breaths and tried to push her image away. The irritating buzzer startled him and the door opened. He stared, shocked to see Harandi enter the cell. Had his mind taken yet another crazed turn?

Harandi stood silent until the cell door closed. "Hello, old friend."

Rowan heaved a sigh. "What are you doing here?"

"I wanted to see you, so I got Foster to agree to a private conversation. We need to talk, damn it. I have some things on my mind."

He couldn't believe what he was hearing. "We have *nothing* to talk about."

"I know you despise me. You'll never understand how sorry I am for not believing you from the beginning. And I honestly can't tell you how I've tried to help you, but you'll always be my friend and brother."

"That's a hell of a speech. Are you finished? Because other than your first sentence, I don't believe a thing you've said."

Harandi leaned against the wall. "Come on, Rowan. Can we cut the crap? I mean it; we need to talk."

He rubbed viciously at the tension in his forehead. "OK. Start talking."

"Thanks. Look, I found out Hancock and Talbot delivered Sa-id to Shemal. I have no intention of letting them get away with that."

"I see. If you'd bothered to ask Chad or me, you'd have known a long time ago, when it might have made a difference. But hell, while you're at it, give those two bastards as much leeway as you did me."

Harandi shoved off the wall and stood in front of him. "One way or another, I am going to rid the world of the pieces of shit who helped kill my uncle."

"Good luck with that. Before you go, take a look around. Because this is more than likely where you'll end up."

"I'm aware of the risks, but I'm not going to stop trying to find real justice. For both you and Sa-id. I wanted you to know."

The back-and-forth stoked his simmering anger. "You want *real justice?* What do you think I've wanted, all this time? We're done. Get out of here and leave me alone."

Harandi countered. "Could you drop the asshole routine for just a few minutes? I took the time to travel here because I want to make things right."

"You think *I'm* the asshole? You did *everything* in your power to put me here."

"Rowan, please. Listen to me. You need to know, even when it looks hopeless, *it's not.*"

He stabbed a forefinger at Harandi. "You know, sometimes it *is* hopeless. And you helped make sure of that. Hell, you should be accepting all sorts of accolades for your role in putting away a dangerous threat to national security."

"You can't stop, can you? I wish you'd wake up and listen. I don't want to end as enemies. Why won't you give me a chance?"

He scratched the stubble on his jaw, the itchy whiskers deepening his smoldering anger. "I seem to remember begging you to listen, to check out Shemal and Ainsley and that bitch Hennessey. But you *knew* I was a traitor."

Harandi pleaded. "I know. I couldn't have been more wrong. And I'm dead serious when I tell you I'm *damn* sorry."

The earnest words had bitterness rising, expanding in his chest, turning his anger to unreasoning rage. *"Goddamn it. I said, we're done."*

"You know what? We *are* done. I gave Whitman my resignation. I'm grateful to be out of the shit show I was dragged into because of you."

He forced himself up and stood wobbling, cursing the pain, cursing his wrecked body. Breathing hard, clenching and unclenching his fists, he glared at Harandi. "The *shit show* hasn't done much for me either. You had a choice, goddamn it. I didn't. Now get the fuck out of here."

Harandi met his glare. "Not until you listen. I haven't said everything I came here for."

He took a step, planting himself directly in front of Harandi. "You've had your private conversation. I can't help you with your guilty conscience. I don't want to hear anymore."

Harandi shuffled backward. "What the hell, Rowan. Back off."

He kept moving, deliberately stomping on Harandi's ankle with his good foot. "I'm so fucking sick of you and your lies. I can't stand the sight of your smug face." He slammed his fist into Harandi's belly as they both lost their balance and crashed to the floor.

They banged against the cell door. Harandi coughed and squirmed. "Get off me."

He struggled to his knees and realized he'd somehow pinned Harandi's arms underneath them. Adrenaline funneled precious seconds of power into his debilitated muscles. God, it felt *good* to *fight.* He took heaving breaths and landed another punch, squarely on Harandi's nose. "You let those two CIA fuckers take me. You let them hand me off to Shemal."

Harandi flailed and grunted while blood spurted from his nose. *"Ouch*, son of a *bitch*, I think you broke my nose."

He heard muffled shouting from outside the cell and ignored it. "You betrayed me, as much as Ainsley and all the rest of them."

Harandi grimaced. "Good Christ, you asked for *everything* you got. Now *get off me.*"

He raised his fist at the callous words, as the adrenaline dissipated and his strength drained away. He could barely keep from tipping over. "And you call me a *brother?* You stupid bastard, I didn't *ask* for *anything* I got."

Harandi twisted an arm free and clamped onto his wrist. "You're *still* so damned arrogant. No one can reason with you, about anything."

The pain roared back, wracking his entire body. He slumped over. "Fuck you."

The harsh buzzer reverberated in the tiny room and the door shoved against them.

A guard yelled into the room. "Clear the door. Move out of the way, *now.*"

Harandi spat blood and hollered, "Stay out. Everything's fine."

The door swung open, pushing them aside. Three guards rushed into the room. Rowan glimpsed the lead guard wielding his club. The hardwood cracked, excruciating, across his shoulders, knocking him flat atop Harandi's sweaty body. The other guards yanked him off, slammed him face down on the concrete floor, and wrenched his arms behind his back. While he groaned and tried to catch his breath, cuffs closed around his wrists and the guards pulled him to his knees.

Harandi, his face smeared with the blood still leaking from his nose, staggered to his feet. "That was uncalled for. Uncuff him, right now."

The lead guard pulled a white handkerchief from his pocket and gave it to Harandi. "With all due respect, sir, any further interaction between the two of you will take place in a proper interrogation setting."

Harandi grimaced and clutched the handkerchief to his nose. "All right, fine. Get him up, and then leave us alone. I only need a couple more minutes."

Rowan clenched his jaws when the other two guards hefted him to his feet and shoved him down on the edge of the bed. He hunched over, desperate to escape the fresh agony vibrating through his shoulders. Sweat dripped down the sides of his face and his nose ran, but no one offered him a hanky. He sniffed and glared at Harandi. "Get the hell out. I'm done talking."

The lead guard eyed him, then turned to Harandi. "Against my better judgment, you've got five minutes. We'll be right outside."

The guards filed out and closed the door. Harandi swung around to face him. "What the hell goes through your mind? You're damn lucky he only hit you once. I swear, I will never figure you out. You're as pig-headed as they come."

He sneered. "You're right. I'm pig-headed, arrogant, the world's biggest asshole."

Harandi retorted. "It never ends with you, does it? When will you face the fact that your own choices created the setup for Shemal? You could have cut your losses, at any time, and had a hell of a career in the Bureau."

Stunned, he couldn't stop the wave of grief rushing through his mind and pooling heavy and cold in his chest. "You think that's what I should have done after losing Michelle on 9/11? *Cut my losses?* I had to *look for her.*" His voice faltered. "I couldn't leave her there." Tears filled his eyes and ran down his cheeks.

Harandi stared, openmouthed. "Rowan, I'm sorry. That isn't what I meant."

"I never found her," he whispered. "I found Danielle, though. And I lost her too. I've paid for every goddamn choice I ever made. The bastards who forced me to make those choices are still out there. Go after them if you think you have to. Just leave me alone. *Please."*

"I'm sorry, Rowan, truly sorry, for everything." Harandi knocked on the door, pivoting back to him one last time after it opened. "Goodbye." Harandi hesitated for a moment, then left.

The door closed. The lock clunked into place, emphasizing his helplessness. His chest heaved, and the tears he hated streamed down his face. "Goodbye, *old friend."*

Harandi limped down the hallway behind the guard, the bloody handkerchief clenched tight in his fist. "Son of a bitch. *Goddamn it anyway."* He looked up, surprised they'd already reached the locked doorway. The guard buzzed it open and he stepped through.

Foster waited on the other side. "From the looks of your face, I'd guess things didn't go quite like you planned?"

"You were right, I should have handled this like an interrogation session. He's still combative, and he's got a big, fat chip on his shoulder where I'm concerned. I said what I needed to, and I tried to make amends. He rejected everything and shut me out. There's nothing more I can do."

Foster escorted him through the elaborate maze of hallways and locking doors to the outside of the imposing prison complex. Harandi's twisted ankle throbbed, and he swore as they hiked across the massive parking lot. They reached his rented Charger and Foster extended his hand. "I hope you got something of what you needed for your trouble. I'd recommend ice for that ankle and something a bit stronger than beer, Mr. Harandi."

He took the proffered hand in a firm grip. "Don't you worry, I'll take care of myself. This is minor. Thanks for your help and cooperation. I've appreciated it. Good luck with Milani."

"I'll keep trying to reach him, but we're almost out of time."

He settled into the Charger and replied before closing the door. "I'm no longer sure he's reachable, but I can tell you he's suffering. Beyond that, I can't figure him out." He gripped the steering wheel. "You know, today I pushed *his* buttons. That is not what I intended."

Foster commiserated. "I think you and Milani know each other too well. Old habits can be tough to break. It was a pleasure to meet you, Mr. Harandi."

"Same here, Agent Foster. Take care." He exited the parking lot and drove mindlessly, heading south on Highway 67. After a few miles, he pulled over and parked the car. He couldn't exorcise the image of Rowan, handcuffed and alone, crying in the bleak cell. From the beginning, Rowan had presented a coldhearted, calculating persona. But the man he'd observed before leaving revealed a depth of suffering he'd been oblivious to and would have sworn did not exist.

He gingerly touched his bruised, swollen nose while memories of their shared laughter and the endless, carefree summers in California echoed through his mind. He pounded the steering wheel. How had they gone so far off course? He stared at the highway stretching southward. He should have had an open mind; he should have listened.

Rowan deserved more than what he'd gotten, not only from the government and country he'd chosen to serve, but from him. He could only hope that the phone call he'd made would make a difference.

CHAPTER TWELVE

A Week Later
Washington, DC

President Whitman walked from the White House toward the Rose Garden podium with Linden beside him, followed by Berenger and Abramson. Harandi brought up the rear of the small group. He'd gathered them briefly in a solemn meeting to reaffirm his intent to pardon Milani and his colleagues. Berenger and Harandi agreed with his decision to announce Milani's indictment by Houston authorities. Abramson frowned, sweated, and uncharacteristically said nothing at all.

Later, he and Linden would travel to Camp David for a long weekend. Together, they'd watch Milani leave ADX Florence and arrive in Houston. He'd asked the warden, the Marshals Service, and the Houston PD Chief to provide video documentation of Milani's transport and final detention. His request may be perceived as petty by some. But since he'd been forced to perjure himself and risk permanent damage to his presidency, he wanted the satisfaction of seeing Milani get what he had coming.

He reached the podium, scanned the roped-off group of reporters with mics ready, and waited while Linden stepped to his left side, remaining slightly behind him. He opened his portfolio and scanned his remarks, having opted to forgo a teleprompter. Why did he feel as though he was attending his own funeral? Or perhaps the funeral of his political career or his presidency? At the very least, his legacy would be blighted, if not demolished by this fiasco.

Linden gave him a barely perceptible touch on the shoulder, and he realized he'd been staring at his notes, fists clenched, while the reporters' faces filled with voracious curiosity. He cleared his throat, forced his hands to relax, and smiled. "Good morning, my fellow Americans. I want to take this opportunity to publicly acknowledge the valuable role James Linden has played in the historic decision I've reached about a matter of grave importance. It speaks well of our country when a sitting President can collaborate with his predecessor."

He paused to flip to the next page of notes. "Many of you are familiar with the saga of former FBI Special Agent Rowan Milani. His career was marred by accusations of terrorism and treason, as well as the death of FBI Director Rodney Ainsley in Milani's Quantico brig cell. Former Special Agent in Charge Ralph Johnston and former Special Agent Chad Cantor were also charged with aiding and abetting Milani."

Forcing conviction into his voice, he continued. "Intensive examination of the charges against Mr. Milani during the tenure of his service in the FBI, as well as the significant contributions made by not only Milani but Johnston and Cantor in our country's covert counter-terrorism operations, in conjunction with President Linden's insight, have brought me to this announcement: There is no basis or substantiation of said terrorism, treason, or aiding and abetting charges."

He surveyed the group of reporters, taking pleasure in their intent stares. "I have therefore chosen to rescind my declaration of Rowan Milani as an enemy combatant. I'm pardoning him for each and every charge of terrorism and treason. I have also chosen to pardon Ralph Johnston and Chad Cantor for the charges of aiding and abetting. In addition, after extensive review, I have pardoned Rowan Milani in the death of Rodney Ainsley. These pardons are effective immediately."

The crowd milled and their murmuring rose in a wave. He raised one hand. "One moment folks. I'm not finished. The seven murders Mr. Milani is suspected of committing in Houston fall under the purview of Texas law enforcement. I chose, therefore, to notify Texas authorities of his pending release. The state of Texas chose to indict him. As soon as we're finished here, Mr.

Milani will be transported from ADX Florence to Houston by the Houston Police Department."

He took a step back and gestured to Linden. "Mr. President, feel free to add your thoughts." He turned to watch his predecessor, wondering if the lyrical voice would woo the reporters in the same way it had millions of voters.

Linden stepped to the center of the podium. "Good morning everyone. It is indeed both a historic and unusual event that President Whitman and I are jointly presiding over, as it were."

The murmuring ceased. Smiles broke out as Linden chuckled. "Don't worry folks, we're not planning to launch a co-presidency. Nor am I campaigning. I'm here to reinforce and add whatever insight I can to an incredibly complex, difficult, and utterly necessary decision your Commander-in-Chief has spent the past six months investigating, reviewing, and agonizing over."

Whitman watched in amazement as the reporters began nodding while Linden crafted a tapestry of commiseration and understanding. "When your President called on me, he'd already done the hard work the people of this country deserve. Because Milani, Johnston, and Cantor served on my watch as well, he asked me to review intelligence spanning the last ten-plus years, so sensitive it remains to this day only for the eyes of the country's chief executive."

Whitman found himself marveling along with the reporters, and he hoped, the entire country, over his own efforts. Linden vindicated him, nullifying the precipitousness of the pardons in a way he'd never considered. And based on his expertise with the national press, they were buying it en masse. Those same reporters would spin Linden's story for the American people. What he'd thought would demolish his legacy now seemed poised to enhance it.

Linden continued weaving his spell. "When I perused the intelligence and saw the efforts of Milani, Johnston, and Cantor in preventing terror attacks in this country, I couldn't help but concur with your Commander in Chief. Each of these three men made invaluable contributions to the safety and security of their fellow citizens. Juxtaposing those contributions against what at first seemed to be incontrovertible evidence of terror-related activities eventually led to President Whitman's choice to pardon these men. I cannot imagine a more magnanimous, as well as courageous, decision."

Linden turned and ushered him forward. "My fellow citizens, let me conclude with this final observation. We are truly blessed to have such a valiant adherent to not only the truth, but the rule of law at the helm of this great nation. Mr. President, I commend you. Thank you for allowing me to have a small part in this momentous day."

The reporters strained at the rope. "Mr. President; President Whitman; sir, have you met personally with Milani, Cantor, and Johnston?"

He observed with a practiced eye and chose one face out of the sea facing him. "Les, you're up."

The CNN reporter wasted no time. "Thank you, Mr. President. Will you consider making the video of Milani murdering Rodney Ainsley available to us, so we may fully understand your decision regarding that specific act being pardoned?"

"At this point, with due respect for former FBI Director Ainsley, I do not believe releasing the video would serve any good purpose. It has been more than adequately reviewed by former President Linden, FBI Director Berenger, and myself, of course."

He pointed at another reporter. "Your turn, Charlotte. How are you feeling today, by the way? You were under the weather at my last presser, if I recall. I missed you."

From CBS, a no-nonsense grande dame of the news, Charlotte liked him. "Thank you, Mr. President. I'm feeling very well. Have you consulted with any of our allies regarding this decision, since Milani may have operated in other countries at your behest? And specifically, how did you ascertain that Milani is not a double agent?"

"Ah now, no sneaking in two questions, my dear. I did not see the need to involve any of our allies in my decision-making process because Milani did not operate in other countries under my auspices. Now, one more question. How about you, Jack?" The FOX News reporter's abrasive attitude galled him, but if he didn't offer the reporter a chance to ask a question, half the country would scream bias.

McKenzie thrust his mic forward. "Mr. President, Milani considers the seven dead in Houston to be part of his efforts in counter-terrorism, and thus they fall under federal jurisdiction. Why did you choose not to pardon him for those specific deaths?"

How did a FOX investigative reporter know anything about what Milani thought? "Aw, come on Jack. Far be it for me to put pressure upon the great state of Texas. I have complete confidence in Texas's legal system and am certain justice will be served. That's it, folks. Thank you for your attendance." He waved, turned in step with Linden, and left the crowd of reporters still clamoring for attention. He'd never felt more relieved, or more grateful.

DC County Jail

Chad looked up from the narrow bed when the lock buzzed and his cell door opened. A tall, blonde woman who looked familiar stepped inside with a guard, but left the door open. The guard carried a plastic bag, but he couldn't tell what it contained. Why hadn't he been asked to approach the door so they could restrain him? "Who are you? What's going on?"

The woman crossed her arms and surveyed him. "Mr. Cantor, I'm FBI Director Berenger. Certain events have taken place, and I wanted to notify you personally."

"What kind of events?"

"You're leaving, Mr. Cantor. The President announced your pardon a few minutes ago. He signed it earlier in the Oval Office. Your personal copy is in the bag with your things."

He stared at her. "Uh, I can leave this cell? I can walk out of County a free man?"

"Yes, you may. I've taken care of the paperwork myself. Your clothes are in the bag. You can change, and we'll escort you out."

He kept staring. "Huh. I don't have any way to get around. I'll need to take a cab or something."

The director said, "I've been informed that transport is waiting. However, I would like to chat with you for a few minutes first. When we're finished, I'll leave so you can change."

"What do you want, Director Berenger?"

She turned to the guard. "Step outside please." The guard obeyed, and she closed the door. "To say that the Bureau underestimated your talent and skill level is an understatement on more than one level. Now that this unfortunate *episode* is over, I apologize, on behalf of the Bureau and the entire intelligence community."

Her words meant less than nothing to him. An apology would never undo the anguish he'd endured or the awful months he'd wasted, sitting in the bleak cell. "I accept your apology."

"Mr. Cantor, I'd like you to consider something as you regroup and reestablish your life."

He knew what was coming. "What's that, Director Berenger?"

"I'd like to welcome you back, reinstate you as a special agent, and offer you a teaching assignment at Quantico. It's my way of expressing gratitude, as well as attempting to repay you for the indignities you've suffered. And in all honesty, the Bureau could use your skillset."

No way would he ever consider rejoining the government agency that had treated him the way the Bureau had. "I appreciate the offer, but right now I want to spend some time, a lot of time, with my fiancée and our baby."

She surprised him by smiling warmly. "I understand completely. I'll leave you to change now. Knock on the door when you're finished."

Thirty minutes later, he stood at the final exit of the DC County Jail with Berenger and the guard. She held out her hand. "Good luck."

He grasped her hand in a firm shake. "Thank you."

Berenger's chin rose, and she let go of his hand. "My offer stands, Mr. Cantor. I hope you'll contact me when you're ready to reengage your professional life."

He resisted the urge to tell her to *piss off.* "I'll think about it."

"Please do. I meant every word. Take care." The guard pulled open the door. Berenger waved him through and remained inside.

He stepped into a confusing mixture of bright sunshine, humidity, grass, trees, and traffic noise. Someone waved from next to a black limo parked on the street. He squinted as he walked slowly down the sidewalk. "Ralph?"

His former boss met him in a crushing hug, then held him at arms' length. "It's damn good to see you. Let's get out of here. Just standing outside the doors of this place gives me the heebie-jeebies."

He followed Ralph into the spacious interior of the limo. "I can't believe I'm out of there."

Ralph faced him from the opposite side. "You're gonna be fine, son. It's all over and done now."

He blinked back unwanted tears and looked away, at the crush of vehicles on the busy street. It felt odd to be outside the confines of the jail, not restrained, with no watchful guards escorting him, gripping his arms. "What about Bettina and our baby? And my dad?" He stopped talking, trying to process his jumbled thoughts. "Wait, where is Rowan? Why isn't he here with us?"

Ralph grimaced. "That prick Whitman claimed he couldn't pardon Rowan for the people he killed in Houston. Bettina and your child are waiting for us in Chicago. Your dad stayed with her."

"I can't wait to see them. But what the hell happened to Rowan?"

"The authorities in Texas want to prosecute him. They're transporting him to Houston today. But don't worry, Johnny took care of that problem, too. They'll be in for a surprise before too long."

"I hope so." He glanced at the driver. "Is this Johnny's doing?"

"It is. Johnny moved everyone back to Chicago from Dubai. He arranged transport for you too, of course. Once we get on board at Reagan, it's a two-hour flight."

As the limo slowed in traffic, he heaved a tired sigh, on edge and frazzled by his sudden freedom. His mind churned with images of Bettina, a baby he'd never seen, and of Rowan, sitting alone and hopeless in a cell. He had questions, but couldn't arrange them adequately in his mind.

Ralph's comment about Dubai brought back the worries he'd never been able to voice to anyone. "Dubai, huh? I never knew where everyone went, or if Bettina was alone or safe. Jesus, Ralph. It was like being in Hell, every day. I couldn't stop worrying. I was helpless. I couldn't take care of her. I wondered, how would I know if something happened to her? Who would tell me? And that son of a bitch Harandi wouldn't believe anything I said. He wouldn't tell me where he took Bettina."

He took a breath, and Ralph intervened. "Easy now. Bettina is fine. She was never alone. The hell is over, and you can relax. You're free. We'll share some drinks on the plane, and I'll tell you everything."

He took a deep breath, then another, and wiped his sweating palms on his pants. He spoke, voice hoarse with the emotions he'd held back for too long. "Thanks, Ralph. I just need to see Bettina and our baby. Then I'll be all right."

ADX Florence, CO

Rowan sat in the interrogation room and waited. He'd refused to leave the cell after his last session with Foster, and the guards hadn't come back until a few minutes ago. He heard the familiar, soft knock, and the guard opened the door. Foster spoke. "I'd like to speak with Mr. Milani alone, please." The guard nodded and left. Foster sat down across from him. "Hello, Rowan. We've only got a few minutes, and I need to inform you of a few things."

The agent's somber expression had his heart rate ticking up. Something must have happened. "OK."

"A couple hours ago, President Whitman announced your pardon for every terrorism charge and Ainsley's murder. He pardoned your colleagues, Johnston and Cantor, as well. Cantor was released about an hour ago."

A frisson of hope shivered through his body and died when he saw Foster's eyes. "What else?"

Foster heaved a sigh. "I take no pleasure in informing you that the President did not issue a pardon for the murders you're accused of committing in Houston. You're being indicted on seven counts of capital murder. Your custody has already been transferred."

He tried to take even breaths while the words wound their way through his mind. His heart sank, remembering the cowboy detective who'd been so pissed off about losing the opportunity to make him pay. "I see."

"Officers from Houston PD are waiting to transport you. I'd hoped to find some sort of mitigation, but none is forthcoming. I intend to keep working on it."

"It's too late. You know it, and so do I."

Foster shoved back his chair and stood up. "As I've said before, the Bureau's investigation is ongoing. We aren't going to stop. We'll keep pursuing the truth. I'm hopeful we may still make a difference in your situation."

He contemplated the dull steel of the cuffs, always cold and unyielding on his scarred wrists. He looked up. "Thank you."

Foster gave him a quick nod. "You're welcome."

The guards led him to the same underground entrance where he'd arrived and handed him off to two uniformed Houston PD officers after a brief exchange of paperwork.

While one officer stood next to him with a firm grip on his arm, the other stood in front of him and spoke in a stern tone. "You have the right to remain silent. Anything you say may be used against you in a court of law. You have the right to the presence of an attorney before and during any questioning. If you cannot afford an attorney, one will be appointed for you. Do you understand these rights?"

He gave the only answer he could. "Yes." The officers led him outside, and he stumbled in the daylight, his heart pounding. They ushered him into a van and left the massive prison complex. As they drove south across the dry Colorado high desert, he closed his eyes. Everything he'd done had been for nothing. He'd lost, once and for all, and no *mitigating circumstances* would save him.

An hour and a half later the guards unloaded him at the FBO on the private side of the Pueblo airport and escorted him to a Learjet 35. He climbed the air stairs with one police officer in front and the other behind him. They shoved him into a seat, secured the seatbelt, and locked the leg irons to an eye bolt in the floor. A headache hammered behind his eyes and stinging tension knotted his shoulders. The chain and cuffs left his arms and hands at an awkward, uncomfortable angle. The leg irons chafed the already-tender skin above his ankles.

The thrust of takeoff pushed his gut to his backbone. His stomach growled, and he smelled coffee. When the jet finished climbing and leveled off, one of the officers took the seat across from him. "Are you hungry? We have some sandwiches on board."

He looked at the officer. "I'm not hungry."

"Suit yourself. We'll be arriving in approximately two hours. One of our detectives, Kyle Matthews, is meeting us. He seems extra-interested in your arrival."

"OK."

The officer lurched to his feet as the jet banked into a turn. "Enjoy your flight."

He closed his eyes. Shemal and the Brotherhood would finally be satisfied. God, how he wished he could go back. If only he'd listened to Ralph, Angelo, and Danielle. She didn't deserve any of what she'd already endured because of him. Now, she'd have more pain and it was his fault.

He thought about the stranger, the *being* who'd come to his cell in Tora. He'd seen a man, heard the tender voice he remembered from before, whispering; *Rowan, redemption is yours, if you choose it.* He knew, for sure now, it had been nothing more than an illusion. Redemption would never be an option for him.

Houston, TX

A rough shake jolted Rowan awake. His head snapped back, and his hands jerked upward. Searing pain enveloped both wrists and shot up his arms. He groaned and blinked. "What?"

The officer hovered over him. "Detective Matthews is waiting. Stand up. Let's go."

His body had gone stiff, and his feet were numb. His hands clenched in paralyzed fists from the unrelenting pain in his wrists, arms, and shoulders. "I can't stand up without help, and I need to use the head."

"We don't have time for that. You'll have to ask your friend for a potty break. I'm sure he'll accommodate you." The officer stooped to release the leg irons, unbuckled his seatbelt, gripped his upper arm, and lifted him upright.

He staggered up the aisle between the two men. They held onto his arms, or he'd have fallen face down. He navigated the steps with the officers supporting him. Blinding sunlight, oppressive humid warmth, and the acrid scent of burning jet fuel assaulted his senses. He squinted and sneezed.

Detective Kyle Matthews stood on the hot tarmac next to a black-and-white van with Houston Police Department emblazoned in black-and-gold on its sides. The guy played the Texas lawman to a T, wearing a short-sleeved white shirt, brown suit pants, cowboy boots, and a white hat. A hefty S&W 1911 .45 pistol hung at his right hip.

The officers shook hands with Matthews and exchanged papers while two burly police officers wearing SWAT vests crawled out of the van. They didn't look at him, just nodded at the officers and took a firm hold of his arms. They loaded him into the back seat behind a metal grate and secured the leg irons to an eye bolt in the floor. One of them jumped into the seat next to his, and the other one trotted to the other side of the van and got in the driver's seat.

Matthews climbed into the front seat and doffed the hat, scratched his head, and turned to gawk at him through the grate. "I've been waiting for this day, Milani. You remember what I told you the last time we talked? You probably don't, since you were doped up. Let me refresh your memory. I said, *someday, you may find yourself extradited back here for these murders. If that day ever comes, I'll find a way to get a few more details from you.* And now, *that day* has arrived. You look tuckered out, but we're gonna get right at it, as soon as you're booked into your short-term forever home."

He ignored the detective and gazed out the window at the cars whizzing by and the endless restaurants and strip malls edging the busy street. He needed a bathroom, a bottle of Jack, and a bed. In that order. The next few hours passed in a haze of all-encompassing pain, combining with hunger and muddling his thoughts, leaving him light-headed. His finger prints and mug shot would live forever in the Houston PD records.

Manhandled by police officers who enjoyed jerking him around, relief came when they released his wrists and ankles long enough for him to pull on a black-and-white striped shirt and pants even more scratchy and uncomfortable than the orange ADX Florence jumpsuit.

Finally processed, he slumped in a chair in a stuffy interrogation room. Matthews entered the room and shut the door. Hatless, his reddish-brown hair stuck out at odd angles. He slapped a legal pad on the table. "How you holding up? You look a little peaked to me."

He shifted in the chair and forced himself upright. He couldn't take another interrogation session. "Let's end this. I confess. I killed every one of those fuckers, and I'd do it again. No one believes they were jihadists in this country to cause harm, because no one believes anything I say."

Matthews pulled a pen from his shirt pocket. "First off, you lie. Marta Pinella was an American citizen who'd committed no crime. She did not deserve to die."

Beyond weary, he eyed the lanky detective. "Like I said, no one believes me, so proceed with your indictment. I'm guilty, and I'm done fighting. I'd give anything for a sandwich and a glass of water."

"Your indictment is already done, and you'll get something to eat and drink later."

"What are you talking about? I just got here."

Matthews' upper lip curled. "Well thanks to David Harandi, I knew over a month ago you were headed here. Our DA jumped on your case, you might say."

It figured. He thought about David's visit to his cell in ADX Florence. "You should remember, David is a CIA tool. He doesn't do anything that doesn't somehow benefit him."

"He believes your pack of lies, in case you didn't know. I halfway believed you too, but I couldn't find any proof of terror-related activities among those six men."

"Speaking of liars, you should also remember, David lies his ass off. And look, Shemal and the Brotherhood have brought people into this country under the noses of law enforcement for years and have kept them off the radar. Did you ever wonder why they went to such great lengths to discredit me?"

Matthews jotted notes on the legal pad before responding. "Because you figured out what they were doing? That still doesn't explain Ms. Pinella's death."

"She collaborated with Shemal. She did everything she could to help him find me and shut me up. You know something, Detective? There are people in this world who need killing and goddamn it, she was one of them."

Matthews scrawled some more on the yellow pad and looked up. "Sounds like retribution to me. You got even with a defenseless woman in a cruel fashion, and you murdered six men whose only crime was being in the country illegally. That's what you're up against with a jury of your peers."

He raised a brow. "A jury of *my peers?* They'd acquit me in short order. I don't have anything else to say."

Matthews slapped the pen down on the legal pad. "I told you, we'd get at the details. I meant what I said."

"You want to water board me, Detective? String me up? My answers aren't going to change. But hell, I can't stop you. Go for it."

The detective stuffed the pen back in his pocket, ripped the page from the legal pad, and folded it into a square before tucking it behind the pen. "Your attorney will be here shortly. Guess I shoulda' told you right off, before you confessed an' all."

Surprised, he stared at Matthews. "My attorney? I don't have an attorney."

"You do now. Some big shot from Austin. I wanted a whack at you before you got all lawyered up. Thought maybe we'd get somewhere, but you're still the same stone-cold killer I saw the first time."

He slouched lower in the chair. For some reason, he thought about the picture he'd seen in the detective's wallet. Not thinking, he said, "You've got a nice family. How old are your kids?"

Matthews glared at him. "You leave my family out of this, you hear? Don't think you can threaten them, or I'll do worse than water board your ass."

Dumbfounded, he wished he'd been smart enough to keep his mouth shut. "Threaten them? No, I saw the picture, in your wallet, in the parking garage that day when I *didn't* kill *you*. I used to want a family. Thought I'd have one, until 9/11." What the hell was wrong with him? Talking to Matthews was starting to feel like a session with Angelo.

"Thanks to you, I don't remember much about that day in the parking garage. Besides all that, a lot of people lost loved ones on 9/11. It's no excuse for what you've done. And I honestly didn't take you for someone with a conscience."

Compelled to defend himself, he kept talking. "Those people weren't offered the chance to avenge their loved ones and every other person killed that day. I was, and I did what needed to be done. I eliminated the threat, wherever I found it in this country and a bunch of other places. I don't regret any of that."

Matthews shoved back his chair and stood up. "Just for shits and grins, tell me. What *does* a man like you regret?"

He thought about barred windows, locked doors, and razor wire. About how his life would end. In his mind's eye, he saw Danielle and wished he hadn't been so hell-bent on doing things his way. He thought of how much life he'd wasted, and how he'd messed things up for his friends. In the end, it had been for nothing. He met the detective's quizzical stare. He wanted to say, *I regret everything.* But the hell with the truth. He'd say what the detective would expect from a *man like him.* "Getting caught."

Matthews snorted. "I shoulda' known."

The door opened, admitting a black-haired man wearing a navy blue three-piece suit with a red silk tie and gold cufflinks that gleamed against a stark white shirt. He'd bet the cut allowing the man's hair to feather precisely across his tanned forehead had cost a fortune. The man dropped his briefcase and placed manicured hands on slim hips, slanting a look from him to Matthews. "I'm attorney Vincent Black. What is going on here? I *specifically* advised Houston PD about not interviewing my client. I was informed exactly ten minutes ago that he'd been booked and was waiting to see me."

Matthews faced the attorney. "And here he is, as promised. We were just having a conversation. You know, sort of like old friends getting reacquainted."

The attorney's eyes narrowed. "Homicide Detective Kyle Matthews, if I'm not mistaken. You have gravely overstepped your authority. I will address your actions with the DA and your Internal Affairs department when I'm finished here. Please remove the cuffs from Mr. Milani's wrists. Then you may excuse yourself."

Matthews opened his mouth, rubbed his jaw while his face reddened, and seemed, for once, to think better of speaking.

Instead, he produced a key and unlocked the cuffs. Rowan massaged his wrists and watched as the detective turned to exit the dreary room.

Black raised a forefinger. "One more thing. According to the officials at ADX Florence, Mr. Milani did not eat before leaving. The Houston law enforcement officers assigned to his transport reported that he did not eat while traveling here. He has now gone over eight hours without food and probably without water. Please see that he has food and water delivered here, immediately."

Matthews glared at the attorney. "Anything else?"

Black dismissed the detective with a wave of his hand. "That'll do, for now."

Matthews left, slamming the door. His attorney chuckled and held out his right hand. "Rowan Milani, it's a pleasure to meet you."

He did his best to raise his hand. "I didn't expect to have an attorney. I told Matthews I was guilty. He said I'd already been indicted."

Black gripped his hand in a firm shake. "Detective Matthews is out of line. He has no business involving himself with you in any way. This entire proceeding is out of the detective's purview, and he knows it."

"OK. What's next?"

"After you have something to eat and drink, you'll appear before the judge and be formally arraigned. You plead *not guilty,* return to your cell, and trust me to do my job."

"But Matthews wasn't lying; I have been indicted, correct?"

"Oh yes. On seven counts of capital murder. The DA in Harris County is looking to add more stars to his already stellar reputation. A grand jury was impaneled a month ago and handed up the indictment. However, you don't need to trouble yourself."

"Mr. Black, I'm not sure what you're planning, but this is a done deal. I know how it's going to end. I know where I'm headed."

Black gave him a fat-cat smile. "You plead not guilty and wait. That's all you need to do."

CHAPTER THIRTEEN

Chicago, IL

Bettina laid baby Cantor on his back and checked him over one more time. She smoothed his satiny black hair and wrapped him in the plush blue-and-white checked blanket, a gift from Marion and Ralph. She picked up the precious bundle and hurried from the room and down the sweeping set of stairs. According to Ralph's text, Chad should be arriving any minute.

She hovered near the double doors in the marble-floored foyer at the bottom of the stairs and hoped she'd found the correct entrance to meet them. Johnny's thirty-thousand square foot home had five or six double-door entryways at intervals along its curving driveway. She could see herself, baby in arms, running from one to the next, desperate to find her fiancé.

After the months of waiting, believing, and holding fast to the hope of seeing the man she loved, knowing he was finally en route had made the last few hours unbearable. Would he be the same man? What would he need? How had he endured, locked in a cell, subject to interrogation, never knowing if he'd be sentenced to life in prison or even executed?

She'd never been able to escape the images of leaving him in Quantico. His helplessness and the desolation in his face had left her staring at the ceiling in the Dubai apartment during too many long nights. She shuddered, then scolded herself. "Get a grip, girl. All that garbage is in the past. *He's free,* and he's going to be here any minute to meet his son. You can both start living again." Above all, she wanted to stay strong for him. And she would, damn it, one way or another. She'd make sure he had whatever he needed.

Chad strained for glimpses of what appeared to be an endless brick structure, tucked behind the tree-lined drive. Anticipation had him tapping nervous fingers on the seat, leaving tiny sweat marks on the smooth leather. When the limo finally slowed to a sedate halt, he fumbled with the door handle and climbed out, not waiting for the uniformed driver. He left the door open and stood on the paved drive, gazing at the massive brick home. It rose three stories in front of him and stretched on either side, edged by a walkway branching off to numerous doors.

Ralph appeared at his side and touched his arm. "Let's go, we're home. Bettina and your baby are waiting."

He felt weak-kneed, afraid to take a step. He looked at Ralph, saw concern in his friend's craggy face. "Uh, yeah. Home."

When he wobbled, Ralph gripped his upper arm. "Let me help you." Together they made their way to a double set of heavy, dark wood doors. He couldn't see through the panes of frosted glass that ran in a narrow band from top to bottom. Ralph entered a code on the security panel and opened one of the doors. "Go ahead, son."

He stepped into the coolness of a large foyer. Bettina stood in front of him, like a vision from one of his hopeless daydreams. But this was no miserable dream. She held their baby, wrapped in a blanket, and smiled while tears spilled down her cheeks. "Oh God. Chad. I can't believe you're here."

He stroked the lustrous, blue-black hair he loved, then folded her and the baby into his arms. He felt her body shaking while she leaned into him. "Bettina." Emotion clogged his throat; he couldn't say anything more. They stood, molded together, until he heard a squeaking cry. Shaken to his core, he drew back.

Bettina placed the warm bundle in his arms. "Here's someone who's been waiting to meet his daddy."

With the baby cradled in one arm, he surveyed the delicate face of *his son,* and breathed in the aroma of baby powder. He touched the soft cheek with trembling fingers. His son's pink lips pursed, then opened in a yawn, ending with another squeaky whimper. Marveling at the tiny, perfect face, he tried and failed to keep from sobbing. His shoulders shook while his tears ran freely. He took deep, heaving breaths, trying to regain control. "Sweetheart, I'm sorry. I'm so sorry I wasn't with you."

Bettina placed a hand on his cheek, then snuggled close beside him. "You don't have anything to be sorry for. Can you tell he's got your nose and mouth? And he's so long. Don't you love his black hair?"

"He's amazing; he's beautiful. I can't believe it." Tears filled his eyes again and ran down his cheeks. "I didn't think they'd ever let me go. I was sure I'd never see either of you."

"Hush, let's go upstairs."

He followed her up a winding staircase and down a broad hallway into the biggest bedroom he'd ever seen. Wide windows faced the drive and sent glowing shafts of sunlight across the white carpet. A king-sized bed sat against the adjacent wall. The baby's crib nestled in the corner. A settee, overstuffed chair, and a rocking chair occupied the other end of the room, along with a huge flat-screen TV.

The bright cheeriness of the room, with its warm yellow walls, billowy white curtains, and comfortable furnishings lent a sense of reality he'd lost in the sterility of the small, bare cell. *His* life, with *his family,* could begin again, and he'd never let anyone, or any entity, separate them, no matter what happened. Bettina laid their baby on the bed, and he stood next to her, unable to take his eyes off of his son. "He is long, isn't he? But he's so little, too. How old is he?"

She smiled at him. "He's two weeks old. If he hadn't insisted on being born, we'd still be in Dubai." She grabbed his hand. "Your dad and Angelo helped me. We recorded everything. We can relax together and watch the whole process. I didn't want you to miss anything."

Staring in fascination at his son's tiny balled fists and spindly, kicking legs, he put his arm around Bettina, reveling in the warmth of her body close to his. “Can we watch right now? I want to sit somewhere and hold him, for a long time.”

“Of course. It’s almost feeding time, and as soon as he’s done eating, we’ll get started. You can rock him to sleep and hold him for as long as you want. We need to decide what we’re going to name him, too.”

He touched the miniature body again, awed by the knowledge that the tiny child was theirs. “I still can’t believe it’s over,” he murmured.

Bettina turned toward him, her body pressing against his. She reached up and cupped his face in her hands. “I love you, Chad Cantor.”

He took the time to gaze at her features. Her dark eyes, so like her brother’s, brimmed with tears even as the lips he’d dreamed of kissing lifted in a smile. He took a shaky breath and wrapped his arms tight around her. “I love you, too.” He met her lips in a kiss he didn’t ever want to end.

Late Evening
Houston, TX
Rowan lay shivering on the bed in the solitary confinement cell he’d been escorted to after his arraignment. He couldn’t sleep. His mind replayed the humiliating process over and over. Guards had surrounded him, two of them gripping his arms tight, making his injured arm throb. His hands were held at his waist by cuffs and a chain. Leg irons made his limping steps into the courtroom even more awkward and his always-running nose added to his misery.

The prosecutor, a sleek brunette in a red power suit, watched him with cold disdain, following his shuffling steps across the courtroom, until the guards pushed him into the chair next to Vincent Black, blocking him from her view. Black had told him about the woman the state had chosen to prosecute him. She’d brought over 250 cases to trial, twenty-six of which had involved capital murder charges. The ambitious attorney had secured the death penalty in twenty-four of those cases. He'd seen utter confidence in her stare.

Restless because of the images he couldn't stop, he forced himself upright and sat on the edge of the bed. He stared at the metal door with its barred grate and sliders for his hands and feet, thinking about the moment when the Honorable Samuel Caito entered the courtroom in a stark black robe. While the judge glared at him, Black lugged him to his feet. He'd been unable to stifle a groan.

The charges against him were read, the prosecutor asked for the death penalty, and of course, bail was denied. The entire proceeding felt surreal. Instead of a thank you, he'd pay with his life for ridding the country of those who meant it harm. In a voice he barely recognized as his own, he'd pleaded *not guilty,* then added *Your Honor,* at Black's whispered admonition.

Black had filed a motion of discovery, afterwards turning to him with a barely discernable wink. The imperious judge set a date for trial and smacked his gavel down hard, making him jump. He couldn't remember the date; his mind refused to absorb it, but it didn't matter because he couldn't sit through even one trial. He couldn't stand the scrutiny of his life and the mischaracterization of not only who he was, but everything he'd done.

Two plastic-wrapped vending machine sandwiches had been dispatched hours earlier to the interrogation room by a young police officer. The food had steadied his shaky hands, but now the stale bread and chipped beef sat like a sour, heavy weight in his stomach. He held his head in his hands while his stomach turned, and bitter saliva filled his mouth. He staggered to his feet and barely made it to the metal toilet in the corner before throwing up the sandwiches. He coughed and heaved until he spat only bile.

Clutching his stomach, he turned the faucet on the sink. A thin stream of water ran, and he cupped it with one hand. He gulped, rinsed his mouth, and returned to the bed. Every ragged breath accentuated sharp pains in his stomach. Hunched over, moaning, he wondered if he could change his plea. Let them serve their fake justice and put him out of his misery. He pushed off the bed as his belly clenched again. He heaved into the toilet, the sour bile burning in his mouth. His stomach had nothing more to give. He didn't either. He'd reached the end, in every way.

The Next Day

Vincent Black opened the door with *Conference Room* printed in gold letters across its glass pane. He pulled a leather chair away from the gleaming mahogany table and sat down, ten minutes early for his 9 a.m. meeting with prosecutor Chrystin Bently. He opened his briefcase and retrieved a pen and legal pad. Over the years, he'd found that doodling cartoon drawings of his wife Melanie's three cats helped him gather his thoughts. While he sketched, he thought about his adversary.

Researching the DA's big gun prosecutor had proven interesting. At fifty-years-old, the attorney had five years on him, had worked her tail off, and from what he'd gathered in the numerous articles he'd read, had risen through the ranks on her own merits. She'd positioned herself as a fierce advocate on behalf of crime victims and their families and was respected by law enforcement throughout Texas. He wanted to respect her too, but would reserve judgment until he'd seen how she presented herself.

At precisely nine o'clock the door opened. Bently had exchanged the red suit of the day before for a black one and looked ready to do battle, which he found amusing. But then, she didn't know the de facto war had already ended. He laid down his pen and smiled. "Good morning, Ms. Bently. I'm glad our respective schedules permitted this meeting."

She closed the door and leaned against it. "Good morning, Mr. Black. Let me be brief. The evidence against your client is, shall we say, overwhelming. The state would like to save the people of Texas the cost of multiple trials. We'd like to offer a plea arrangement. If Mr. Milani admits his guilt, the state is willing to forgo the death penalty in exchange for consecutive life sentences."

He picked up his pen and toyed with it, pretending to consider her offer. After a few moments, he laid it down and affected a sober, thoughtful countenance for her benefit. "As Mr. Milani's attorney, I am obliged to inform him of your offer. I will certainly discourage him from accepting it, however. I believe everyone is entitled to a fair trial, and the cost should never be an issue as far as I am concerned."

Bently struck a regal pose, reminding him of Melanie's blue-eyed tabby. He wanted to laugh, but kept his demeanor respectful while she spoke. "In addition, you may not realize this, but your client has privately admitted his guilt more than once to Homicide Detective Kyle Matthews."

"Yes, regarding Detective Matthews. I have spoken with the head of Internal Affairs. The detective overstepped his bounds by a wide margin when he attempted to interrogate my client, as you are certainly aware."

"While that may be true, if Mr. Milani does not accept my offer, the state will be relentless in its pursuit of the death penalty."

He would have expected nothing less from the state or its hot-shot prosecutor. "I understand."

"May I ask you a question, just between the two of us?"

"Of course you may."

"Why did you choose to represent Mr. Milani? He's a home-grown terrorist and a cold-blooded killer. Certainly not your typical client. If you are looking to make a name for yourself, may I suggest you've made an ill-advised choice of clients with which to accomplish that goal?"

He was ready for her. *"Alleged* terrorist and killer. Mr. Milani's situation piqued my interest early on. He has never been afforded the opportunity to defend his actions. I intend to see that he is given that chance. And may I add, ego is most certainly not the driving force behind my decision to represent him."

She replied, "I intend to serve as the voice of the seven people your client murdered. Is there anything further we need to discuss this morning?"

He retrieved a sealed envelope from his briefcase and held it out. "Although I filed a motion of discovery at the arraignment yesterday, I wanted you to have our request in writing."

She took the envelope and tucked it in her suit pocket. "Very well. The District Attorney's office will act to provide what you have requested as soon as practicable, as I am sure you understand."

He'd decided she was a bitch and a half. *Oh stick it,* he wanted to say. Instead, he gave her his best sham smile. "Thank you. Mr. Milani and I are grateful to the District Attorney's office, and you personally, for your prompt attention to our request."

"Very well. My office will be in touch."

"I look forward to that. Thank you for your time this morning, Ms. Bently."

She left, closing the door firmly behind her. He finished his sketch, adding bared fangs and chuckling. Mel would get a kick out of this one. He couldn't wait to see the prosecutor groveling before Judge Caito, asking for the charges against Milani to be dismissed. That would take her down a notch or two, and he'd thoroughly enjoy it.

Since he had a few minutes before he saw Milani again, he hit the contact he wanted on his phone and waited. The Boss answered promptly. "Vinnie, how goes the battle? Let me put you on speaker. Now, go ahead."

"You were right about the detective. Matthews had Milani in an interrogation room yesterday, working him over, before I could get to him."

"You put the screws to that son of a bitch. Whatever it takes. I'll talk to Sam. We'll make Detective Matthews sorry he ever laid eyes on Milani."

"I met with the prosecutor a few minutes ago. The discovery process officially starts this week. I told her about Matthews, and I've spoken to the head of Internal Affairs. The cowboy doesn't know yet how badly he stepped in it, but he'll find out. Boss, are you confident of the work your crew did?"

"Damn straight. Roberto confirmed when everything was completed. You don't have anything to worry about. The DA and his prosecutor are in for one hell of a surprise."

A voice he didn't recognize said, "Mr. Black, this is Ralph Johnston. How's Rowan doing?"

"Hello, Mr. Johnston. He's thin and in quite a lot of pain, but cognizant of his situation. I wish I could reassure him, but it's vital he remain unaware of how this is going to end."

Ralph said, "He likes to live on peanut butter and jelly sandwiches. You'd surprise the hell out of him if you brought him one."

"I can do that for him, Mr. Johnston. Thank you for the tip."

Ralph replied, "You need to know a couple other things. I swear he's got a death wish. Besides that, he's stubborn like a mule. If he's retained anything of himself through this, he'll try to bully you into doing things his way."

"That's good information. I appreciate your insights."

Johnny said, "You keep us informed, Vinnie. Thanks for calling."

"I'll do that, Boss. Have a nice evening."

The guards shoved Rowan into the hard metal folding chair in the interrogation room, secured his hands and feet, and left him alone. Exhausted after a sleepless night, he hunched over and closed his eyes. He hadn't been able to face the cold eggs and dry toast shoved through the slider earlier, and his stomach growled and burned. He leaned down and scratched at the stubble growing out of control on his jaws, driving him crazy with its itching.

The lock turned and he looked up. A guard entered, followed by his attorney, carrying two covered cups of what smelled like coffee, with his briefcase stuffed under one arm. Black addressed the guard. "Remove the cuffs, please, before you go."

The guard complied. He rubbed his wrists and gazed through burning eyes at the attorney that he guessed Johnny Giacopino had procured. Black looked as sharp as the day before, in a steel-gray suit with a crisp white shirt and blue silk tie. "Why are you here, Mr. Black? Like I said yesterday, I know how this is going to end."

Black handed him one of the cups of coffee. "Good morning, Mr. Milani. If you'll recall, I asked you to trust me to do my job. Speaking of which, I am required to inform you of the plea deal proposed by the great state of Texas. The prosecutor informed me this morning that if you change your plea to guilty, the state will spare you the death penalty in exchange for consecutive life sentences. You will, of course, decline their magnanimous offer."

He took a cautious sip of coffee. Surprisingly still hot, it cut through the awful taste in his mouth. "I want to change my plea to guilty. I can't— I mean, I don't want a trial. And I don't want consecutive life sentences. They can execute me. I don't have anything to live for."

Black sat his briefcase on the table and opened it. He rummaged inside, pulled out a brown paper bag and shoved it toward him. "I'd have been here earlier, but was informed that you have a penchant for peanut butter and jelly sandwiches. I brought two, one with strawberry preserves and one with grape jelly."

"How would you— never mind." His mouth watered while he pulled the sandwiches from the bag and unwrapped them. The first one tasted like Heaven on Earth. He licked grape jelly from his fingers and took a huge bite of the second one.

Black watched him devour the sandwiches. "As your attorney, I am advising you to decline this offer. It is imperative that the discovery process is allowed to go forward. I cannot emphasize enough the importance of you allowing me to do my job. You most certainly have a great deal to live for."

He finished the second sandwich and smirked at Black. "What do you know about what I have to live for?"

The attorney's cordial manner vanished. He spoke, his voice laced with menace. "Listen carefully. I'm in charge, I'm here to do a job, and you will follow my instructions to the letter. Do I make myself clear?"

His shoulders slumped. The future stretched ahead, bleak and empty. He'd go crazy sitting in the cell thinking about facing a jury. He met the attorney's glare. "Thank you for the sandwiches. I am not interested in changing my plea to guilty. What's next?"

"That's better. The DA's office has received my formal motion for discovery to begin. They'll delay as long as they think they can get away with, but will be forced to comply, probably within a week or so. My first request is to examine the limo where Ms. Pinella was found. I've also requested copies of DNA evidence gathered from the mosque. I'm asking to see your pistols and knife, as well."

"And then?"

"After the prosecution complies, we'll take the next logical step. Building a solid defense is my goal. The discovery process is crucial to that."

None of what his attorney proposed made sense. Whether Black realized it or not, the outcome was a foregone conclusion. "Any chance you could ask about pain medication?"

"Yes. I spoke to the infirmary doctor at ADX Florence. He contacted the infirmary doctor here. You'll receive regular doses of pain medication, starting as soon as you return to your cell."

He'd give anything to take the entire bottle and end the charade his life had become. An idea tickled the back of his mind. Maybe he'd been given an opportunity to accomplish just that. "Thank you. I appreciate it." He yawned and sniffed. "I'd like to go back to my cell if we're done."

Black snapped his briefcase closed and stood up. "I believe we're finished for the time being." He knocked briskly on the door.

The guard stepped inside. "What do you need?"

"Mr. Milani and I are finished."

The guard didn't answer, just cuffed his hands and released the leg irons from the eye bolt in the floor. The other guard entered and helped him stand up. He clenched his jaws when the man latched onto his wounded arm. Complaining would only give them reason to abuse him more. He didn't look at his attorney as they led him from the dingy room.

Back in his cell, he lay down on the bed and yawned. The guards surprised him by leaving and then returning with two white pills and a glass of water. The medication dulled the pain, and he couldn't keep his eyes open. As he drifted toward sleep, he tried not to think about the ugly ordeal ahead.

The Next Day

Captain Shirley Lavoe hung up her phone, took a deep breath, and closed her eyes. She'd just received the worst ass-chewing of her career, and she intended to pass it along, as soon as possible. She exhaled, opened her eyes and dialed the phone. "Detective

Matthews, my office. *Now.*" She hung up before Matthews could respond.

While she waited for her insubordinate detective, she reflected on her career, upon which his reckless actions had placed the only stain. The first member of her proud African-American family to graduate from college and pursue a law enforcement career, absolute integrity meant everything to her. Always feeling the need to prove herself as a woman, and especially as a black woman in a position of authority, she did not need Matthews going off on his own, directly against *her* orders, like a loose cannon.

The more she considered his ill-advised interview of Milani, the angrier she became. She stood and prowled her office, smoothing her gray suit jacket, wiggling her toes in the heels she abhorred but wore because she'd earned the right to dress the part. She watched as Matthews headed toward her office, observing the hitch in his long stride, courtesy of Milani's attack the previous winter. He paused in the doorway. "You wanted to speak to me, Captain?"

She returned to her desk. "Shut the door and close the blinds, Detective, and then sit down." She waited while he scowled and closed the floor-to-ceiling blinds, isolating them from curious passersby, all of whom knew about Matthews' obsession with the Milani case. When he'd finished and sat facing her, holding his hat, she said, "Do you know why you're here, Detective?"

He scratched his head. "Not for sure, ma'am. Am I going to be chastised by that city-slicker lawyer? All I did was take a few minutes to grill Milani."

"Chastisement by a city-slicker lawyer is the least of your worries, Kyle."

He protested. "Shoot, Captain. You know as well as I do that Milani deserved a hell of a lot worse than what I gave him for five minutes."

She raised an index finger. "That's quite enough. Answer two simple questions, please. Did I specifically tell you not to interact with Milani? And did I instruct you to allow HPD to transport Milani from the airport to Harris County?"

"But, I needed to question him. That despicable son of a bitch *owed me.*"

She sat up straight. "Answer the questions Detective, and watch your mouth."

He glowered at her. "Yes, you told me to stay away from him and yes, you told me to allow HPD to transport him."

"Yet you took it upon yourself to disobey not one, but two direct orders. From me."

"I apologize, Captain. But I didn't cause any problems. Milani admitted his guilt. He's a sorry pile of… I mean, he hasn't changed. I'm grateful he's finally going to get what he's got coming to him."

"Oh yes, I'm sure he will. And now, so will you. Effective immediately, you are suspended, indefinitely and without pay. You're on shaky ground, Kyle. I suggest you go home and give your career some serious thought."

"What? For taking a few minutes to grill Milani?"

She clasped her hands together and gave him a hard stare. "You seem incapable of understanding the seriousness of what you've done. The head of Internal Affairs just spent fifteen minutes altering the shape of my ass. You have put my career in some jeopardy. Your reckless actions have cast aspersions on my ability to manage my squad."

He blushed to the roots of his reddish-brown hair. "Oh. Well. Ma'am. Uh, Captain, I had no intention of making you responsible for my actions."

"Yet, as your captain, I am responsible. You interfered in an important multiple murder case involving a high-profile defendant. The judge in the case, the Honorable Samuel Caito, has filed a complaint as well."

He finally had the grace to squirm. "Oh. I'm sorry, Captain."

She clenched her hands together. "You know, Detective, in this instance, *sorry* just doesn't cut it for me. I need your badge and firearm, please."

He swallowed hard. "All right."

She'd also heard directly from the Chief of Police and wouldn't soon forget his exact words: *If you value your career, this type of insubordination will never happen again. Do you understand, Captain Lavoe?* She'd understood perfectly. "In this instance, you have no recourse, Detective, and neither do I. What's done is done, and you earned it."

He placed the hat on his head and stood up. He unholstered and unloaded his pistol and laid it on her desk, along with his badge and ID. "If we're finished, I'll clear out my things and be on my way."

"We're quite finished, Detective."

He nodded and left without saying more. Hopefully, he'd learn from a few months without pay and choose to get over his obsession with making Milani pay for almost killing him.

Two Weeks Later, Mid-September

Chrystin Bently sat behind her desk, paging through the pile of papers atop the stack of files she'd planned to work on that afternoon. However, her phone had not ceased ringing since lunchtime. Even with her savvy assistant fielding most of the calls, she'd spent much too long on the phone. A glance at the clock on the wall opposite her desk told her she had only minutes before Vincent Black arrived to examine the evidence she'd promised to produce. She'd taken as long as possible to respond to his request. Two weeks might have been pushing it, but the District Attorney's Office handled many such requests, and Vincent Black needed to understand that.

A knock on her closed office door enhanced her irritation. "Come in."

Her clerk opened the door and slid through, closing it behind her. "Sorry to disturb you, ma'am. I thought you'd want to know right away."

"Where have you been, Sydney? Is the evidence locked in the conference room, as I requested?"

The young woman wavered in front of the door. "Ms. Bently, the police officers did not find a record of the evidence you asked for. Also, they were not able to locate the limousine or any record of it."

Her irritation reached full-blown status. She glared at her clerk. "Did the officers say they found no *record* of the evidence or that the evidence was not in its assigned location?"

"The officers were quite specific. They both said no record of any such evidence had been logged into the system, either digitally or on paper, including the limousine."

"That *is not* possible. Inform them that they need to look again. No, inform them that they *will* look, until they find the evidence. Accompany them and make sure they collect the evidence and bring it here."

"I'll tell them exactly that, Ms. Bently."

"And one more thing."

"Yes ma'am?"

"Keep me informed of your progress. I'll expect to hear from you within the hour."

"Absolutely, ma'am." Her clerk fled the office.

She scrambled to collect her thoughts. The Houston Police Department dealt with corruption and incompetence in its handling of evidence, even after serious efforts to correct the problems. The items she'd requested had most likely been misplaced somehow, somewhere in the vast Property Room. Except for the limo. How did an automobile, especially one as distinctive as a limousine, get misplaced?

Her phone buzzed and she answered. “Yes?”

Her secretary said, “Mr. Black is here to see you ma’am.”

“Escort him to the conference room, please.” She smacked the receiver down, harder than she intended, and strove to rein in her burgeoning angst. The last thing she needed was the über-confident attorney accusing her of obstructing the discovery process.

She left her office, walked slowly down the hall, and stopped at the closed conference room door. Vincent Black must not see either her irritation or her uneasiness. However, the missing or misappropriated evidence left her in unfamiliar territory, which she needed to navigate with care. She was accustomed to using her tactics and skill to place her opponents behind the eight ball. Yet it seemed that through no fault of her own, she’d been placed there. She opened the door and stepped inside.

Black waited, seated at the table. “Good afternoon Ms. Bently. Thank you for meeting with me. I’m looking forward to examining the evidence you’ve procured on our behalf. Also, may I offer you a ride to the impound lot to examine the limousine?”

She tried for a gracious smile. “It’s my pleasure to meet with you.”

Black replied. “I’m ready to get started. Or would you prefer to visit the impound lot first?”

“Mr. Black, please accept my apology. We are not in possession of the evidence you asked to see.”

His voice took on a hard edge. “Excuse me? I’m not playing that game, Ms. Bently.” Black stabbed a forefinger on the table. “If memory serves, we’re meeting here for the express purpose of examining Mr. Milani’s weapons and the documentation of DNA evidence gathered at the mosque, and then traveling to the impound lot to look at the limousine he supposedly commandeered while allegedly at the mosque.”

She glanced at the door, uneasy being alone with him, for no reason she could understand. "I'm certainly not interested in game playing, Mr. Black. However, as you are probably aware, the Houston Police Department has had issues with evidence storage."

"I'm from Austin, Ms. Bently. I'm well-acquainted with *issues* within police departments. However, I find your inability to produce evidence for discovery after two weeks to be quite disturbing. In fact, it smacks of obstruction."

Leaning against the door with her arms crossed made her more comfortable, or perhaps less wary. She'd best keep his Dr. Jekyll and Mr. Hyde personality in mind as they approached trial. "I am interested in nothing other than moving this process forward in a timely manner. My clerk is overseeing the police officers as we speak. I expect to hear from her within the hour."

Black shoved his chair back and stood up. "My time is valuable, Ms. Bently. I suggest we proceed to the impound lot to inspect the limousine. When we return, I expect to see the evidence and documentation I requested."

Should she mention the missing limo? No, the police officers had probably made a mistake. "Yes, I'll follow you there."

Black's congenial nature returned. "My driver is standing by. No need to take two cars. Allow me to offer you a lift."

Still uneasy, she agreed. "Thank you."

Two dispiriting hours later, they stood in the broiling heat on the concrete, in the middle of the impound lot. Accompanied by the supervising officer on duty, they'd spent the previous almost hour-and-a-half searching the lot. Located on a tree-lined property in a shabby area of Humble, surrounded by a six-foot chain link fence topped with razor wire, the lot housed numerous vehicles, storage sheds, and flatbed trailers.

At first, she'd insisted they see the records for vehicles delivered, as well as the towing companies involved. She'd been stunned to find no record, either on paper or in the supervisor's computer, for either delivery or removal of a Cadillac limousine. Certain a mistake had been made, she'd insisted on searching. Black had emphatically agreed. No vehicle even close to the description she'd been given existed within the impound lot.

Both she and Black questioned the supervising officer, but he explained that different officers rotated through shifts and assignments at the lot every day.

Black mopped sweat off his forehead with a pristine white handkerchief. "Ms. Bently, this is beyond strange. I suggest we return to your office."

In the air-conditioned back seat of his spacious Lincoln Town Car, grateful for the respite from the relentless heat, she remembered her phone. She listened with increasing dismay to her clerk's messages.

The officers had shown her the logs from the Property Room. She'd perused the computer records. According to the logs and digital records, the evidence did not exist. The police officers had balked at continuing to search for non-existent evidence and had finally deserted her. She'd gone to the forensic lab at Methodist Hospital and found the same situation. No record existed showing any DNA evidence entered in the Milani case.

Bently laid her phone in her lap and stared out the window. She needed time to regroup before informing Black that no evidence would be forthcoming.

Black conversed quietly with his driver, then turned to address her. "Perhaps the limousine is parked in a different impound lot. I'd like you to look into that, Ms. Bently."

"I will make it a priority, Mr. Black." She hesitated, and decided to wait until safely returned to her office before informing him that the evidence he'd requested was still missing. Within forty minutes, they were back at the table in the conference room. She left the door open and faced him. "I spoke with my assistant regarding the evidence you requested."

"And?" His lean frame put him at least a half a foot taller than her five-foot-six-inch height *with* heels. Never before had she felt intimidated by an opponent, but there was something about him that kept her on guard. His taciturn driver had given her pause as well. He wore a cap drawn low with sunglasses, had a stocky frame, and thick black hair that stuck out in tufts beneath the cap.

Together, the two men gave her a different sort of inkling. She couldn't put her finger on it, and she didn't have time to think about it. "A diligent search did not produce the evidence. The police officers were correct. My assistant found no record of Milani's weapons ever being entered into the system. She found the same scenario at Methodist Hospital's forensic lab when she sought the DNA evidence documentation."

Black regarded her for a long moment. "Well then, Ms. Bently, expect my written request to arrive on your desk first thing tomorrow morning. I insist the remainder of the evidence in Mr. Milani's case be produced post-haste. Certainly, I don't need to remind you that examining the evidence is a vital part of building a strong defense."

"I need no reminders on criminal trial procedures, Mr. Black, and I will entertain your request in a timely manner."

"See that you do. I'll be on my way."

Intending to chastise him for treating her like an associate in a low rent firm, she fired back. "If we encounter further difficulties with the evidence, perhaps you'll entertain the possibility of the plea agreement we spoke about earlier."

The attorney's eyes widened visibly and his mouth dropped open. "Ms. Bently, if you choose to employ tactics to delay the discovery process in order to force a plea deal, we have a serious problem."

His zinger hit home. She felt the burn in her cheeks. "I will not dignify that statement with a response. Good day, Mr. Black."

He stalked from the room. She slid into one of the leather chairs and stared unseeing down the length of the table. The cheery bouquet of daisies in a bright yellow pitcher went unnoticed as she considered the possible ramifications of missing evidence. Milani's weapons must have been misplaced, labeled incorrectly, or simply lost.

And the DNA evidence must exist somewhere. It had to. Perhaps it had been sent to another lab, or mislabeled, or lost. But the limousine? She had no shortage of coincidences in place of evidence. Should she call her boss? The District Attorney took a no-nonsense approach to his prosecutors. She'd had no trouble living up to his stratospheric standards in the past, but she'd never found herself in this kind of situation before.

She stood up. *No.* She wouldn't trouble her boss with what tomorrow's evidence retrieval would reveal as a simple anomaly in a complex case. Mind made up, she returned to her office. On a whim, she made a call. A deep Texas drawl answered right away. "Kyle Matthews. How may I help you?"

"Detective, this is Chrystin Bently. I'm prosecuting the Milani case."

"Ms. Bently, as you must know, I'm on indefinite suspension from Houston PD."

"Yes, I am aware of your status. However, I have a question, if you don't mind."

"Anything to help, Ms. Bently."

"After Milani's initial arrest, did you examine any of the evidence collected?"

"I did. Why?"

"The limousine, his weapons, and DNA evidence is missing."

Matthews exploded. *"What?* I entered his weapons and the limo into evidence myself."

"The police officers sent to retrieve the weapons and DNA evidence found no record of those items ever being admitted into evidence storage. We were unable to locate the limousine today. Is it possible the vehicle was moved to another lot in the city?"

"Not likely. It has to be there. Same with the weapons and DNA evidence. Some bonehead could have moved things around, been sloppy with storage and what not. If there's no record of check-out of the evidence, then like I said, it has to be there."

"Thank you, Detective Matthews. You've eased my mind, somewhat. But I have to tell you, I searched the impound lot myself. The limousine is not there. I will follow up on the check-out records, just in case. And we'll double down on our search."

"Well that's a head-scratcher. If I hadn't been declared persona non grata, I'd help you out. Good luck. Put that SOB on death row where he belongs."

"I intend to do that. You have a good day, Detective."

CHAPTER FOURTEEN

Vincent Black slid into the rear seat of the Town Car and let Gino shut the door. He leaned back against the cool leather and grinned. He couldn't have written a better script than what Bently had provided. Her comment about the plea deal gave him the foundation for any number of insinuations of corruption on the part of the District Attorney, in connection with a certain suspended detective.

Gino flopped into the driver's seat with a grunt and put the car in gear. "Where to now, Mr. Black?"

"Gino my man, I'm in the mood for a bit of celebration, but first I'd like to check on Mr. Milani. Next stop Harris County Jail, please. After that we'll find a liquor store."

Gino pointed the big car smoothly into traffic and eyed him in the rearview mirror. "I know a downtown spot. You let me know what you want, and I'll pick it up while you hang with Milani."

"How do you know about a downtown Houston liquor store?"

The young man shrugged. "It's what I do. The Boss told me you like a fine liquor now and then, so I scoped out a few places."

He grinned again. "If you ever decide a move to Texas would suit you, let me know."

Gino's eyes narrowed. "I don't think the Boss would like the idea of you stealing me away from him."

He laughed. "You're a good man, Gino. In our business, you can't put a price on loyalty. Don't you worry, I wouldn't think of trying to steal you away."

"I'm loyal, you can count on that."

"And here we are at the jail. You make driving in this insane city seem easy. Thank you."

"No problem."

Rowan sneered at the backs of the two guards who'd shoved him into the uncomfortable chair in the interrogation room and left him cuffed and shackled to the table and floor. The guards never told him why they were taking him or where, just gripped his arms tight, as though they thought he'd try something. How stupid were they? How stupid did they think he was? He bent over and wiped his nose, sniffed, and shivered.

Enduring endless days in the solitary confinement cell, he'd had time for honest consideration of the choices he'd made. In retrospect, he'd been pretty damned shortsighted. He could hear Ralph. *Don't be an idiot.* Why hadn't he listened? Probably because he was, in all actuality, fairly stupid. He'd finally faced the facts. He was where he was because of the things he'd done.

Not that it mattered anymore. Aside from hating himself for the pain the conclusion of his life would cause Danielle, he'd come to terms with the entire mess he'd created, with help from Shemal and an intelligence community determined to see him destroyed. He'd pay, for things he had and hadn't done. He couldn't stop the process and neither could Vincent Black.

But he could control the final chapter of his life. Every time the guards gave him a pair of pain pills, he stashed one of them in a tiny pouch he'd made in the mattress, up against the wall. When he'd accumulated a few dozen, he'd end his story by his own hand and deny Shemal, the government, and the goddamned state of Texas the privilege of taking his life.

The decision gave him a kind of peace. He couldn't stand the thought of sitting through multiple trials showcasing the actions he'd taken, the sacrifices he'd made, and the life he'd lived, holding it all up for scrutiny, misunderstanding, and harsh judgment.

He'd be damned if he'd be declared a traitor to the country he'd given up everything defending and he wouldn't be called a murderer for ridding the country of the real traitors. No, he'd end it before they could torture him one more time.

The lock grated, and the door opened. His attorney stepped in and gestured to the police officer standing guard outside the door. "Please remove the cuffs."

The officer entered and removed the handcuffs before leaving and locking the door. He rubbed his wrists and gazed at the attorney. "What now, Mr. Black?"

Black gave him the fat-cat smile he'd come to expect, sat down across from him at the scarred wooden table, and opened his briefcase. "How are you holding up?"

"I'm OK." He'd figured out the attorney's modus operandi and kept his opinions to himself and his answers brief. Maybe he wasn't stupid after all.

Black produced two plastic-wrapped sandwiches and shoved them across the table. "My hotel restaurant makes a mean PB&J, so help yourself. I wanted to stop by and see how you were doing and let you know everything is proceeding as planned."

His mouth watered while he unwrapped one of the sandwiches. "OK."

Black continued. "The prosecuting attorney, along with that cowboy cop have unwittingly created the perfect storm. They're building your defense for you, in a manner of speaking."

He regarded the attorney with a raised brow. "I see." But he didn't. His future was cut and dried.

Black chuckled. "You will. Hang in there and don't lose hope. Things are going well, even better than planned."

He finished the first sandwich and unwrapped the second. He wanted to tell the slick attorney that nothing he did could change anything. But instead he nodded. "OK."

Black closed his briefcase and set it on the floor. "Preparing for this case, I studied your resumé and your background in detail. Before all this started, you had a hell of a career going. Not to mention your clandestine work."

He didn't know how to respond. Black sounded like another interrogator starting in on him. "Yeah. So? You have a question you want to ask me?"

The attorney replied. "I've spoken to your former boss, Ralph Johnston. He informed me of your stubborn nature and the death wish you carry around."

No wonder Black knew how much he loved peanut butter and jelly sandwiches. "Ralph thinks he knows more than he does."

"Oh no, I think he knows you quite well. Perhaps better than you know yourself."

He stuffed the last bite of sandwich into his mouth and mumbled, "OK. If you say so."

"I've spent some time trying to understand what drives a man like you, to do the things you've done. *All* the things. You've risked your life over and over, for years. Why?"

Drawn into the conversation because he had no choice, wishing for another sandwich, he chose, once more, to be honest. "I've always done what I believed needed to be done."

"At great risk. Not to mention, recklessness to the point of absurdity."

"In your opinion."

"You disagree?"

"Like I said, I did what I believed needed doing. Sometimes things get messy. If you don't take chances, you don't get anywhere."

Black said, "I can't decide if you're a courageous American hero or the President's hired killer."

"Let's just say the President's goals and mine happened to coincide."

"Ah, now that makes sense. However, I still don't understand the death wish."

He stared past the attorney at the grungy, yellowing wall. Black could never understand what truly drove him. "No, you probably don't," he murmured.

"Keep talking, Mr. Milani. I'm interested."

He dragged his mind back to the present. "I lost everything that mattered to me on 9/11. After that, I didn't care anymore whether I lived or died."

Black stared at him, intent. "Hence the risk and reckless abandon."

"I've said over and over, to anyone who'd listen; I want to kill the fuckers before they can make another 9/11. If I die trying, so be it. If that's a death wish, then I guess I own it."

"Yet, you met another woman. You gave up your freedom in order to secure hers and suffered for your choice."

The blunt comments surprised him; brought his carefully hidden pain to front and center. "I'm not having this conversation. Are we done here?"

Black raised a forefinger. "Not so fast. That's the part of your death wish I don't understand. Any woman that a man like you would walk into certain hell for seems like someone worth living for, in my book."

He stared at the attorney, struggling with the private pain tightening his chest. "You have *no idea* what motivates me. I'm done talking."

Black continued as though he hadn't spoken. "As your attorney, I pay attention to a lot of things. As I mentioned, I've studied your background, as well as the more recent events which are concluding here. I've studied *you,* and it's been educational."

Helpless anger overlaid his pain. "I don't care what you've studied."

"I believe in preparing to the max, but also learning everything I can through interaction with my clients."

"Good for you."

"When I told you to plead not guilty, and you balked, I let you know in no uncertain terms that you'd do as you were told. You acquiesced immediately."

"It's a skill I learned the hard way."

Black grimaced. "I can only imagine. Now think about this. One of the perks of being your attorney is my access to the video recordings which monitor your cell."

"What the hell does that have to do with anything?"

"I find great value in observing my clients. Every day the digital recording is emailed to me. I watch and learn."

He managed a weak shrug. "So, you're a voyeur as well as an attorney. *Nice.*"

"After that particular conversation, I got to thinking about what a resourceful man you are. You gave in so readily, I became somewhat suspicious. Eventually it dawned on me that you may choose to enter a guilty plea in your own way."

"I don't follow."

Black chuckled. "I have a feeling you do. You're collecting pain pills, have been for a couple weeks. By now you've probably got enough to make your death wish a reality."

He stared. "How did you figure that out?"

"I've studied you. And I saw you, on the recordings, stashing something. Then it dawned on me. As you stated, a man like you does what needs to be done. What I still don't understand is why, with a woman like Danielle Stratton waiting, you would choose to end your life."

"Oh, for God's sake. We both know what kind of evidence the DA has. My fingerprints, my weapons, and everything else proves my guilt beyond any reasonable doubt. And goddamn it, if you have to know, I'm trying to save Danielle from more pain because of me and my fucked-up life."

Black leaned forward and his voice took on an earnest tone. "I didn't plan to give you details, but since you're determined to take matters into your own hands, listen carefully. *You're going to walk out of here a free man.* It's a done deal."

"Don't blow sunshine up my ass, Mr. Black."

"Mr. Milani, let this one thought permeate your stubborn mind: Things you know nothing about have taken place over the last couple of months. These things guarantee your freedom."

He shifted in the uncomfortable chair, thinking about the stash of pills. "OK. If you say so." He'd keep his stash and see if what the attorney had told him turned out to be the truth or wishful thinking.

Black continued. "You are a most predictable man. I've instructed the guards to remove the pills from your hiding place in the mattress. From now on, they'll make certain you swallow both pills. As an added benefit, you'll feel better getting the amount of pain relief you need."

The attorney sure as hell knew how to piss him off. "Thanks for your concern. Now, are we done? I'd like to go back to my cell and lie down."

"Yes, I believe we've covered everything. We'll talk again in a few days, or maybe a week, depending on how quickly the prosecution handles my request. And like I said, you hang in there and trust me."

"Oh, hell yeah. No worries." Back in his cell, he checked the hidden pouch in the mattress and found it empty. He stared at the camera high up in the corner and raised his middle finger.

A Week Later

Bently gazed at the lean, sculpted features of her boss from across the expanse of his desk. His dark brown hair swept back in an imperious wave above his forehead. She tamped down the inane desire to ask him about his hairdresser. "Good morning, sir."

Bartholomew Newton, the Harris County District Attorney, known as Bart to his close friends and Newt to a special few, regarded her with the deceptive calm she'd learned to expect. "May I ask why you didn't bring this issue to my attention at the outset, Ms. Bently?"

"Thank you, sir, for seeing me on short notice. I chose not to concern you because I believed we were dealing with an anomaly. You are perhaps more aware than most regarding the issues Harris County faces with evidence storage and retention."

"Yes. However, need I remind you that we are dealing with a high-profile case involving the most wanted man in Texas, which by the way is a national story as well?"

Houston's rumor mill put the thrice-elected District Attorney in contention for the governorship of Texas. His political ambitions would not be denied, and she'd find her career on the ash heap if she didn't follow the correct script. "Of course not, sir. I am fully aware of the ramifications of this case on both a state *and* national level."

"Good. See that you keep those ramifications at the forefront as we proceed. Now, you stated that further requests for evidence have produced zero results?"

"Yes sir, that is correct. Milani's defense attorney has requested the evidence in its entirety. He is insisting on dismissal of all charges if we are unable to comply."

The DA rose from his chair. At six-foot-six, he towered over the desk. "Of course, any defense attorney worth his salt will press aggressively at even a whiff of a problem."

"Yes, sir. Mr. Black is a forceful advocate for his client."

Her boss adjusted his tie and glanced at his watch. "This situation is untenable, Ms. Bently. The state is not prepared to lose a case of this magnitude because of evidence storage problems."

"Agreed, sir. How would you like me to proceed?"

"You will initiate a search of the entire Property Room and Methodist Hospital Forensic Lab. Supervise it yourself and involve as many police officers as necessary to complete the search in two weeks."

"Yes sir. I will keep you informed of our progress."

His hand sketched a curt wave. "Unnecessary. Results are my only interest, Ms. Bently. The state demands them. See that you achieve them. We will meet again, two weeks from today."

She stood up and met his implacable stare. "Certainly, sir. Understood."

Two Weeks Later

Bently wandered her office, pausing to gaze out the window at the busy street four stories below, while she addressed the Property Room supervisor on her cell phone. "Sergeant Jenson, are you absolutely, unequivocally certain that the officers I assigned have completed a search of the entire building?"

She pictured the harried supervisor in his cluttered office. "Yes, ma'am. The team finished this morning."

"And you're telling me the search produced no physical evidence?"

"Correct. In addition, no paper or digital record exists to show that the evidence you seek was ever admitted."

"What about evidence check-out? And the cyber-security team? Did they discover any discrepancies involving the PD's server? What did your team find at the forensic lab?"

"Well now, let's take one thing at a time. If evidence hasn't been entered, obviously no check-out records will exist. The cyber team found no evidence of hacking into our server. Nothing untoward appears to have happened at the lab. Their records reflect the same as ours; no evidence in or out concerning the Milani case."

Taken aback by his snide response, she retorted, "Are you ready to sign an affidavit swearing to this? The District Attorney requires absolute proof."

"I stand by my word and my men. I'll sign whatever worthless scrap of paper you and your boss require. With due respect ma'am, this search has set us back a full two weeks. The evidence backlog affects other cases, and that becomes my problem. I need to attend to it. That is, if you and the DA don't mind."

Hating to grovel, but wanting to placate him, she affected a soothing tone. "Of course, Sergeant. Your hard work will not go unnoticed by either myself or the District Attorney."

He remained peevish. "Now that makes my day. Thank you, ma'am."

She ended the call and noted the time. Her boss expected her in precisely fifteen minutes and she had nothing. She rode the elevator to the sixth floor, her mind reeling with the gravity of the situation she faced. Her career teetered on the brink of disaster for reasons so bizarre she found them difficult to comprehend. She refused to believe the evidence had never existed. Her gut told her someone or some entity had scammed the Texas justice system in a magnificent and despicable way.

The District Attorney's secretary escorted her into his office. She surreptitiously wiped damp palms on her skirt and perched on the edge of an overstuffed armchair facing his desk while her boss perused a paper and made notes. She'd never been on the receiving end of his trademark, deliberate indifference; part and parcel of the DA's ability to demean his opponents without saying a word. Her record of success gave him no right to treat her like opposing counsel, or a clerk waiting for reprimand.

The office door closed and he looked up. "Good afternoon, Ms. Bently."

"Good afternoon sir."

He didn't waste any time. "Your results?"

"I spoke moments ago with Sergeant Jenson. The officers I assigned were unable to locate or account for a single piece of evidence. I'm sorry to report that PD digital and physical records show no such evidence ever entered into or removed from the system."

"And the evidence from Methodist Hospital's forensic lab?"

Her stomach tightened at the telltale red invading his face. "Non-existent, sir. In addition, the PD server shows no signs of hacking and neither does the forensic lab or the hospital server."

He rubbed his hands together. "In other words, we have no basis upon which to charge Mr. Milani with seven counts of capital murder."

"You are correct."

He slammed both hands on his desk and yelled. *"Well, Jesus H. Christ! Your answers are unacceptable, Ms. Bently."*

She couldn't stop her reflexive startle or the fierce heat crawling up her face, burning into her scalp. "I'm sorry, sir."

The District Attorney's lips formed a thin line. The muscles in his jaws bulged and contracted. "Apologies are for losers. Do you have any plausible ideas on how this travesty may have occurred?"

"Detective Kyle Matthews informed me that he logged some pieces of the evidence into the system. That means someone had to remove it."

"Matthews destroyed his credibility by getting himself suspended. A clever defense attorney would site Milani's pardon by the President and suggest that he'd been set up for the murders committed here by a zealous detective bent on making a reputation. Unfortunately, I must give that possibility serious consideration."

"Yes. I mean, *no.* I find it hard to believe Milani is not responsible for those murders."

"And yet, we find ourselves at this juncture, left with only one option."

"Are you contemplating an investigation of Matthews?"

"Regarding the circumstances within which we find ourselves, do you think I have a choice, Ms. Bently?"

Heat burned in her face again. "I'd have to say no, you probably don't."

The DA straightened his tie. "We will take the high road. I do not intend for this office to become a laughingstock."

"Meaning?"

"You will meet with Judge Caito and Mr. Black, informing them of our decision to dismiss the charges against Milani."

"Sir, there must be a way…"

He raised a hand, stopping her. "I'll hold a press conference after your meeting, announcing that the District Attorney's Office is magnanimously extending the same exculpation to Milani that the President chose to do."

"How will you explain the missing evidence?"

"Explain what, Ms. Bently? The District Attorney has recognized, as did President Whitman, the value of Mr. Milani's service to his country. Mitigating circumstances, in the form of a derelict former detective with an axe to grind, have encouraged me to follow the President's lead and dismiss the charges against Mr. Milani. Period. End of story."

If anyone could turn a looming disaster into a win without losing his gravitas, it'd be Bartholomew Newton. "I'll meet with Judge Caito and Mr. Black at the judge's earliest convenience."

"Get it done. We need to put this behind us and move on, as quickly as possible."

"Yes sir."

"One more thing, Ms. Bently."

"Yes?"

"Inform Mr. Matthews' superiors that he faces a criminal investigation due to his interference in this case. Someone is going to pay for this debacle and it is not going to be the office of District Attorney, or any of its standard bearers."

"I'll make the call right away."

The Next Day

Bently waited in the anteroom outside Judge Samuel Caito's chambers, dreading the meeting she'd requested. The double doors opened and Black sauntered into the room. She tried for a civil tone. "Good afternoon, Mr. Black."

"Hello, Ms. Bently. I understand you requested this meeting? Does it have anything to do with the evidence I'm still waiting for the District Attorney's office to produce?"

The door to the judge's chambers opened, and she bit back an answer to his impertinence. An aide summoned them. "Judge Caito will see you now."

Black motioned for her to enter ahead of him, and they proceeded into the quiet chambers of the Honorable Judge. The dark wood book shelves lining two walls, the heavy, chocolate-brown leather sofa and armchairs bespoke somber authority. One cream-colored wall held a gallery of framed degrees and accolades. A leather-topped desk took up one end of the room.

The Judge waited, seated in his high-backed chair with his hands folded on the desktop. "Ms. Bently, Mr. Black, please sit down. Ms. Bently, the District Attorney's office requested this meeting. To what do we owe the pleasure this morning?"

"Thank you, Judge Caito. The District Attorney's Office is asking you to dismiss the charges against Mr. Milani."

Caito's brows rose. "This is most unprecedented, Ms. Bently. Please expound, if you would."

"Certainly, Judge. District Attorney Newton has spent considerable time examining Mr. Milani's case. After extensive review of his service to our country, and in light of the President's pardon, the District Attorney believes this is the best course."

Black stirred in the chair next to her. "Judge Caito, if I may?"

Caito gestured toward Black. "Please address this situation."

Black said, "The prosecution has been unable to comply with my motion for discovery. They have not produced a single piece of requested evidence. I believe this is because the evidence does not exist."

Caito addressed her. “Ms. Bently, other high-minded deliberations aside, am I to understand the District Attorney’s Office has no evidence with which to pursue a prosecution of Mr. Milani?”

She withered inside. “Judge Caito, DA Newton understands the importance of the President’s decision to exonerate Mr. Milani. He has thoroughly researched Mr. Milani’s career and contributions to our country. While attempting to comply with Mr. Black’s motion for discovery, we were unable to locate any of the evidence. This cemented District Attorney Newton’s decision.”

Caito scowled. “This is disturbing, to say the least. Have you exhausted every possible means of determining whether this evidence ever did exist?”

She continued the downward spiral. “Yes, Judge. We conducted a systematic examination of physical and digital records, as well as a complete search of the Property Room, the Sheriff’s Impound Lot and Methodist Hospital’s forensic lab. No physical or digital record of evidence exists.”

Caito shifted his fierce gaze to Black. “Do you have anything to add, Mr. Black?”

Black replied. “Homicide Detective Kyle Matthews grossly overstepped his boundaries and attempted to force a confession from Mr. Milani through an unauthorized interrogation. I believe that for reasons we may never be privy to, Mr. Milani is the victim of a well-planned and executed setup.”

Caito shifted his gaze to her. “Ms. Bently?”

Black had performed exactly as Newton expected. She didn’t look at the attorney, although she felt his smug gaze. “The District Attorney is certainly aware of Mr. Matthews’ egregious overstepping of his authority. Whether he is guilty of the crime Mr. Black suggests is another matter, one we are prepared to investigate, but is not the reason I requested this meeting.”

Caito replied, "Yes, the detective's actions are indeed another matter. This is a most, shall we say, *interesting* development. I see no point in disagreeing with the District Attorney's assessment and recommendation. The charges against Mr. Milani are dismissed. I will inform the senior warden. Milani may be released immediately. Do either of you have anything further?"

Black said, "Thank you, Judge. I will inform Mr. Milani of your decision."

She met Caito's gaze dead on. "Thank you, Judge. I have nothing further. Good day."

Caito stood up. "Ms. Bently, Mr. Black, I believe we're finished here."

She stood, pivoted away from Black, and left without giving him the satisfaction of smirking at her incomprehensible, humiliating defeat.

Rowan waited, hands cuffed to the table, feet shackled to the floor in the interrogation room. His days and nights ran together, alternating between a medicated haze and a fog of unrelenting pain when the pills wore off. How long had it been since his attorney told him he'd walk out of the jail a free man?

The door opened and instead of his attorney, Detective Matthews barged into the room, slamming the door behind him, rattling the chalkboard on the adjacent wall. The detective grabbed the chair opposite him at the table and straddled it. "How is it you always manage to slither out of things?"

"I don't know what you're talking about."

"Don't screw around with me."

"I'm not."

Matthews glared at him. "You make my ass tired."

"You're at the end of a long line with that problem."

The detective gripped the top of the chair with both hands. "Your crooked lawyer has spent the last month mucking around with discovery, asking to see the evidence of your vile crimes, so he could prepare your flimsy defense."

"Normal procedure, if I'm not mistaken." He tried to gesture with his hands and winced. The cuffs dug into his tender wrists. On purpose. He'd seen cruel satisfaction on the guard's face as the cuffs clicked tight.

"And you'd be correct. It's normal until the evidence *disappears,* including every physical piece, every scrap of paper, and all the forensic evidence. The stinking limo is missing too. Would you care to explain?"

Now he understood what Black had been trying to tell him. "The evidence against me is gone, as in, it doesn't exist?"

"That's right, and I'll ask you one more time. Care to explain?"

"How would I destroy your evidence, erase the documentation, and lose a limo? In case you're unaware, I've been locked up and incommunicado for oh, I don't even know how long anymore."

"Stop being a smartass and answer my question."

"I told you, I don't know what you're talking about."

Matthews banged the top of the chair with a fist. "Stop with the lies."

"I'm not lying. Besides, why are you here? Aren't you suspended for doing what you're doing now?"

The detective shoved out of the chair and stalked around the room. "Kiss my ass, Milani. You're the reason I'm suspended, but you know what really pisses me off? The case against you was *airtight,* and somehow it's been dismissed. I don't know how you did it, but you get to go scott-free." Matthews returned to the chair and glowered at him.

He observed the red face and the veins bulging in Matthews' temples. The man had fallen off the deep end concerning *him* to a degree he hadn't realized. "Are you sure about that? I walk out of here?"

"Yes, you do. I can't figure it out. I swear, you've got the luck of the Irish."

The thickheaded cop's animosity toward him would never end. "While you're trying to figure things out, remember one thing. I've never lied to you about anything."

"All you do is lie, Milani, and I'm done listening. I'm sure your friends are waiting and your crooked lawyer will be wondering where you've gotten to." Matthews pulled a key from his pants pocket. "Are you gonna cooperate?"

"Yes. For God's sake, I'm not going to kill you."

"You won't ever get a second chance at that. I've only got one more thing to say. I'm sure whoever stole my evidence will give you back your pistols. Stay out of my city with them, you hear? Hell, keep out of my state, because next time, I will *have* your ass. And seriously, *Glocks?* Try a real pistol sometime, made in America, like a 1911."

The detective looked like he wanted to keep ranting. Rowan slouched in the chair. "Fuck you."

Matthews grabbed his wrists, wrenched them flat on the table and flourished the key. "Right back at ya."

He drew a sharp breath and clenched his jaws, but couldn't suppress a groan at the excruciating pain. He tried to breathe while the scowling detective unlocked the cuffs from the table and crouched beside him to release the leg irons from the eyebolt in the floor.

Matthews scrambled to his feet. "Let's go. Back to your cell."

He stood and met his enemy's angry glare. "You were right, you know?"

Matthews gripped his arm and jerked him toward the door. "About what?"

He stumbled, forcing Matthews to shove him against the wall. "You know, what you said about my cell. It did turn out to be my *short-term* forever home."

"By God, Milani, you've earned this much from me."

He flinched and tried to lean away when Matthews drew back his fist. The door burst open. Two police officers bounded into the room and grabbed Matthews. Black loomed in the doorway with a third officer.

Matthews twisted in the officers' grasp. "Get your hands off me. I'm escorting Milani to his cell."

While the police officers held onto Matthews, Black spoke. "Mr. Matthews, I suggest you leave immediately, before you find yourself in handcuffs."

One of the officers muttered, "Come on Kyle, let's go, before you think of any other stupid things to do."

While he leaned against the wall, wanting more than anything to get the cuffs off his throbbing wrists, Matthews yanked one arm free and shook his fist. "I'll figure out how this happened, Milani. When I do, you better be looking over your shoulder, because I'll be gunning for you. And on that day, no one's going to step in and save you."

Black said, "That is enough. Get him out of here." The police officers dragged Matthews out of the room. The other officer lingered in the doorway. Black addressed him. "Please release Mr. Milani."

He held out his hands. The police officer unlocked the cuffs and pulled the unyielding steel away. He grimaced and held first one wrist, then the other while the officer squatted beside him and removed the leg irons.

The officer stood up, holding the restraints he hated. "Anything else, sir?"

Black replied. "That'll be all. Thank you." The officer left and closed the door. Black placed a large paper grocery bag on the table. "I'd planned on meeting you in your cell with the good news. Somehow, Matthews got wind of it and beat me to it. The sack contains a shirt, a pair of pants, and your shoes. As soon as you change, we're out of here. I'll step outside and give you a couple minutes."

"OK." As the door closed he slid into the chair and stared at the paper sack. "Out of here," he whispered, then closed his eyes, took a deep, shuddering breath, and let it out slowly.

Matthews watched from a hidden vantage point as guards buzzed Milani through the final locked door of the jail, his slick attorney at his side. A black Lincoln Town Car with smoked windows waited. The driver jumped out, and a stocky man climbed out of the back seat. The two men greeted Milani and his attorney with handshakes.

Milani and the stocky man slid into the back seat. The attorney waited for the driver to open the front passenger side door. Watching how the men conducted themselves, dressed like they were packing, heads on swivels as they moved around, the answer clicked in his mind. They'd been bushwhacked by a Mafia operation, or he wasn't an Irish Texan.

Somehow, somewhere along the line, someone had prior knowledge. And they must have had help from inside his police department. He dug his phone out of his pants pocket and punched the contact he wanted.

Harandi answered. "Kyle, what's up?"

"I just watched Rowan Milani walk out of our lock-up a free man, the charges dismissed."

"Say what? You can't be serious. What happened?"

"I'm as serious as I've ever been."

"This is unbelievable. How could he skate? You had a massive amount of evidence. What's going on in your department?"

"All I can come up with is dirty cops and some kind of Mafia deal. I'm not letting this thing go. I'm gonna get to the bottom of whatever kind of tomfoolery got him off. I told the prosecutor I'd help her if I could."

Harandi countered. *"Mafia deal?* That's crazy talk."

"You might think it sounds crazy, but you didn't see what I did. He crawled into the back seat of a Town Car, along with his attorney and a couple of goon-looking guys in suits."

"Look Kyle, in my dealings with Milani, there's never been even a whiff of Mafia involvement. But you be damn careful digging around, because whoever orchestrated this must have a hell of a lot of influence. People like that don't take kindly to scrutiny."

"I don't give one crap whether the *people* who fixed this like scrutiny or not. I didn't see you ever backing down on Milani."

"Come on, what I'm trying to say is that you need to proceed with caution. Someone or some entity capable of this wouldn't think twice about harming you or your family."

Somewhat mollified, he continued. "I'm always careful. But this sticks in my craw. It ain't right."

Harandi replied. "On the flip side, none of the things that happened to Rowan were right, but they still happened. What happened to my uncle Sa-id wasn't right either. Same with Patricia's assassination."

He turned away from the window. "What are you getting at?"

"What I'm getting at is this, Kyle. Count the cost *before* you decide to dig in your heels and go after whoever pulled this off. Before you get in too deep and find yourself regretting what you've done."

"Milani *earned* every damn thing that happened to him. I can't speak about your uncle or Patricia Hennessey. Tell me why you're pussyfootin' around this shit."

"I'm not pussyfooting. I'm trying to caution you. Regardless of what you think of Milani or what you think he did, it's not worth risking everything you cherish. Let things lie. You may look back in six months or a year and feel differently."

"Jaysus, what I *think he did?* If I didn't know better, I'd put you square on Milani's side."

"You know better than that, my friend. I'm on your side."

Matthews pulled the phone away from his ear and scowled at it before smacking it back against his head. "You coulda' fooled me."

"Look, I'm out of the shit show, and it feels good. It didn't do me any favors, and I hate to see you take the same path. If I've spoken out of turn, I apologize."

Still disgruntled, he replied. "An' I halfway expected you'd be fixin' to head down here and help us."

Harandi chuckled. "I gave Whitman my resignation and can't wait to put some serious distance between me and the entire mess."

"Guess I can't blame you. DC is a pressure cooker, and I can't imagine being at the President's beck and call."

"Exactly. Think about what I've said, all right? And keep me in the loop. If nothing else, I can be a sounding board."

"I'll think about all this, and I won't go off on any tangents."

Harandi sounded relieved. "Take care and stay in touch."

Matthews ended the call and stuffed his phone in his pocket. The subtle, ongoing pushback from the man he'd always thought of as a solid ally puzzled him. Something Milani said poked at the back of his mind. *Speaking of liars, you should remember, David is a CIA tool. He lies his ass off.* What kind of underhanded deal had he stumbled into?

CHAPTER FIFTEEN

Rowan closed his eyes and listened to the jet engines winding up. Once airborne, he'd believe what Black had told him. Until then, he expected the jet to make an abrupt stop and for Detective Matthews to board with his .45 and a set of cuffs.

The engines whine turned to a roar. The Lear 75 careened down the runway and lifted, pushing him back in the seat. He opened his eyes and stared out the window. The city receded quickly, and with it his sense of dread. Every second took him further and further away from the jail, the capital murder charges he didn't deserve, and the pissed off, crazy detective.

Johnny had outdone himself in Houston, and Matthews wouldn't get over being blindsided. What if the vindictive cop found a discrepancy? What if someone talked? Roberto came down the aisle and placed a bottle of single barrel Jack Daniel's whiskey and two glasses on the table in front of him. "You wanna drink with me? I think you could use a shot or two."

"OK." He sank lower in the cushy leather seat and tugged on his shirt. "Thanks for the clothes. And for the shoes." He'd hung onto and cherished the battered slip-on leather shoes for too many years. Michelle had insisted he buy them, only a few weeks before she died.

Roberto sat in the seat opposite him and poured carefully while the jet continued to ascend. "You're welcome. I'd have salvaged your jacket, but it was ripped and covered with blood."

Uneasy, he took the glass of whiskey and breathed in the pungent, soothing aroma. How in God's name had he stayed sane without it? Hell, maybe he hadn't. He tossed back the shot, feeling the burn all the way down. "What happened to all the evidence? Such as my jacket, the limo, assorted DNA evidence, guns, casings, the whole works?"

Roberto poured more Jack. "Gino and I took care of it. It's been disposed of, erased, made non-existent, however you want to look at it."

He took another hefty swallow of whiskey, conscious of Roberto's watchful gaze. "How?"

"You don't need to know, and you don't want to know. The Boss has business associates in Houston. Gino and I helped them, and we took care of it. Trust me, you don't gotta worry about a thing."

"How did you alter the evidence chain or eliminate it? I can't figure out how you managed to fix everything in such a short time."

Roberto frowned. "You know, you think too much. We had a month, give or take, before you got to Houston. I gotta say, though, once we got in, we took care of things in a few days."

"A month *before* I got to Houston? How did you know that's where I was headed?"

Roberto drank some whiskey and set the glass on the table. "The Boss got a call from the guy in charge of you, what's his name? A couple of months ago."

He stopped, the drink halfway to his mouth. "David called Johnny?"

"Yeah, he told the Boss the President planned to pardon you but wouldn't give in on the Houston deal. Said he didn't have a choice about notifying that detective, and asked the Boss if he could fix things."

He thought about David, repeatedly telling him what he'd never believed. "What about cleanup and any possible loose ends?"

"Believe me, that's taken care of too. All of it. Like I said, you got nothing to worry about."

"If you say so. Hey, I'm sorry I fucked you over when I left Key West."

Roberto grabbed the glass of Jack and drank more. "Yeah. You can forget about it. What's done is done."

"OK." He finished his whiskey and let the glass lay in his lap while he looked out the window at the blue sky stretching to the horizon and the clouds crowding together far below. A huge yawn overtook him. Flying always made him sleepy. The whiskey had reduced his pain to a dull ache and he could almost relax.

Roberto stood up. "We've got a couple more hours to O'Hare. The Boss is putting us up at the Four Seasons. He wants to have a meet. After that, you can do whatever the hell you want."

He yawned again and gazed blearily at Roberto. "Thank you, for whatever you did. I'm grateful."

"You're welcome. Relax and get some rest. None of those pricks can touch you now, or ever. The Boss made sure of that."

"OK." He reclined his seat and closed his burning eyes. If he could, he'd stay at 40,000 feet and keep flying, for a long, long time.

Captain Lavoe waited at her desk, steeling herself for the unpleasant task she faced. Kyle Matthews had served under her command since making detective six years earlier. They'd formed a professional bond which occasionally delved into the personal. She'd met his wife and two kids. She'd thought of him as a rising star and had enjoyed mentoring him. And now, he'd managed to ruin everything. The Chief's bellowed words still echoed in her mind and she winced, remembering the angry frustration in his voice. *He's DONE. I want him OUT.*

Matthews appeared at the door, flanked by two uniformed officers. "Captain. You wanted to see me?"

She'd already closed the blinds in anticipation of their meeting. "Yes. Come in and shut the door. Thank you, officers. Please wait outside."

Matthews took a seat. "Look Captain, I need to apologize…"

"Stop right there, Kyle. Before we get to the gist of this meeting, I have a few questions."

"Sure, anything. Shoot."

"First, who informed you of Milani's imminent release?"

"Uh, well, the DA's office."

"Specifically?"

"Ms. Bently, the prosecutor. She called me during the discovery process with a few questions, and I told her…"

"That's enough. Why did you choose to interrogate Mr. Milani *after* the charges against him were dismissed? In addition, where were you when you received the phone call from Ms. Bently?"

Matthews frowned. "The evidence against him *did* exist. I know that for a fact."

"Answer my questions, Kyle."

"Yes, ma'am. I wanted to make that SOB tell me *how* he got rid of the evidence."

She couldn't hide her incredulity. "Listen to yourself. Milani has been incarcerated for months."

"I know. But damn it, somehow he managed to screw around and corrupt our system."

"How amazing. A prisoner with the power to what, snap his fingers and cause evidence to disappear? Never mind. Where were you when you received Ms. Bently's call?"

"Waiting at the lockup."

"How is that possible? You turned in your ID and badge. You have no access."

Matthews wouldn't look at her. "I still have a few friends in the department. You know how it is."

"I see. You're telling me that members of the Houston Police Department gave you unfettered access to a prisoner while on suspension. Did I understand you correctly?"

He cleared his throat and still wouldn't meet her gaze. "Uh, yes, ma'am."

"And you're worried about corruption? That's laughable. You don't seem to mind corrupting the system when it benefits you."

"Oh, come on Captain, it's not the same thing."

"Don't insult my intelligence, Detective. My last question is this. What on Earth gave you the idea that assaulting Mr. Milani was within your purview?"

"I didn't assault him, but I wish I had. He's a smart-mouthed jerk, arrogant as hell, even when he's helpless."

"I'm quoting the officer who intervened. 'Matthews had the prisoner up against the wall and was about to pile-drive his fist into Milani's face.' Assaulting a prisoner is *never* acceptable behavior for a Houston PD detective. Whatever your reasoning, I'm done with this."

Matthews stood up. "Thank you, Captain…"

"Sit down. We aren't *quite* finished."

Matthews sat. "Oh, sorry."

"Kyle, I know Milani made a permanent impact on your life, but you've gone round the bend and off the rails. Your continuing obsession with him, your lack of discipline, and most importantly, your disobedience of *direct orders,* leaves me no choice. You are done. Fired. Your employment with Houston PD is officially over."

He finally met her hard stare. "Captain, you and I go back a long way. I know I overstepped my bounds. If you suspended me for six months or something, I'd understand. But I can't believe you'd fire me."

"Some of us don't disobey direct orders, no matter how distasteful. I have no choice in this matter. I have one other issue to discuss with you."

Matthews snorted. "What else is there if I'm fired?"

She couldn't believe what she had to tell the man she'd mentored and trusted. "The DA's office is contemplating a criminal investigation of you."

Matthews leaped from the chair. "Captain, you've got to be *kidding* me. How do I end up being the criminal here?"

"Kyle, if you are not able to control yourself, I will request assistance."

He sprawled in the chair and muttered, "Son of a *bitch.* This *stinks.* What's going on, Captain?"

She glared at him. "The District Attorney's Office informed me that they intend to investigate whether you have anything to do with Milani being set up. I'm sure you'll learn the details once they formalize their investigation."

He kept muttering. "That arrogant jerk. He can't do this to me. I'll have his ass."

"Kyle, I'm truly sorry for how this has played out. You may wish to retain legal counsel. However, we are finished. The officers who escorted you here will see you out of the building."

Matthews gripped the arms of the chair. "This isn't right. The DA can find another scapegoat. I'll investigate on my own. When I figure out what happened, I'll be back. You can mark my words, Captain."

"I wish you the best, Kyle. Give my regards to Erin." *Don't let the door hit you,* she wanted to add.

Matthews stood up and left without saying anything more. She stared at the door as it closed. Something had gone terribly wrong in the Milani case. If her former detective hadn't lost all traces of a reasonable perspective, he may have been able to retain credibility and play a part in rectifying the situation. She hoped he didn't end up serving time for something she knew he hadn't done. But at this point, she intended to keep her mouth shut and do whatever she could to keep her own career intact.

London, UK

Shemal watched the breaking news report in shock. The reporter must have it wrong. Milani could *not* have been freed. The Jinn could not have walked out of the Houston jail and disappeared into thin air. "But that is what a Jinn would do," he murmured. Bands of familiar agony tightened around his chest and beads of sweat popped on his forehead.

He sank down on the sofa in his front room and stared out the window at the unending flow of vehicle lights in the darkness. "This cannot be happening. This cannot be true." He reached for his phone with trembling fingers and punched the contact he wanted.

Abramson answered after only one ring. "Hello Muusa. You must have heard the news."

"I am watching it now. Tell me a mistake has been made and that Milani is back in custody. He cannot have been exonerated."

"It's true. He was released several hours ago. I'm afraid we were outwitted."

"Outwitted? Yes, we have been thwarted by this man and his cohorts at every turn. We must find him. And this time, he and his friends and his woman *must die.* I will accept *nothing less."*

Abramson replied. "Agreed. We will find and punish whoever is responsible for this travesty."

"After everything we've done, the resources I have sacrificed, and the losses I have sustained to neutralize this man, defeat is not an option. He is not even a man. He is a Jinn who walks into the shadows and disappears. *I cannot stomach this... ahh."* His words became a moan as the anguish in his chest intensified. He bent over and struggled to breathe. Sweat dripped from his face onto his pants.

"Muusa, are you all right? Do you need a doctor?"

"No, no, I'll be all right," he whispered. He took shallow breaths and forced his body upright.

Abramson said, "You understand, of course, that my role is limited. Any action on my part could expose our plans to unwanted scrutiny. Allahu akbar, my friend. We will find a way to succeed."

"Certainly, your role must remain hidden. Our jihad has come too far. The Brotherhood's goals are within reach as they have never been before. We will succeed. Allahu akbar." He ended the call and leaned back against the soft leather, exhausted.

Chicago, IL

Ralph stalked the confines of the Four Seasons presidential suite on the forty-sixth floor, waiting for Rowan to arrive. He could only imagine his friend's state of mind and the condition of his abused body. And he still couldn't get their last, rancorous conversation out of his mind.

Johnny sat at the elegant, dark wood table, puffing on a Cubano, sending a cloud of fragrant smoke across the seating area. "What's the matter, Ralphie? Nervous about seeing Rowan after everything he's been through?"

He paused in his tour of city-to-lake views, wishing his private thoughts weren't so transparent. "Hell yes. I can't imagine how he's survived. And on top of that, our last conversation left an ugly taste in my mouth. I've regretted it ever since he left Kauai."

"I don't think you need to worry. I'd wager he's looking for a bottle of booze, a bed, and the knowledge that he's out of the reach of Shemal and the government."

"I'd like to agree with you, but there's one thing you have to remember about Rowan. He doesn't forget *anything.* If he did, none of us would be here today, and the last screwed-up year would never have happened."

Johnny held the cigar between his fingers. "We'll see. How about you and Marion join El and I for dinner at my restaurant after we get him settled in?"

"I think we'd like that. Thank you."

A soft knock ended their exchange. Johnny rose from the table and ambled to the door, checking the viewer before admitting Roberto and Rowan. Johnny held out his hand. "Rowan Milani, it's been too damn long. How the hell are ya?"

Ralph hung back. Relief hit him in an overpowering wave as he watched the man he loved like a son step into the room and shake Johnny's hand. "I'm OK."

Johnny ushered Rowan further inside. "Ralphie and I have been looking forward to this day for quite some time. I'll leave you two for a bit while I meet with Roberto."

Ralph stepped forward, hoping he could hold it together. "God almighty, son. You look better than when I saw you on that jet in Cairo."

A smirk flitted across Rowan's gaunt face. *"Ralphie?"*

He spoke, voice hoarse. "It's a long story, so don't start. Let me be glad to see you, at least for a few minutes. You want to sit down?"

Rowan scratched at the stubble on his jaw. "Yeah, sure."

They sat facing each other on adjacent sofas. "So how did that detective in Houston react when he found out you were leaving?"

Rowan peered at him, the dark circles beneath his eyes enhancing the younger man's palpable aura of exhaustion. "He's not letting it go. He'll dig around until he finds something."

"Johnny assured me his people took care of everything. You don't have anything to worry about on that score."

"Roberto told me the same thing, but I don't know. Matthews is pissed off in a big way, and he's nobody's fool. Eliminating the evidence is one thing, but destroying the evidence chain is something else."

"If there's one thing I've learned about Johnny, it's that he doesn't leave a damn thing to chance. You can relax and try to enjoy living for a change."

"I sure as hell hope so."

Unsure how to proceed, he floundered. “Uh, Marion made your favorite cookies. You know, the ones with all the stuff mixed in. Monster cookies, I think she calls them.”

Rowan’s demeanor softened. “I haven’t thought about those cookies in a while. Tell her thanks for me.”

“I put a plateful in your room, which is across the hall. You can relax and recuperate for as long as you want.”

“OK. Sounds good to me.”

He hesitated, then plunged into the mess he wanted to fix. “You know, our last conversation left something to be desired and I…”

Rowan interrupted him. “Stop, Ralph. You and I both know you were concerned, and I was an ass. Had to do things my way. I’ve had plenty of time to regret that conversation, and a lot of other things too, in case you’re wondering.”

Tears brimmed in his eyes and escaped, coursing down his cheeks. “Well, see, I thought it might be the last time we talked.”

Rowan spoke so quietly he had to lean close and strain to hear. “It’s OK. I’m sorry for what I put you and everyone else through. If I could undo it, I would.”

He wiped the wetness from his face. “You’re alive, and you’re going to be well. Son, that’s the only damn thing that matters to me and everyone else to boot.”

Rowan’s dark eyes bored into his. “I’m done trying to fight or find my own version of justice. I just want to be left alone.”

“You’ve got the opportunity to do lots of things, thanks to Johnny.”

“I’ve never understood why he did all this for me.”

He smiled through the tears. “You’ll have to ask him about that.”

Rowan asked, “Where is Chad? Is he all right? What about Bettina?”

"Chad and Bettina and their bouncing baby boy are staying at Johnny's home in Lake Forest for the time being, along with everyone else. Of course, they're all anxious to see you."

"A boy, huh? How's Chad?"

"He's a cute little bugger. You'll see for yourself, as soon as you're up to it. Chad suffered in Quantico and DC's County lockup. He'll be all right, but it's going to take some time and maybe a few sessions with Angelo."

Rowan's voice contained a hint of resignation. "Yeah, I need to have a conversation with Angelo."

"Angelo is anxious to see you, too."

"I don't want to see anyone, but I guess it's inevitable. What about Mike and Gabriel? Are they here?"

The absence of Rowan's stubborn personality unnerved him. "Gabriel is in Mexico with his family. Mike and Asal are staying temporarily at Johnny's home, too."

Rowan shifted on the sofa and winced. "Asal is here?"

"Yes, she is. Mike brought her to Dubai after they picked up Angelo and took care of a problem in Sioux Falls."

"Oh, right. I heard about that."

The answer surprised him. "How did you hear about *that?"*

A thin line of sweat made its way down the side of Rowan's face. "The new FBI Director came to ADX Florence. She, uh, she knows way more than she should."

"Derek chattered like a little monkey. He told the Bureau everything he knew and caused problems for Mike's parents at their ranch in South Dakota and for Jerry and Bryan's business."

Rowan replied. "Yeah, I heard about that, too. We should have left that useless piece of shit in Sioux Falls at the very beginning."

"Well, hindsight is always twenty-twenty."

"Tell me about it."

Concerned about the level of pain obvious in Rowan's face, as well as his friend's seemingly altered personality, he forged ahead. "What, ah, have you thought about what you'd like to do?"

Rowan arched a brow in the expression he knew so well, bringing the lump back to his throat. "What can I do besides wait for Shemal to come after me again?"

Rowan's words only deepened his unease. "Maybe Shemal has gotten the message to leave you alone. We, I mean Johnny, caused him a lot of heartache for what he did to you."

The muscles in Rowan's jaws tightened. "Yeah, I know."

"How did you know? Johnny kept the whole operation on the down low. His closest crew were the only ones involved in both mosque explosions."

Rowan absently rubbed his thigh. "Shemal asked me who was blowing up his mosques. You might say he put me on the spot. I could only think of one person capable of pulling off something like that, so I spilled my guts and told him."

Dry-mouthed at the meaning inherent in what he'd just heard, Ralph swallowed hard. "I'm sorry."

"No worries. In the larger scheme of things, it was nothing. It didn't matter then, and it sure as hell doesn't matter now. Nothing much does anymore."

"Aw, you can't mean that. You being here, alive, matters to all of us. Uh, have you thought about when you're going to contact Danielle?"

"I'm not going to intrude in her life again. She's been through enough with me. Besides, I don't want to put her in danger."

He frowned at the finality in Rowan's voice. "Maybe you should give yourself some time to recover before you make major decisions. You know what I mean? Who knows how you'll feel about that in a month or two."

"I've had plenty of time to think about my life. It's essentially over. There's nothing I can do about that anymore. Like I said, I'm done."

Dismay over Rowan's matter-of-fact analysis overlaid his relief at seeing a glimpse of the younger man's stubborn character. "It's all right. You don't have to do anything you don't want to."

Rowan's shoulders slumped. "I need to move on and think about how to survive. Like I said, the cowboy detective isn't going to give up. And Shemal probably already knows where I am."

Thoroughly disquieted, he kept his voice low. "You're not alone in this situation. Remember that. For now, all you need to be concerned with is recovering."

Rowan opened his mouth to respond, but Johnny chose that moment to thrust his jovial presence into their conversation. "Roberto tells me you had a chance to relax on the flight, but you must be exhausted. We won't keep you long."

Rowan replied. "Best flight I've taken in a while. Thanks for the ride."

Johnny puffed on his cigar and grinned. "You're welcome. I've been wanting to tell you, Rowan, taking Linden and Whitman to task was more fun than I've had in a long time. You probably don't remember, but I told you last winter in Chicago: it was my pleasure, meeting a bona-fide American hero. Whatever you need, just ask."

Rowan inched his way off the sofa to face Johnny. "You saved my life. You went out of your way, risked your resources, and spent a lot of money on my behalf. I honestly don't know how to thank you or even begin to repay you."

Johnny flung his arm in an expansive wave, scattering ash to the carpet. "Consider it my gift. We'll talk more after you've had some rest. My doc will check you out, and whatever he says you need, we'll arrange. You can stay here as long as you want to while you recover."

Ralph waited for Rowan to protest, but his friend surprised him. "OK. Sounds good. After that, if I could, I'd like to return to the beach house in Key West. Right now, I'd like to get some rest. My room is across the hall?"

Johnny replied. "I rented the entire floor. Your *suite* is across the hall. Roberto and Gino have the adjoining suite. They'll be outside your door 24/7, in shifts. Anything you want, you tell them. *Anything.* Capisce?" The Don's voice became solemn. "And Rowan, the door locks from the inside. You're not a prisoner here."

Ralph saw the first glimmer of something other than despair cross Rowan's face. "Thanks."

Stricken once more by his run-amok emotions, Ralph cleared his throat and faced Rowan. "I hope you'll be ready to see everyone soon. They're anxious to welcome you back." He stepped close and embraced his friend, biting his lip and holding his breath to keep from sobbing when Rowan tentatively returned the hug.

They parted, and Rowan gave him a barely discernable wink. "Thanks Ralph. See you soon."

Rowan gave Gino thumbs-up and shut the door. He turned the deadbolt and listened to the solid clunk with satisfaction. The lock, along with Gino's imposing presence and the full-size Glock .40 the young man carried left him with the assurance of safety. God only knew what other security measures Johnny had put in place throughout the Four Seasons. No one would disturb him, at least for a while.

He wandered barefoot from room to room, wiggling his toes in the thick carpet. He touched the leather sofa, gazed at the shimmering reaches of Lake Michigan from the big windows, and shook his head at the whirlwind of the previous month. He still couldn't quite believe Detective Matthews wouldn't appear, or maybe Special Agent Foster, apologizing while guards cuffed and shackled him.

He shuddered and rubbed his still-aching wrists. None of that would happen. He stopped at the bedroom door and grimaced. The room, appointed with heavy oak furnishings, brought back too many memories. A lavish arrangement of pillows festooned the head of the king-sized bed above the white comforter. They'd had a lot of fun with the pillows. He stepped inside and hesitated, not wanting to confront the buried emotions evoked by the bedroom and hell, the entire suite.

Of course, Johnny hadn't known. No one did, except him… and Danielle. They'd spent a weekend in a suite a few floors below. He'd had three precious days of carefree happiness. The nightmare had begun almost immediately after they'd returned to Sioux Falls. But that weekend he'd been happier than he'd been since before 9/11. He stared unseeing, remembering how Danielle had slid her fingers over his body, unconditionally loving every part of him.

He drifted through the bedroom and ventured into the bathroom, larger than either his ADX Florence cell or his recently vacated solitary cell in Houston, and appointed with marble countertops, glittering lights, and huge mirrors. He looked at his image in the mirror and sucked in a quick breath. His eyes seemed sunken into his head. The thin, livid scar on his cheek remained as a permanent reminder of Shemal's dagger.

He tugged the shirt from his sweat-dampened body. With a fist over his mouth, covering the groans he couldn't stop, he twisted and turned, looking at the scars the bastard had left on his chest, sides, belly, and arms. He faced the mirror. What would Danielle think of his body now? He already knew. She'd be sad, wanting to help him, and then angry because someone had hurt him.

He shucked out of the jeans and god-awful tightie-whitie underwear and gazed with bitter hatred at the scar up high along his inner thigh. Shame still burned in his face when he remembered the terror he'd felt at the slice of the cold dagger. He'd broken after that, and Shemal had reveled in making him talk. Not that it mattered. As he'd known, Johnny could take care of himself.

He found a plush bathrobe in the walk-in closet, next to what must be several thousand dollars' worth of clothes. He wondered who had picked out the variety of shirts, t-shirts, shorts, jeans, and dress pants. His mouth hung open when he saw the black leather jacket. How had the cunning man found almost the exact match of the jacket he'd worn for over a decade? He dropped the robe and pulled the jacket from its hanger.

Taking his time, cursing the pain, he struggled into it. The jacket felt big, but the soft leather molded to his body. If he ever found a way to regain any semblance of muscle and weight, it would be perfect. Why had the powerful Don concerned himself with his situation? He left the closet and bedroom, wearing the jacket and a fresh pair of boxers he'd found with a dozen or so other pairs in the five-drawer dresser.

Thinking about his former boss, he nabbed the plate of monster cookies from the polished oak table and sank down on the sofa. Ralph had always cared, way more than a boss should, for both him and Chad. He couldn't believe how broken up Ralph had been, yet still wanting to give him directions and tell him what to do. At some point, his hard-ass ex-boss needed to figure out that those days were over. But hell, in his own way, Ralph was just as damned stubborn as he was.

Exhaustion overtook him and muddled his thoughts. He reluctantly exchanged the jacket for the bathrobe and snagged the full bottle of single barrel Jack Daniel's whiskey and a glass. He sat on the sofa and ate cookies until he was stuffed and drank until the biting agony in his shoulders, back, and hips receded.

When his lips were numb, and his arms and legs felt heavy, he shoved the stopper into the bottle and set it on the coffee table. He lay down, his hands folded on his belly and his ankles crossed. From his spot on the sofa he could watch the mellow dusk fading to darkness beyond the big windows.

The Next Day
Camp David
Whitman dropped his phone on the table and slammed his fist on the arm of the chair. "This can't be happening."

Linden said, "What's going on?"

Whitman shoved himself out of the chair and stalked angrily to the fireplace. He jabbed at the crackling logs, causing an explosion of sparks. The two men had agreed to meet a month or two after their joint appearance to assess how the media, political opponents, and the country had dealt with the conclusion of the Milani affair, or *debacle* as he thought of it.

He stabbed at the logs one more time before turning to face his colleague. "Milani was released from Houston's lockup yesterday morning. He's free, and no one has any idea where he's gone."

Linden's jaw dropped. *"What? Why?* And more importantly, *how?"*

He shot the former President a grim look. "No evidence exists to prosecute him. It's gone. The judge presiding over the case released him at the request of the District Attorney. They didn't have a choice."

Linden replied. "Evidence doesn't just disappear. Do you realize the implications? Johnny Giacopino must have orchestrated this, but who tipped him off?"

"Your guess is as good as mine. The only people who knew about the plan are Abramson, Berenger, and Harandi." He sat down and glared at Linden. "Abramson despises Milani.

Berenger is a strict law-and-order type. But Harandi is another matter. I trusted him, confided in him."

Linden's features were partially obscured in the muted lamplight and flickering shadows of the fire. He spoke quietly. "Are you sure, Gil?"

"It couldn't have been anyone else. He tried to convince me of Milani's innocence. They grew up together, for crying out loud. I've been played for the fool."

Linden leaned forward. "Stick to the plan, Gil. Give it a couple years and take care of both of them."

"I'm not sure I can do that. It's one thing to bow to a Mafia Don. But Harandi betrayed me *personally.* Who knows how much information he funneled to Giacopino? He may have been in contact with him all along."

"What are you going to do?"

"I'm going to talk to Leigh Berenger first thing in the morning. We'll bring Harandi in for questioning and find a reason to keep him."

Linden gave him a crafty smile. "That's a start."

CHAPTER SIXTEEN

The Next Day
Washington, DC
Harandi surveyed his open duffel bag, ticking off the items on his list, making sure he hadn't forgotten anything. A road trip appealed to him, and he'd mapped out a back-roads-route to Chicago, after making one more call to Johnny Giacopino. He'd made the impulsive call, surprising himself, not entirely sure of what he planned to accomplish, but the Don had agreed to meet with him. His meandering route would give him some time to gather his thoughts.

Besides, he wanted to see Rowan in a setting other than a prison cell, and the Don would surely know his former friend's location. Gnawing, persistent sadness stuck with him, and the guilt pressed in every time he pictured Rowan's haggard face and the tears running down his cheeks. Somehow, he had to get past it, and he hoped that freedom might soften his old friend's heart. Knowing Rowan, it was a crapshoot, but he had to try, for his own peace of mind.

He zipped up his duffel bag, hoisted it to his shoulder, and swiped his car keys from the coffee table. His phone rang, and he dug it out of his shirt pocket, glanced at the ID and sighed. "Hello Director Berenger. What can I do for you?"

"Hello Mr. Harandi. I'm sure you're as stunned as I am over Milani's unprecedented release yesterday."

Something in Berenger's tone seemed off. He plopped the duffel bag on the floor. "You've got that right. I don't know how it could have happened. Matthews called me. He says something dirty went on."

"Obviously. I cannot begin to imagine who accomplished this, but it cannot stand. We need to meet today. I'd like you to consider traveling to Houston, maybe collaborating with Matthews to find out what went on."

An all-too-familiar sensation in his gut had him striding to the windows overlooking the street. He stood out of view and scanned as far as he could see. No tell-tale black Suburbans or nondescript four-door sedans waited on the street. "You want me to go to Houston, Director?"

"Yes. How soon can you meet? Whitman is furious and he wants action, sooner rather than later." While she talked, he made his way to the patio, checked his tiny, fenced backyard, and then closed and locked the door.

"How about your office, 3 p.m.?"

"Thank you. I'll see you then."

He winced at her brusque tone. "Goodbye Director, I'll see you this afternoon." She ended the call before he'd finished talking. His phone rang again, and he cursed at the ID. "Hello Mr. President. I wasn't expecting to hear from you so soon."

Whitman's voice contained an alarming, false heartiness he hadn't heard before. "Hello, David. I'm calling in one of those favors I mentioned as a condition of your resignation."

"What may I help you with, sir?"

"I've arranged for a new advisor, and he's ready to hit the ground running. I'd like you to meet with him today."

An almost unbearable sense of urgency hit him. He needed to get the heck out of DC, and fast. "Certainly, sir. I'm planning on meeting with Director Berenger at three o'clock. Do I need to reschedule that meeting, or do you have a time in mind?"

"Let's make it four-thirty. You can brief me on your meeting with Berenger."

"Very well, sir. I'll see you this afternoon." He ended the call, grabbed his duffel and keys, and headed out the door. If things went his way, he'd be safely out of DC long before either Berenger or Whitman could take him into custody.

Two Days Later
Chicago, IL
Rowan shifted from one foot to the other while Roberto knocked on the door of the presidential suite. Johnny, clad in an impeccable Italian suit, ushered him inside. “Good afternoon, Rowan.”

“Hello, sir.” His jeans and t-shirt felt shabby and out of place, in the same way he felt out of sync with any sort of normal living.

The Don intruded on his unhappy thoughts. “Have a seat and make yourself comfortable. I’ve been looking forward to this.”

“Me too.” He gravitated to the grouping of leather sofas where he’d sat with Ralph, unsure what to expect from the man who’d spent hugely in dollars and personal capital to secure his freedom.

Johnny conversed quietly with Roberto, then pulled the door shut and turned toward him with a grin. “You wanna drink? Or maybe a cigar? I got a stash of Cubanos I believe you’d like, along with a bottle of single barrel Jack.”

“Jack sounds good, but I’ll pass on the cigar.” He’d never developed a taste for smoking, although he’d tolerated Ralph’s penchant for what his former boss called a good cigar. And after every op, he’d put up with Michael and Gabriel puffing on fat cigars while his eyes burned and his clothes stank.

Johnny held out a squat glass filled with whiskey. “Here ya go. I believe a toast is in order.”

“Thank you.” He took the glass and inhaled the pungent fumes.

“Here’s to your freedom.”

“I’ll drink to that, for sure.” He clanked his glass against Johnny’s and tossed back a swallow. Long ago, he’d decided that unless someone had experienced *real pain,* they’d have no idea how to appreciate the potent whiskey.

Johnny took a drink and smacked the glass down on the coffee table. “Ah, that’s good. Now, I know you’ve only had a couple days to rest, and I've got a feeling that freedom is tough to handle after what you've been through. Speaking of that, I've set up an appointment for you with my doc."

He took a long drink of whiskey. "I see." But he didn't see anything. Nothing came without a price, and he wondered what his rescue would end up costing him.

"I wanna be sure you get the care you need. He'll see you in a private clinic the family has used for years. He understands discretion, too."

"Sounds good." Increasingly on edge, he finished the whiskey.

Johnny said, "Our whole ragtag group can't wait to see you. But there's no rush. Ralphie and I told them we need to give you some time to re-acclimate."

"I appreciate everything you've done for me, sir, although I've never understood why you chose to help me."

The Don shook a forefinger at him. "I've told you more than once, *you* call me Johnny. I have my reasons for the things I did, for you and the whole bunch."

He held his empty glass in sweating hands. "But I'm nobody to you. And yet you took extraordinary risks, pulled strings, called in favors, and expended tremendous resources, *for me.* Why? What do you want or expect from me?"

"One of the things I like about you is that you're direct. You don't pull any punches." The Don plucked the bottle of whiskey from the table and stood up. After refilling both their glasses, he strolled around the suite. "I told you the first time we met, I did my research on you and liked what I heard. And I hate goddamned injustice. Always have."

"You and me both," he muttered.

The Don swung around and gestured with his glass. "I have my own code, and I see that it's enforced. What happened to you had less than nothing to do with any kind of justice. I wasn't going to let that conniving Whitman dink around and screw you over."

Rowan drank more whiskey and wiped his mouth with the back of his hand. "Whitman, and probably Linden too, wanted to get rid of me."

Johnny replied. "They're a couple of cocksuckers. Neither one is worth the bullets it'd take to whack 'em. And you represented the potential for one hell of a lot of questions, requiring embarrassing explanations."

"The US government will never admit to illegal black ops like the ones we handled. Especially when those ops involved allies and trespassing on foreign soil."

"You're right. I gotta tell ya, Rowan, I had a damn good time fixing everything for you."

He took another swallow of whiskey and kept watching the Don's ambling progression around the suite. "I'm grateful."

The Don caught his eye and gave him a cagey smile. "You know I'm not a do-gooder. When I decide to do something, I stack the deck in my favor."

Wondering where the hell the conversation was headed, he replied. "So I've noticed."

Johnny returned to the sofa and sat down facing him. "You may not remember, but during our brief meet at O'Hare last winter, I offered you a job in my organization."

"I remember." He wanted to add that he'd changed his mind. The only thing he needed was the assurance that *no one* could *ever* put their hands on him again.

"Here's the thing. I respect my Arab business partners in Dubai and a few other places. They filled me in on the Muslim Brotherhood. I did my own fact finding, too. I read the *Memorandum,* and it kinda pissed me off, if you wanna know the truth."

Rowan stared at the glass of whiskey in his hand. "How does this involve me?"

Johnny replied. "When we talked before and I offered you a job, you said I could count you in, anywhere, anytime. You remember that?"

What the hell could he say? "Yeah, I remember."

"After we talked, I dug into the shit pile, and found out how far down the pike our spineless politicians have gone, letting the Muslim Brotherhood get its hooks into the country."

"I've been beating that drum for ten years, but no one listens."

"I'm here to tell you, I'm listening, and like I said last winter, the Brotherhood isn't the only player with a global organization. I wanna fight fire with fire. That son of a bitch Shemal needs to go down first, hard and fast. Then we'll take on the Brotherhood's infiltration of the country."

He contemplated the artful man. "You want to start your own war."

Johnny slapped a hand on the arm of the sofa. "Damn straight. We're gonna put a stop to those motherfuckers. This is my country too, and I'm not about to step aside so the Muslim Brotherhood can take over."

He thought back, to a year-and-a-half earlier, sitting on a hard bench in the bowels of the Denver airport, trying to figure out why he'd been yanked from his flight. He'd felt like a pawn on a chess board, being manipulated by forces he couldn't see. He felt the same way now, except this time the man who owned the chess board stared intently at him. The suite seemed unusually quiet, and he thought there should be a clock ticking away the seconds, marking the exact time that he surrendered once again to a powerful man because he had no other choice. "All right. I'm in."

Johnny gave him a sharp nod. "I knew you'd see things my way. You're part of the family now, and I take care of my own. You can trust me when I say you'll never lack for anything you want or need."

The only thing he needed was more Jack, so he could erase the utter humiliation draining away his self-respect. "Thank you. I appreciate everything you've done for me, and I'm happy to work for you."

Johnny waved a hand. "No, no. El and I discussed this. You and I are partners in this venture. You're not some flunkie or part of a crew."

Even more surprised, he replied cautiously. "You want me as a partner, an equal? What about one of your sons?"

"My sons are already partners. Each of them plays an integral role in the family business. Besides, none of them has your resumé when it comes to this kind of fight." As if on cue, the door opened, and a shapely woman proceeded into the suite. "El, honey, come meet one of my favorite people. He's agreed to be my partner."

Eloisa Giacopino sat down next to her husband. She looked every bit the wife of a global businessman in a chic black-and-white suit. Her thick black hair, stylishly strewn with silver covered her head in a trendy cut. Diamonds glittered at her ears and throat. She spoke in a cultured voice. "Hello, Mr. Milani. It's a pleasure to finally meet you."

He winced as he stood and reached across the table, offering his hand. "Thank you, Mrs. Giacopino, and please, it's Rowan. It's my pleasure to meet you as well."

She shook his hand with a firm grip. "I'm happy you've decided to become Johnny's partner. Welcome to the Giacopino family, Rowan."

He sat back down, exhausted, the whiskey weighting his muscles and dragging him toward the empty state of mind he craved. "I'm happy to be a part of the family, ma'am, believe me." He hoped to God he could escape to the seclusion of his own suite, now that he'd agreed with the man who controlled his future.

Johnny said, "It looks to me like Rowan needs a break, El. If you'll excuse me for a minute, I'll see him out."

The elegant woman patted her husband's knee. "Of course. Then we can discuss our dinner plans."

Johnny stood up. "Whatever you'd like, dear. Rowan, this has been a good meet."

He clenched his jaws and pushed himself off the sofa. "I look forward to seeing you again, Mrs. Giacopino. Thank you again uh, Johnny, for everything. I can see myself out." He nodded at both of them and retreated.

Gino had replaced Roberto, and let him into his suite with a nod and grunt. He made his way to the sofa and slouched down, covering his face with his hands. The far-sighted Don had set him up as cleverly as Shemal, and he'd never seen it coming. Johnny owned him now, in the posh prison of the Four Seasons, as surely as Shemal had in the horrific confines of Tora.

He let his hands drop to his lap and gazed at the door to his suite. It might as well be locked from the outside. At least he knew what regaining his freedom had cost him. He shook his head at the irony. No matter how long it took, he'd find a way to disappear, off the grid, for the rest of his life. Johnny couldn't own him any more than Shemal could. Somehow, he'd find a way.

Three Days Later
Seattle, WA
Danielle looked out the rain-spattered front windows of her cheery bistro. The rain fell steadily from low clouds, subduing the fall orange, gold and red of the trees, succeeding in turning the world outside a dreary gray. Or maybe it was her mood. The aroma of fresh-brewed coffee, the muted voices of her customers, and the occasional clink of glass from behind the counter normally enveloped her in workaday pleasure, but not today.

She rubbed her arms against the damp chill beyond the windows. She felt like she'd just climbed out of the front-row seat on the worst emotional rollercoaster ride imaginable. From thinking Rowan was dead to learning he was alive and imprisoned, reading about his indictment in Texas, and finally discovering he'd been freed left her mind reeling and her heart, first hopeful, then crushed. He could have contacted her. Of all people, he had the resources to find her, if he wanted to.

Forcing a bright smile, she turned from the windows and nodded at the clusters of people enjoying the warm ambience of her shop as she made her way to her office. Leo padded along behind her. Once inside, she closed the door and slid into the chair behind her desk. She lost the smile and closed her eyes. Maybe the chapter of her life that included Rowan was over, and she could move on, like she kept telling herself she wanted to.

Grief rolled over her in a wave. How could she let him go? How could she not? Bitter tears crept, hot and wet from her squeezed-shut eyes. She hadn't allowed herself to cry over Rowan since she'd first heard from Angelo that he'd been killed. She felt Leo's warm bulk pressing against her leg. The Rottie whined and laid his head in her lap.

She patted the dog's furry head. She loved Rowan *so much.* Why wouldn't he call her? She *knew* he loved her. What if she tried to find him? She hadn't used the phone Chad programmed for her since that final conversation with Angelo. Blinking back more tears, she thought about Bettina, Marion, and Ralph. They'd been so close. She had no idea what had become of anyone associated with Rowan.

If she'd stayed in touch, would she know his secret whereabouts? Would she be with him? She shook her head, angry with her teenage angst and silly, ambiguous thoughts. She would give Rowan all the time he needed. If he didn't want her in his life, she'd survive the hurt-filled truth, and she would keep going. She tugged her phone from the back pocket of her pants, wiped the remains of tears from her cheeks, and called the man who'd told her he'd always be there. "Hey Tom, it's me. Are you up for dinner tonight?"

Chicago, IL

Rowan heard knuckles rapping hard and fast on the door to his suite. He figured it had to be Michael and Chad. He checked the viewer, turned the deadbolt, and opened the door. His brash friend stood tapping a foot impatiently. Chad waited behind him. "Hey, my brothers. Come in."

His friends stepped inside, and he led them to the grouping of sofas where he spent most of his time. On the low table between the sofas a bottle of Jack waited, with three glasses. He sloshed whiskey in each glass and motioned to the two men. "Here's to us. Drink up. Somehow, we made it out alive. I just wish Gabriel was here."

Michael perched on the edge of one of the sofas, tossed back the whiskey, and coughed. "Gabriel hasn't returned any of my calls for the last six months. But, I've been waiting for *this* moment for too long."

Chad smiled, restoring his faith in his friend's optimism. "Same here."

Michael splashed more whiskey into his glass, took a long swallow, and stifled another cough. "Damn Rowan, this shit will kill you. Give me an ice-cold Budweiser any day. How the hell are you?"

He needed to get everything off his chest at the outset. "Relieved mostly, I guess, and tired. I owe both of you, and Gabriel too, a huge apology for being a dick and blowing you off. I don't know, anymore, what I was thinking."

Chad slouched on an adjacent sofa and held his glass of whiskey in both hands. "You don't owe me anything, brother. I'm the one who lost focus and got all of us caught."

Michael rolled his eyes and muttered, "Fuck me. I wish both of you would shut up. I should have done more when you were in

Houston. Besides, I figured you'd be pissed because we didn't nab you when we had the opportunity in Cairo. It sucked to leave you with Harandi and those two CIA jerks."

"Oh hell, no worries. You didn't have a choice." He frowned at Chad, who had only sipped his drink. "Hey brother, I've had plenty of time to think about how and why I ended up where I did, and not once did it cross my mind that it was in any way *your* fault." He turned to Michael. "Or yours. If I'd listened or just said fuck it all and stayed put… well, it doesn't matter now, does it? So, both of you drink up." He gestured at Chad. "Tell me about your little kid. Did you name him yet?"

Chad pulled his phone from his pants pocket. "I've got a few pictures. We named him Carson, which is my grandfather's name. His middle name is Khalil."

He smirked at Chad as he took the phone. "You know he's going to hate you for that name one day." He scrolled through the pictures, relieved to see Bettina looking happy. The infant looked like every tiny baby he'd ever seen. He passed the phone back to Chad. "Nice."

Michael ditched his shoes and put his feet up on the coffee table, then tugged his phone from his shirt pocket. "Imma call downstairs and get some Bud."

He pointed vaguely toward the opposite end of the room. "Your beer is in the fridge. Help yourself."

Chad downed his glass of whiskey and stood up. "I'll get it. A cold beer sounds good. For once, we don't have to plan anything or go anywhere." A genuine smile brightened his friend's face, and he spoke over his shoulder, heading for the refrigerator. "Bettina told me I could stay as long as I want. Marion and Janice are helping her with baby Carson."

Hoping levity would get rid of the sad emptiness dogging him, Rowan put his feet up on the table and nudged Michael's white-socked foot. "Can you believe it? My sister has taken over for Ralph."

Michael snickered. "I'd rather have her bossing me around than either Ralph or Johnny. Those two are a hell of a pair. Talk about kickin' ass and takin' names."

Chad retorted. "You should see Asal lead Mike around by the nose. He's like a little puppy dog with her."

"Yeah, well, we all have our weaknesses, right?" He smiled, but the banter didn't have the effect he'd hoped for. Instead, his friends' comments only deepened his sadness and emphasized the lonely emptiness of his life without Danielle. He tipped his head back and finished the glass of Jack, determined to blunt the pain.

He was with a couple of the people who meant *a lot* to him, and for once he wanted to do what Ralph said. So goddamn it, he was going to enjoy living. He reached for the bottle and poured more, watching the elixir he depended on flow into the glass. "Let's just drink."

Michael caught the beer Chad tossed and popped the top. After gulping the foam, burping, and wiping his mouth, he said, "What's your plan? Got any ideas on how you want to proceed?"

He'd forgotten how Michael's frat boy attitude hid his sometimes irritating, always-assessing nature. "I don't have a plan. But you need to know what the Bureau's up to."

Michael swilled more beer. "What do you mean?"

"The new director is hot to get her hands on you and Gabriel. Asal, too. She grilled me for hours, wanting info on all of you. She suspects that you and Gabriel killed Hennessey, and that Asal killed Derek. Thanks for both of those, by the way."

Michael replied. "My pleasure, brother, always. They were righteous kills. She got anything remotely resembling proof?"

"I don't think so. She's smart, though, and she's tough. Just be careful."

Michael raised his beer and grinned. "Where's the fun in that? And I know she doesn't have any proof because we *were* careful. She's fishing."

Chad commented. "My dad picked up a new laptop for me, so I'm back in business, as far as hacking the Bureau's servers and access to Berenger's private emails. I'll stay on top of whatever she's planning."

Michael replied. "All right, looks like we've got that covered. Have you contacted Danielle yet?"

He put his feet on the carpet and sat up, scowling at Mike. "No, I haven't contacted Danielle. We ended things." He turned to Chad. "Can you get a line on Shemal's communications, too?"

Chad gave him an eager nod. "Yeah, I can hack CAIR and his personal emails. No problem. One way or another I'll keep tabs on him for you."

"OK, good. I just need to know if any of them decide to come after me again. Same with that cowboy cop in Houston."

Michael pushed off the sofa and headed to the fridge. "You aren't serious about Danielle, are you? Because *you* may have ended things, but I'm here to tell you, she didn't want to."

He waited until his friend returned and hunkered down with two cans of Bud. "Danielle and I talked. We both agreed it was over. I'm not going to sit here and rehash it."

Michael passed one of the beers to Chad before answering. "All right. Let me ask you this. Are you up for seeing everyone before you head out of here?"

He finished his whiskey and poured more. "I told Ralph I would. I'd like to see Bettina. Asal, too."

Chad blurted, "We can't wait for you to meet Carson, and Bettina is dying to give you a hug. You know how she is. And my dad wants to meet you."

Michael added his two cents. "These are the people who care about you, brother. They've been through hell, ya know? First, they thought you were dead. They watched you get executed, in the worst way possible, then saw you come back, in the hands of those two CIA jerks and Harandi. Make that three jerks."

He only half-heard Michael. His mind rushed him back, to the filthy, stinking cell and the cruel guards. He heard the rope creak as it stretched; heard his groans; felt the agonizing rip and tear through his shoulders. The buzzing roar started in his ears and blackness shimmered in front of his eyes. He spilled whiskey, cold and wet on his hands.

"Rowan, are you all right?" He felt the warmth of a hand on his arm and shuddered. His heart banged in his chest, out of control. They'd take him. He couldn't stop them. The pressure on his arm increased. Michael's concerned voice cut through the panic careening through his mind. "Rowan. Hey brother, come on back."

The blackness faded, the roaring subsided, and he pulled away. He couldn't miss the compassion in Chad's eyes and the disquiet in Michael's. Weariness overtook him, and a headache thumped in his forehead. He took a shaky breath. "Sorry. I'm OK." He set the glass of whiskey on the coffee table and wiped his hands on his jeans. "Sure, I'll talk to everybody, or see them. Whatever."

Michael responded. "Look, we don't know what happened in Tora, but let us help you. I know Shemal did a number on you. I can see a few of the scars. And something blew your circuits just now."

Embarrassed by the pointed words, he pulled his shirt tight around his body. "I said, *"I'm OK.* Just leave it at that."

Michael raised his hands. "Understood."

Chad murmured assent and raised his can of beer. "I get it, Rowan. Like you said, here's to us."

He took a deep breath, forced a smile, and picked up his glass of whiskey. "Right."

Seattle, WA

Tom looked at Danielle, seated across from him in the wooden booth. They'd found their way, on the cool, wet night, to the old cobblestone streets of Pioneer Square and an Italian restaurant he loved. Its cramped interior featured old, varnished wood booths and red-checked tablecloths. A tiny lamp mounted on the wall above the booth cast a warm, intimate glow over their table. The waiter took their orders and deposited a covered basket of fragrant bread and a carafe of house red wine before rushing off. Tom poured wine in both their glasses and raised his. "Here's to fabulous comfort food on a rainy night in Seattle."

Danielle tapped her glass against his and took a sip. "I love funky little places like this. Thanks for suggesting it."

"You're welcome. They've got the best lasagna *ever.*"

She slipped out of her rain jacket and fluffed her hair. "I've been chilled all day. Couldn't seem to drink enough coffee to get warmed up."

He replied. "I appreciate you thinking of me. You saved me from an evening of boring stats on a new project I'm organizing at work." He'd heard the strain in her voice when she'd surprised him with the invite to dinner and wondered what had happened involving Rowan Milani this time. If he ever ran across the guy, he'd like to give him a piece of his mind. Or maybe his solid right hook.

Danielle uncovered the bread and chose a slice. "I'm happy to help. Besides, I received some interesting news today, and I'm dying to share it."

He grabbed a piece of crusty bread, inhaling the garlicy aroma. "Do tell."

"Small-Batch wants to open another store in Seattle, and they're considering a couple other locations, too. They want me to move up a couple notches and become their official trainer. My boss said the CEO is impressed with how my shop is performing, and they love the neighborhood bistro concept. They think I'll make a great trainer because of how my kids are working out."

He gnawed on the bread while she talked, enjoying the way her eyes changed with the shifting expressions on her face and how she couldn't help using her hands to talk. He would love to feel her hands on him, too. And her lips. Maintaining a platonic friendship with her got harder by the day. He realized she'd stopped talking and sat with her head tilted, gazing expectantly at him. He responded, hoping he hadn't missed anything. "I'm impressed. Congrats. When do you start?"

She smiled. "Where were you just now? I told them I'd consider it and let them know in forty-eight hours."

What would she say if he told her he'd been in bed with her? And that even now, he couldn't stop thinking about pulling her sweater over her head and unfastening her bra. "Shoot, I think I'm too hungry to concentrate. Sorry. Are you seriously thinking about taking the new position?"

"Yes. I didn't want to give them an immediate answer, but I plan on taking the position. This is one more way for me to move forward, with both my life and career."

"Dani, that's fantastic." He hesitated, sensing a new independence in her attitude. This might be a good time to ask her something he'd been thinking about. "Hey, I've got an idea for you. Every year my family celebrates Christmas at our place on Orcas Island. Why don't you come, too? You can't imagine a more magical Christmas."

Her chin lifted in what he'd swear was an act of personal defiance. "I'd love to come. I don't have any plans for Christmas, and it sounds like a wonderful way to spend the holiday."

The waiter arrived with two steaming plates of lasagna, and they dug into the food. He kept a surreptitious eye on her and wondered what had prompted her subtle but definite change in attitude. Had she heard from Milani? Would she tell him about it if she had? He tapped his fork on his plate. "I wasn't lying about the lasagna, was I?"

She shook her head, eyes wide. "No, it's unbelievable. This is a perfect way to end the day. Thanks again for bringing me here."

Feeling like some sort of breakthrough had happened in their relationship, he grinned. "Anytime. Thanks for sharing your awesome news with me."

"Of course. You're my best friend."

Her words put a tiny pin-prick in his ballooning happiness, but he didn't let it show. "He'd made the choice of being *in it* with her for the long haul. Every day she was with him and not with Milani gave him the advantage. He raised his wine glass. "Here's to best friends. Forever."

She raised her glass and touched his. "Yep, here's to us."

The Next Day

Tom smiled at his twin sister Christina as she slid into the booth across from him. He'd asked her to meet him at their usual spot, a trendy pizza eatery mid-way between their respective offices. A few times a month they shared lunch and caught up. Christina stayed in touch with his other two sisters and their mother, which saved him a lot of time. He and his father met for coffee every other Saturday morning, thus keeping his connection to the only other male in his family intact.

His sister always looked chic, yet somehow down home, with her honey-streaked brown hair arranged in what looked to him like some kind of crazy braid that wrapped part way around her head and trailed down her back. Her slender frame made the short denim jacket, leggings, and knee-high boots eye catching in a way that he, as a protective brother, always bristled over. "You're looking way too sexy, as usual. Thanks for meeting me. I need your expert advice."

Christina pursed her perfectly glossed lips. "Thanks for noticing, and you're welcome. You still hung up on your way-too-sexy *friend* Dani, who can't give up the terrorist guy?"

He scowled at her. "No, I'm not *hung up* on her, I'm just not sure how to proceed."

She rolled hazel eyes that matched his and said, "Right. Did you order our favorite pizza?"

He could never pull anything over on her. "OK, you're right, Tina. And yes, of course, I ordered the seafood specialty."

"Oh good, I'm starving. Why don't you invite her over to your place for dinner this weekend? I'll stop by. After I leave, I'll text you what I think, and you can put the moves on her."

"Put the moves on her? Are you kidding? I think I'm falling in love with her, and you're the only one I've talked to about it." Their server arrived with their favorite steaming pie.

After flopping a wedge of pizza on her plate, Christina delicately licked her fingers. "You *are* serious, aren't you? I'm sorry. Here's what you need to do. Take things a simple step further."

"I've been trying to accomplish that by spending quality time with her. Yesterday, she called me. We had dinner, and I got the definite feeling she's about had it with waiting around for Milani. He's footloose and fancy free now. As far as I can tell, he hasn't contacted her."

"Yeah, I've seen a few news reports. The whole thing is creepy. Who knows what he really did or didn't do? So. Are you going to take my advice?"

"How am I supposed to take it a step further without scaring her away?"

"Oh geez, think about it. She doesn't exactly sound like someone who scares easily. Have you ever invited her to your place?"

He helped himself to more pizza. "Not yet. I've thought about it, though."

She pointed her fork at him. "Do it. Keep the lights low, have some wine, suggest watching a movie. And then, you know, take it a step further. You're a guy, you know what you want. Who knows? She might surprise you."

As close as he was to his twin, he'd never be able to tell her the things he'd dreamed of doing with Danielle. He gave her a faint smile. "I guess it's worth a try."

"See? Problem solved. Aren't you glad you decided to buy me lunch?"

"Whoa. I believe it's your turn, hot-shot Seattle marketing queen."

Christina waved her fork again. "Hey, if any of my clients found out I was giving free advice, I'd be in deep trouble. Besides, I'm your kid sister."

He chuckled dryly. "Yes, by seven minutes. Fine. Lunch is on me. And I do appreciate your time. I know you've got a busy schedule with the holidays coming up."

Her eyes widened. "That's it! You've got to invite her to the family Christmas on Orcas."

While his gregarious sister did everything but jump up and down in the booth, he tried to keep his response low-key. "I already did."

Christina flung her arms wide. "It's the perfect setup. Meeting someone's family signals a further step in a relationship. Good for you."

"She said she'd love to come."

"This is fantastic. She'll get to meet all of us. I can't wait to meet her. Neither can everyone else."

"You better not gang up on her. Dad will keep Mom from going overboard. I think."

She blew him a raspberry. "I keep telling you, Dani does not sound like the kind of woman who is easily deterred or frightened." Christina paused, and her eyes went wide again. "Oh my goodness. Maybe you're the one who's scared. You aren't still thinking about how things ended with Whitney, are you?"

He cringed inwardly, hoping it didn't show. Count on his twin to figure out what was really eating at him. "I don't think so."

"Oh stop. I know you better than that. I should have figured this out weeks ago. Tom, she let you down, I know. But that was five years ago. You've dated other nice women since then."

"But not one I've felt this way about. And Whitney didn't just *let me down.* She ended our engagement after two years. After we planned the wedding and our lives together."

Christina reached across the table and put her hand on his. "I know how awful it was for you. If you love Dani, she must be someone very special and worth fighting for. Maybe sharing your experience would help her."

"She is special. Sometimes, seeing the hurt in her eyes, I just want to say, forget the guy who jerked you around and *look at me.* I'll dedicate my life to making the best possible life for you. Whatever you want or need, I'll do my best to give you. I've never felt that way before, not even with Whitney."

"Tom, that's beautiful. Did you ever consider telling Dani how you feel?"

He laughed. "Oh yeah, and every time I make up my mind to tell her, we meet, and she's upset over one more thing that's happened to this loser Milani."

Christina squeezed his hand. "I'm a firm believer in the right timing. Keep the faith and be patient with her. Dani sounds like a keeper to me."

"Thanks Tina." The server laid their check on the table as she passed by, and he glanced at it while he dug his wallet from his back pocket. "I'll seriously consider taking your costly advice."

She patted her mouth with a napkin. "You better."

CHAPTER SEVENTEEN

Chicago, IL

Marion Johnston faced her husband from a foot below his chin and poked him in the chest.

"Ralph, no matter what you think, I'm going to visit Rowan today."

Ralph looked down at her, his face reddening. "Now you listen to me, Marion. He's not the Rowan you remember. He's in a lot of pain, and he's had at least one flashback we know about. Damn it, I don't want you to feel bad."

"Oh, for crying out loud, Rowan will always be Rowan. He just needs to see someone who loves him. I'm going to do this, Ralph. Don't think you can stand in my way." She emphasized each word with a jab to his chest.

He scratched his chin and glared at her. "God almighty. You're as damn stubborn as he is. I think you're on a doomed mission, but you go ahead. Good luck."

"You can drive me to the Four Seasons right now. I can't wait to see him. I've got another batch of cookies all ready to go."

"Fine. Michael and I already have a meeting scheduled with Johnny. He's sending the limo, so you don't have to worry about me driving you."

An hour and a half later, she shooed Ralph and Michael impatiently away to their meeting and stepped across the wide, carpeted hallway to Rowan's suite. She gazed up at the bald-headed man standing in front of the door, hands folded, feet planted at shoulder width. He carried a pistol openly at his side. "Hello Roberto. I brought you some cookies too."

The big man grinned. "Thank you, Marion. Nice to see you again. Go ahead and knock. Rowan's in charge here."

She knocked on the door. After a few seconds, she rapped again. The door opened slowly. She couldn't stop a sharp intake of breath, then coerced her lips into a genuine smile. "Hello Rowan. I come bearing one of your favorite gifts. May I come in for a bit?"

Johnny watched as Michael and Ralph filed into the presidential suite. They took seats at the table, facing him. Windows with sweeping views of the city below framed their meeting. For reasons he couldn't explain, he'd felt compelled to stay in the suite, catching up on his business interests, enjoying the peace and quiet. "Thanks, you two, for humoring me. I'm looking for your take on Rowan."

Michael deferred to Ralph. "Go ahead."

Ralph began. "He's different. Penitent. Subdued. I guess I'd have to say, he's essentially given up on damn near everything. Whether that will change over the next several months remains to be seen."

Johnny shifted his gaze to Michael. "What did you get from your meet with him?"

Michael replied. "It pains me to say it, but Rowan has some serious problems. He reminds me of a guy with PTSD, but you know, guys like Rowan aren't supposed to get PTSD. They bounce back and keep going."

Ralph added, "You can tell his body hurts in a big way."

Johnny considered. "My doc gave him a thorough exam. MRIs on his shoulders, back, and hips. Those sons of bitches in Tora did a number on him. It's a fuckin' miracle he can still walk around. But the doc said they must have known how long his body could stand up to the torture and stopped short of completely debilitating damage. It's damn gruesome when you think about it."

Michael replied. "I'm not surprised. Torture is a science for the Egyptians. We'll probably never know what he endured."

Ralph snorted. "Not if we wait around for Rowan to tell us."

Johnny looked from one man to the other. "I've gathered that he's a very private man. Here's what concerns me most. The doc said he needs extensive rehab. Rowan told the doc he'd do what he needs to. I asked for input from you two because I'm questioning whether Key West is the best place for him to recover. Help me out here."

Michael replied. "My usual experience with Rowan, in almost every situation, is this. If you try to tell him he can't do something, he's going to find a way to do it. But now, I don't think he wants to do anything except remain free."

Ralph said, "I agree. The stubborn, hard-headed man we all knew and loved is pretty much gone."

Johnny replied. "You think we ought to let him head for Key West, keep tabs on him, and give him some time to think things through?"

Ralph countered. "He's going to be out there, wandering around wounded, in both his mind and body. I'm not sure that's a good idea."

Michael leaned forward, intent. "I don't think you have to worry about him going much of anywhere. Besides, do we want to risk him acting *in character* and telling us to go and fuck ourselves?"

Ralph grimaced. "Point taken."

Johnny said, "My next question concerns the redhead. What about bringing her here, or sending her to Key West?"

Michael replied. "He told me in no uncertain terms that it was over between them. And believe me, he meant it."

Ralph muttered, "He's still as stubborn as a mule. God forbid anybody help him with any of this crap. I give up."

Johnny observed his friend. "Aw Ralphie, we gotta be optimistic. I get the picture of one tough son of a bitch who's been pushed to the end of his endurance or his limits or what have you."

Ralph replied. "You may be right. It's just— Well, I've known Rowan for a long damn time, and I've never seen him quite so beaten down. I'm concerned he won't cooperate with Angelo or any of us, simply because he's given up."

Johnny tapped restless fingers on the table. "Before we jump to any foregone conclusions, I say we give your psychiatrist the opportunity to work with Rowan. I'm betting he'll have a handle on things."

Michael replied. "Like Ralph said, *if* Rowan will cooperate."

Ralph added, "And that remains to be seen, but I agree, we need to give Angelo a chance."

Johnny surveyed the two men. "Gentlemen, I believe we've reached the optimum solution for the time being."

Rowan gazed into the kind face of one of the few people he'd always felt completely at ease with. "Hey Marion. Come on in."

She proceeded with high energy into his suite and flourished a plastic container. "It's so good to see you. I brought you a whole batch of cookies. I figured your supply must be running low."

He'd always thought of Marion as a miniature force of nature and probably the only woman in the world who could make Ralph stand down. He accepted the container of cookies and pried open the lid. "Thanks. Chad and Mike finished off the first batch when they were here." He nabbed a cookie and stuffed half of it into his mouth.

Marion said, "I've been wondering how you're doing. I'm so glad you still like the cookies."

Somehow, from her, it didn't sound like, *I'm here to see how screwed up you are.* Seated with the container of cookies between them on the sofa, he panicked for an instant, wondering what he could even talk about. "The cookies are great. Thanks again."

"You're welcome. I've always loved making them for you because of how much you enjoy them."

"You're right. I enjoy the hell out of them."

She smiled at him. "I see you like wearing your new jacket. Do the jeans fit you, and the shirts?"

"Did you find this jacket for me? And the other clothes too?"

"I searched online until I found a jacket most like the one you had. I shopped for the other clothes too. I had a blast picking things that reminded me of you."

She'd managed, through her sweet kindness, to damn near undo his untrustworthy emotions. "Huh. Thanks."

Marion gave him an airy wave. "Of course." She stood up and reached out. "Come on, let's look out the windows. I love being on the top floor of hotels, especially in a city like Chicago."

He hesitated, then took her hand, the warm contact sending a jolt through his gut. Contact with another person's *hand* had been anything but pleasant for a long time. He stood up, unable to stifle a groan and wince. "Ouch. Damn it."

"Rowan, I'm so sorry. I didn't realize that would hurt."

He kept a hold of her hand, surprised because he didn't want to let go. "It's OK." They walked together to the windows. He stood close beside her and blinked back hot tears, mortified at his reaction to her genuine concern.

Marion stayed at his side, gently disengaging her hand from his and easing it around his waist. She was close to a foot shorter than he was, but felt like a tower of strength next to his hurting body. "I'm so glad you're here safe and sound," she murmured.

"Me too."

"Isn't the water beautiful? The lake seems to go on forever."

He stared at the sparkling expanse. "I love the water."

"It's so peaceful. I hope you can rest here."

He heaved a sigh. "I'm trying."

Marion looked up at him and he saw tears on her cheeks. "I know it must be hard." She wiped the tears away. "Goodness, I'm sorry to be such a wet blanket. It's just a huge relief to have you here, in the flesh."

He flicked one last tear from her cheek with his thumb. "I'm relieved too. How else would I get the cookies?"

She waggled a forefinger at him. "Rowan Milani. You'll never change. It's always about the cookies with you."

He winked at her. "Always. Don't tell anyone, though, OK?"

She chuckled. "Your secret is safe with me. Ralph mentioned you'd like to head south? To Key West?"

"Yeah."

"Soon?"

"I'd leave today, if I could."

"What's holding you back?"

"I need to see everyone before I leave, and I can't bring myself to do that. Yet."

"Well, there's no rush, is there?" She gave him a gentle hug. "You know something, Rowan? You're the most amazing, honorable man."

His brows shot up and he stared down at her. "You may be the only person on the entire planet who holds that opinion of me. Especially now."

"I disagree. After everything you've endured, you're choosing to fulfill an obligation to others instead of doing what you want and need."

"Marion, I'm not *honorable*. Far from it."

She shook her finger at him. "You stop right there, young man. Everything you've done has been to right the wrongs committed against you and get rid of the real terror threats." Marion pulled away. "Are you taking anything for your pain?"

He eyed the bottle of whiskey on the counter. "Yeah. Johnny's doctor gave me a prescription."

"Oh good. It's no fun hurting all the time."

"You're right about that."

Marion made her way back to the sofa and he followed her. "We're all hoping for the best for you. I believe you have a great future ahead of you."

"Thanks. I hope you're right."

"Speaking of the future, have you talked to Danielle yet?"

He searched for the right answer. The one that would end the conversation. "No, I haven't talked to her. As far as I know, she's somewhere in the northwest, Seattle maybe. I don't plan to intrude in her life."

"Oh Rowan, I think you're making a mistake. Danielle loved you very much. She was devastated when you left Kauai."

"We talked after that, a few times. I told her, I mean, I encouraged her to move on. We ended our relationship."

"But now you're free. You have a chance to start over. Don't you want to be with the woman you love?"

If nothing else, her gentle probing helped solidify his resolve, and clarified the painful decisions he'd battled with while he sat alone with his thoughts. "No. I'm being realistic. My future is anything but certain. I'm the last thing Danielle needs."

"But don't you think Danielle has the right to decide what she needs?"

"Danielle doesn't think clearly when it comes to me."

"Oh Rowan, I think you're denying yourself a partner who wants to be involved in your life."

"I ruined things between us, you know? For too long, I only thought about what *I, by God,* wanted. Then, sitting in Tora, *wishing* they'd kill me, I realized what a jerk I'd been. What a fool. How I'd thrown everything away."

"I'm so sorry," she whispered.

He saw tears welling in her eyes again. "Hey Marion, it doesn't matter. I shouldn't have brought up Tora. Besides, it's over now."

She sat up straight and folded her hands in her lap. "I understand. You need to do what you think is right."

He nodded, relieved that she'd backed down, but suspicious of her quick assent. "I don't want to interfere in Danielle's life. She's been through enough with me."

Marion stood up. "Well, I've got to retrieve Ralph."

He walked her to the door, wondering what she might be planning. "Thanks for the cookies."

Marion gave him a light hug. "You're welcome, sweetie. You know we love you. Listen, when you're ready to see everyone, I'll run interference for you with your parents."

He laughed. "Damn, I'd appreciate that. *A lot.*"

She reached up and patted his cheek. "You know I've got your back."

He opened the door, and she left after giving him a wave. He nodded at Roberto, shut the door, and turned the deadbolt. He poured a glass of whiskey and found himself staring out the windows at Lake Michigan, wishing it was the turquoise water surrounding Key West. "I need to get out of here," he muttered.

Restless, anxious to get past the obstacles in his way, he stared at the silky, rolling waves far below. As the day drifted toward sunset, the slate-blue water took on a coppery sheen. A few sailboats dotted the glistening surface. He envied the people out there, enjoying the day, maybe going out for dinner, or home to a family.

What must that be like? He could no longer even conceive of what constituted a *normal* life. The actions he'd taken with such confident certainty had guaranteed he'd never have any of the things other people took for granted. He left the windows and grabbed the bottle of Jack. Well, goddamn it, *fine.* He'd own that.

But he couldn't ask Danielle to leave her life again and live the way he knew he had to. He poured more whiskey, gulped it, and poured more. The gloom of the suite fit his mood, and this time he slouched down on the sofa, leaving the lights off.

He took a couple more deep swallows of the potent booze, while his bitter thoughts continued. Not one of the people *out there* enjoying life would give a shit that he'd sacrificed everything on their behalf, for the benefit of their country. His country too, not that it mattered. He'd be damned if he'd care anymore.

His jaws cracked with a huge yawn. He closed his eyes, grateful for the whiskey working its magic one more time, easing the tension from his aching body, leading his mind away from the painful thoughts and into peaceful darkness. Long ago, he'd found it to be the one thing; the *only* thing he could rely on. His breathing slowed, and the glass slipped from his fingers, tumbling silently to the carpeted floor. Only his soft snores punctuated the stillness.

A staccato trio of knocks had Johnny rising from his chair. He ambled to the door and checked the viewer, then grinned and opened the door. "Come on in, Marion, and join us."

Marion marched into the suite. "Thank you. I want to add my two cents to whatever you three have concocted concerning Rowan."

Johnny caught Ralph's glance and chuckled at the consternation on his friend's face. "Now this I'm dyin' to hear. Fill us in." He pulled out the chair next to his.

Marion sat down. "I know exactly what Rowan needs."

Ralph cleared his throat. "Now Marion."

Johnny watched, fascinated as Marion shook her finger at her husband. "Hold it right there, Ralph. Don't you *Marion* me. Rowan needs Danielle." She paused to frown, then continued. "He's got too much honor to allow himself to do what's best for him. So. I'm going to call Danielle and tell her to get her fanny to Chicago. Chad should be able to find her phone number for me."

Ralph scowled but didn't say anything. Johnny stepped into the sudden quiet. "You get that phone number, pronto. The minute his woman agrees to make the trip, I'll send the jet."

Marion flashed him a thousand-watt smile. "Thank you. I'm going to text Chad before we leave. The sooner we find Danielle and get her here, the better off Rowan will be."

Michael spoke up. "We've got a number for Danielle. She has the same kind of phone as the rest of us. Chad set them up for everyone at the Kauai estate."

Marion replied. "I know, but I've tried calling her, multiple times. Bettina tried calling her after baby Carson was born. The phone goes directly to voice mail. Angelo said he isn't surprised."

Ralph said, "That's just it, Marion. Maybe Danielle isn't interested anymore. Maybe she wants to be left alone, the same way Rowan does."

Marion waved a dismissive hand. "Nonsense. Relationships get twisted for silly reasons. I know one other thing, too."

Johnny leaned forward, intrigued. "What's that?"

Marion's eyes filled with tears. "Oh goodness, I'm sorry. Rowan is so alone, and he's so sad. If we don't try to help him by bringing Danielle here, he's going to dive deep into the whiskey. I saw him staring at the bottle while we talked."

Ralph heaved a sigh. "I'd have to say, she's right."

Michael bent his head for a moment and wiped his eyes, then gave Johnny a weak smile. "Yeah, I agree. It's harder than hell to watch him suffer. I'd love to see the old Rowan. I'll text Chad right now. We gotta do whatever it takes to get Danielle out here."

Johnny observed each one, reading surprisingly tender compassion on Michael's face, fierce determination on Marion's, and renewed hope on Ralph's. Deeply pleased, he addressed the threesome. "Good job people. Ya know, we make a damn decent crew."

Mid-October
Seattle, WA
Danielle's phone rang, and she plucked it from her desk. She'd forced herself to spend the morning in her office with the door closed. Small-Batch had emailed her mountains of information, and she couldn't wait to get started in her new position. Before long, she'd be traveling to Spokane for training. The challenges the promotion offered distracted her, and she loved it.

She frowned at the *Unknown Caller* message and hesitated. It might be someone at corporate. They had her personal number. "Hello, this is Danielle."

"Hi Dani. It's me, Marion. How are you sweetie? We've all missed you so much."

"Marion? Oh wow, I can't believe it. I've missed you, too. Where are you? How's Ralph? Is everyone still together?"

"We're in Chicago. Ralph's fine, and we're all still together."

She couldn't bear to ask about Rowan. "I've always loved Chicago. What about Bettina and the baby? Is Chad with her now?"

Marion replied. "Their baby boy was born just over seven weeks ago, right before we left Dubai. His name is Carson. Yes, Chad is here, and they both say hello. But that isn't why I called."

She clutched the phone in her damp hand. "Um, really, Dubai?"

"Dubai is a long story. Listen sweetie, Rowan is here. He needs you."

Fresh hope warred with the old hurt, and she said, "I haven't heard from him since he was released. The last time we talked he was adamant about how I needed to move on."

"The reason he hasn't reached out to you is because he doesn't want to intrude on your life. He actually admitted to me that he ruined things between you."

She replied, her voice shaky. "Well, it was sort of a two-way street. I said mean, hurtful things, threw Derek in his face, and then later, I pushed him into a corner."

Marion's tone became business-like. "It's time the two of you stopped beating yourselves up and robbing yourselves of each other. Are you willing to make the first move?"

The longing she'd tried so hard to suppress rolled through her in waves. "What exactly do you mean?"

"Fly out here and see him. Be with him. I know Rowan. He loves you, Dani. Every day without you is killing him."

"Um, I don't know. He was so angry with me." A kaleidoscope of memories swept her away. The way she'd felt, seeing him in the airport lobby in Sioux Falls. The urgency in their first kiss. Making love on the beach in Kauai. The warmth of his body covering hers, the taste of him in her mouth, the rough brush of the stubble on his cheeks contrasting with the soft exploration of his lips. The times they'd spent in companionable silence with his arms snug around her. And then, the harsh, cutting finality in his voice. *We're done.*

Marion's insistent voice interrupted her painful memories. "He's not angry, sweetie. He's lonesome and hurting."

She closed her eyes. "This is so hard. Since I haven't heard from him, I decided he must have meant it when he told me it was over between us."

"Oh Dani, what are you saying?"

"I don't know. I accepted a promotion at my job. I love my career and my life in Seattle. I miss him too, but what if he doesn't want me?"

"Give yourselves a chance. You don't need to be afraid or worried about how he feels about you. Trust me, I've seen him and listened to him. You are all he truly wants."

After all the lonely months, she had the opportunity to see the man she'd never stopped loving. What was wrong with her? "I'll come. I just need to make a few arrangements with my job. If he doesn't want me, at least I'll know."

Marion sounded relieved. "Dani, that's fantastic. Let me know when you can leave. A private jet will pick you up."

"Wow. That sounds interesting. I'll call you as soon as I get things organized."

Chicago, IL

Rowan heard the quiet knock and made his way to the door, wiped sweaty hands on his jeans and braced himself. He pulled the door open and greeted the compassionate man who always seemed to know more about him than he did himself. "Hey, Doc. Come on in."

Angelo entered the suite, his slender face breaking into a grin. "Ah, Rowan. Seeing you is a special kind of blessing. If you can tolerate my exuberance, I would like very much to give you a hug."

"OK, Doc. Just this once."

Angelo embraced him gently, murmuring while patting his back. "It is good to have you safely home, and I am grateful you agreed to see me."

He worked to keep from cringing at the contact and hesitantly returned the embrace. When Angelo gave him a final pat and stepped away, he met the shrink's perceptive blue eyes. "Uh, I've got coffee. And an endless supply of Marion's cookies."

"I never turn down an opportunity for either your coffee or Marion's cookies."

"Well then, it's your lucky day." He couldn't say the same for himself. Talking with Angelo usually left him painfully blindsided by something the psychiatrist ferreted out of the depths of his mind. He led his guest to the grouping of sofas where he spent each night.

While he shoved his blanket and pillow aside and lowered himself gingerly, Angelo dunked half a cookie in coffee. "Mm. What a delicious combination."

He sipped the hot brew and contemplated the psychiatrist, wondering what kind of instructions Angelo had received. "I'm guessing you're here so you can report back to Johnny. Before we get started, I've got a few things to say."

Angelo sat his coffee cup down and shoved his glasses further up his long nose. "Rowan, you are proceeding from a false premise. I am here solely for your well-being. I have received no instructions other than to care for you in whatever way you may want or need. You must also understand, anything you share with me is held in strictest confidence, *by me.*"

"OK. Whatever. Look Doc, I need to apologize for the things I said the last time we talked. As I recall, I threw you out and slammed the door in your face."

"I certainly accept your apology. I know you were quite angry that day, for a variety of reasons, which I came to understand later." Angelo settled back, one leg crossed over the other, his hands laced together over one knee. "This is your time, Rowan. Why don't you tell me what's on your mind?"

He tried to get a gauge on the earnest man sitting relaxed and confident across from him. Could he trust him? Or was he in cahoots with his new master, interested in searching out his condition, finding his weak points, and exploiting them? "I'm sorry, Doc. Sometimes it's hard for me to think. All I want is the beach on Key West."

Angelo replied gravely. "What draws you to Key West?"

He stared unseeing, thinking about the peace he'd felt walking in the sand, enjoying the heat from the sun, the color of the water rolling in endless waves past his ankles and the three scraggly palms rooted in a pile of rocks. He blurted his thoughts. "I love the turquoise water and the palm trees."

"I take it you have spent some time in Key West?"

“Yeah, and I’m heading back as soon as I jump through whatever hoops I have to for Johnny.”

“You have an interesting perspective on Mr. Giacopino’s involvement in your life.” The words and tone held no condemnation or judgment. The psychiatrist had simply stated the facts.

And so would he, if he could get his scattered thoughts to cooperate. He shrugged. “Don’t get me wrong, I’m grateful. But I’ve been passed from one keeper to another and then another. First Shemal, in Tora, then the government, and now I guess it’s Johnny’s turn. I have to do whatever he wants.”

“Is that what Mr. Giacopino told you?”

“Not in so many words, but I can read between the lines.”

“Your reaction now is not like it would have been six or seven months ago.”

He grimaced. “My reaction to damn near everything is different now. Spending a few months in Egypt’s version of a supermax has given me a completely different outlook.”

Angelo replied. “In a bit, we will come back to the significance of the turquoise water and palm trees. First, though, I would like to further explore a few initial things. Do you mind?”

He resisted the urge to wipe his still-sweating hands and swallowed more coffee instead. “No, of course not.”

“Thank you. What changed your mindset in regard to authority, specifically in the form of Mr. Giacopino?”

He tried not to fidget while one eye twitched uncontrollably. Somehow, the shrink always knew how to cut to the heart, *his heart,* and it made him damn uncomfortable. “I said, spending time in Tora gave me a different outlook.”

Angelo gave him the patient smile he remembered. “Yes, you have now used the word *different* three times. If you can, please enumerate for me the things that brought you to this new or altered perspective.”

He stared, dry-mouthed at the psychiatrist. His hands holding the coffee cup shook. Lying alone in his Tora cell, he'd longed for only one opportunity, far out of his reach. "In Tora, it was, uh, difficult. I remembered, you know? I realized what a jerk I'd been, to everyone. Danielle, Ralph, you, Mike and Gabriel, my parents, *everyone."*

Angelo said, "Continue, please."

He swallowed hard and spoke, his voice hoarse. "I swore, if I could come back, I'd be a different man. But it hasn't worked out that way."

Angelo gazed at him, brows furrowed. "Why not?"

"Nothing changed, except no one tortured me in ADX Florence. Then they took me to Texas. If not for Johnny, I'd be headed for death row."

"But you are not in that situation. You are free."

Despair crushed him. He took a final swallow of the coffee before answering. "But don't you see? There is no opportunity for me to be any kind of *different man.* And I'm not free."

Angelo sat back, and his look turned thoughtful. "Yet, the first thing you did was apologize to me for your previous actions. No matter the outer circumstances, if your heart has changed, then you are indeed the *different man* you swore you would become."

"Nah, Doc. I'm just a coward. I learned that in Tora, too." He couldn't believe the words had fallen from his mouth. He should have known he'd spill his guts. It happened every single time they talked.

Angelo responded. "I must emphatically disagree. I know you, Rowan, and would wager that you conducted yourself with courage in the face of unspeakable acts against your person."

"Yeah, well, Shemal found my breaking point. I told him what he wanted to know, in exchange for, never mind. I can't, I don't want to talk about it." Gooseflesh rose on his arms and legs. He shivered and swiped at the perspiration on his forehead, felt it on his chest and back.

"How about if we take a break. Would you like more coffee? I could use more, along with another cookie."

The kindness in the calm voice, along with the empathy in the psychiatrist's lean face only heightened the raw emotions overtaking his mind. His eyes strayed to the bottle of whiskey on the counter and he wished he could be alone. "OK. Just coffee for me."

Angelo refilled their cups and returned to the sofa. "Would you like to revisit the connotations of the color turquoise and your affection for palm trees?"

"Sure." He'd take any kind of diversion from the awful memories of the cowardice he'd been forced to confront at the point of Shemal's dagger.

"You are probably unaware of the significance of your words and choices. In the parlance of color psychology, turquoise is most often associated with emotional healing. It is said to rebuild a person's spirit during times of mental stress. Turquoise is also purported to relieve loneliness."

The psychiatrist's complete change of direction jarred his mind away from the desperate thoughts. "You're kidding, right? You can't be serious about *color psychology,* Doc."

Angelo appeared unfazed. "From a negative perspective, turquoise relates to a lack of communication skills and deception."

"Well, that part sounds about right."

The shrink's response came smoothly, leaving him with a hot core of anger in his chest. "I am not subscribing any of these characteristics to you. I am simply offering an alternate way of exploring your mind's inclinations. Food for thought, you might say."

"Of course. What the fuck do the palm trees mean?"

Angelo's face creased in a grin. "For a minute, I thought you might throw me out again."

He drew a deep breath and let it out slowly, realizing his hands were clenched in a death grip around the china cup. "You have the ability to piss me off like no one else, except maybe, well never mind. Tell me about the palm trees."

"Ah yes. Back to the palm trees." Angelo slurped more coffee and held the cup in both hands. "We delve into interesting territory here. The palm denotes a righteous man. One who does not stoop or bow earthward, a man governed by true and abiding principles, I believe is how the explanation goes."

He felt inexplicable heat in his face. For no reason he could understand, he thought about the man who had appeared in his Tora cell. He shoved the thought aside, done with his worthless delusions. "You aren't making any sense. Do you think you could speak English?"

As usual, Angelo sidestepped his bluster. "The delineation continues with the strength and elasticity of the palm. Although weighed down with many things, the good man withstands them all and continues to rise."

"You're still not making sense. Maybe you're right, and I'm a different man than I was six months or a year ago, but I haven't been a *good man* for a long time."

The psychiatrist continued, maddeningly serene. "Surely you know, Rowan, many options exist for you to rebuild or restore your life."

Irritated that he couldn't affect the shrink's calm demeanor, pissed off at his inability to grasp or decipher the message embedded in the obscure explanation, he countered. "Just what the hell is all of this supposed to mean? Can you give it to me in plain words instead of psychobabble?"

Angelo spoke in a soothing, quiet voice. "In simple terms, I'm saying that redemption is yours, if you choose it."

The cup dropped from his fingers. He watched, from far away, as it fell and crashed in slow motion on the low table, spilling steaming coffee across the glass top. His heart pounded at double time. He felt the grit of the cold, filthy concrete pressing against his pain-wracked body, saw the man bending down beside him, and heard the gentle voice whispering through his mind. *Redemption is yours, if you choose it.*

"Rowan, are you all right? How can I help you?"

He felt the leather sofa beneath him and saw coffee dripping from the table to the white carpet in a rush of tiny brown splotches. Angelo sat beside him with one hand resting gently on his arm. He turned, meeting the concerned eyes above the glasses that had slipped once more down the narrow nose. *"Why would you say that?"*

"Say what, Rowan? What exactly did I say that triggered your flashback?" Angelo's voice held familiar, exhausting enthusiasm. The shrink's singular purpose, his determination to help him, had brought him to another agonizing blindside he couldn't handle.

This time the revelation had come with a sledgehammer, worse than any of the other times, punishing him with every heartbeat. He hunched over and rubbed his forehead, staring at the accumulating drops of coffee on the pristine carpet, thinking he might heave his guts out. "It's a long story Doc, and I'm not up for it right now."

Angelo spoke with less intensity. "I understand. You have only just been released from cruel circumstances, and I am afraid that in my desire to help you, I have inadvertently caused you even more pain. I am sorry, Rowan, and hope you will consider seeing me again."

He knew he didn't have a choice about whether or not he'd see the shrink again. "No apologies, Doc. You didn't cause any of what's going on in my screwed-up head. Just give me a couple days to think about this, OK?"

"Absolutely." Angelo patted his arm, then stood up. "You need rest more than anything. Are you able to sleep?"

He gaze drifted once more to the bottle of whiskey. "Yeah, I've been able to sleep."

The psychiatrist followed his gaze. "I see. Well, good. I am certain the beds in this lovely hotel are supremely comfortable."

The Four Seasons was another version of a prison as far as he was concerned. "Right you are. Thanks for everything."

"It has always been my pleasure to help you. If I may make a suggestion?"

He nodded, anxious to be alone. "Say what's on your mind."

Angelo replied. "Be patient and kind with yourself. You have only just emerged from a hellish half year, preceded by an equally wretched year. Take all the time you need to decompress and adjust to your new circumstances. And please, do not hesitate to call me if you need anything."

He walked the psychiatrist to the door and opened it. "Thanks. I'll do my best, and if I need anything, I'll let you know."

He read doubt on the wise face, but Angelo only said, "Very well. I will see you soon."

"Sounds good." He shut the door noiselessly, turned the deadbolt and leaned against the doorframe. His focus went immediately to the bottle of whiskey and single glass on the countertop. He'd never found a better way to expunge the misery from his tormented mind.

After pouring a generous glass-full, he wandered across the suite, drawn invariably to the big windows overlooking the waterfront. He took a long swallow of the biting liquid and sniffed at the pungent aroma invading his sinuses. Somber, low clouds had turned the water deep gray-blue. The sky and the water suited his mood. *Turquoise water be damned.*

The psychiatrist's comments left him disturbed, unsettled, and if anything, *more* wounded. He shuddered, tossed back more whiskey, and sneered at his image reflected in the window. "If you weren't such a coward, you'd figure this shit out and be that goddamned *different man.* But hell, what's the use?"

In a few days or maybe a week, he'd meet with Johnny again and begin his new role as partner. Some *partnership*. He'd do whatever the Don required, starting with rehab and continuing on with Angelo. He'd take the shrink's advice and lay low in Key West as long as possible before taking the lead in Johnny's private war against the Islamists. After that, it would be only a matter of time before he found a way to disappear permanently. Unless he was taken out or succumbed for the last time to Shemal and the Muslim Brotherhood.

He grimaced at the hopelessness of his situation. Angelo had said, *you are free.* For once, the shrink was wrong. He would *never* be free. And regardless of the other mumbo-jumbo he couldn't unravel and the delusion he'd experienced in Tora, he would *never* be a different man. He tipped his head back and drained the glass of whiskey.

He brooded at his reflection. He was nothing more than a broken man, in every way. His body, his mind, and his life. All broken. The empty darkness, always present at the edges of his consciousness, pressed in, hovering at the periphery of his sight. He rubbed his eyes, yawned, and snagged the bottle of Jack Daniel's before sliding onto the smooth leather sofa.

He poured more, took a long swallow, and swirled the whiskey in his glass. "You're a cold bitch of a lover, aren't you?" But it gave him what he needed, and for that, he would be forever thankful. He gulped until the glass was empty, then pitched it. Leaning back, staring at the ceiling, he let the darkness pull him into painless oblivion.

Angelo stood in front of the heavy wooden door of Rowan's suite as it closed quietly. He winced when he heard the deadbolt turn. An overpowering sense of urgency gripped him, and he raised his hand to knock, then stopped. At this point, Rowan did not trust him and most certainly would not endure more probing, painful questions. However, leaving the desperately wounded man alone with a bottle of potent whiskey went against every part of his being, not to mention his ethics as a psychiatrist.

His years of experience, including his own path to recovery after suffering at the hands of the Viet Cong, told him he should have addressed the alcohol issue with his patient. He should never have allowed himself to be ushered out of the room without saying anything. Even in his diminished state, Rowan had remained in charge of this first session. He was ashamed to admit he'd allowed it because he feared; no, because he *knew* he'd lose connection with the hurting man if he'd tried to assert any kind of control.

Roberto cleared his throat. "You want I should ask him to let you back in, Doctor Blevins?"

He turned away reluctantly. "No, but thank you for asking, Roberto."

The big man peered down and cracked his knuckles. "He drinks too much booze. I first noticed last year, in Key West. On the jet on the way back here, too, he tanked it right down. I'm a little worried about him, to tell ya the truth. But I haven't mentioned anything to the Boss, because I don't want to smear Rowan's good name. You get what I'm sayin'?"

The tenderness in Roberto's voice surprised him. "Oh, I get it. No question. Thank you for sharing your concerns with me. I hope he will connect with his friends and family more often now that he is a free man."

Roberto nodded. "I'm glad you're here to help him. Rowan's a standup guy. He takes responsibility for his doings, and I admire that in a man."

"I must say, I am glad you are here, making certain Rowan remains safe." He held out his hand, eyes widening as Roberto reached out with a thick paw.

Roberto's hand enveloped his, but the handshake was gentle. "We'll take good care of him. Nobody will get close who isn't supposed to. You got nothin' to worry about on that score."

"Good. Now I must have a chat with your Boss." He headed down the hallway, organizing his thoughts and marshalling his courage. The Mafia Don had asked for an analysis of Rowan's mindset. But he had a feeling the man wanted more information than he was willing to divulge.

He knocked firmly on the door and waited, tapping one foot soundlessly on the carpeted walkway. The door opened, revealing the Don, in a black suit and white shirt, sans tie. "Please come in, Doctor Blevins. I've been looking forward to meeting with you."

"Thank you, Mr. Giacopino." The lavish suite seemed quite appropriate for the vigorous man who ushered him to a heavy, dark wood rectangular table surrounded by six white-stitched leather chairs. A crystal vase of white and yellow roses graced the center of the table. The dizzying backdrop of Chicago's skyline, partially obscured by low rainclouds completed the palpable ambience of sophisticated power. No wonder Rowan felt *owned.*

The Don slid into a chair across the table and gestured to the bar. "Would you like a cup of coffee, or perhaps something stronger?"

"I am fine, but thank you."

"All right. Have a seat. How's Rowan doing?"

He clasped his hands together on the table, sat ramrod straight in the deep cushion and chose his words with care. "Rowan is suffering on several levels, as you might expect, given his experience of the previous six months or so."

Johnny observed him with narrowed eyes. "I want to know what it's going to take to fix his problems and get him back up to speed."

"Define *up to speed* for me, if you would please."

"Capable of handling a job or career, you know, life in general, without losing it or going off some deep end."

"I see. I do not have a good answer for you. Each of us processes the things that happen to us according to our unique personalities, backgrounds, and capabilities. Rowan is no different in that regard."

Johnny frowned. "What exactly is wrong with him?"

He realized he'd started sweating. "Mr. Giacopino, my analysis of Rowan at this stage is incomplete at best. And in every instance, my first and foremost commitment is to doctor-patient confidentiality."

"You mean you can't tell me what's going on in that head of his? I've got a lot riding on Rowan's recovery, and I'd like to be sure he receives everything he needs in order to get up to speed on the things we're planning."

He gazed steadily at the forcible man. "Cannot is the wrong word. I *will not* betray Rowan's confidence. Nor will I discuss his treatment program. He is a highly functioning adult, capable of making his own decisions. You are not his legal guardian. If he chooses to discuss his needs with you or gives me permission to share his treatment regimen when one has been developed, I will comply with his wishes, not yours."

The Don methodically rubbed first one jaw, his chin, and then the other jaw. Finally, he stopped and smiled. "I'm pleased to see you've got a backbone, Doctor, because as you most likely already know, you're going to need one when dealing with Rowan. Although, I'd have to disagree on one point. I'm not so sure Rowan is capable of making his own decisions right now."

He replied. "Thank you, sir. And yes, I am aware of the strength of Rowan's personality." He wouldn't add that he'd allowed himself to be temporarily bulldozed by said personality. "I understand your concern regarding his decision-making capabilities. I disagree. He is making decisions daily. So far, he has chosen to remain here. He has also chosen to remain under your auspices, which appears to be a wise choice."

"I like you, Doctor. Are you willing to continue working for me, as Rowan's psychiatrist?"

Relief had him struggling to maintain his equanimity. He'd wondered if the Don would have him escorted out. The powerful man could have him killed on a whim. "Yes, I would very much like to continue working with Rowan. I believe his desire to return to Key West is a healthy one, and I would like to accompany him there, as soon as it is feasible."

Johnny nodded sharply. "Consider it done. I want him to receive whatever medical care he needs after what those motherfuckers in Egypt put him through. Excuse my French, Doctor, but it sickens me to see him try to move around. He's in a lot of pain."

Grief threatened to engulf him when he thought about the humbled, hurting man he wanted so badly to help. God only knew what savagery had been visited on him. "My heart's desire, from the first time I met Rowan, has been to help him regain his emotional health. He is a most passionate, courageous man. I confess, I have come to care very deeply for him."

"You aren't alone there, Doctor. I'm going to tell you something I haven't shared with anyone besides Rowan and Elouisa."

Surprised to be taken into the Don's confidence, he said, "I shall keep your information to myself."

"Thank you. See, Rowan has agreed to be my business partner. He and I haven't hashed out all the details yet, but I've got some plans."

The admission flabbergasted him. He remembered Rowan's despondent words. *I'm not free.* "Hmm. I see. That's interesting."

Johnny sounded deflated. "He didn't mention it?"

Aware that he'd ventured into uncertain territory, along with unfortunately revealing something he and Rowan hadn't discussed, he considered quickly, then said, "We spent our time becoming reacquainted and sharing memories. The only current event we chatted about was his desire to return to Key West. May I remind you, this is privileged information? I will not discuss it further."

"Of course. Thank you for your discretion. It is a rare quality and one I value highly in my choice of business associates."

"You are most welcome. If you have no other concerns, I believe I will ask your driver to take me back to the residence." The meeting with Rowan and the subsequent grilling by the overpowering Don left him exhausted.

Johnny snapped his fingers. "That reminds me. Would you like to stay here? I've rented the entire floor. The suite at the end of the hall is empty. This would give you 24/7 access to Rowan if necessary."

"You are most kind. Yes, I would consider it beneficial to be close to Rowan during this transition."

"Good. I'll send my driver for your things. Roberto has the key card. He'll let you in and you can make yourself at home. Order whatever you need from room service." The Don pulled a thick roll of cash from an inside suit pocket and tossed it onto the table. "This should cover anything else you need. Consider it your first month's salary." Johnny glanced at the gold watch on his wrist. "And now, I've got a date with the Missus at my restaurant."

He hesitated, then picked up the cash. He glimpsed fifty- and hundred-dollar bills before stuffing it in his pants pocket. "Thank you, sir, for everything. Have a lovely evening with your wife. I hope you don't get rained on."

Johnny walked him to the door and gave him a crafty smile. "That's what curb-to-curb service is for. Besides, I own the business."

"Very good sir. Thank you again, for everything."

An hour later he sat at the desk in his own opulent suite, reflecting on the adventure his life had become since he'd first met Rowan in the study of the sprawling home on Kauai's coast. He remembered the angry, wounded man with the Glock pistol holstered beneath the unbuttoned, wrinkled shirt. They'd spent hours together in frequent sessions in the quiet room. He frowned, thinking about how Rowan had played him then.

While he'd been patting himself on the back at what he perceived were positive changes in his patient, Rowan had simply been biding his time, recovering from the injuries he'd sustained while in the CIA's custody. When he was ready, Rowan's personality reasserted itself, and he left Kauai to pursue justice in his own, flawed way. That pursuit had concluded, finally, with Rowan a humbled and even more wounded man. He'd glimpsed the reservoir of anger still residing, deeper than ever in his patient. The addition of Jack Daniel's made for what he considered an explosive situation.

He perused the notes he'd jotted while sipping the hot chamomile tea he'd ordered from room service. Rowan presented the biggest challenge he'd faced in his career, and he'd welcomed it from the beginning. How would he fare this time? How would Rowan respond to the very first thing he needed to address, which was the alcohol? His patient needed to acknowledge that he had a problem before they could proceed.

His tea had gone cold, and he set it aside. He rubbed his eyes, glanced at his notes one more time, and switched off the light. Beyond the large windows, the city glowed and pulsed with never-ending activity. Endless lights flowed like a busy river throughout the streets. Jets on approach to O'Hare blinked through the clearing clouds. The skyscrapers resembled jeweled towers in the early evening darkness.

He absently shoved his glasses further up his nose. Somehow, without intending to, he'd floundered into deep waters with Rowan in their first meeting. What had he said to trigger the distress he'd witnessed? Yawning hugely, he decided to check on his patient in the morning. The familiar energy, the enthusiasm for assisting in the healing process had burned itself out. The suite's bedroom was his next destination.

CHAPTER EIGHTEEN

The Next Day

Harandi pulled into the parking garage on Walton Street and crawled out of the Santa Fe he'd rented with a bogus ID to ensure Berenger couldn't find and follow him to Chicago. He handed the keys to a valet and headed for the Four Seasons. The hotel was a scant tenth of a mile away on Delaware Place, and the walk would allow him to gather his thoughts before meeting with Johnny Giacopino.

He crossed Walton, heading for the imposing hotel complex. Before entering, he paused beneath the *Four Seasons* sign, glittering above the doors. How the next chapter of his life began depended on the powerful Don. He'd come halfway across the country to offer his commitment to a cause. And to the man who'd suffered for that cause and rejected him with uncompromising certitude.

Entering the foyer, he paused to gain his bearings. He allowed himself to appreciate the ambience created by gleaming gray-and-black marble flooring, massive crystal chandeliers, and the creamy gray-and-white walls showcasing colorful pieces of the hotel's private art collection.

A stocky, bald-headed man wearing a black suit walked toward him. His instincts told him this was Giacopino's emissary. The man came to a larger than life stop in front of him, and he looked up, into blue eyes devoid of emotion.

The man spoke in a low voice. "Harandi, the Boss sent me down to meet you. Come with me."

Before he could answer, the man turned and walked away. He hurried to keep up and followed him past a massive profusion of white blooms he couldn't identify, the entire arrangement set in mirrored glass and metal vases on a heavy, dark wood table, then past the black marble check-in counter to a bank of elevators.

Once inside, the man slid a key card, punched a button, and then faced him with his hands folded in front of him. The man's stoic face forbade conversation, which suited him. He'd save his thoughts, his *pleas,* for Giacopino.

They exited the elevator and headed down a wide hallway, the muffled clump of their shoes on thick carpet the only sound. He spotted another man with black hair, wearing a shirt, tie, and suit pants, armed with a full-size Glock .40, standing squarely in front of a door. The big man he was following kept walking.

The black-haired man frowned at him, and he wondered if Rowan was behind the guarded door. They continued to a door on the opposite side of the hallway. His escort knocked and waited until the door opened. The gravelly voice he remembered said, "Thank you Roberto. Send him in."

The big man stepped aside and jerked his thumb toward the door. "The Boss will see you now."

He slid past the imposing bulk and entered the suite, taken aback at the disconcerting aura of raw power emanating from the man in front of him. He held out his hand. "Hello Mr. Giacopino. Thank you for agreeing to meet with me."

Johnny ignored his outstretched hand and gestured toward a grouping of sofas. "Have a seat. In the interests of being upfront, I'll tell you now, the one and only reason I agreed to see you is because of the phone call you made regarding Rowan's situation."

He took a seat. "Thank you. I appreciate your kindness."

"Mistaking remuneration for kindness would be a tactical mistake on your part, Mr. Harandi. I took you for someone smarter than that."

A brisk knock saved him from replying. The Don returned to the door. "Ralphie, thanks for coming. Our visitor has arrived."

Ralph entered the suite and tromped to where he sat. "Harandi, what the hell are you really doing here?"

Johnny answered for him. "He said he has a proposition. We're going to evaluate its merits."

Ralph sneered. "How do we know he's not wired? He's working for Whitman, after all."

He raised both hands. "Whoa. Listen, I'll strip and go naked if you want. I swear, I'm not wearing a wire, and I don't work for Whitman anymore. I resigned when Rowan was transferred to Houston."

Ralph said, "What's your angle?"

He replied. "Somehow, Whitman figured out I had something to do with Rowan's release from Houston."

Johnny said, "You're looking for protection."

Ralph chuckled. "It figures."

He looked from one formidable man to the other. "You're partly correct. I don't know how Whitman put two and two together, Mr. Giacopino, but I contacted you before that happened."

Johnny perched on the edge of the sofa facing him. "Keep talking."

He met the Don's calculating stare. "If I hadn't wanted to *undo* the things I helped do, why would I have called for help getting Rowan out of Tora? Or contacted you about Whitman's decision to allow Rowan to face charges in Houston?"

Johnny glanced at his watch. "I've seen stranger things. You've got five minutes left before I hand you off to Roberto."

He shifted his gaze to Johnston. "Ask Rowan. He can attest to how many times I've tried to make amends."

Ralph glared at him. "The last damn thing I'm going to do is bother Rowan with any mention of you."

Johnny added, "I'm inclined to agree with you, Ralphie. Tell me, Mr. Harandi, why I shouldn't leave you in Roberto's hands as just compensation for how Rowan has suffered."

He affected an ease he didn't feel. "Respectfully, sir, I want to work for the man who brought two presidents to heel and masterfully thwarted the criminal justice system of the state of Texas."

Ralph snorted. "Of course you do, now that the tables have turned."

Johnny said, "Whitman is a vindictive son of a bitch. How do I know you're not his boy, sent here to infiltrate my outfit?"

He appealed to Ralph. "I convinced the FBI director to bring your contact, Jack McKenzie, into an investigation with the aim of exposing Shemal and exonerating Rowan."

Ralph replied. "You began an investigation with Director Berenger to *clear* Rowan's name? That doesn't sound like something she'd sign off on, especially after the way she grilled Rowan in Colorado."

He dug in his pocket for the burner phone he'd purchased. "Let's call Jack and ask him. I know he'll vouch for me."

Johnny said, "Make the call, Harandi."

He punched McKenzie's number and put the phone on speaker. "Jack always answers."

The phone rang six times before McKenzie picked up. "McKenzie here. Who's this?"

Hoping his relief didn't show, he said, "Jack, it's me, David. I'm with a couple of people who need verification of our investigation into Shemal on Rowan's behalf."

Ralph spoke up. "Jack, it's Ralph Johnston. Long time no talkie. Can I trust this guy? Is he on the up-and-up, or should I tell him to go to hell?"

McKenzie responded. *"Ralph Johnston,* as I live and breathe, I *never* thought I'd hear from you again."

Ralph said, "I'm still around. Too damn stubborn to go away."

McKenzie replied. "Listen buddy, you can trust David. We're collaborating with Leigh, and I'm juiced about getting the full scoop on what's happened to your friend Milani."

Ralph retorted, "First-name basis with the director, huh? Sounds like you're damn sure getting the full scoop of something."

Johnny cut in. "That's all I need to hear."

McKenzie said, "Who's your other friend, David?"

He replied. "Need to know, Jack. Thanks for vouching for me. I'll be in touch again, sometime." He hit END before McKenzie could ask any more questions. He looked at Johnny. "Are you satisfied?"

Johnny said, "You've had your meet. I'm going to discuss your situation with my friend here while you take a ride with Roberto. I'll text him with my answer to your proposition. You'll either come back here or get let off somewhere."

He protested, "But I haven't told you my proposition. At least hear what I've got to say before you decide whether I live or die."

Johnny stood up and headed for the door. "Who said anything about dying? You hear anything about dying, Ralphie?"

Ralph shook his head. "Can't say I did."

Johnny chuckled. "You've got thirty seconds, Harandi. Spit it out."

He replied. "I found out that the same people who targeted Rowan killed my uncle Sa-id. The CIA agents who abducted Rowan helped make that happen. I intend to see them pay for those choices."

Ralph said, "It's a free country. Go for it."

He ignored the jab and continued. "These same people and entities are powerful. They've made deep inroads into our intelligence community and our entire government. They need to be taken out."

Johnny paused at the door. "Those are the first smart words out of your mouth. Keep talking."

He'd gotten a reprieve. "I'm certain Abramson at CIA is deep into this, which is what McKenzie is investigating on the sly.

Whitman is concerned about his legacy, period. Berenger believes Rowan is innocent of the terrorism charges, but she's strictly by-the-book."

Ralph said, "I used to be that way myself. But God almighty, Rowan went after those people and entities too, and you know firsthand how it turned out for him."

Johnny added, "Rowan's methods left something to be desired, but he had the right idea. He just needed effective backing."

Harandi replied, "I'm ready to commit. I'll put my skills at your disposal. I'm loyal, and I'll do what needs to be done. This is my way of showing Rowan, once and for all, that I'm on his side."

Ralph started to protest, but Johnny stepped in. "You take a ride, and then we'll talk some more." The Don opened the door. "Roberto, take him out and about. I'll text you in a bit."

An hour later he sat sweating in the rear seat of a black Lincoln Town Car, wondering where they were headed. Roberto swung the car off the Eisenhower Expressway and headed south. After a couple more turns, they pulled into Mt. Carmel Catholic Cemetery. "Perfect," he muttered. "Just perfect."

They drove into the cemetery, past a mausoleum with CAPONE etched in the granite, and among other heavy tombstones bearing Italian names, some he recognized. Roberto followed the narrow-paved road further into the cemetery and parked. The big man turned sideways in the seat. "The Boss's father and grandfather are buried right over there."

He followed Roberto's pointing forefinger. "How interesting."

"I've worked for the Boss for a long time now. He's always played it straight with me. He doesn't think much of people who aren't up front. You get what I'm saying?"

"I have a lot of respect for Mr. Giacopino. I wouldn't be here otherwise."

Roberto gazed at him with the cold eyes. "Rowan's a good guy. My job right now is to make sure he stays safe and sound. I take my job pretty seriously, if you get my drift."

He stroked his goatee and nodded. "I do. I share the same level of commitment when I'm given an assignment."

Roberto cracked thick knuckles and kept talking. "In case you're thinking of screwing around with Rowan or the Boss, I wanted to let you know something."

"What's that?"

"You do, and I'll put you in the ground." Roberto turned around, started the Lincoln, and put it in gear.

He opened his mouth to respond and thought better of it. What could he say? He watched Roberto pick up his phone and glance at it before tossing it back on the seat. They drove in silence to the hotel. Roberto escorted him once more to the lavish suite.

Johnny motioned him inside. "Did you and Roberto have a nice drive and chat?"

He sat down on the sofa. "We did. He's not much of a talker, though."

"He usually says what he needs to. Roberto's a man of his word, you can count on that."

"Good to know."

Johnny relaxed on the sofa opposite him. "Ralphie had another obligation, otherwise he'd be here."

"Ralph is a good man. His team had an exemplary reputation."

"So it did, before Shemal took it upon himself to destroy Rowan."

He replied. "Look, I want to take out the people responsible for killing my uncle and targeting Rowan, but I don't have the resources to do it on my own."

Johnny studied him. "What makes you think I'm interested in committing my resources to this kind of an endeavor?"

He raised his hands and let them fall. "After everything you did for Rowan, I thought it might be a possibility. You have the means, and I thought maybe I could persuade you." Observing the man who'd personally forced Whitman to back off, he felt silly for even *thinking* what he'd just said.

"Mr. Harandi, I'll give some thought to hiring you. For now, hang around Chicago. I'll let you know what I decide."

He stood up. "All right, sir. I'll wait to hear from you."

Johnny saw him to the door. "You take care. Chicago can be a dangerous city."

He nodded, unsure whether the Don was issuing advice or a warning. "I'll be careful."

Early Evening
Seattle, WA
Danielle tried to relax in the back seat of the hired car Tom had sent to pick her up. He'd invited her to his home for the first time, and she'd agreed to an evening of popcorn and wine. The car might be a bit extravagant, but she appreciated his thoughtfulness. Cocooned in the toasty warmth while rain spattered against the windows, with no tasks to distract and occupy her mind, her thoughts veered to Rowan, and the trepidation she couldn't shake.

For nine agonizing months, she'd done her best to put their relationship behind her. Thinking about seeing him had her thoughts careening from hope to despair. Rowan had left her standing alone in front of the home on Kauai where she'd thought they were building a life together. She'd been terribly wrong about that.

She closed her eyes, hating the memories, but helpless to stop them. They stood out in her mind, as stark and painful as if they'd happened yesterday. Rowan had as much as accused her of loving Derek instead of him. Of course, she'd stupidly brought Derek into the fight they'd had over how Marta died.

Marta had been one of her Legacy employees in Sioux Falls. She'd confronted Rowan about her death, and he responded with chilling indifference. Marta was nothing more than another jihadist to him. The entire conversation had been a huge mistake on her part, but his attitude about brutally killing someone she knew horrified her.

Derek had been her house mate. She'd offered him a room after his divorce, and for four years they'd comfortably shared her home in Sioux Falls. They commiserated about the airline industry, and she thought of him as a good friend, nothing more. Derek had eventually told her that he loved her.

Rowan had never liked Derek. She'd always thought his jealousy was irrational, but in retrospect, she was sure Rowan had sensed Derek's feelings for her. On the awful morning before he left, Rowan responded to her desperate attempt to apologize by savagely kissing her until she could only whimper, and then reminding her that he was a *monster*. She'd watched in stunned silence as he climbed into the sleek black Escalade and made his final exit from the estate.

After that she'd wandered inside to their living quarters in the rambling home. In a daze, she'd drifted into the bedroom and found his closet emptied, everything gone. Then she'd found the half bottle of Jack Daniel's whiskey he'd left on the kitchen counter. For the first time, that morning, she'd understood why he drank such copious amounts of the potent whiskey. She'd finished the bottle and passed out; her body numb to everything.

She tried reaching out to him. At first, he wouldn't answer his phone. Then Michael attempted to intervene on her behalf, and Rowan hung up on him. Only after Bettina, unintimidated by her brother's mercurial temperament, chewed him out, did he respond by calling her. At first, she thought he'd be reasonable. She tried to tell him how much she loved him, and wanted to be with him.

He'd been resolute, uncompromising, and finally, she foolishly backed him into a corner. *You know, I have never met anyone more pig-headed than you. How about if I just leave and start over?* She should have known better. Rowan was a proud, stubborn man, and she would never forget his sarcastic chuckle and harsh, cutting words. *Now you're talking. How's this – we're done.* His words seared her heart and still hurt as much as the day he'd uttered them.

She'd done her best to move on, the way he wanted her to, but she'd always felt hollow inside, with a permanent ache in her heart. She listened to the steady slap-slap of the windshield wipers and opened her eyes. An endless stream of vehicles rushed along in the darkness, illuminating the rain-slicked freeway ahead of them. She heaved a sigh as the driver hit the turn signal and swung the car onto an exit ramp, then a side street. The promotion Small-Batch offered had seemed like a step in the right direction, almost like a lifeline she could cling to.

And then Marion called and sent her mind into its endless, spinning debate. As if she needed more complications, Tom had sounded like he had more on his mind than a fun evening when he asked her to come over. None of her problems were his fault, and she didn't want to hurt or mislead him. He'd been a friend when she'd needed someone to help her get a new start, and rightly or wrongly, she'd come to depend on him.

She tipped her head back, staring unseeing. His kind, steady nature was diametrically opposed to Rowan's intense, volatile personality, but she knew which man would always have her heart. She couldn't imagine loving anyone other than Rowan. So what was she doing? Had she made a mistake by hanging out with Tom, spending an occasional afternoon on the Harley, or having dinner? Was she leading him on or implying that she too, wanted more than a friendship?

The car came to an abrupt halt and the driver spoke. "We've arrived, Ms. Stratton."

She realized she'd been wringing her hands, dampening the ten-dollar bill she had ready for a tip. "Thank you. I guess we'll call later, when I'm ready to head home."

He accepted her tip. "I'll get the door."

"Oh, all right." She waited until he'd opened her door and then climbed out. "Thank you, again." He smiled and returned to the car. She stared at the two-story brick home, mellow light glowing in its windows and spilling into the rainy darkness. As she made her way up the curving sidewalk, she tried to marshal her thoughts. Maybe she was overthinking everything. After all, she and Tom had been friends since the previous spring. Spending an evening at his place was no big deal, right?

She rang the doorbell and Tom opened the door right away, sucking on his thumb. "Hi, Dani. I burned my thumb on the popcorn. Come on in. How was the car?" He surprised her with a hug and a kiss on the cheek.

She returned the hug, even as she thought she probably shouldn't. "The car was fun. You didn't have to do that, you know. I could have driven my trusty Escape, or taken a cab."

"Aw, heck, it was my pleasure. I thought it might be a fun treat for you. Let me take your jacket. The popcorn's ready, and so is the wine."

She slipped out of her jacket, uncomfortably aware of his appreciative once-over. His demeanor put her on guard. She didn't want to mislead him any more than she apparently already had. She gave her arms a quick rub. "Mm, the popcorn smells delicious. It's perfect for a cold, rainy night. Thanks again for inviting me over."

Tom led her further into the house. "I've been looking forward to this. How do you like my man cave? It's supposed to be a family room, but I don't seem to have the knack for decorating."

She surveyed the room. Heavy leather sofas squatted like linebackers in an arc in front of the lit fireplace, and a matching loveseat sat squarely in front of the sixty-inch curved-screen TV at the opposite end of the spacious room. Hardwood shutters covered the huge picture window. Subtle lighting gave the room a welcoming feel. "I think you could say it's a handsome room. Ruggedly so. It's comfy, too."

"I'm glad you like it. Grab a seat and I'll get our stuff." They laughed and chatted, devouring the bowl of popcorn between them on the sofa in front of the fire while they finished off a bottle of her favorite Shiraz. When only seeds were left in the popcorn bowl, Tom said, "You want to head to the other side and watch a movie? Or would you rather keep talking?"

She moved the bowl and turned to sit half-way cross-legged, facing him. The eagerness in his eyes confirmed her thoughts about the evening. How had she been so dense and stupid? God, it was her and Derek all over again. At least Rowan wasn't there to hate Tom, or hurt him. "I've got more news, and I'm wondering if you could take Leo for a while. He loves being with you, and I'm going to be out of town. I hate to think of leaving him in a kennel."

"Leo can stay here anytime. Is Small-Batch sending you somewhere exciting?"

She looked down for a moment, tracing the seam of her jeans, then met his gaze. Her next words would probably ruin the evening. "I'm going to see Rowan. I'm not sure yet how long I'll be gone."

He opened his mouth, closed it, frowned and said, "What about the new position you accepted with Small-Batch?"

"I'm taking a brief leave of absence. I honestly don't know what's going to happen. The company isn't quite up-to-speed yet with their planning, so it's all right."

His voice turned despondent. "Huh. You heard from him."

"From someone close to him."

"He didn't have the cojones to call you himself?"

She felt the heat rising in her face and settling in her cheeks. "It's a little more complicated than that."

"I'm sorry. It's just, well I'd like to meet him, you know? Because I'd like to tell *him* how much *you've* suffered."

She finished her wine and held the glass in both hands. "It's nice of you to feel that way, but trust me, you do not want to meet Rowan. *Ever.*"

He bristled. "Oh, I don't know. I've got a pretty damn good right hook, and I know how to take care of myself."

She twirled strands of hair between her fingers and met his peeved stare. "You're out of your league with Rowan."

"Apparently. In more ways than one." He shook his head. "Look, I'm sorry Dani; that was out of line. I'm a clod."

"No, don't be silly. On the way over tonight, I realized how important our friendship is to me. I depend on you, probably too much. Thank you for always being there. You've made some hard situations easier for me to get through."

"Dani, can I tell you something?"

She sat the wine glass down and clasped her hands together. "Sure. You can tell me anything."

He leaned forward, gently peeled her hands apart and held them. "Before you make this trip, I want you to know a few things."

She braced herself and didn't pull away. "All right."

"I've enjoyed getting to know you. The time we've spent together has always been special to me. And, well, here it is: I've fallen in love with you."

She stared at him for a long moment. "Oh Tom. Oh my. I love you, too, *as a friend.*"

He gazed at her, then shrugged. "Of course, I understand. But, I have to say this. I've rehearsed it so many times. Just know that I'd love to dedicate my life to making the best possible life for you. Whatever you want or need, I'd do my best to give it to you."

She should probably tell him that *she* was the clod, for being so utterly clueless. "You're so sweet. I don't know what to say."

He tossed the popcorn bowl, scattering seeds across the carpet. In a quick motion, he slid next to her and pulled her into his arms. He murmured into her hair. "You don't have to say anything. I'm not going anywhere."

Her body tensed. Why couldn't he leave things the way they were? She murmured, "I'm glad," and pushed away from him.

His hands slid to her shoulders, then he leaned in and kissed her on the lips.

She pulled away from his mouth and gasped. "Oh no. What are you doing?" She pushed him away.

He spoke, his voice hoarse. "*Shit.* My bad. I'm sorry." He touched her cheek with light fingers. "The last thing I would ever knowingly do is hurt you. I just want to love you."

"No, don't apologize. I'm the one who's sorry. I should have known better, depending on you so much. I don't know what I was thinking."

He grasped her hands and held them. "Whoa, stop with the guilt. You don't have anything to apologize for."

"Maybe not to you," she replied softly.

He tightened his grip on her hands. "You don't owe *anyone* an apology. Promise me you'll remember that."

She withdrew her hands from his and stood up. "I better call a cab and head home."

"Nonsense. I'll give you a ride. If you want, I can bring Leo home with me. That's one less thing to deal with before you leave."

"That would be wonderful. Thank you." She couldn't believe how their conversation had gone from two friends chatting to what felt like a stilted exchange with an acquaintance in a matter of a couple minutes.

Tom retrieved her coat and gave her a lopsided smile. "I'm glad you came over. At least now you know how I feel. And Dani, I'm not going anywhere. Don't forget that."

Tom sat in Danielle's driveway in his Outback, watching from behind the rain-spattered windshield as she waved. Leo sat behind him in the back seat, alternately breathing on his neck and licking the side of his face. He waited until she'd stepped inside and closed the door before putting the car in reverse. He scratched Leo's head and drove mindlessly, his thoughts churning.

He'd waited so long for the right moment, had embraced his sister's belief in timing, and decided to take her advice about a simple step further in their relationship. Then the bottom had fallen out of his carefully constructed plans. Could he have been more off-base? Could his timing have been any worse? In hindsight, his meticulous planning of what he'd envisioned as the perfect evening seemed ridiculous. "I'm a loser. What the heck was I thinking? Why did I kiss her?"

He gripped the steering wheel, remembering how Danielle looked when she arrived and took off her jacket. Wearing a white sweater that clung to her body, skinny jeans, and lace-up boots, she *still* had him doing a double-take. She turned him on, made him want to dive into her, and at the same time hold her tight and protect her. But for some crazy reason, he couldn't compete with the man who'd hurt her over and over. What could she possibly see in a guy like Milani?

He pounded the steering wheel while his resentment overflowed. Leo growled, then woofed and poked his snout against his face. "Sorry, buddy. I just can't figure this crap out." Her crack about him not ever wanting to meet Milani made him feel like the butt of a private joke he wasn't privy to. "I'm not afraid of him. I'd *like* to meet him. I'd give him a piece of my mind. And I *can* take care of myself," he muttered.

He wondered what might happen when she saw Milani. If the guy had any brains, he'd hang onto her for good this time. That's what he'd do. He shrugged. Milani was *nothing* like him, so anything could happen. Would he ever see her again? Had he become Leo's owner? He patted the big head resting on his shoulder. "Hey buddy, you might be stuck with me." Leo whined and licked him one more time.

Two Days Later

Danielle stretched out in the deep leather seat and closed her eyes as the jet's twin engines revved. She'd been shocked when Michael greeted her in the lobby on the private side of SEA-TAC. He'd sauntered up, wearing a black leather jacket and dark jeans, reminding her of Rowan and bringing unwanted tears to her eyes. After escorting her to the Learjet and taking her two suitcases from her, he'd bounded into the jet, conferred with the flight crew, and asked if she wanted anything. He told her they'd talk on the way, then slid down the spacious aisle to take a seat somewhere behind her.

She'd always loved to fly. The roar of the engines and the powerful take off felt good. But for the moment, she needed the opportunity to unwind. The previous few days had been hectic and now she was headed at 500 mph to see the man she loved. The jet leveled off, and Michael plopped down in the seat facing her. "How've you been, Danielle?"

"Oh, you know. I've been fine." She had always felt more comfortable with Gabriel, Rowan's other partner in his clandestine operations. Gabriel reminded her of a big teddy bear, while Michael maintained a flinty hard edge. She felt constantly analyzed in his presence.

He continued his steady gaze. "Good. You've probably got some questions, so shoot."

"Um, sure. I do. How's Rowan? Is he all right?"

Michael hesitated. "Rowan's in a lot of pain. We don't know what exactly happened to him in Tora. He's had a couple flashbacks that we know about, so be aware."

Her heart broke again, thinking of the brave man she'd known and the unimaginable things he must have endured. "All right."

"We'll be in Chicago in about another three hours or so. Johnny's limo will take us to the Four Seasons. Rowan's in a suite there."

She gaped at Michael. "The Four Seasons?"

He frowned. "You all right?"

She hurriedly shook her head. "No. I mean yes, I'm fine." Flustered, she changed the subject. "Who's Johnny?"

"As far as I know, he's the Mafia Don to end every damn Mafia Don. He got Rowan out of all the trouble he was in, and in case you don't know, that's sayin' something. He also picked everyone up in Kauai when it all went sideways. Well, except for that monkey ass Derek. And me."

"Marion mentioned something about Dubai."

Michael nodded. "Johnny hauled everyone to Dubai for the duration. The UAE doesn't have an extradition treaty with the US. The government couldn't demand Ralph's return, or anyone else's for that matter."

Weariness overwhelmed her, and she yawned. "I haven't slept very well, thinking about seeing Rowan. If you don't mind, I'm going to take advantage of the flight time to catch up, before we get to Chicago."

Michael's cobalt eyes flicked over her face. "I'll wake you when we're close to landing."

"Thanks." She reclined the seat and closed her eyes, shutting out the uncomfortable man who'd probably read every one of her thoughts.

Late Afternoon

FBI Headquarters Washington, DC

Berenger waited for her call to connect. She could imagine the scramble at the other end of the line. A call from the director of the FBI generated an immediate response. A female voice said, "The District Attorney will speak with you now, ma'am. Thank you for holding."

The line clicked and Bartholomew Newton spoke with a hearty Texas drawl. "Good afternoon, Director Berenger. To what do I owe the pleasure?"

Small talk had never been her thing. "Hello, Mr. Newton. I'm calling about your decision to dismiss the charges against Rowan Milani."

"What may I help you with regarding that decision?"

"You may explain what precipitated your decision to dismiss seven capital murder charges."

"I'm sorry you were not made privy to my public statement. My secretary will forward a copy as soon as we've finished speaking."

She couldn't believe he'd take that tack with her. "I've read your public statement. Spare me the pablum, and tell me why you dismissed the charges."

Newton cleared his throat. "The evidence against Mr. Milani did not exist anywhere in our system. His attorney appeared poised to create a ruckus about corruption within the police department and implied that Milani may have been set up. We had no choice but to dismiss the charges."

The magnitude of the deception his words portrayed set her back. "Mr. Newton, this is extraordinary news."

"Yes, ma'am. We are not happy about the situation."

"What do you believe actually happened?"

"Only one of two things could have happened. Either Milani was the victim of an elaborate setup or the beneficiary of a massive con."

“Neither option speaks well of the legal system in Texas.”

“Hence my public statement, ma’am.”

“I’m beginning to understand. Who was Mr. Milani’s attorney?”

“His name is Vincent Black. He told my prosecutor he’d taken an interest in Milani way back at the beginning.”

“Interesting. Are there any other pertinent details that may be germane?”

“Kyle Matthews, the detective who initially handled the murder cases went rogue. He interrogated Milani before his attorney had access. Immediately before Milani’s release Matthews interrogated him again and damn near assaulted him. He swears the evidence existed.”

“Do you believe him?”

“I’d like to believe him, ma’am, but when Milani’s attorney started squawking about a setup, we had to consider that Matthews may have had a vendetta. He and Milani had an encounter when Milani was in Houston around the time of the first five murders. Milani injured Matthews so severely he spent several days in ICU and needed six months of rehab.”

“Good God,” she murmured. “The extent of your dilemma is much clearer to me now. Thank you for speaking candidly with me.”

“It’s my pleasure, Director Berenger. We are weighing our options and are planning to begin a criminal investigation of Matthews. I cannot ignore the possibility, however far-fetched, that he may have set up Milani.”

Grasping at straws came to mind, but she couldn’t afford to discount anything. “That does seem a bit out of the realm, but I’ll keep an open mind. I may contact former detective Matthews.”

“We’re happy to comply if you need more information. May I ask whether you intend to investigate this further?”

"If I decide to proceed with further investigation, you'll be the first to know."

"Thank you, ma'am. You take care now, you hear?"

"You do the same, Mr. Newton."

After ending the call, she left her desk to gaze out the windows. A run in the crisp fall air would clear her head, but McKenzie expected her to arrive within the hour for an early dinner. She'd accepted his invitation a week earlier and had been looking forward to spending more time with him.

But that was before Harandi skipped his meeting with her and the President. He must have disabled or tossed his phone, because her agents hadn't been able to track it. She'd stupidly begun to trust Harandi even though she should have known better. How could she, after decades of professional service, have been so foolish? Power had a way of negating common sense and she'd tripped and fallen headfirst into a predicament of her own making.

Had McKenzie known about Harandi's dealings? Had he been a party to any of it? Would he have done something like that and concealed his participation from her? For all she knew, either Harandi or McKenzie, or both of them had been secretly cooperating with whomever had facilitated Milani's release. The potential jeopardy she'd placed herself in by teaming up with Harandi *and* starting a relationship with McKenzie left her breathless.

She exited her office and hurried to the waiting Suburban. As her service drove to McKenzie's residence, she considered and discarded numerous ways to confront him. Giving him the benefit of the doubt would be the kindest approach, but she wasn't in the mood to be kind. She needed answers, and he'd better supply them, because if she'd been hoodwinked, someone was going to pay.

Woodley Park, Washington, DC

McKenzie opened the door before she could ring the bell. "Leigh, come in. I've been looking forward to this all week."

"Hello Jack." He leaned in to give her a peck on the cheek, but she swept past, taking petty pleasure in his pursed lips and furrowed brows. She strode into the airy kitchen-family room she'd fallen in love with on her first visit. A chilled glass of white wine waited on the granite counter. She grabbed it, took a long swallow, wished she hadn't, and turned to face him.

He frowned. "Are you all right? Long day? How can I help?"

She clutched the bowl of the wine glass. "You can help by telling me the truth right now."

"Leigh, what happened? What is this about?"

Why not, she thought, and took another swallow of the exquisite wine. "How about you tell me?"

He scratched his chin. "A little context here? I have no clue what you're talking about or why you're angry."

She drank more wine, enjoying the warmth it created, even though she didn't want to. "What do you know about David Harandi's *real* involvement with Rowan Milani?"

"Real involvement? I still have no idea what you're getting at."

"When did you know about Milani's release?"

"Me? I knew when you did. When everyone did. I heard it on the news."

"Are you sure about that?"

He said, "Wait a minute. Did you march in here all wound up because you think I had something to do with Milani's release?"

"Jack, please. Tell me the truth."

"I just did. Leigh, what sent you down this particular rabbit hole? I'd really like to know."

She downed the rest of the wine and smacked the glass on the countertop, too hard. The base shattered. “Oh God. Jack, I’m sorry.”

He rushed to her side. “Are you hurt? Watch out for broken glass.” He took the remains of the wine glass from her and wiped up the mess she’d made on the granite. “What’s wrong, Leigh?”

She took off her suit jacket, draped it over the tall, padded chair, and sat down. “Almost two weeks ago, I set up a meeting with David, at the request of the President. David didn’t make the meeting. I’ve been unable to reach him since then.”

McKenzie whistled. “That’s unbelievable. I wish you’d let me know earlier. David called me two days ago.”

She stared. “That’s incredible. What did he want?”

“He asked me to vouch for the fact that he and you and I are investigating Shemal on Milani’s behalf. Ralph Johnston piped up and asked me if he could trust David. Then someone else spoke up. David cut me off and hung up when I asked who he was with.”

“Do you have any idea who it was?”

“No, unfortunately I don’t. But you can bet it’s whoever helped spring Milani. David told me he’d be in touch again, although he wouldn’t give me any kind of indication as to when.”

“If or when David calls, would you be inclined to probe for more information? I’d love to know where he is and what he’s up to.”

“I’ll do what I can.”

Reading the concern in his eyes, her earlier suppositions seemed over-the-top. “Apparently, David has never been completely honest with me. I should have known. He’s CIA, through and through. Not to mention, of course, his undying quest to prove Milani’s innocence.” She sighed. “I *really* should have known.”

He reached in the fridge, producing the bottle of pinot grigio and another chilled glass. He poured and gave it to her. “So, you thought David and I were in some kind of partnership to deceive you and free Milani?"

She sipped the wine and set the glass gently on the counter, hating to meet his quizzical gaze. "It sounds silly when you say it out loud. I think I'd better leave."

"Nonsense. Dinner is ready. You need to decompress with a decent meal and excellent company. Besides, the information I've dug up will enhance our investigation."

She conceded. "I could use whatever news you've come by. I'm starving, and your dinner smells heavenly."

An hour later, she relaxed on the sofa in his family room. "Thank you for the fabulous meal. I'm discovering that you're quite the chef."

McKenzie refilled her wine glass and settled at the other end of the sofa. "You're welcome. Are you ready to hear my news? My quiet investigation has yielded a ton of information for you on the connection between Abramson and Shemal."

"I'm more than ready. Please, fill me in."

"Seems that Abramson and Shemal go way back, as in *thirty years* ago, when Abramson attended American University in Cairo. He met a young, up-and-coming Islamic scholar named Muusa Shemal."

"You don't say," she murmured.

"Oh yes, and they've maintained a close friendship ever since. My sources tell me Abramson converted to Islam while in Egypt, but kept it under wraps."

She shook her head. "That's not an indictment against him. I understand why he'd keep it quiet, given his position and the fickle mood of the country."

McKenzie concurred. "Quite right."

"How does this information help us in determining whether Abramson has ulterior motives regarding Milani, in conjunction with Shemal?"

"I'm getting there. I've had to dig pretty damn deep to come up with what I think may be the root cause of Milani's troubles."

She stifled an unexpected yawn and settled further into the comfy sofa. The wine and dinner had unwound her overwrought mind more than she realized. "It's been a long week, Jack. Get to it before I tip over."

"My sources directed me to people who've attended mosque services with Abramson. On more than one occasion, Shemal was their speaker, encouraging the ongoing plan of the Muslim Brotherhood, via CAIR and a bevy of other Islamic groups, to turn the United States into their Islamic Caliphate. In addition, Abramson is regularly a participant in private meetings held after the regular prayer service."

"And Milani has claimed all along that his battle against those plans put the target on his back."

"Exactly. Abramson actively, although quite discreetly, supports the Brotherhood's plan."

She sat up, sleepiness forgotten. "Abramson could have planned the destruction of Milani, in partnership with Shemal, convincing Ainsley and Hennessey, who in turn convinced Whitman."

"Yes. And there's more."

"Your sources are a godsend. Are you certain of the veracity of *their* sources?"

"I'd plan a FOX News special around their information. Which brings me to another idea."

She said, "One thing at time. How does this tie in to whoever David was with?"

He chuckled. "That's next. You'll recall that no one ever claimed responsibility for the mosque bombing in Houston last year. The House of Allah was destroyed. That was the mosque where Milani allegedly killed four people. Shemal taught there."

She replied. "We conducted an exhaustive investigation and ended with no viable leads."

"Are you aware of the bombing of the Al-Azhar mosque in Cairo?"

"I remember that, but you're confusing me. How do these threads come together?"

"Shemal was at Al-Azhar that day. He sustained minor injuries. Later, he bragged to his compatriots that he'd forced Rowan Milani to reveal who was responsible for the bombing of both mosques."

She frowned. "Why wouldn't Shemal bring that information to the FBI?"

"I won't pretend to understand Shemal's motivations."

"Did Shemal tell your sources who bombed the mosques?"

"They told me that for some reason Shemal played it close to the vest. It made me wonder if he'd been threatened with further bombings or wanted to carry out his own revenge."

She considered. "This has to be someone with a massive array of resources."

He added, "Taking this full circle, it's at least plausible that the same person or organization responsible for the mosque bombings facilitated the dismissal of charges against Milani in Houston. Both operations required extensive resources and influence."

"Here's another twist for you. I spoke with the DA in Houston today. He informed me that he's planning a criminal investigation of Kyle Matthews, the former detective who worked with Harandi to apprehend Milani. He's been accused of setting up Milani to take the fall for those seven murders, which I find difficult to believe."

McKenzie rubbed his hands together, reminding her of a little boy. "Why don't I interview the former detective? I'm between projects at FOX, and I'd enjoy taking some time off. I still have to tell you my initial idea, too. I'm juiced about this, Leigh. We can do some real good, for Milani and the country."

"Take it easy, Jack. My head is already spinning, so lay your ideas on me one at a time."

"All righty. First, I believe our answers lie with Milani himself. I want to find him and conduct an interview. And, I have a feeling Danielle Stratton is the key to locating Milani. She can't be hard to find."

She raised a forefinger, planning to protest, then stopped. "That's a great idea. Although, my agents debriefed her at SEA-TAC last winter and she held her own with them. Much as I've questioned her loyalty to Milani, I have to admit, she's a smart woman. You'll need all your skills to get anywhere with her."

"Interviewing Milani has always been at the centerpiece of my investigation. In my opinion, he has lost the most and has the most to gain from the truth becoming public knowledge. I'm guessing Ms. Stratton knows where he is and what he's up to. But tell me, would you consider sending me to Houston?"

"Yes, I'd like you to start with Matthews, then find Stratton, get as much information from her as possible, hopefully interview Milani after that, *and* find Harandi. I have a serious bone to pick with him."

"Excellent. I'm ready to go."

A stray thought bubbled up. "Jack, I just remembered something. Milani used a bogus ID to travel around the country. Posing as James Hawthorne, he embarrassed Harandi, boarded planes, *and* rented a house in Key West."

"You don't think he'd use that name again, do you?"

"No, but what if he returned to the same property? He's been pardoned by the President and freed from prosecution in Texas. He must have chosen Key West for a reason; for all we know, he likes it there and went back. We have the address of that house."

McKenzie replied. "It's worth checking out, that's for sure. This is great, Leigh. I can't wait to get going."

She needed to be honest with him. "As you know, I've been reluctant to involve a news organization in my investigation. I came over here today planning to end our collaboration and distance myself from you personally."

McKenzie chuckled. "Is that political-speak for saying you were planning to dump me?"

"Actually, it's too many years in government service. I don't know how to converse in an ordinary way anymore."

"Obviously, we're continuing our professional, albeit clandestine collaboration. What about our budding, unprofessional relationship?"

She smiled. "You, on the other hand, have such a way with words. I apologize for my snarky entrance this afternoon. A number of scenarios were going through my mind, none of them good."

McKenzie took her hands in his. "Leigh, I understand. You've got a tremendous amount of responsibility riding on your shoulders."

She'd never dreamed of finding a partner who understood, let alone accepted, the way she needed to conduct her life. "Thank you."

"If at any time, you say pull the plug on this entire thing, then that's what I'll do. Above all, I respect you and the position you hold as director of the FBI. Don't forget that."

She clung to his hands. "You may never realize how important your support has become to me."

McKenzie said, "Good. Although you haven't answered my final question, I'll pose one more. Are we officially off the clock now, Director Berenger?"

She couldn't stop staring at his lips. "I believe so, Mr. McKenzie."

"Hot damn. Using your vernacular, I'll call that a tacit answer to both questions." He closed the distance between them and kissed her.

CHAPTER NINETEEN

Chicago, IL

Rowan wandered, aimless, throughout the suite, increasingly restless and unhappy. He paused at the windows to watch a storm approaching the city. The American flag, atop a building on the pier, whipped straight out in the blustery wind. Lights along the shoreline had come on early. Lightning zigzagged through the gray-black clouds and fat raindrops pelted the windows.

A soft knock on the door pulled him away. “Goddamn it.” He didn’t want a visit from anyone. Knowing he’d get no peace until he responded, he checked the viewer and pulled the door open. “Hey Marion.”

“Hi sweetie.” She didn’t wait for an invitation, just brushed past him with another container of cookies.

He started to turn, then saw Michael coming down the hallway with two suitcases. He scowled at Gino. “What the hell. Does he think he’s moving in here?”

Gino snickered. “I don’t think so, boss.”

Michael reached the door. “Hello Rowan. Excuse me. I have to get these inside. Wait out here, would you?”

His irritation deepened at the smug grin on his friend’s face. “What’s going on? What are you doing?”

Michael didn’t answer. Gino moved fast, following Michael into the suite and closing the door. Perplexed and uneasy at their strange antics, the hair rising on his arms at his vulnerability, he wondered why they’d leave him standing by himself outside the door. He glanced first one direction, then the other, down the wide hallway. Danielle walked toward him, wearing a sleeveless dress in his favorite shade of blue. He stared unblinking, afraid she’d disappear.

Instead, she stopped in front of him. Her chest heaved, and the eyes he loved filled with tears. "Rowan. Oh… My God. I can't believe… It's really you."

He remembered his vicious anger and deliberately cruel retaliation for how she'd hurt him, and his brutal words, ending their relationship. He'd hated himself afterward. And now he couldn't wait another second to tell her what he'd wanted to, for so long. "Danielle, I'm sorry. I'm *so sorry. For everything.* I never stopped loving you."

She gave him a shaky smile. "I thought so. I mean, I hoped so. I love you and I'm sorry, too."

He drew her into his arms. "Shh, hush. You have nothing to be sorry for."

She laid her head on his chest and wrapped her arms around him. "I've missed you so much."

He let his chin rest on the top of her head and inhaled the strawberry scent of her hair. "Oh God, I missed you too. Every single day."

After a while, Danielle stirred and pulled back. She placed her hands on his chest and moved them slowly upward, pausing to gently cup his face. "Rowan, kiss me. Please."

He could only whisper, "OK," while she drew his head down. When their tongues touched, she moaned softly and crushed him even closer. Her body fit perfectly against his, awakening desires he'd shoved aside for too long.

Intoxicated by her lips, warm and gentle at first, then burning his mouth with their urgency, he forgot about the pain and forgot they were standing in the hallway, until a gentle hand touched his shoulder. Startled, he broke away from Danielle, his pulse pounding in his throat. "What?"

Michael, Marion, and Gino milled around them. Michael said, "Hey brother, why don't you take it inside? We'll get out of your hair."

He nodded. "Oh, right. OK."

Danielle kept one arm wrapped tight around him. She spoke, barely above a whisper. “Thanks for coming to pick me up, Mike. See you soon, Marion.”

He led her into the suite, and she gravitated to the windows. “When Mike told me you were staying at the Four Seasons, I was so surprised. This suite is almost identical to the one we shared.”

He went to stand beside her. The cold rain fogged the windows, shutting out the city, shrinking their world to the suite and the two of them. “I know. It was hard, at first, being here.”

She slipped out of her shoes and tossed them aside. “I can imagine.” She shivered and rubbed her arms. “Talk about memories.”

“I’ve never slept in the bed. I couldn’t.”

She gazed up at him. “We will, tonight.”

“Sounds good to me.”

She squeezed his hand in hers. “Hey, I brought you coffee. I’ll make some for you.”

“That sounds good, too.” He wanted to forget the coffee and continue what they’d started. But she seemed shy all of a sudden, so he stayed quiet and watched how her dress clung to her body in all the right places. Desire dampened his palms while she retrieved a bag of coffee from one of her suitcases, fiddled with grinding beans, and brewed the coffee.

She brought him a steaming cup. “Here you go. This is one of my favorites from Seattle.”

He inhaled the steam and sipped. “It’s perfect.” He tried to focus on talking, but he just wanted her in bed. Alarm sizzled through him, and the cup shook precariously in his sweating hands. He almost spilled the coffee. How the hell could he do any of the things he wanted to with her?

She settled cross-legged beside him, not seeming to notice his panic. “I’m glad you like it. Gosh, I’m starving. Let’s have a picnic, like we used to, on the beach.”

"You want peanut butter and jelly sandwiches? Room service does a hell of a job." He waited for her reply, enjoying how the floaty bottom of her dress hiked up her thighs. He could give a rat's ass about food.

"Potato chips, too. I love peanut butter and jelly with chips."

"All right. Give me a sec. Gino will get everything for us." He held his breath, shoved off the sofa and made his way to the door without groaning. He scowled at Gino's leering smile and told him what they wanted, including a case of Bolgheri Sassicaia to surprise her.

He slid back down beside her and put his feet up on the low table. Danielle cuddled close and stretched her legs next to his. While he stared, mesmerized, at her slender, bare legs and wondered how long he could keep up the charade of civilized behavior, she said, "I watched everything that happened to you on TV."

Her words jolted him. "Oh. Hell. I'm sorry. Every time they moved me, I hoped to God you wouldn't see it."

"The YouTube video was the worst. I thought you were dead."

He heard the bleak anguish in her voice, saw fresh tears dripping down her cheeks. "Hey, it wasn't real. Nothing happened."

"But I didn't know. I thought you were gone. Forever." She reached up and touched the thin scar on his cheek. "I can't imagine the awful things you've been through."

He grasped her fingers and kissed them. "It's over and done. In the past." A sharp knock interrupted their conversation. "I think our picnic is here." He forced himself up again and opened the door. Gino entered with a covered platter. "Here ya go, boss. Hold the door, and I'll grab the vino."

He wondered what Johnny would think of his underling calling him *boss*. "Thanks. You can leave everything on the counter. Have a good night."

Gino winked at him. "Sure thing. You too."

"Whatever." He pulled the door shut and turned the deadbolt with satisfaction. No one could disturb them. For a while, he could forget about everything but her and goddamn it, that's what he intended to do.

Danielle put her arms around his waist. "I have an idea."

He turned to face her, looped his arms around her and raised a brow. "Oh yeah?"

"Yep. How about take our picnic to the bedroom?"

"I could go for that."

She slipped away from him, noticed the case of wine, and pulled out one of the bottles. She clutched it to her chest. "When you sent a case of this wine to the house in San Francisco, I knew, no matter what you said, that you still loved me."

"Oh God, Danielle, I was such a jerk. I hoped you'd forgive me someday, and I guess the wine was my stupid way of asking you to."

"Of course, I forgave you. I understood, eventually, that you had to do certain *things,* and the last thing you needed was me."

Her sad acknowledgement sent pain ricocheting through his heart. "Danielle, you'll never know how sorry I am for how I hurt you. I know I don't deserve you, and I don't know why you're here. But I will never stop loving you. Don't ever forget that."

"Rowan, I'm here because *I love you.*" She pointed at him. "Don't *you* ever forget."

Their conversation felt too cryptic, too laden with the kind of things neither of them wanted to admit or God forbid, talk about. "Look Danielle, let's have our picnic and go from there. OK?"

She grabbed the platter of sandwiches. "OK."

He uncorked the wine, grabbed a couple glasses, and followed her into the bedroom. She ditched the platter and piled the sandwiches and chips on the bed. He poured wine in both glasses and handed one to her. "Here's to us."

She took the glass and clinked it against his. "Here's to us, forever."

He didn't want to disagree or start an argument with her, so he didn't say anything and took a drink of wine. "Now I remember why I got that first bottle."

"Mm. It's been my favorite ever since. Out of my budget range, but I've never forgotten how lovely it is."

"We've got plenty. You can have as much as you want." They ate in silence for a few minutes, and his doubts rushed back. Would she be disappointed with his ruined body? What if he couldn't…?

Danielle placed her hand gently on his arm. "Hey, I've got an idea."

"OK. Let's hear it."

"I'll show you." She turned the lights down low, then stood next to the bed, hands on hips. He could barely see her seductive smile. Behind her, the light he'd left on earlier in the bathroom cast a shaft of light through the doorway. It highlighted her silhouette and reflected in the dark windows. "Rowan, do you remember how nervous I was, the first night we stayed in our suite here?"

"Yeah. Why?"

"Well, um, you helped me feel comfortable. I want to do it this time, for you."

"What do you mean?"

"Just come here, next to me, would you?"

"OK." Trying not to wince, he shoved off the bed and stood up. Facing her, feeling awkward, he frowned. "Now what?"

She ran her hands up his arms and across his shoulders, while he concentrated on not flinching. She stopped at the top button of his shirt and spoke quietly. "Try to relax. I know this is hard for you. But I love you just the way you are."

He resisted the desire to clutch the shirt around him in the semi-darkness. "I'm not the same man."

She undid one button and moved to the next. "I know you're in pain. You try to hide it, but I can tell. Let me help you. Please."

"You can't help me, Danielle. No one can do anything about the pain."

She put two fingers on his lips. "Hush. Just come along with me on this. It'll be all right. I promise."

He took hold of her fingers, reluctant, but not wanting to disappoint her. "OK. I'll try."

She wiggled her fingers out of his and undid another button, her hands brushing his belly. He shivered and took a quick breath. When all the buttons were undone, she slid the shirt off his shoulders with gentle hands. "Oh no," she whispered.

"I told you, it's done, in the past. It doesn't matter."

She replied, her voice fierce. "I'd gladly kill Shemal myself."

He couldn't help a dry chuckle. "I'm sure you would."

She trailed her fingers, feather light, from his shoulders to his belly and then to the button on his jeans. He held his breath while she unfastened it, unzipped them, and tugged them down. He stepped out of them, and she placed warm fingers inside the waistband of his boxers. "You all right?"

He released his breath in a sigh. "Uh-huh."

She slid the boxers down, then helped him shove them aside. She pulled back the covers. "Go ahead and get in bed. Then it's my turn."

He gingerly lowered himself to the bed and pulled the covers to his chest. "I'm as ready as I'll ever be."

"Oh, I don't know about that." She shoved her hair forward and raised her arms behind her head. He watched, fascinated as she unzipped her dress and let it drop to the floor. She undid the front clasp on her bra, shimmied out of her panties, and stood there, as breathtaking as the first time he'd seen her naked. She lifted the covers and slid into the bed next to him, warm and close. "How'd I do?"

"You're amazing." He held his breath and turned on his side, barely able to stifle a groan. But he didn't care about the pain. His hand roamed from her shoulders, down her back to the roundness of her hip, then glided back up from her abdomen to her ribs and the fullness of her breasts. She was *so soft*, all over, and he couldn't get enough.

She propped herself up on one elbow and gave him a lazy smile. Her hand rested lightly on his back, then zigzagged across his side, while gooseflesh rose on his arms and legs. "This is so much fun. It's still hard to believe I'm with you. I want to make love to you for hours and hours."

He took uneven breaths and whispered, "Me too, but I'm not sure. I mean, I don't know if…"

She interrupted. "Rowan, just let me love you."

"But I…"

She cut in again. *"Shut up.* All I want to do is make love to you. So let me."

He gave up. "OK."

She gave him a gentle shove. He lay on his back with his fists clenched and wished like hell he could slit the throats of the two guards who'd ruined his body. Danielle began kissing him, her lips making their way from his cheek to his shoulders, chest, and ribs. Tears stung his eyes when he realized she'd found each scar left by Shemal's dagger. She raised her head and gazed down at him. "I fell in love with you the first time we kissed," she whispered.

"I'll never forget that," he muttered. "You damn near bit through my bottom lip."

She giggled, her fingers teasing him, kicking his heart rate into triple digits. "Um, that was our second kiss. After you told me how unprofessional you were for kissing me in the first place."

"Oh, right." His body responded to her in spite of the pain and despite his awful fear. She took her time, leaving him dry-mouthed, sweating with anticipation while she worked her way from the stubble on his face to his collar bone, swirled the hair on his chest, and trailed fire from his ribs to his belly.

His breathing turned ragged as her hands slid lower, gently caressing him, then moving up, tantalizing him, leaving him desperate for more. While his heart pounded, she leaned over him. "Think you're ready for me now?"

He could barely form coherent thoughts, let alone words. "Uh, yeah."

She laughed out loud and straddled him, her knees snug on each side as she lowered her body, using her hands to guide him, moaning as he slid inside the hot, wet part of her. She moved rhythmically, with her hair flung back and her breasts thrust forward. He couldn't reach up with his hands and found her thighs instead. She grabbed his hands and took him to a place beyond his deep, abiding sadness, beyond everything he'd lost. A place for only the two of them.

They finished with him gasping and her shrieking and then laughing, her hair swirling around his face and tickling his chest. Her mouth found his, and her toes curled on his calves while his arms went around her. Exhausted, he clung to her while his heartbeat slowed, and his pulse ticked in his neck with less force. "Oh God, Danielle. You're beautiful. I love you."

"I love you, too," she murmured. "Always. Forever."

The Next Day

Rowan became aware of the burning, crawling misery in his shoulders first. He opened his eyes and gazed at the ceiling. His hand found cold, empty space next to him. He rolled to his side and forced himself upright. Squeezing his eyes shut against the pain, he managed to scoot to the edge of the bed.

He rubbed his eyes and gazed at the new day through the big windows. Low, gray clouds muted the sunrise glowing dully behind them. He smelled coffee and decided he'd better take a quick shower. Standing under the hot water, he tried to clear his mind and think about the conversation he needed to have with Danielle.

She couldn't stay with him. It would kill him to see her go, but he wondered whether she didn't already know they couldn't be together. He'd seen something in her eyes that he couldn't quite put his finger on. He stepped from the shower and wrapped a towel around his waist, while water dripped from his hair and ran in rivulets down his neck, making him shiver.

He wiped condensation from the mirror and squinted at his image, wondering why he hadn't shaved first. He was standing with his jaws covered with shaving cream, razor in hand, when Danielle appeared in the doorway with a steaming cup of coffee. She looked sexy in a long white t-shirt, her denim shorts barely visible beneath it. "Good morning. I brought you some coffee."

He scraped carefully with the razor and glanced at her. "You're up early. Thanks. I better finish this first."

She leaned against the doorway, watching his progress. "I'm used to waking up early. You know, I always loved watching you shave. I've missed the scent of your aftershave."

He finished and rinsed his face. "I know what you mean. I thought all the time about how your hair always smelled like strawberries."

She handed him the cup of coffee and gave him a quick kiss. "Mm, even your shaving cream smells nice."

He sipped the hot brew. "You gotta tell me about this coffee. It tastes as good as my favorite Italian Roast."

Sadness flitted across her face, but she gave him a bright smile. "I'll tell you about it over breakfast, which by the way, is the monster cookies Marion brought yesterday. And I ordered some fruit. I talked to Roberto. He seems like a nice man."

"Yeah, Bobbie's a good guy." He swallowed more coffee. "I'll get dressed, and then we can talk."

The smile seemed pasted on her face. "All right. That sounds good." She turned and left the bathroom.

He stared after her, frowning. What the hell was that about?

An hour later, he faced her across the tiny table nestled in one corner of the suite. She'd just refilled his coffee and moved the remains of the cookies and fruit to the counter. "OK, tell me about this special coffee. Tell me about your life."

She stared into her cup for a moment, then looked at him. "The coffee is a special batch from beans harvested in Peru. My new career is with a company called Small-Batch-Love Coffee. I manage a bistro, their first one, in Seattle. We're establishing a niche market, right beneath the noses of the coffee giants."

He gripped the cup with both hands. "Interesting. Tell me more."

She hesitated, then became animated. "I've wished for so long that I could tell you everything." She chattered on about the bistro, the kids she managed, and the damn Rottweiler she'd adopted. As she talked, it dawned on him that she'd done exactly what he'd insisted she do. She'd begun a new life and *moved on.*

He watched how she talked, how she used her hands, how her hair framed her face. He needed to absorb everything about her, drink in every detail, to guard against the empty, aching days he'd endure after she left. Because the more she talked, the more the certainty sank into his gut. She would leave. Caught up in his abysmal thoughts, he realized she'd stopped talking. "Uh, what else is going on? What's next for you?"

She flung her hair back before answering. "Well, I was recently offered a promotion, but that was before Marion called me. And um, I guess what's next depends on what you and I decide."

"I'm not sure what you mean."

She waved an arm. "You know, how we work things out."

"You've built a new life and career. I'm happy for you, and I'll always love you. I don't know what else to say."

Her chin tilted up. "Rowan, you're leaving a huge *but* hanging there, and you know it. I've done exactly what you wanted me to do. From now on, maybe *you* should do what *I* want you to do. You're free. What's stopping you from moving to Seattle?"

Nonplussed, he opened his mouth and closed it. She'd said the very last thing he expected. *"But* I can't be a part of your life in Seattle."

She fired right back. "Why not? What's holding you here? The Mafia guy Michael told me about?"

"What? No. Johnny doesn't care where I go." He wanted to take back the words as soon as he said them, because she was already nodding, and he'd just lied to her.

"All right then. What's your problem? Why did Marion have to call and beg me to come?"

He heard the hurt in her voice. "Because, don't you see? Being with me puts a target on *you.* And the last damn thing I'm going to do is put you in danger. I don't want you to be hurt by all the garbage surrounding me."

"You think being left out of your life doesn't hurt? Besides, you've been exonerated, right? No one is coming after you anymore. Honestly, Rowan, you're always so fatalistic."

He tried another tack. "OK. I'm going to get a rehab program set up, through Johnny's doctor. Then I'm heading for a beach house in, uh, south of here. You can come with me. Johnny's crew will protect us. How about it?"

He saw the answer on her face, before she spoke, confirming his thoughts and stabbing him deep inside. "I love Seattle and my career. But I love you more…" Her voice trailed off.

"Enough. I won't ask you to leave the life you've created and what you've worked hard to achieve. And if I'm in Seattle, I put you in danger. There isn't a good solution for us."

"I guess not," she whispered, fiddling with her cup, not meeting his gaze.

He reached across the short expanse and grabbed her hand. "How long can you stay?"

She held onto his hand, still not looking at him. "A week or so, I guess. I'd like to stay longer, but my new boss was a bit anxious. And I left Leo with a friend."

He kept his voice on an even keel while jealousy flooded his mind. "I understand. Tell me about your friend."

She looked at him then, with a mixture of guilt and apprehension. "There isn't much to tell. His name is Tom, and he's a good friend. He's an engineer at Boeing. Once in a while, we have drinks or dinner. He has a Harley. He loves Leo, so I knew he'd be in good hands while I was here."

He forced a smile, thinking about her arms around another man. "A Harley, huh? I had one, years ago. It's why I don't drive anymore, at least not legally."

Real curiosity lit her features. "I'd love to hear *that* story."

"Maybe later. For now, I want to know more of your story."

She met his gaze directly and reached for his other hand. He let her take hold of it. "Rowan, I will never love anyone else. You need to believe me, all right?"

He'd bet her engineer friend had other plans. Instead of protesting, he gripped her hands tightly. "I believe you, Danielle. If there's one thing I've learned, it's that I was an ass about a few things. Maybe more than a few."

"Maybe. But I know you had your reasons."

He pulled his hands away. "I was a fool. Threw away everything that mattered. Didn't figure it out until I was…" He stopped short of saying, *until I was strung up a few times.* "I mean, I figured out a few things in Tora."

Her eyes went huge. "I can't begin to imagine."

He tried for a nonchalant tone. “We both need to move on.” He hesitated, then decided to finish it. “Danielle, I want you to know something.”

“What’s that?”

He had to hurt her again, but at least this time he’d do it for the right reasons and not because he was a stupid, foolish jerk. “I want you to live your *life.”*

She nodded. “I know. I am. I will. With you. We’ll figure it out.”

“No, what I mean is, I want you to experience everything you deserve. A great career, sure. But along with that, a family, a place to settle and call home. You’ve got part of that going on. Don’t be afraid to let the rest of it happen. You get what I mean?”

Her lips trembled. Tears brimmed in her eyes and slid down her cheeks. “No. I love *you. No one else,”* she whispered.

“I know. And I love you. I always will. But look, what we have, what we *had* is a crazy, once in a lifetime thing. I’ll never forget it, and I hope you won’t either. But I want you to go back to Seattle and live your life to the fullest. You deserve to have a normal, wonderful life with someone who loves you *and* can give you that.”

“Then last night meant nothing to you? I thought, I wanted…” She closed her eyes.

His gut tightened and tiny beads of sweat popped on his forehead. “No, you’ve got it wrong. Last night meant everything to me, and I’d give *anything* for a different outcome. But I’ve learned, the hard way, to face reality. I want you to face it, too. So you can keep moving forward with your life.”

She opened her eyes. “You don’t want me.”

“For God’s sake, I don’t know how to get through to you. Here it is in the simplest terms I can put into words. Because I love you, I feel responsible for you. I want to make sure you’re safe and have the best life possible. I need to make the right decisions on your behalf, for you, not me.”

She ducked her head. "You want to make the best possible life for me." She scrunched her eyes shut again. Her lips kept moving, but he couldn't make out her mumbling introspection.

He watched the tears seep out of her tightly closed eyes and trickle down her cheeks. They glistened in the light from the window, making him aware for the first time that the storm clouds had broken up, leaving a crystal clear, sunny morning. "I'd give my life for a different ending. Please believe me."

She took a shuddering breath, opened her eyes, and gazed at him with more composure than he'd expected. "I believe you, and I understand." She grabbed the white linen napkin lying on the table and wiped her cheeks. "Now *you* need to understand a few things."

"I'm listening."

She held the napkin in trembling hands. "I'm staying here, with you, for the entire week. After that, I'll go back to Seattle. I want to give this new venture my best shot. I owe it to the people who hired me and believe in my ability."

Relieved, he said, "Good. You'll be great."

"And," she shook her index finger at him, "I'll make my *own decisions,* thank you very much, about who I love and how I want to live the rest of my life. I refuse to be pressured in one direction or another by you or, or anybody. Do you get that, Rowan?"

He'd be willing to bet good money that her friend Tom had done some pressuring of his own. "Yeah, I get it." He sketched her a vague salute. "Understood."

Her voice sank to a whisper. "And please don't cut me out of your life, ever again."

"I won't."

"I want to call you when I'm lonesome for you, or even plan a visit, someplace where no one can find us. *Promise me* you'll stay in touch."

"I promise."

She leaned back in the chair and tipped her head toward the ceiling. "Thank God." Her face softened and her voice became pensive. "I'm starting to understand something else, or something more."

"Such as?"

"You aren't *really* free, are you?"

"No."

"And you're not actually fatalistic or even paranoid, are you?"

"No, I'm not."

She grasped his hand. "I understand completely now, not just why you won't come to Seattle, but why, from the beginning of all this, you pushed me away."

"You do? Are you sure?"

"You're frightened, aren't you?"

He'd never admitted his gut-level fear to anyone. "Yes. I'm scared to death. Have been ever since those two CIA bastards grabbed me in Sioux Falls."

"I never realized it before now because you've never acted afraid. Angry, for sure. But I've always thought you were one of the most courageous people I've ever known."

"Oh hell, I'm not brave. I just did what I had to, what needed to be done. I couldn't let fear stop me."

"Come on Rowan, deciding to do something even when you're afraid is how most people define courage. You don't seem so angry anymore, either."

He slanted a careless smile her way. "Well, as you've figured out, I'm not a lot of things anymore." Anxious to steer the conversation away from himself, he said, "As far as I'm concerned, you're the brave one."

She pulled her hand away from his and splayed it across her chest. "Me? Why on Earth would you say that?"

"Because you picked up the pieces of your life after I shoved you away. You started a new career, made new friends, and now you're poised to go even further. All of those things required courage."

She folded the napkin and laid it back on the table. "Well, it was either start a new life or live forever with my parents. I couldn't let *that* happen." She pushed back her chair and stood up. "Let's move this conversation to the sofa. I want to hear some of those stories you have."

"We can exchange as many stories as you'd like. I want to hear more about your coffee shop and your big mutt."

"I get first pick. Tell me about your Harley and why you don't drive *legally* anymore."

He chuckled, and for the moment it felt good. "OK. I need another cup of coffee if I'm going to tell you that tale."

Two Days Later

Rowan stared at Lake Michigan, shimmering blue-green in early afternoon sunlight. Gauging the number of people on the pier, he thought it must be the weekend. Danielle stood beside him and put her arm loosely around his waist. He drew her close, enjoying the way her body fit next to his.

She hadn't mentioned leaving, and he'd grown too quickly accustomed to waking up with her soft, sexy warmth beside him. A staccato series of knocks on the door to the suite ended his contemplation. Danielle gave him a quick squeeze and pulled away. "It must be Bettina and Chad. I'll get the door."

He smiled his agreement and braced himself for his sister's entrance. He hadn't seen Bettina since leaving Kauai the previous January, and he never knew what his sister would do or say in the best of times.

Danielle opened the door. Bettina squealed and held out her arms. The two women hugged, shrieking their excited greetings. Behind them, Chad waited, carrying the baby. Bettina saw him and left Danielle. She opened her arms wide while her eyes filled with tears. He accepted her embrace, surprised at her gentleness. "Oh Rowan. Oh God, it's so good to see you," she whispered fiercely.

He held her close and murmured in her ear. "Hey Bettina, it's good to see you too. Congratulations. Your baby is beautiful."

She pulled back and held onto his arms, her smile huge, even as tears continued spilling down her cheeks. "Thank you. I can't believe you finally get to meet him. He's your nephew, you know?"

He nodded. "I do know that."

She grabbed his hand. "Come and sit so you can meet him properly. You need to hold him and get to know him."

"OK." He looked to Danielle for help as he settled on the sofa.

Bettina perched on the arm of the adjacent sofa, and Chad stood in front of him. "You ready for this?"

"Uh, sure." He'd never held a baby before and had no clue what he was supposed to do. Danielle slid down next to him while Chad carefully placed baby Carson in his arms. He gazed at the chubby face, framed by thick black hair. Deep brown eyes stared up at him and a miniature hand clutched Danielle's finger. He sniffed at the scent of baby powder and smiled at the blue t-shirt stretching the length of the tiny body, even covering the baby's diaper. Emblazoned in red were the words *My Daddy is the Best!*

He leaned back, trying to ease the taut muscles in his shoulders. Carson weighed more than he'd expected for such a small person. Danielle pressed closer. "He's so sweet. Feel his cheek. I want to hold him next."

Supporting the little body with his right arm, he moved gingerly and stroked the baby's cheek. The velvety skin surprised him. Carson turned his face toward his fingers, making tiny suckling sounds. "Uh oh. Here, Danielle. You take him."

Danielle eagerly took the small bundle, bringing relief to his shoulders. He leaned back and caught Bettina's worried frown. "Are you in a lot of pain?"

"Nah, I'm OK." Curious, he watched Danielle. She'd become completely engrossed, making cooing sounds and leaning over Carson, head bent, her hair blocking her face. He gently tucked it behind her ear, marveling at the simple joy in her eyes. He'd never thought of Danielle in the role of mother. Unexpected memories rose in his mind like a flash flood.

He saw Michelle, her eyes glowing with happiness when she placed his hands on her abdomen. Her voice whispered through his mind. *I'm pregnant, Rowan. We're going to be a family. I can't wait.* He felt the pliable warmth of her belly while he imagined the life, a part of him, growing inside. Her voice whispered once more, their last conversation. *I'm having breakfast tomorrow morning at Windows on the World, at the top of the World Trade Center.*

He'd been with Ralph. They'd seen the televised report from their hotel room in Ohio. He'd never forget the straining roar of the jet's engines as it barreled into the north tower. He'd clung to Ralph, watching the live images of the tower imploding, knowing his family was gone forever.

Bowled over and sucked under by the wave of raw emotion, he stared blindly. Carson squawked, and he blinked back to the present. He met Chad's uneasy gaze and knew he had to say something. "You did well, my brother. He's quite the little kid."

Chad grinned. "He's amazing, ya know? I never dreamed being a father, a *dad,* would be like this. I wouldn't trade it for anything. It's the best thing that's ever happened to me."

His pain-filled memories lingered, and he didn't know how to respond. "I'm happy for both of you."

Chad seemed to relax. "Thanks brother. I'm happy for you, too. It's nice to see you and Danielle together. I hope you don't mind if we hang around for a while. Those two have a lot of catching up to do."

He wished he could shut himself away with his bottle of Jack, crawl into bed and under the covers. "Stay as long as you want."

Bettina chimed in. "Mom and Dad are dying to see you, and Chad's father Clifton wants to meet you. They'd all love to see Dani, too."

He'd put off seeing the people whose lives had been irrevocably altered because of him, but he could face them with Danielle. She'd never know how her presence gave him the vaunted *courage* she was so sure he possessed. "OK. Let's do it, before Danielle has to go back to Seattle."

Bettina said, "Oh Dani, you aren't staying?"

Danielle replied. "For a few more days, then I need to head back."

Before Bettina could launch an argument or blame him for *anything,* he added, "Danielle just got a big promotion in her career. She needs to get back. We'll handle things long distance for now."

Bettina's cherry red lips formed an 'o.' Danielle slanted a surprised glance his way and said, "Yep, for now we've decided that's the best."

Chad observed them both. "Sounds like you've got things settled. How about we meet up with everyone tomorrow afternoon?"

The ordeal of facing everyone was one more thing he didn't have a choice about. "OK. Sounds great."

Bettina added, "You'll be interested to know, Mom became quite the lush for a while. Good ole Johnny introduced her to his favorite bourbon. She took to it, bigtime."

His brows shot up. "Our mother started drinking?"

Bettina giggled. "Yep. She quit, though, after I refused to let her help when Carson was born because she was sloshed. Thank God for Angelo and Clifton."

"You mean, they, uh, what about a doctor?"

Bettina replied. "Our American lady doctor and extremely proper Arab midwife came to Johnny's apartment, just in time. We made a video, so I could show Chad. We can show you, too."

"You what? No, it's OK. I mean, that's nice. I don't need to watch it, though." His sister giving birth was the last damn thing he'd ever want to see. Just the thought had his hands sweating. He heard Danielle's soft snort of laughter and shot her a dirty look. "What's so funny?"

She gazed back at him, biting her lower lip. "Childbirth is the most beautiful thing in the world. I cry every time I watch it on TV."

He stared, unable to wrap his mind around what she'd said. "You watch it on TV? Are you crazy?"

Danielle threw her head back and laughed. "After all you've done, childbirth gets to you? Wow, I never would have thought."

"What the hell is that supposed to mean?"

She laughed harder. "Never mind. Forget I said anything." She bent her head and began cooing at Carson, pointedly ignoring him.

He noticed Chad and Bettina grinning at him. "I give up," he said, then realized Danielle had distracted him, taken his mind away from the memories. He didn't know if he could stand the suite anymore without her. She not only made him feel like a man again, she made him feel like a *person.* With her, life seemed like it could be peaceful, maybe even normal.

A brisk knock on the door startled him. Chad stood up. "I'll see who it is."

A moment later, Johnny came into the suite. "Ladies, excuse me. I'd like to borrow Chad and Rowan for a few minutes if you don't mind." The Don stopped in front of him and Danielle. "Ms. Stratton, it's my great pleasure to meet you." He held out his hand.

Danielle shook Johnny's hand. "It's a pleasure to meet you, Mr. Giacopino. Thank you for sending your jet to pick me up. The Lear 75 is a beautiful aircraft."

The Don's chest puffed at the compliment. "You're welcome, young lady. It was my pleasure." Johnny angled his head. "Now, Rowan, if you don't mind."

He rose stiffly to his feet. "Sure." He followed Chad and Johnny down the hall to the presidential suite. Johnny entered, then held the door open, giving him a searching look as he stepped inside.

Michael and Ralph waited at the dark wood, rectangular table. Michael scowled at him, and Ralph gave him a wary, sideways glance. He looked further and saw David Harandi. "What are you doing here?"

Chad came to a stop beside him. "Why would you come here? You can't do anything more to us. You should get the hell out of here. Now."

He nodded. "I couldn't agree more. Leave now."

Harandi took a step back. "Wait, you don't understand. I'm on your side. Rowan, you should know that by now."

Johnny stepped in front of him and Chad. "Mr. Harandi asked for a meet last week. He wants to work for us. You remember, he informed me of Whitman's plans to screw you over for good. It's thanks to him that you're free."

He didn't care. "David's CIA. He lies his ass off about damn near anything. You can't trust him, believe me."

Johnny gave him a hard stare. "I'd like to hire him. I believe we can trust him, or he wouldn't be standing here. You need to give him a listen, Rowan. You too, Chad."

Harandi gave him a pleading look. "He's right. You can trust me."

The suite door opened and closed. He heard his sister. "Chad, honey, I don't mean to interrupt, but Dani and I were thinking…" Bettina gasped. *"You. I thought I'd never have to see you again."*

Surprised at the depth of animosity in her voice, so unlike Bettina, he turned to stare at her. She glared at Harandi, her face flushing deep red.

He reached out. “Hey, Bettina, it’s OK.”

Ignoring him, she headed for his ex-friend. *“I will always hate you.”* Rowan winced at the sharp crack of her hand making contact with Harandi’s face and snapping his head to one side. She sucker-punched him next, the force of her fist sending her staggering and dropping Harandi to his knees, gasping and choking.

He sneered at Harandi, still on his knees, holding his face with one hand, clutching his gut with the other. “Thanks Bettina. I’ve been wanting to return that particular favor for a long time.”

Beside him, Chad snickered and put his arm around Bettina as she rushed to his side. “Way to go, sweetheart.”

Harandi staggered to his feet and coughed. “Nice to see you, too, Bettina.”

Johnny interjected. “Well, now that we’ve all said hello, I’d like to have a quick meet. If you’d excuse us please, Bettina?”

Bettina gave Harandi a final glare. “Of course.” She stepped away from Chad. “I’ll see you in a bit.”

Rowan winked at her as she swept away, then turned to Harandi. “You’ve had that coming. For a damn long time. It’s less than you deserve, but it’s a good start.”

Johnny gestured toward the three of them. “You’re all gonna have to let bygones be bygones. Come and sit so we can talk.”

He and Chad took seats across from Mike and Ralph. Johnny resumed his place at the head of the table, and Harandi sat at the opposite end. The Don shifted his gaze from Mike to Ralph, then to Chad and finally him before speaking. “Like I said, Mr. Harandi came to me last week. Seems that Whitman put two and two together somehow and blames him for your release.”

Rowan turned to Harandi. “So, Whitman wants your ass? Welcome to my world.”

Harandi frowned and rubbed his jaw, but didn’t answer.

Johnny said, “Mr. Harandi has expressed a strong interest in our goals regarding Shemal and the Brotherhood. Because of that and in the interests of keeping him out of the hands of the feds, I want to hire him.”

He replied. “For all we know, he’s still working for Whitman. Agents may be converging here as we speak.”

Johnny responded. “I’ve checked him out. He hasn’t made any calls I don’t know about, and no one has met with him. Rowan, think about it, if he hadn’t called me, you’d be in Houston facing those charges. That’s worth something, in my book.”

He’d had enough. “Right. OK, I get it.” He turned to Harandi. “If it were up to me, I’d hand you over to Whitman myself. Or maybe even Shemal. He turned his back before Harandi could reply, and addressed Johnny. “If you are determined to hire him, be advised that he always has an ulterior motive.”

Harandi said, “Come on, Rowan, you know…”

He interrupted, still addressing Johnny. “I’m seeing my sister for the first time in damn near a year, so Chad and I are leaving.” He shoved back his chair and smirked at Ralph, staring wide-eyed at him and at Mike, gazing at him with his mouth open.

Johnny nodded. “Thanks for entertaining my request, Rowan. We’ll chat again later.”

“Sounds good.” He stood up, turned, and left the room, with Chad following him.

CHAPTER TWENTY

Late That Night

Danielle leaned against the pillows she'd stuffed behind her back and clutched the covers to her chest. Rowan lay flat on his back next to her, taking deep, even breaths. The glow of neighboring skyscrapers illuminated the bedroom with their lesser version of moonlight, allowing her to study his features. While he slept, the constant tension of pain slid away from his face, and he looked relaxed, even peaceful.

She smiled at the expressive brows that shot up whenever he was surprised or confused; the prickly whiskers he hated, and she loved; the lips that felt like fire when they glided across her skin. Her smile faded when she thought about their first night together. The confident, powerful, sometimes terrifying man she loved had become wounded and hesitant.

That night she'd shoved aside her shock and grief and poured out everything she had; given him every part of her body, mind, and heart. She smoothed the hair on his forehead. Had she helped him? With Rowan, she couldn't tell. Sharing his thoughts, or God forbid, his heart, did not come easily for him.

Rowan showed his love in ways that had taken some time for her to understand. Surrendering to secure her freedom and suffering for his unselfishness; pushing her away to keep her safe; freeing her to pursue her life; those were his ways of showing how much he loved her. She wished with all her heart that, for once, he'd say how much he wanted her. Because she'd stay with him. For all the effort she'd put into her new career and life in Seattle, if he said he wanted her with him, she'd leave everything behind. Again.

He'd closed the door to those possibilities with his insistence that she return to Seattle and her career. Was he right? Seattle held a special place in her heart, and she loved what she thought of as *her* coffee bistro. Managing and sometimes mentoring the crowd of kids who worked for her provided huge satisfaction.

Rowan didn't deserve further wounding. He needed every bit of healing she could offer by being with him. For four more days. Fresh indecision tore at her mind and heart. She didn't want to leave him. What would he do if she refused to go? She touched her lips with two fingers and pressed them feather-light against the scar on his cheek.

He jerked his head away, and she gasped. Eyes still closed, he twisted his head back and forth. *"Who are you?"* He frowned and his voice tapered off in an agonized whisper. *"I don't understand."*

She waited a moment, then whispered, "Rowan, are you awake?" She hoped he'd fallen back to sleep.

He stretched and groaned. "Yeah."

Hearing the weary discouragement in his voice, she slid down close beside him and laid her hand on his chest, felt his heart pounding. "I'm sorry you woke up. I know you don't sleep much."

He yawned. "Can't seem to."

"Nightmares? You were talking in your sleep."

"Maybe. Probably."

Surprised he'd admit anything, she ventured further. "This time?"

He grunted and turned to face her. "I dunno."

She saw the pain-tension in his face again. "I wish I could help you forget. I wish I could take your pain away."

"Not gonna happen." He hesitated, then continued. "Can I tell you something?"

"You know you can tell me anything. What is it?"

"Are you sure? I don't want you to feel bad."

She grasped his hand. "I'm tough. I can handle it. Go ahead."

"OK. One time, in Tora, I was lying on the floor of my cell. I knew it was over for me and I wanted to die. I heard footsteps and thought it must be the guards coming again to, to..."

She tightened her grip on his hand, determined to help him. "It's all right. You're safe. No one can hurt you anymore."

"I know, it's just, I hate thinking about it. But see, it wasn't the guards. It was a man. He appeared in my cell, without opening the door."

Not wanting to break his concentration, she murmured, "Wow, how amazing."

"His voice got to me. When he spoke, I somehow felt this unbelievable kindness, directed toward *me.*"

She smiled at his incredulity. "That's not hard for me to understand."

"He touched my face, and the pain went away, for the first time in months."

"Do you remember what he said?"

"I do, but it's crazy, or I'm crazy, or maybe it was a delusion, something I made up because I was desperate and in bad shape."

"That doesn't sound like you. What did he say?"

"He said my name, from inside my mind, not out loud. I've heard the same voice a couple times before, when I knew I'd reached the end."

"I remember you telling me about that last fall, when we first got to Kauai. I can't even imagine how that feels. What else did he say?"

He pulled his hand away from hers and began a slow exploration of her body. "Oh hell, I don't know. I don't remember. Let's not talk about this anymore."

She tried to ignore her reaction to his touch, recognizing his attempt to distract her from the lie he'd just told. "I'd love to hear more. I've always wanted to know what happened to you."

"No. You don't want to know. I don't want you to know. I wish I could forget."

Hoping to keep him talking, she added, "You said something interesting in your sleep."

"Oh yeah?" He trailed his fingers along her side, and she could tell he had no intention of continuing their conversation.

"Yep. You said, 'who are you,' and then you muttered something that sounded like, 'I don't understand.' You think you were dreaming about the person who came to you?"

Even in the dim light, she saw his eyes widen and felt his body go still. "Nah, I doubt it. I can't even remember what I was dreaming about."

His reaction told her he knew exactly what he'd been dreaming about, and the finality in his voice told her he didn't plan to share it with her. Crushed by his decision to shut her out, not wanting him to know, she faked a yawn. "Maybe you'll remember later. Guess I'll try to get a few more hours of sleep."

He raised a brow. "You don't want to waste the rest of the night sleeping, do you? I can think of a few other things we could do."

Much as his effortless deception stung, she couldn't— she didn't want to disappoint him. He was probably unaware he'd hurt her, and his touch made her ache for more. "I bet you're thinking about the same things I am. Shall we find out?"

He snickered, sounding almost lighthearted, or relieved. "I think we should."

The Next Day

Rowan stood at the windows, feeling the usual restlessness in his mind and heart as he watched the sparkling waves far below. His suite felt more and more like a luxurious prison that he needed to escape. He wanted to walk the beach at Key West, feel the hard-packed, warm sand beneath his feet and let the water rush over his ankles. He wanted to feel the pull of the ocean as the waves receded.

Danielle came to stand next to him and put her arm around his waist. "Bettina just texted me. Everyone's waiting for us. Are you ready to go?"

He winced and lifted his arm so she could sidle closer and rested his chin lightly on the top of her head while he stared at the varying shades of water. "No, I'm not ever going to be ready. I don't want to see anyone."

"I know," she said. "I wish I could help you."

"I couldn't do this without you." Her presence, warm, close and sexy helped him, more than she'd ever know. And he'd never tell her, because he didn't want her to feel obligated to stay.

"Sure, you could." She turned to face him and cupped his face in her hands. "You've done things much harder than this. Kiss me before we go. You can think about what we'll do when we get back. That'll help, right?"

"Right. That sounds good. Well, actually it sounds great. Best idea you've had all day." He let her draw his head down, closed his eyes, and focused on the softness of her lips. She teased him with her tongue until he wrapped his arms tight around her and deepened the kiss.

He didn't know how long they stood in front of the windows. He couldn't get enough of her mouth and her body. When Danielle drew away, he tipped his head back. His pulse pounded, and he took a deep breath, willing his heart to slow. "Damn it. Now I really don't want to go."

She laid her head on his chest. "Neither do I." Her tone became businesslike and she stepped back. "We have to go. My phone keeps vibrating in my pocket. I'm sure it's Bettina wondering where we are."

"Oh man, is *that* what I felt? Hell, I thought it was you."

She giggled and led him out of the suite and down the hallway. “You’re terrible. Come on, let’s hurry up so we can come back and take up where we left off.”

“I’m all for that.” He squeezed her hand and stepped into Johnny’s suite. The Don had vacated for the afternoon, offering his suite as a place for him to meet with everyone.

She gave him a reassuring smile. “It’ll be all right.”

“I don’t know about that.” Panic set in when he saw the entire group gathered near the long rectangular table in front of the windows. What would he say to everyone? What did they expect from him? Angelo caught his reluctant gaze, waved, and touched his mother’s arm. Janice turned and put her hand over her mouth. He heaved a sigh. “Oh great. Here we go.”

Danielle gripped his hand. “She’s just being a mom, Rowan. Don’t worry about it.”

He hoped he could withstand his mother’s emotional outburst. Janice reached him first while his father hung back. He saw the tears in his mother’s eyes, the quiver in her lips. For the first time ever, he noticed permanent worry lines in her face and felt sad. He’d helped put them there and wished he hadn’t. “Hi, Mom. It’s good to see you again.”

Danielle extricated her hand from his and stepped away. Janice embraced him, hesitant, her tears spilling over. “Oh Rowan. It’s wonderful to see you.” He tried not to shrink away while she patted his back. “Having you here is a miracle.” She pulled away. “I have to tell you something.”

Uneasy, not wanting to hear her endless apologies, he said, “OK.”

She bit her lip, reminding him of Bettina, then met his gaze. “When we heard you were dead, when we saw the video…” She closed her eyes. Tears squeezed out and ran down her face. She shuddered and opened her eyes. “I thought I’d never be able to tell you how much I love you. And I realized, while we were in Dubai, how selfish I’ve been, for so long.”

No way could he listen to any more confessions from her. “It’s all right, Mom. The past is over and done. How about we move on?”

She gripped his arms, and he flinched. Her eyes widened, and she let go. “Oh my, I’m sorry. You’re right. I want to move on, too. I just want you to know, I’m doing my best to be a different person.”

Her words stunned him. At first he didn’t know how to respond. Then he knew. “Me too.”

She smiled through her tears. “Thank you for seeing us.”

“Of course. What are you and Dad planning to do now? Do you want to move back to Cali?”

“We’ve had some time to see my family, here in Chicago, and Bettina and Chad and little Carson will be living here. It’s nice to be close to family again, although we loved Carpinteria.”

“That sounds good for you and Dad.” He hadn’t known about Chad and Bettina choosing to settle in Chicago. For some reason, it jarred him. He couldn’t help but feel out of sync with everyone. Inexplicable weariness hit him, head on, along with a dull ache behind his eyes. He needed the bottle of whiskey. And Danielle.

Janice motioned to Khalil and his father stepped forward. “Hello son.”

His father’s voice left his mind awash with memories he hadn’t thought of in more than twenty years. Khalil teaching him to surf, laughing with him over some teenage escapade, or exhorting him to love the country he’d been fortunate enough to be born in. Khalil had been a good father. How had that eluded him until this moment? Feeling guilty, he could only say, “Hi Dad.”

The longing in his father’s eyes compelled him, and without thinking, he reached out. Khalil embraced him with a light touch, lingering until he returned the hug. “I love you, Rowan, and I’m proud to be your father.”

Khalil's whispered words, along with the unexpected memories had him blinking back tears. He held onto his father, mortified once again at his lack of control. When he could finally speak, he whispered back, "Thank you. I love you too, Dad."

The entire situation felt surreal. The resentment he'd harbored for years had disappeared. His mind drew him back to Tora. Lying in the filth on the cold cement floor, he'd wished with all his heart that he could go back. Somehow, he'd been granted the opportunity. Had Angelo been right? Had he become the different man he so desperately wanted to be?

Bowled over by the revelations tumbling one over the other, he stood in front of Janice and Khalil with no idea how to continue. Danielle came to his rescue. "It's lovely to see you, Mr. and Mrs. Milani. I'm so glad I could be here. Rowan needs to say hello to a few other people, but I know he wanted to talk to you first."

Danielle took his sweaty hand in hers, and he held on tight. "Mom, Dad, I better catch up with everyone else. Maybe we can talk more, later?"

Khalil and Janice were nothing if not polite. His father spoke. "Absolutely. Everyone wants to see you."

"OK. Thanks." He let Danielle lead him toward the group clustered around the table. He didn't see Mike and tried to ignore Ralph, Marion, Bettina, and Angelo giving him interested and happy stares. Instead, he gravitated to Chad, holding Carson in his arms, standing next to a man who could have been his friend's twin.

Danielle squeezed his hand and pulled away. "I'm going to say hello to Marion and Bettina. You'll be all right."

He wanted to tell her he needed her. Didn't she know that she gave him the strength to confront the people whose lives he'd ruined? Instead, he said, "Don't go too far," and continued his slow trek.

Chad said, "Hey brother, come meet my father."

The man standing beside Chad held out his hand. “Hello Rowan, I’m Clifton Cantor. Welcome back. I’ve waited a long time to thank you for your service to the United States. There are many who appreciate the things you’ve done on behalf of our country and I am one of them.”

He shook the proffered hand. “Thank you, sir. It’s a pleasure to meet you. I’m grateful for everything you did for me, and I’m sorry, too. My problems caused you a lot of trouble.”

Clifton replied. “I made my own choice to get involved in your situation, and I have no regrets. We’re all glad to see you home safe and sound. I hope you’ll be able to enjoy your freedom. You’ve certainly earned it.”

“I’ll do my best. What are your plans for the future?”

Clifton smiled at Chad and Carson before responding. “I’m loving my new role as grandpa. I’ve got my family, and they mean everything to me. I can’t think of a better outcome for us.”

Clifton’s heartfelt words left him feeling more out of touch, more empty, than before. “I’m glad to hear that. Thanks again for everything you did. Guess I better talk to a few more people.”

Chad said, “Catch up with you later, brother.”

“OK.” He turned and saw Mike near the door with his arm around Asal, grinning and gesturing to him. He wished he could escape all of them. He couldn’t understand or handle their happy togetherness.

Mike greeted him. “It’s good to see you again, brother. How’s it going?”

“Oh, you know. It’s going.” He hadn’t seen Asal in a couple years, and as far as he could tell, she hadn’t changed or aged. “I’ll be damned. Hello Asal.” He couldn’t resist a smirk. “Don’t tell me you’re still letting this creeper hang around. You could do better, you know.”

Asal laughed in her breathless way and spoke in the voice he remembered well; soft, yet strong, and intimately sexy. “Rowan, it's nice to see you in the flesh. I did not have that opportunity in Cairo." She gave him a hug.

When they parted, he saw Danielle heading toward him, giving Asal an intense once-over. She drew close, and he grasped her hand. "Danielle, meet Asal, the love of Mike's life. She's the other member of our infamous team."

Asal swept her thick black hair over one shoulder. "It's nice to finally meet you, Danielle. I'm glad you're here with our Rowan. He needs a woman like you by his side. You have his heart, and always will."

Danielle stiffened beside him. "Rowan never, ever mentioned another member of his team."

He heard the subtle accusation in her tone and frowned. "Asal works behind the scenes doing what she does best, which is infiltrating jihadist chatrooms and gleaning valuable intelligence. I never had a reason to talk about her. To you. Or anybody." Why did he feel like he had to defend himself? And against what? Danielle couldn't tell he'd ever been involved with Asal, could she? Did she have some kind of radar alert?

He'd been deep into perfecting the art of what he'd dubbed *incidental sex,* and Asal had been one of more women than he could count. None of them had meant squat to him, including Asal. She'd figured that out and ditched him in short order. She and Mike had been together ever since.

And besides *that,* their brief hook-up happened at least seven or eight years ago, which qualified as ancient history as far as he was concerned. He wiggled his fingers out of Danielle's tight grip and put his arm around her waist.

Mike helped him out. "We swore to each other we'd never talk about Asal. I created a new identity for her, similar to what I did for you last summer, Danielle."

Danielle's body melted against his, and she nodded. "I get it. Wow, how amazing."

Asal clasped Danielle's hand with both of hers. "Rowan and Mikey and Gabriel helped me escape from Iran when my own operation was compromised. They brought me to the United States in absolute secrecy. In order to protect me, they all agreed never to mention me to anyone else."

Danielle replied, "It's nice to meet you. I'd love to talk more. Your story sounds fascinating."

Trepidation wound its way through his mind, and his headache ratcheted up. "Yeah, that'd be nice. Maybe later. Right now, I think we need to say hello to Ralph and Marion. Nice seeing you again, Asal. Keep Mike in line for me."

As they made their way across the suite, he couldn't help noticing that the people who'd suffered because of him, whose lives had been forever altered, had become a family. His mother sat in comfortable conversation with Chad and Bettina. He heard her soft laughter. His father held Carson and chatted with Clifton. Both men looked content.

Ralph and Marion lingered in conversation with Angelo, gazing out the windows at the city. He'd bet good money they'd discussed him to death. Angelo saw him first. "Hello, Rowan. Hello, Danielle. It's nice to see you two together again. But if you'll excuse me, I haven't seen Carson in much too long."

He tried with no success to rub the tension from his forehead. "Yeah, Doc. It's nice to see you, too. Go. Enjoy the baby."

Danielle spoke up. "I'll go with you. I've only held Carson once."

Angelo smiled. "That would be nice, Danielle. Let's go."

He faced Ralph and Marion, unsure what to say, wishing the whole ordeal was over. "Hi Ralph. Good to see you again, Marion. Uh, it's nice to see everyone."

Ralph's upper lip curled and his mouth opened, but before his friend could say anything, Marion took over. "Yes, isn't it wonderful? You're looking good. Thank you for agreeing to see all of us."

Ralph added, "She's right. You're looking much better. Been eating those damn cookies by the dozen, I'm sure."

He chuckled. "Yep, and we need some more. They make the best breakfast."

Marion gave him a sly smile. "No worries, sweetie. I brought more."

Ralph snorted. "Of course you did."

The endless charade wearied him, and he spoke without thinking. "Well, I've asked everyone else about their plans. What are yours? You gonna rejoin the Bureau, Ralph?"

His former boss gave him a hard stare. "Are you shitting me?"

"Hell, I don't know. Didn't they invite you back? Since they offered Chad a job, I dunno, I thought maybe they'd contacted you, too."

Marion laid her hand on Ralph's arm. "Now, now dear."

Ralph brushed her aside and pointed a finger at him. "It might interest you to know, I've come over to your side of the fence as far as our government entities and what constitutes true *justice."*

He raised a brow, headache momentarily forgotten. "I see. Do tell."

Ralph lit up, reminding him of their final confrontation on the stormy afternoon in Kauai. "I've been made privy to how things operate. I sat with that ass James Linden in Dubai and listened to his bullshit. I've also seen how Johnny operates."

He couldn't wait to hear more. "And?"

"Johnny knows more about justice than Linden and Whitman and our entire law enforcement apparatus ever will."

"We do seem to be on the same page now. Does this mean you're collaborating with Johnny?"

Ralph glanced at Marion again. She stood with her arms crossed, lips pressed together. "In a manner of speaking, but we haven't finalized our plans yet."

He took his cue from Marion. "You'll have to tell me more another time. It's been great seeing everyone. And now I'm ready to relax. Maybe have some more of those cookies." And a glass of whiskey, *extra-large,* he wanted to add. But that was nobody's business except his. He winked at Marion. "Thanks."

An hour later, he lay sprawled on the sofa with Danielle close beside him. At her insistence, he'd taken a couple pain pills. He'd also poured a generous serving of Jack Daniel's. She watched him pour, and he thought she wanted to say something. She hadn't, probably because she didn't want to argue any more than he did. She poured wine and scooted next to him with a plate of cookies.

He took a deep drink of the pungent whiskey and enjoyed the burn from his tongue to his belly, the heat radiating outward, easing the tension throughout his body. "Damn, that feels good."

Danielle put her arm around his middle and laid her head on his shoulder. "Does it help the pain a lot?"

He tossed back another hit and coughed. "Yeah, more than anything else, ever. The pills help too."

"Good. I'm glad. So, tell me more about Asal."

"Nothing to tell, really. She's Iranian, grew up in Karbala with a strict Imam father. Her mother died in an ugly way when she was a teenager. She had a younger sister who committed suicide. Asal escaped her father and snuck out of Iran."

Danielle murmured, "How did her mother die?"

"You sure you want to know? I wasn't exaggerating about the ugly part."

She pressed closer. "I think so."

"Well, OK. Her father had her mother stoned to death because he thought she was becoming too westernized. She questioned some things about his fundamentalist Islamic beliefs. Asal and her sister were forced to witness her execution. Her sister couldn't handle it."

Danielle shoved away from him and stared, eyes wide. "That's one of the most horrifying things I've ever heard."

"Yeah, like I said, ugly."

She sank down next to him again. "No wonder she seems so tough. It sounds crazy, but something about her reminds me of you."

He hunkered down further on the sofa and put his arm around her. The booze and pills relieved the pain and left him in hazy relaxation. "Huh. I can't imagine what that'd be." He wouldn't tell her that she'd nailed it. Both he and Asal could kill jihadists with cold efficiency and zero remorse.

She tapped on his chest with light fingers. "You two didn't ever, you know, have anything going on, did you?"

He swallowed more Jack and tried to think. He didn't want to lie to her. "Once, a long time ago, for a couple days. Literally. She ditched me for Mike."

She somehow snuggled closer. "I don't know how anyone could prefer Mike to you. He's got some kind of hard edge about him. I always think he's analyzing me or something."

He tipped his head back and finished the whiskey. "Yeah, I know what you mean. He's always got the gears turning, thinking of every contingency or whatever. It's helpful in the field. Not so much when it comes to personal stuff. He can be a real ass."

"Some people would say it takes one to know one. But they'd be wrong, don't you think?"

"Nah, I think they'd probably be right on. But as long as you prefer this ass, I'm OK with it."

She finished her wine and pitched the glass onto the carpet. "Mm, I love your ass, and you. How about we finish what we started a while ago? It turned out all right seeing everyone, don't you think?"

He followed suit with his whiskey glass, watching it bounce and roll across the carpet. "I always finish what I start. Or you start. And yeah, I guess it went OK, but I don't want to talk about it right now."

"Me either. Let's go to bed." She started to push away, but he held onto her.

"Hey, wait. I know for a fact that I can't get up and walk anywhere." He propped his head up with a throw pillow. His arms and legs felt heavy, his entire body was pain-free, and relaxed. "We're gonna have to make do on the sofa."

She slid down next to him. "We're going to do more than make do. A *lot* more. Just so you know."

The Next Day

Rowan answered the brisk knock on the door without checking the viewer. He stood still, shocked to see Harandi standing in front of a scowling Roberto. "What do you want?"

"I'd like to come in, for starters. We need to talk."

He held onto the door. "For God's sake, do you want a repeat of our *chat* in ADX Florence?"

Harandi shook his head. "I don't want to fight. I just want to talk."

"We do not need to talk. Ever." He tried to close the door, but Harandi took a quick step forward, stopping him.

"Please don't shut me out. I just spent an hour getting briefed on what sounds like a hell of an assignment. The opportunity to disrupt the Muslim Brotherhood in this country and destroy their inroads is fantastic."

"You're out of your mind if you think I'm going to include you in any operation I'm in charge of. Now get out of here."

Roberto clamped a meaty hand on Harandi's shoulder. "I'll take care of this for you, boss."

Harandi twisted away from the big hand. "I've got some things I need to say. Things you need to hear. I won't stay long. Just humor me for a few minutes."

He let go of the door. "I might as well be sitting in a cell. I can't get away from you. It's OK, Bobbie. I'll give this jerkwad ten minutes. Starting now."

Roberto nodded. "I'll let you know when his time is up."

He gave the big man a quick wink. "Thanks. All right David. Get your ass in here. The clock is ticking." He turned and walked into the suite, heard the door close behind him. When he got to the windows he swung around to face his ex-friend. "Say what you need to and make it quick."

Harandi perched on the edge of the sofa. "Come sit down, please, and hear me out."

He crossed his arms and leaned against the window. "I'm quite comfortable here."

Harandi shrugged. "All right, fine. Look, I've had lots of time to think about you and me. I remember so many things from when we were kids. After my parents died, it was tough. Sa-id did his best, but you were something else."

"Where are you going with this?"

Harandi continued. "You stood up for me. Even though you're younger than me by a couple years, you always seemed older, or tougher. I'll never forget that."

"Good for you. That was then and this is now."

"Come on, Rowan. Remember the kid on the bus who smacked me on top of the head with a book because I wouldn't answer his taunts about being I-*ranian?* Or the time those little creeps ganged up on me? They tormented me over and over because I didn't know what songs were popular, and I wore clothes that were different."

He said, "Yeah, I remember saving your sorry, skinny ass more than once. But when I needed help or *saving*, you as much as told me to go fuck myself. So that's what I'm telling you now."

Harandi stood up and approached him, arms outstretched. "I know I let you down. If I could undo it, I would. Please Rowan,

I'm begging you. Can't you give me a chance? Together, we can get rid of those two corrupt CIA agents and put Shemal away, for good. Let me help you. Please."

He glared at the man he'd grown up with. "There are certain things you can't undo and this," he gestured between them, "is one of those things. Look, I appreciate you calling Johnny about the Houston deal; I really do. But I don't need or want your help. Ever."

Danielle heard Rowan arguing with someone. She left the bedroom and stopped, surprised to see a man she didn't know facing Rowan. He looked familiar, and she didn't know why. "Is everything all right? I don't mean to interrupt."

Both men swung around. Rowan's eyes had the black look she'd been frightened by on more than one occasion. "No, you aren't interrupting anything. This asshole is leaving right now."

The other man ignored Rowan. "You must be Danielle." He held out his hand. "I'm David Harandi. It's nice to finally meet the woman who means so much to Rowan."

She held out her hand, realizing she'd seen him in the video of Rowan returning to the United States. He'd been on the plane. "It's nice to meet you."

Rowan exploded. "No, goddamn it. Don't you even *think* of touching her."

She jumped and jerked her hand back. "Rowan, please. What's going on?"

Rowan shoved Harandi aside and turned his fierce gaze her way. "This is my old friend, who couldn't wait to arrest me."

Harandi stumbled back. "He's right, but once I figured out the truth, I went to bat for him with the President and the Bureau. Did you tell her who started the process that got you out of Houston?"

"None of this concerns her. Just get out of here and don't *ever* approach me, or anyone close to me, again."

Harandi said, "You'll have to take that up with our boss. He wants me to help you."

Rowan sneered. "That's *Mr.* Giacopino to you. He may be your boss, but I'm his *partner.* That makes me *your boss* as well." Rowan stepped in front of Harandi. "Let me ask you something. Do you remember my answer, on that goddamned miserable flight from Houston to DC, when you asked me what I'd do if you removed the cuffs and shackles?"

Harandi's face reddened. "That's not fair. I had no idea you were innocent. I did what the President hired me to do. Nothing more, nothing less."

Rowan took another step and thrust his forefinger against Harandi's chest. "Oh, I don't know. You seemed to take pleasure in causing me pain. But that's not what I asked. *Do you remember my answer or not?"*

She saw Harandi swallow, then look at Rowan. "Yes, I remember."

Rowan gave him a sharp nod. "Good. Don't ever forget. You keep fucking around with me, and I'll do exactly what I said. You got that, *old friend?"*

Goosebumps rose on her arms. She remembered this Rowan; the powerful, confident, and terrifying man she'd thought was gone forever.

Harandi locked eyes with Rowan for a moment longer. "Yeah. I got it." He backed up and nodded at her. "It was nice to meet you, Danielle. Take care."

She didn't say anything. Rowan pointed at the door. "Get out."

Harandi left the suite. Rowan turned the deadbolt and leaned against the door. His shoulders sagged. "I'm sorry you had to witness that, Danielle."

"He must have caused you a lot of trouble. Do you want to tell me about it?" She wished he'd talk about the things that kept his terrible rage so alive and raw.

"Sure. But I gotta sit down."

She followed him to the sofa and sat next to him. He grunted with pain, but put his arm around her. She laid her head on his shoulder. "What happened between the two of you?"

He propped his feet on the coffee table. "David and I were friends growing up. That's why he was here today. He wanted to play me by bringing up old memories. The President hired him to find me, and he did, because I made a couple stupid mistakes. He treated me like a traitor, wouldn't believe anything I told him."

She spoke quietly. "Do you think he's sincere now? That you should try to make amends?"

"He ruined any chance of that."

She grasped his free hand. "When you called me, from Houston; that was right before he found you, wasn't it."

"Yes, it was."

"What did you tell him on the plane, on the trip from Houston to DC?"

Rowan's body tensed beside her. "That's between David and me. But I meant every word."

"I think he knows." She wiggled her hand out of his and snaked her arm around him. "Let's go to bed. Let me love you and help you forget all of the awful things that happened."

"He drew her close. "OK. I need to forget about a lot of things."

"I'll make sure of that," she whispered.

CHAPTER TWENTY-ONE

The Next Day
Rowan knocked on the door to Angelo's suite. He'd agreed to meet with the shrink on a regular basis, and they needed to get this meeting over with so he could get back to Danielle. Their time was winding down, and he sensed her restlessness. She must be thinking about her new career and maybe her Boeing engineer friend, too, for all he knew.

Angelo opened the door. "Come in, Rowan. It's good to see you. I hope you and Danielle are enjoying your time together."

"We are, Doc, so let's get to it, OK?"

"Absolutely. Sit wherever you're comfortable. Would you like some coffee?"

"No thanks." He'd like a glassful of whiskey, but if he knew Angelo, he'd soon be listening to a lecture about his drinking. He sat on a purple armchair facing the purple-and-white sectional, glad the sofas in his suite were black leather. The swirls of color would enhance his nightmares, for sure.

Angelo sat down on the sofa. "As I've said before, this is your time. Tell me what's on your mind this afternoon."

In more than one interrogation session, he'd looked at his interrogator and decided, *what the hell,* and told the truth. Eyeing the kind psychiatrist who'd tried so hard to help him, he made the same choice. "I'd rather be in my suite tossing back a glass of whiskey."

Angelo tucked strands of graying hair behind one ear. "I'd hoped to address your dependence on Jack Daniel's. I'm intrigued that you brought it up."

"I'm not as obtuse as you might think."

"I've never thought of you as obtuse, Rowan. Stubborn to a fault and sometimes too proud to admit when you're wrong, but never obtuse."

"OK. What's your game plan? Are you going to tell me to knock off drinking? Maybe take up meditation or yoga?"

A smile lit Angelo's face, then vanished. "My only game plan is to explore what you need."

"What I need is to spend as much time with Danielle as possible, because she'll be gone soon. I have my doubts as to whether I'll ever see her again."

Angelo frowned. "You sound definite. Why?"

"She's moved on, with a new life, like I insisted. I can't ask her to leave that behind, and I can't be with her."

"And you think drinking whiskey helps you cope with her absence from your life?"

"Look Doc, whiskey is the only thing that's ever helped me deal with life. It's a simple fact. And going forward, I think I'm going to need it."

"I see. Tell me more."

"It's like this. The only thing I have to look forward to is living, if you want to call it that, in the shadows, hunting jihadists, hunting Shemal. Until one day, when the bullet with my name on it finds me. Or Shemal finds me, in which case the bullet meant for me will come from my own gun because I'm not ever going to be taken by that bastard again."

Angelo prodded. "If you could, what would you do differently?"

"Oh hell, Doc. Why do you ask me shit like that? You and I both know I can't do anything differently. But if I could do whatever the hell *I want,* I'd start by going wherever Danielle is happiest. I'd live with her and support her in whatever she wants to do and goddamn *love* her for the rest of my life."

"I firmly believe you owe it to yourself and Danielle to make that happen."

He stared at the psychiatrist in disbelief. "And how would I do that? Tell Johnny to stick it? If I tried something like that, I'd end up hiding from him for the rest of my life, too."

"Rowan, you find yourself at this juncture with a woman who loves you with all her heart. I find myself unable to comprehend why you would substitute Jack Daniel's whiskey for her in order to satisfy someone else's demands."

"I don't have any kind of answer for you."

Angelo replied. "You are not required to have an answer for me, Rowan. You need to have an answer for yourself. Think about it the next time you pour a glass of whiskey."

The Next Day

Danielle retrieved her two packed bags from the bedroom and pulled them slowly into the living area of the suite. Placing her carefully folded clothes in the suitcases had been difficult, especially the blue dress she'd worn when she arrived. Her hopes had been so high. But now, their time together had a terrible feeling of finality about it.

She left her suitcases next to the door and turned. Rowan waited on the sofa, staring at the floor. When she approached, hesitant, he raised his head. The desolation in his face had her faltering. She sat on the sofa facing him. She couldn't bear to sit beside him, to feel the warmth of his body and his touch. The pain inside expanded, wrenching her heart, taking her breath away.

"I wish I didn't have to go." Her voice trailed off, and she waited for him to speak.

"It wouldn't be right for you to stay," he said, so quietly she barely heard him.

She said, "I still don't understand why— Well, I guess there's no point in talking this over again."

He replied, voice still low. "I don't know how to make it any clearer. I love you, Danielle, too much to ruin your life. You have so much talent, so much *life* ahead of you. Just go and live it, OK?"

The pain inside felt hard, immovable. "I can't change your mind, can I?"

"No."

"Did it ever occur to you that maybe what I want is *you?"*

"No. Once you get back home, you'll know I'm not what you want. Or need."

"You're wrong about that." She couldn't think of anything more to add. "I guess it's time for me to leave."

"Yeah, Mike is on his way up." He stood and reached for her hand. She clutched it in hers, and together they walked to the door.

She turned and faced him. He put his arms around her. "I don't want to go," she whispered.

He held her close and murmured into her hair. "Yes, you do. You need to go home and live your life."

She put her hands on his chest and pushed away, so she could look up at him. "You promise me, Rowan Milani, that you will answer your phone when I call."

His dark eyes met hers. "I will. I promise."

She saw the fine lines at the corners of his eyes; hated the thin red scar on his cheek. She reached up and cupped his face in her hands, loving the rough stubble on his cheeks. "I already miss you."

"I know. Same here." He kissed her, deliberate and careful, like he needed to commit their last kiss to memory.

The gentle touch of his lips undid her fragile control. She broke away and clung to him. "I can't do this. Please, *please* don't shut me out of your life."

He stepped back. "I won't, Danielle. I promise."

She dug in the pocket of her pants. "I meant to give this to you when I got here and kept forgetting. I hope you still want it." She held out a gold, oversized coin.

He drew a sharp breath and plucked the coin from her palm. "I never thought I'd see this again. Of course, I want it. I couldn't take it with me when I left Kauai, in case, well you know, don't you?"

"I know. At first I thought, well, it doesn't matter. I'm just glad you still want it." A soft knock on the door ended their conversation. "Oh no. That must be Mike."

He reached out and touched her cheek. "If you want, give me a call when you get home and settled in. I'd like that."

"I will." She turned away and opened the door. "Hi Mike. I'm ready."

A sober-faced Michael nodded and stepped inside to retrieve her suitcases. He gave Rowan a brief glance. "You want to ride with me to the airport?"

Rowan shook his head. "No. Thanks for taking care of Danielle."

"Sure brother, no problem." Michael edged out of the suite with her suitcases. "All right, let's go."

She looked at Rowan for the last time. "Goodbye. I love you," she whispered.

His smile was more of a grimace. "I love you too. Always. Goodbye."

She followed Michael from the suite and shut the door behind her. Would she ever see him again?

Rowan stared at the door. The suite already felt unbearably empty. When he was sure Danielle wasn't coming back, he turned and walked mindlessly to the sofa. He slouched down and stared at the gold coin she'd returned to him. The Twin Towers, etched into the coin, glowed in sharp relief. He turned it over and read the familiar words. *We will never forget. 9/11/01.*

She'd given him the coin the first time wrapped up as a gift while he lay in the hospital bed in Sioux Falls, after he'd told her she couldn't come with him, because he didn't know where he was going or what might happen. He stuffed the coin in his pants pocket. How could they be reliving the same goddamned nightmare scenario?

He clenched his jaws and shoved off the sofa, making his way to the counter where the full bottle of Jack Daniel's waited. He glared at the empty glass sitting next to it, grabbed the bottle and wrenched it open, pouring until the glass ran over. The sharp tang of the whiskey filled his nostrils. He raised the glass and sneered at it before taking a deep swallow.

He snagged the bottle and headed back to the sofa. He sank down, tossed back more, and stared at the door. "For God's sake, she's gone," he mumbled. He tipped his head back, forcing himself to drink it all, impatient for the inevitable numbing.

Anguish squeezed his heart, worse than the torture, worse than every betrayal. He poured more whiskey, drained the glass, and waited, but the awful pain continued unabated. Hot tears filled his eyes and ran down his cheeks. He threw the glass to the carpeted floor and shoved off the sofa, groaning and wobbling.

He clutched the bottle of Jack and made his way into the bathroom. He held the bottle upside down over the sink and watched while the amber liquid he'd depended on for too many years choked and glugged its way down the drain. When the last of the pungent whiskey dripped into the sink, he tossed the bottle into the waste basket. "There, goddamn it."

He gazed at his image in the mirror. "You're a different man, right?" He blinked through reddened eyes and wiped his nose on the back of his hand. "That's why she's gone. Because I want what's best for her, instead of me." He weaved his way out of the bathroom, ignored the bed with its rumpled blankets, and slammed the door.

At the big windows, he rubbed his arms and stared at the lake. The water sparkled in the late afternoon sunlight, but it wasn't what he wanted. It wasn't what he needed. He needed to sink his bare feet into the warm, white sand and stare at the turquoise water. And yes, he needed to see the three scraggly palm trees, somehow remaining upright, holding on despite the buffeting wind, in their rocky anchor. And now, he'd go tell Johnny his plans. After all, the Don had told him he wasn't a prisoner. "We'll see," he muttered.

He turned away, wavered, and leaned against the window. After straightening his shirt, he made his way to the door and opened it. Roberto regarded him with a frown. "You need something, Rowan?"

"I need to talk to Johnny. Right now." He started out the door, but the big man stepped in front of him and placed a gentle hand on his shoulder. "How about a cup of coffee first?"

He glowered at Roberto's calm face. "I don't want any coffee. Get the hell out of my way."

Roberto somehow propelled him back into the suite and shut the door. "Look, if you want to see the Boss, you need to sober up, because you don't want to say a bunch of shit you'll regret later. Have a seat, and I'll make you some coffee."

He couldn't fight Roberto. "OK." He walked unsteadily to the sofa and sat down.

While the coffee brewed, Roberto leaned against the door, alternately observing him and messing with his phone. "How much whiskey have you had since Danielle left?"

He raised a brow. "What do you care?"

Roberto cracked his knuckles and replied. "You oughta know by now that keeping you safe *and* sound is my job."

"Oh. Hell, why didn't you say so? I drank the entire fucking bottle."

"That's quite a bit of booze. You sure about that?"

"Yeah, what difference does it make?"

"It's going to make a big difference in how you feel tomorrow."

"I'm not going to feel anything tomorrow. Or any day. I'm going to make damn sure I never *feel* anything again. So, you see, it doesn't make any difference."

"You aren't talking sense."

A quiet knock stopped him from replying. His keeper pivoted away from the door and opened it. Angelo stepped inside. "Hello, Rowan. I hope you do not mind my stopping by."

"Cut the crap, Doc. Bobbie sent you a text and here you are."

Angelo nodded at Roberto and murmured something he couldn't hear. Roberto left the suite. Angelo carried two steaming cups of coffee to the sofa and handed him one before sitting on the edge of the adjacent love seat. "I came right away when Roberto texted me because I am concerned. But I had planned to stop in to see you."

He took the cup and blew on the hot liquid. The aroma took him back. He heard Danielle, excitedly telling him about her coffee, saw her smile. The pain stabbed him, and he couldn't stop the tears filling his eyes again. They dripped down his cheeks while his lips quivered. He couldn't sip the coffee, couldn't look at Angelo. "I'm not in the mood to talk, Doc. You might as well leave."

Angelo settled back and propped his feet on the low table. "I am generally not a betting man, but I will wager that you are not going to kick me out if I refuse to leave."

"You win the bet. Stay as long as you want." He took a tentative sip of coffee and wished he could make the tears stop leaking from his eyes.

"You are clearly not dealing well with Danielle leaving."

He chuckled harshly. "You're observant, I'll give you that. I can't spend another day here. I need to be in Key West."

"If you like, I will convey that message to Mr. Giacopino on your behalf."

He wiped the tears from his cheeks. "OK."

"You didn't actually drink the entire bottle of whiskey, did you?"

"No. It didn't help this time. I dumped it down the bathroom sink."

Angelo nodded. "I understand, believe me. It took great courage for you to do that."

"Well, I'm a different man, remember?" He smirked at the psychiatrist. "I have to keep reminding myself."

Angelo swallowed more coffee before replying. "Allow yourself to embrace that man."

He shook his head. "I don't even know what that means. Why are you here, Doc? What do you want me to say?"

"I am here because I care for you. There is no need for you to say anything."

He fought a hard, painful lump in his throat, managing only a hoarse "thank you."

"You are my first priority, Rowan. You have been for quite some time. My heart's desire is to see you whole and at peace. Or even, dare I say, happy with your life."

He gave up on the coffee and placed the cup on the low table. "You're on a doomed mission."

"Would you like me to keep talking? Or would you prefer that I keep my thoughts to myself?"

He eyed the shrink. Angelo's quiet presence helped take his mind off the painful emptiness of the suite, and his life. "Keep talking."

"I firmly believe that the things you value, the things you want most, are yours for the choosing."

"That's because you are an eternal optimist. I'm a realist. Always have been."

"I believe you are more cynical than anything. Because of that, you oftentimes miss things that are obvious to others."

"Such as?"

Angelo finished his coffee and set the cup on the table. “First, that a positive outcome is possible, even for you. Second, you can live your *life*, not some sort of permanent black ops mission, and finally, you can choose to be with the woman who loves you.”

He gazed tiredly at the psychiatrist. “You said a mouthful there. The truth is, I need to give Danielle the opportunity to live her life unimpeded by me. Much as it kills me, it’s what’s best for her.”

“And what about you, Rowan? What’s best for you?”

The whiskey had succeeded, finally, in numbing his body, leaving only a dull, tight ache in his chest. He yawned and rubbed his burning eyes. “Key West. Or not. I don’t know.” He stretched out on the sofa and crossed his arms. “Stay if you want, Doc.”

Angelo said, “I will stay for the night. Tomorrow we can tell Mr. Giacopino your plans.”

He closed his eyes. “OK. Thanks.”

Late Evening
Seattle, WA

Danielle let herself into her home, dragged her suitcases to the middle of the living room and wandered into her bedroom. She collapsed on the bed, covered her face, and cried. She cried until her voice squeaked, and she couldn’t cry anymore. She took ragged breaths and remembered her promise to call. She dug in her purse for her phone and punched his contact.

He answered after too many rings, and she wondered whether he’d been sleeping or maybe drinking. “Hey Danielle. Thanks for calling.”

“Hi Rowan,” she whispered.

“Are you OK? How was your flight? How’s Seattle?”

The longing in his voice made it impossible for her to control her raw emotions. “I’m sorry. I miss you so much already. I’m not sure I can do this anymore.”

“I know. Me either. But we don’t have a choice.”

"I can choose to be with you. I'm not afraid of what might happen. I've always felt safe with you."

He was silent for a moment, and she wondered if he'd hung up. Then he spoke, his voice bleak. "Right now, we just can't do it. So, live your life, OK? That's what I want, more than anything."

Sitting cross-legged, her tears dripped on the phone while she stared at it. Why couldn't he understand? She sniffed and shook her head. "I'll try. But really, I want to live my life with you. Why is that so hard for you to accept?"

"You know why. I can't offer you any kind of life because I'm always hiding, waiting to be either abducted or killed. I'm not going to endanger you."

"I understand. I love you, Rowan. Please don't forget that."

"I won't forget. I love you too. Call again soon, OK? I want to know how your big mutt is doing, and how your promotion goes."

She closed her eyes and whispered, "I'll call soon. Please take care of yourself."

"I will. Good night, Danielle." The connection died, and she laid her phone on the bed. Emotionally spent, she pulled off her clothes and slid under the covers. She stared at the ceiling, covers at her chin. The chill emptiness of the bed magnified her loneliness.

Did she belong here, in Seattle, pursuing her new career, living the life she'd built over the last year? Was expanding the footprint of a coffee company her life's passion? Or did her passion lie in loving and living with Rowan?

She sniffed and wiped away the tears dripping down her cheeks. Rowan was still a secretive man. Had he ever been completely honest with her? She knew the answer, and it brought more tears. In his mind, keeping things from her amounted to protecting her. She understood that, but on another level, it hurt.

She wished he could see her as the one person he could share anything with. But Rowan would never be that kind of man. He had lived with too many secrets for too long. She saw Tom's easy smile and clear hazel eyes. He'd already shared his heart with her. Tom was that kind of man. But he wasn't the man she loved.

Wide awake, she flung back the covers. She couldn't stand to be in her bed alone. Rowan had promised to be available anytime she needed him. She tugged the comforter off the bed and made her way to the sofa. Wrapped up in the heavy, warm blanket, she clutched her phone and hit his contact.

This time he answered right away. "Hey Danielle, what's up? Are you OK?"

"I'm OK. I can't sleep, and I need to talk to you."

His reply came without hesitation. "I'm listening. Talk to me."

"Where are you?" Had he been able to sleep in the bed after she left? She needed to know.

He sighed. "On the sofa. I can barely stand to go through the bedroom to get to the bathroom. But it's all right. I'm leaving here tomorrow, or later today, I guess."

"Where are you going?" Would he be truthful?

"To a place where I feel halfway comfortable. That's all I can say."

"Rowan, why don't you trust me? You can tell me anything."

"It's not that simple."

Before he could say more, she interrupted. "It is for me. I wish you could trust me, because I hate all the secrets."

"I trust you, Danielle. I'm worried about someone forcing you to reveal where I am. I can't put that on you."

Why hadn't she picked up Leo right away? Her cozy house always felt warm and safe. Now every shadow seemed sinister. "I never thought about it that way. But when I'm with you, I feel safe."

She heard sadness, tinged with frustration in his voice. "Look, I'm sorry. I shouldn't have been so blunt. It's just, we've talked about how this crap won't ever end for me. That's why I want you to live your life with, uh, with someone who won't put you in danger."

"Don't say that. Would you tell me no if I made the choice to be with you, understanding the possible consequences? Be completely honest with me. Please."

He didn't answer right away. When he spoke, she felt his bitter anger, overlaid with raw pain. "You want honesty from me? All right then. You mean everything to me, but Johnny Giacopino *owns* me. He wants a partner, and I can't say no. I'm going back to what I've been doing for the past decade. That's a hell of a joke, don't you think? Now you know the truth, and that's as goddamned *honest* as I can be."

Eyes closed, she huddled on the sofa, listening to his harsh breathing. "Thank you," she murmured.

"I'm sorry, Danielle. I should have told you all this when you were here. If I could, I'd tell everyone to fuck off and be in Seattle with you right now."

"Mr. Giacopino must be an incredibly powerful man."

"Yeah, I don't think I'll ever be free. That's why I want you to go for it with your career, and live your life to the fullest."

"I get that, I do. I've been lying here thinking about what I want. And I'm not sure it's my career."

"Give yourself some time, Danielle. And remember: I don't have a future."

"You remember this, Rowan. You'll always have a future with me."

The Next Morning
Chicago, IL

Rowan stood in front of the door to Johnny's suite. A fierce headache pounded behind his burning eyes, despite the handful of Ibuprofen he'd tossed back with a few sips of water. This hangover, although not as ugly as the two previous involving Danielle, was bad enough. Apparently, he'd never learn.

He knocked, massaged his forehead, and waited for the Don. Angelo had wanted to come with him, as promised, but once he was sober, he knew he needed to face his partner on his own. After talking to Danielle, he'd stared at the ceiling until the blackness outside the windows shifted to gray, thinking about what he needed to do. As the hangover set in, he'd pulled his head out of his ass and put a few things in motion.

The door opened and Johnny waved him inside. "Good morning, Rowan. Breakfast just arrived, and the coffee's fresh. Let's eat and talk."

He followed Johnny to the table and swallowed bile at the whiff of eggs and sausage. "Thanks, but I'm not hungry."

Johnny raised a forkful of scrambled eggs. "You're missing out, but suit yourself. What brings you by this morning?"

"I'm ready to leave Chicago and head to Key West as soon as possible. Actually, I'd like to leave today, if that's feasible."

"You got a crew in mind to go with you?"

"Yes. Angelo, Mike and Asal, and of course Roberto and Gino. Once I arrive, I'm planning to contact my colleague Gabriel Hernandez. He's a medic, and he's taken care of me more than once or twice. If he's agreeable, I'd like him to oversee my rehab."

Johnny took a drink of coffee. "Sounds like you've got a damn good crew in mind. What about Harandi?"

"Harandi won't be part of my crew. You hired him, so find a place for him."

The Don's face reddened. "I hired him to help *us* achieve *our* objectives regarding Shemal and the Muslim Brotherhood's infiltration of the country."

"I understand." He bit back the word *sir*. "However, I don't trust him, and I would not have hired him. I'm neither interested nor willing to negotiate that point." He met the Don's glare without blinking.

Johnny patted his mouth with a white linen napkin. "I'll find a spot for Harandi someplace besides Key West."

He pushed back his chair. "Perfect." He'd be damned if he'd say thank you. Johnny had called him an equal partner, so by God, he'd act like one. "When can I reasonably expect the jet to be fueled and ready to go?"

"What do you think about taking a chartered jet? No reason to advertise the fact of our jet flying to Key West, would you agree?"

"I do. Who handles the arrangements?"

"My personal assistant Georges handles my travel. Would you like him to take care of it for you?"

He stood up. "Yes. I'll expect him to notify me with a departure time." He didn't add that he'd already told each member of his new team to be ready within two hours. Mike and Asal were excited. Roberto had grunted and said he'd tell Gino to get his ass in gear. Angelo was thrilled.

Johnny said, "Before you go, I've got something for you. The Don pushed back his chair and stood up. "Give me a minute."

"OK." He watched the older man stride away and rolled his tense shoulders.

Johnny returned, carrying a cardboard box. "I've been keeping a few things for you." Johnny sat the box on the table. "Take a look."

He pulled back the stiff cardboard and peered inside the box. His brows rose. "I'll be damned." He reached in and grasped his Glock 36, the sub-compact .45 he'd always treasured. It felt cold, solid, and comforting in his hand. The box also held his Glock 18, the 9mm full-auto pistol that had saved his life on more than one occasion. His Karambit, the lethal knife he sometimes preferred when facing jihadists up close and personal lay next to the 18. He looked at Johnny. "I don't know what to say."

"A man deserves to have the weapons he needs to defend himself. I wanted to make sure you had yours."

He stroked the smooth steel slide of the 36 and reveled at the empowerment, the confidence he felt with the pistol in his left hand. "Thank you."

Late Afternoon
Seattle, WA

Danielle answered the knock on her door, surprised to see Tom, holding a bouncing, tail-stub-wagging Leo on his leash. "Hi, come in. You didn't need to bring him back. I could have come over and picked him up." She sank to her knees and embraced the wiggling dog, ending up cross-legged on the floor, taking endless, slobbery kisses. "It's good to see you, too. I think you missed me."

Tom said, "I'm sure he did. When we got close he started whining. I hope you don't mind me dropping him off."

She scrambled to her feet. "No, of course I don't mind. Do you have time for a glass of wine or a beer?"

"Actually, I had a spontaneous moment and picked up a pizza. If you have other plans, I'll take it home."

"No way. I'll grab some plates. Wine or beer for you?" Gazing at him, buff as usual in his bomber jacket and jeans, she felt a ripple of longing for Rowan.

Tom replied. "I'll rescue the pizza from the car. And a beer would be perfect."

They sat at her breakfast nook in the kitchen while they devoured the pizza. Leo laid *on* her feet. She wiggled her toes. "I'm not sure if Leo wants to be close to me or wants to be sure he doesn't miss a treat."

Tom nudged Leo with his foot. “Probably a combination of the two. I enjoyed keeping him. If you ever need to travel for work, or whatever, you can always leave him with me.”

“Thanks. I appreciate that. I am not sure when I’ll need to visit the new shops, but I’ll give you as much notice as I can.”

“It sounds like you’ve decided to keep going with your career? Did your visit go well?”

She opted for what she hoped was a carefree shrug. “Heck yeah, I love my career. I’m committed to pursuing my goals with Small-Batch. And yes, we had a nice visit. It was fantastic to reconnect for a while.”

Tom studied her, one elbow on the table, his chin propped against his fist. “Good for you. Is Rowan doing all right?”

“He’s doing OK. It’s going to take him some time to recover from everything. He’s been through a lot, especially in the last six months.”

“I bet.” Tom downed the rest of his beer and shoved back his chair. “I’ve got a meeting first thing tomorrow morning, and my prep is lacking. I better get at it. Oh, before I forget, my mom is taking an early head count. Are you still up for going to Orcas Island for Christmas?”

Relieved he was leaving and trying to quash the guilt she felt for feeling that way, she nodded. “I’ve been looking forward to it.”

Tom stood up. “I’ll keep you up to date.”

She followed him to the door. “Thanks again for taking Leo, and for the pizza. It’s nice to be home.”

He lingered, one hand on the door knob. “Is it, Dani? Nice to be home, I mean? You seem sad. Or distracted. Maybe both.”

She met his gaze, so full of kindness, so honest. The opposite of Rowan’s dark, always enigmatic look. “Oh sure, I’m fine. Just overwhelmed with the promotion and thinking about getting back into it.”

"Even now, you seem like you're somewhere else."

She wondered how he'd react if she told him she'd been comparing him to Rowan. She faked a yawn, patting her mouth with her fingers. "I'm super tired. I've got a series of meetings tomorrow, too. They must be weighing on my mind. Sounds like we both need some serious desk time."

"You are so right. Take care Dani. See you later."

Houston, TX

McKenzie surveyed the tree-shaded, flagstone patio and paused next to a cluster of potted baby palm trees. He leaned on the wrought-iron fence overlooking the pool area. The water sparkled in the warm sunlight, wafting a chlorine-laden breeze his way. Maybe he'd take a swim later, to clear his mind and make more plans. He might as well take advantage of the amenities offered by the Omni Houston Hotel. Although average by his international standards, it was a decent place to stay.

He hated to admit that he'd become somewhat jaded because of his travels, but it was true. He'd stayed in the best hotels in the world as well as the worst hovels a third world country could serve up. A pang of guilt stabbed him. He hadn't been to the cemetery to visit Anne since the first time he kissed Leigh. Somehow, he didn't think Anne minded. He could see her smiling and saying, *go for it, Jack.*

A tall man entered the patio area, caught his eye, and raised a hand. He appraised the man as he strolled across the flagstone in a shirt, jeans, boots and a bona-fide cowboy hat. Matthews walked with a slight hitch in his long stride, and looked like a lawman. Too bad the guy had screwed that up. He left the wrought-iron fence and headed across the patio. "Hello, Mr. Matthews."

Matthews held out his right hand. "Howdy, name's Kyle."

"Nice to meet you, Kyle. I'm Jack McKenzie. Thanks for meeting with me. And by the way, our conversation is off the record, unless the two of us and FBI Director Berenger agree differently. That work for you?"

"Sounds fair enough. I'd like to thank the director for taking me seriously. And by the way, I've seen you on the news, more than once."

They sat in adjacent, matching rattan chairs, and he addressed Matthews. "Believe me, Director Berenger takes what's happened in Houston regarding Rowan Milani very seriously. And you're correct, my day job is with FOX News."

Matthews stretched long legs and clasped his hands in his lap. "I'm glad somebody is taking this pile of horse hockey with more than a grain of salt. The DA's prosecutor told me they weren't going to pursue it any further. But they'll gladly investigate me."

He decided to go for the jugular at the outset and gauge Matthews' reaction. "Milani pled not guilty at his arraignment. Did you set up Milani because of a personal vendetta against him after he almost killed you?"

Matthews face flushed deep red, and he jabbed a forefinger in the air. "I'll swear on a stack of Bibles and take a lie detector test about that evidence. I know it existed because I catalogued some of it and checked it in. Can't you ask David Harandi? He was working with the feds. He caught Milani and saw the evidence. But shoot, he went all squirrely on me at the end."

He ignored the extraneous comments. "What do you mean by squirrely?"

"When I told him I suspected Mafia involvement, he told me I was crazy and to be careful. Plus, he backtracked, said what happened to Milani wasn't right."

He hadn't seen this coming. "Why did you suspect Mafia involvement?"

"You'd a had to see the two goon-looking guys who crawled out of the Town Car to greet Milani and his lawyer. They were wearing suits, packing pistols, and keeping an eye on everything. My gut told me. That's all I can say."

"Let's go back to your first interview with Milani after his arrival in your jail. Obviously, there was no love lost between the two of you."

"I don't know if you've ever had any personal dealings with Milani, but he's got a way of getting under a person's skin."

He replied. "I've never had the pleasure of meeting Mr. Milani."

"I wouldn't classify meeting Milani as a *pleasure.* He cost me six months of rehab and a permanent hitch in my get-along. I know I went too far after we got him back. But I don't regret it. Seven people are dead, and he's free. That's not justice in my book."

"Setting aside the legality of what you did, were you able to garner anything of value in your two conversations with him?"

Matthews snorted. "No. Milani is a hard case, the worst I've ever run across. And his slick lawyer managed to stick his nose in before I got very far."

"Did Milani deny he'd killed those seven people?"

Matthews lit up. "Hell no. He admitted it. In his words, '*I killed every one of those fuckers, and I'd do it again.*' That seems damn straightforward to me."

"That's fascinating. Why would Milani admit his guilt to you, and then enter a not-guilty plea at his arraignment?"

"You can thank his lawyer for that. For all I know, he's got Mob connections. He crawled into that Town Car right along with the two goons and Milani. Besides that, Milani seemed surprised when I mentioned his lawyer."

"Everything you've told me is interesting, to say the least. "Can you think of anything else, no matter how insignificant, that happened before Milani arrived in Houston that seemed out of the ordinary?"

"Hmm." Matthews stared into space, brows furrowed. "There was one thing. I put it out of my mind, but I wonder…"

"Keep talking."

"A few weeks or a month before Milani got here, a couple cops were killed during a robbery at a CVS pharmacy."

He prodded further. "How do you think this may be related to Milani?"

"I don't know if it's related, but those cops called me the same night they were killed. Said they had information on a case and wanted to drop by the precinct for a chat."

"Is that a common occurrence?"

"It happens once in a while. I did take a gander at the crime scene. One of the cops died right next to a copy machine. Just for the heck of it, I lifted the lid and found a scrap of paper that had *Evidence Release Form* printed on it. But I had no reason to tie that to Milani."

He said, "What happened to the scrap of paper?"

"I handed it off to the detective who caught the case."

"Do you know anything about the two officers who were killed? May I have their names?"

Matthews replied. "I don't know anything about them. But I do remember their names, Ed Nelson and Juan Morales. I jotted them down in case anything ever came to light. To be honest, I never gave it another thought."

His investigation had grown legs and was about to take off. He had more to follow up than he'd dreamed possible, and he couldn't wait to get at it. "Thank you again for meeting with me, Kyle."

"Anytime, Mr. McKenzie. This whole thing is a puzzle. I promised Milani I'd get to the bottom of it, and I intend to."

He stood and faced Matthews. "I take it you're planning to conduct your own investigation?"

"Yes, I am. Something stinks to the high heavens when the evidence I *know* exists disappears, a man like Milani skates, and I can't take my family to West Texas for Thanksgiving or Christmas because *I'm* the one who's under investigation."

He handed Matthews a business card. "Would you consider keeping me apprised of your progress? I know Director Berenger would be grateful as well."

Matthews took the card and stuffed it in his shirt pocket. "I'd be glad to. Tell Director Berenger I appreciate her interest."

"Will do. You take care, Kyle."

"Yes sir, I will. You do the same."

He watched Matthews saunter away. The former detective had created way more questions than he'd answered. After a swim, he'd start digging into the tantalizing clues Matthews had dumped in his lap.

He grabbed his phone and hit Berenger's contact for her private cell. "Jack, how's Texas?"

"Hello Leigh. Texas is warmer than DC, and that's about all I can say for it. However, I've got a pile of leads to dig into, if you approve."

"Tell me what you've got."

"According to Matthews, a couple cops wanted to give him info on a case, but were killed before they could talk to him. I'd like to spend some more time here and dig into their backgrounds."

Her response made him smile. "Go for it. You never know what you might turn up. But be careful."

"Don't you worry, I'll be careful. I've got a couple more nuggets of information for you. For starters, Matthews seems to think the Mafia was somehow involved in getting Rowan out of jail."

Berenger said, "The Mafia, huh? That's one for the books."

"Isn't it, though? He also told me Harandi got, in his words, *squirrely* when he told him about Rowan's release. He said one other thing that intrigued me. Apparently, Milani was surprised when he heard about his lawyer."

"That is interesting. Take a closer look at Milani's attorney while you're there. Someone had to hire him. Sounds like you've got enough to keep you occupied for a while. Keep me informed and enjoy the weather. I miss you, by the way."

"I miss you, too, Leigh. I'll talk to you soon." He wondered how long it'd be before they'd be ending their phone conversations with *I love you.* He was darn close to being ready for that.

A Week Later
Leôn, Mexico
Gabriel strode back and forth on the deck, eyeing the half-empty bottle of tequila and shot glass on the table. He'd spent the morning drinking and planning. The phone call from Rowan the previous week had lit a fire inside. He would leave in a few hours, to help his brother recover and become healthy again. Then he would be part of a new clandestine operation with Rowan and Michael. Though he did not yet know how, he and his brothers would achieve their goals.

The sliding door to the house opened, and Sherie stepped onto the deck. He watched her approach, filled with dread. She knew nothing of the plans that would take him away from his family one more time. How would he justify leaving?

Eight-year-old Sophia, barefoot and dressed in a bright yellow sundress, bounded out the door. "Papa!" He caught her as she jumped into his arms. Folding his squirming daughter into his bulky, six-foot frame, he inhaled the sweet aroma of her little girl body. The guilt pressed on him even harder.

Sophia snuggled in his arms, and he hugged her close. The pain of leaving his children and his wife would be his to bear. How could his heart be torn in such opposite directions? His duty to another family, one he loved as much as this one, called him away, and he would go. To stay would mean a steep slide into the darkness of alcoholism. In his heart, he knew he had already traveled a long way down that bleak pathway.

Sophia pushed against his chest with sturdy arms. "Papa, you smell funny." She wrinkled her nose and tapped his chest with a forefinger.

He smoothed her curly black hair and cupped one hand behind her head. *"You* smell good, little one. Like your mama's flowers."

"Can you take us to the park to play on the swings and in the pool? Mama says it's your turn. After that, we get to have ice cream with Nana and Grampy." Sophia tilted her head and smiled at him, simple adoration and trust in her child-eyes.

Instead of answering, he drew her close again, conscious of Sherie observing them. The choice, his only choice, had been made, but it hurt him to disappoint her. And it was only the beginning of a much larger disappointment. "Oh, my sweetheart, Papa needs to take a surprise trip today."

His daughter wiggled out of his embrace and frowned. "But Papa, it's *your turn.* You can't miss."

Sherie stood in front of them, arms crossed. He loved the way her hair framed her face, the fullness of her lips, and the contour of her cheekbones. He met her grim stare. "Can you take my turn today?"

He saw pain mixing with anger in her eyes, heard it in her voice. "Tell me, for how many days or months will I be taking your turns this time?" She held up both hands. "Wait. Don't speak. Sophia, darling, go and tell Jamie to get ready. Fetch your swim suit and a towel. Go wait with him on the front porch."

Before Sophia could squirm out of his arms, he kissed her forehead and her cheeks. "I love you, little one. Now go and do what your mama says. I will see you on the front porch in a few minutes."

He sat her gently on the deck. "OK Papa, see you!" She scampered to the house.

He faced Sherie, hating himself, hating the situation. "I'm sorry, mi Amor. I got a call."

She interrupted him. "You told me this was finished. You said you were done. You have a life here. Your family is here. We need you. This Rowan Milani, this *hombre* does not deserve you. *We* are your family, and *we deserve more.* Why are you doing this?"

He shrugged. "I have to go. You know I do. You know it is killing me to be here."

"Oh, so we are *killing you?* Being a father and a husband, raising your children, living with your family is killing you? No, you're wrong. I had no idea."

"Sherie, please, you know what I mean. I love you. I love Jamie and Sophia more than anything else." He stopped. Did he? Unsure of himself, flustered with how she twisted his thoughts with her accusations, he gripped her arms. "Being here while my brother Rowan suffers is killing me. The alcohol is killing me. Can't you see? *I need to do this."*

She wrenched free of his hold. "I have always believed in you. I have waited for you more times than I can count. I will wait again. But *this time,"* she shook her finger at him, "don't come back until it is *finished.* I don't want to see you again until this is *over.* Now go. Say goodbye to your children and leave."

"Sherie, please. Try to understand. Rowan and Michael are my brothers. They need me. I owe them my life. I have to go."

Sherie faced him, delectable in a sleeveless white blouse and blue shorts. He saw marks on her arms from his hands and tried to reach out to her. She backed away, waving her finger again. "Don't ask me to understand why you place these people above your family. I love you, Gabriel Hernandez. Now please, just go."

She left him standing there, his head pounding and his mouth dry from too much tequila.

Two miserable hours later, he stood on the pavement outside Del Bajío International Airport, sweating in his black t-shirt, black leather jacket, and jeans. He pulled a stack of pesos from his wallet and paid the taxi driver. After hugging Jamie, seeing the letdown in his ten-year old son's face, and telling both children as they stood, solemn and sad in front of him, that Papa had to leave, Sherie swept them away, leaving him to make his own way to the airport. He had expected nothing less.

Looking beyond the wire fence surrounding the airport, he spotted a jet parked on the tarmac, its big engines roaring. He and Michael had stolen the crown jewel of the CIA's fleet, a Gulfstream G650. They'd painted it iridescent black, with a new tail number provided by Chad, with a dummy corporation recorded as owner. The jet waiting on the tarmac had seen better days. Its scarred body had been painted robin-egg blue and dark gray in patches, as though the painters had applied a couple different primer coats. The number on its tail looked old and worn. This junk heap couldn't be their ride.

Wondering what the hell had happened to the G650, he headed into the terminal with his field bag. A man he recognized sat in a chair, hunkered down with his hands in his lap, wearing sunglasses, clothed in a black leather jacket and jeans; a slimmer, slightly taller, Anglo version of himself. He couldn't help a smile as he approached. Michael gave him a quick nod and stood up.

They clasped hands and bumped shoulders. "Holy Mother of God, it's good to see you. What happened to the jet? We're not flying in that piece of junk, are we?"

Michael clapped him on the back. "It's good to see you too, amigo. Don't start whining already. That *is* our jet. Jerry and Bryan had to get creative with hiding it from the feds. They did a number on the paint job and parked it in a bone yard somewhere near Phoenix."

He grinned. "Jerry and Bryan are here? It's going to be a good trip after all."

"Who did you think was going to fly us, Aeromexico? We aren't exactly commercial flight material, in case you've forgotten."

"I'm not stupid. I thought they were under close scrutiny by the FBI, after that chicken bastard Derek spilled his guts."

"Jerry and Bryan are damn skilled at clandestine ops, which you seem to have forgotten as well. They gave the Bureau losers the slip, and voila, here we are." Michael gave him a sideways glance as they strode out of the terminal and onto the tarmac. "Mexico has made you soft, brother. Looks like I've only got a couple hours to harden your ass up before we get to Key West."

He followed Michael's bounding steps up the air stairs and into the luxurious interior of the G650. The jet's Captain, Jerry Reynolds, six feet tall with wavy, dark brown hair and blue eyes, stood outside the flight deck door. "Damn Gabriel, it's great to see you."

From the farm country of central Indiana, with a friendly, open face, Jerry had joined the Air Force straight out of high school. He'd flown F-16s during Operation Iraqi Freedom and earned a reputation as a fearless pilot. He'd guided all of them in and out of hostile countries many times.

"It's good to see you, Jerry. Shitty paint job on the jet. But it'll fly the same, si?"

Jerry laughed. "You bet it will."

The flight deck door opened, and Bryan DeMuth stepped out. "Aw Gabe, how's it hangin' brother?" Shorter than Jerry and stocky with short, spiked blond hair and brown eyes, Bryan managed the financials of the business he and Jerry co-owned. Quick-thinking and smart, a small-town Ohio boy and decorated wing-man in Operation Enduring Freedom, he made the perfect First Officer.

Gabriel drew both men into back-slapping hugs. "Si, si, it's good to be here."

Michael interrupted. "Hell yeah, and if you ladies have had enough time to get reacquainted, I'd like to hit the road."

Jerry and Bryan snapped salutes and headed into the flight deck. Gabriel gave Michael a shove. "Fine, let's go." He started down the aisle and stopped, staring at the slender woman smiling at him from beneath a sweep of long black hair. She sat in one of the deep leather seats, legs crossed, a glass of red wine on the low table in front of her. "Asal? Is it *you?"*

Michael shouldered past him and sat down next to her. "No, it's my mother. Sit down and give your tequila-soaked brain a rest."

Asal touched Michael's arm. "Mikey, be kind. Hello Gabriel, my sweet. It's magnificent to see you."

He sank down in the seat across from Asal and closed the seatbelt around his mid-section as the engines whined and the jet lurched into motion. He glared at Michael. "My brain is not tequila soaked. Why are you being such a prick?"

Michael pulled a toothpick from his jacket pocket and started gnawing on it. "We've all had a hard time dealing with this situation. Over the last seven or eight months, I've damn near lost my mind, first thinking Rowan was dead, then finding out he'd been tortured for *months* while we sat on our asses in Dubai. Chad was stuck in DC County jail, and I had no idea how you were faring, living the dream down in old Mexico, because you never returned my calls."

Gabriel read the challenge in Michael's eyes. "Why do you want to fight? It hasn't been a party for me." He shook his head. "I love my ninôs. I love my wife. I thought Rowan would get us all killed. He went loco, don't you remember?"

Michael pulled the toothpick from his mouth and pointed it at him. "You bailed. I did everything I could to hold it together with Chad. Rowan needed us and you quit."

The engines roared, the jet rocked back and forth, and he felt the lift as they took off. He looked at Asal. She winked at him. He met Michael's cold stare and answered, talking loud over the engine noise. "I didn't call you, amigo, because I was drinking myself to death feeling guilty about leaving and trying to be a father and husband. I'm here now. If that doesn't satisfy you, then go fuck yourself."

The engine noise leveled off as the jet finished its initial climb. Michael stuffed the toothpick back in his pocket. "Fortunately, thanks to this lovely lady, I have no need to do what you're suggesting. I just had to get this shit off my chest." Michael gave him a lopsided smile. "I love you brother, and I missed you. More than you'll ever know."

"I love you too, my brother. I know where I belong now, and it's not in Mexico."

"Enough said. We need to get you up to speed on Rowan and the new op we're starting. You'll be hung over by the time we arrive, but we'll make do."

Gabriel opened his mouth in mock outrage, then leaned back and smiled. "It's good to be back."

CHAPTER TWENTY-TWO

Key West, FL

Rowan stood on the beach and took a deep breath, inhaling the intermingling scents of fish, seaweed, and salt air. He wiggled his toes in the warm sand and squinted at the endless expanse of sparkling water. He'd made a good decision, his first in a long time, to leave the stifling confines of the suite in Chicago.

When Michael and Roberto politely asked if he wanted them to take care of the details, he'd been grateful. With Asal, Gino, and Angelo contributing, they set up the household and made the property secure while he spent hours each day wandering the beach. He felt almost free of the obligation to his new master. *Almost.*

Acting in domineering character, his *partner* had finagled a deal to purchase all three properties; the fenced and gated home where he stayed and the houses on either side. *El and I will enjoy a winter break now and then.* Yeah right. More likely, the Don wanted to keep an eye on his investment. He didn't care, though. The additional homes meant he could enjoy the solitude he craved. Except for Angelo, who insisted he needed some form of human interaction. He'd grudgingly agreed that the shrink could stay in the house with him.

His phone vibrated, and he dug it out of the back pocket of his cutoffs. A text from Michael confirmed that they'd arrived at the Key West airport with Gabriel. That Gabriel had agreed to leave his family in order to help him had both surprised and relieved him. He hoped to God his friend's expertise would undo at least some of the damage done to his body by the bastards in Tora.

Shimmering blackness blinded him. He heard the rope stretching. Tearing pain engulfed his body. He staggered, dropped his phone and rubbed his eyes. Abject terror wound its way through his mind and squeezed his chest. *He couldn't stop them.*

The blackness dissipated, and his heart pounded. "They can't hurt me anymore. It's OK. *I'm OK,"* he whispered. He shivered and pulled his shirt close, buttoning it with shaky fingers. A parade of puffy clouds covered the sun, and the breeze raised gooseflesh on his arms and legs.

He retrieved his phone and took heaving breaths, willing his heart rate to slow. The flashbacks hit with no warning and left him drained. He gazed at the water, turned deep jade-green by the clouds obscuring the sunlight. They'd be back from the airport soon, and if he didn't head back, one of them would come looking for him.

He felt out of touch with their good-natured banter and the growing camaraderie between Roberto, Gino, Michael, and Asal. He smiled and played along, but they would never understand the abysmal grief he carried in his heart, or the painful emptiness of his life. He'd lost too much, and it had finally caught up with him.

He heard a faint shout on the breeze and turned, reluctant to leave the solitude of the beach. Michael stood waving at him from the patio. He trudged away from the rolling waves and limped through the deep sand to the crushed-shell walkway. The walkway, edged by tall sea grass, wove its way to the tiny yard and the patio off the kitchen.

Gabriel met him on the patio. "Holy Mother of God. I never thought I'd see you again in this life. It's like you've come back from the dead."

"Hey, que pasa my brother? Thanks for coming."

Gabriel drew him into a hug, murmuring in Spanish, then pulling away. "Ah, mi amigo. It's good to be here."

"How's the fam? Your kids must be getting big. How's Sherie?"

His emotional friend's eyes filled with tears. "Mexico turned me into a drunk. Sherie doesn't understand why I had to come. I love my niños, and I love her, but you are my family too. I should have stayed and helped you."

The honest distress in Gabriel's voice shocked him. "I'm sorry, brother. I don't want to come between you and your wife or hurt your family. You sure you want to be here?"

Gabriel let loose a string of Spanish, some of which he recognized as curse words. "No, no, no, it's not you. *This* is where I belong, helping you and my pain-in-the-ass brother Michael. I know that now."

He decided to take Gabriel's proclamation at face value. "OK. Look, there's something I need to say, before we go any further."

"I'm all ears."

"I'm sorry for how I ended things in Chicago. You know, drawing down on you and Mike. I apologize for being a jerk."

The expressive eyes went round. *"You are apologizing?"* Gabriel made the sign of the cross. "I can believe in miracles again."

"Yeah, I know, because I'm a living, breathing, fucking miracle."

Gabriel nodded. "Si, you are different. I can sense it."

"Whatever," he muttered, anxious to change the subject. "When you get settled in, we can start on rehab. I've got the report from the doc in Chicago. You'll probably understand it better than I do."

Gabriel gave him a disconcerting once-over. "We'll get started tomorrow. I'll examine you myself. For now, I want to relax and hear about how you ended up here."

"Not much to tell. You're right, though. I am back from the dead, in more ways than one."

Michael stepped onto the patio. "You two girls done kissing and making up? Because we need to figure out a few things."

Gabriel responded before he could. "You're such a prick. You need to get over yourself."

Michael snorted. "You're just hung over. No more tequila for you."

Rowan took a stab at their old repertoire. "Yeah, we're done. Too bad you weren't here, we could have made it a ménage á trois."

Michael scowled. "Fuck you both."

He raised a brow. "I believe that's the basic purpose of a threesome."

Gabriel guffawed and slapped Michael on the back. "Your loss, brother."

He should be laughing, but the smack-talk didn't do anything for him. The emptiness and pain stayed front and center.

A Week Later

Rowan didn't think he could move. He lay face-down on the massage table Johnny had purchased and sent to the beach house at Gabriel's request. His friend set it up in an empty bedroom and glibly informed him that proper massage techniques would enhance his rehabilitation. He'd just lived through Gabriel's rehab exercises and experienced his first massage.

Every time Gabriel's hands touched him, his body tensed and his heart rate exploded. He couldn't exorcise the memories of the brutality done to his body, and he couldn't stop his reaction. Gabriel placed a hand, feather light, on his shoulder, and his body tensed again. He spoke, voice muffled by the headrest. "What now? I think you've done enough damage for one day."

Gabriel said, "Let me help you sit up. We can talk about your exam and what the hell's the matter with you."

"OK." He couldn't stifle his groans as Gabriel half-lifted him upright. He sat on the table with a towel over his lap, feeling exposed and vulnerable without his clothes. "Why is this necessary? I can't believe it helps anything."

Gabriel tut-tutted in the mother-hen way he remembered. "No, no, amigo. This will help you, trust me. Your body remembers what your mind forgets, and your muscles react because of how they've been traumatized. Massage will help retrain your brain and muscles."

"My mind hasn't forgotten a damn thing. I wish it would. What's the prognosis?"

"Johnny's doctor gave you a thorough exam. I've studied the X-rays and MRIs. How much detail do you want?"

He rubbed his forehead in a futile attempt to stop the hammering behind his eyes. "The doc in Chicago told me a lot of things, but I'd just been released and was in a lot of pain. I don't remember much of anything he said, except that rehab would repair most of the damage, if I stayed with it."

Gabriel said, "Why don't you get dressed, and we can take a walk on the beach. You need to drink some water and keep your body moving."

"OK. If you say so." Gabriel left him alone, and he pulled on his t-shirt, boxers, and cutoffs, grateful for their protective covering. It had damn near killed him to shed every piece of clothing in order for Gabriel to work on his damaged body.

As they trudged along the hard-packed sand, Gabriel started in. "You got yourself hurt bad. You can't raise your arms above your head, can you?"

"No. I manage to shave and comb my hair, but even that hurts, some days worse than others."

"What about your hips?"

"My lower back and my hips hurt all the time. Shooting pains go down my legs every once in a while, depending on what I'm doing."

"Why did you quit drinking?"

"Long story. I try not to take too many pain pills, but sometimes I can't stand it."

"You should have had treatment as soon as you arrived stateside. It's been almost four months. That doesn't help things along, ya know?"

"Yeah, well trust me, no one at ADX Florence or Houston gave a rat's ass about rehab for my body. I got out of Chicago as soon as I could, and here we are. What's next?"

Gabriel stopped walking and faced him. "I talked to the doctor in Chicago because I'm a medic, and he's an expert. He suggested we start with conservative treatment. You've got over-stretched tendons and ligaments, but fortunately no tears. He's concerned about your shoulders and a couple vertebrae in your lower back."

"Meaning?"

"The short answer is that we'll give conservative treatment six months or so, but you may need surgery at some point."

"Great. Do I have to put up with more massage?"

Gabriel managed to look insulted. "Don't be a pussy. Massage is good for everyone. I'd have one every day if I could."

"And you think I'm loco."

"You used to be. Not anymore though. I said it before, and I see it more every day. You're a different man."

"OK. Whatever."

Gabriel touched his arm. "What happened to you in Tora? I have an idea, but it would help me to know specifics."

He shook his head. "I'm not having that conversation. Go with your idea. I'll catch up with you later."

Gabriel handed him a bottle of water. "All right, you stubborn jerk. I should have known you wouldn't tell me. Don't drown out here in the ocean. I'm going to go back and have some tequila."

He took the water and smirked at Gabriel. "How about when I get back, we talk about why you're here instead of in Mexico with your sexy wife and two kids?"

Gabriel's eyes widened. "Sure, and then we'll talk about why Danielle isn't here. How about that? You up for it?"

"Touché. Never mind, forget I said anything. Thanks for the water."

"You're welcome. I gotta tell Michael I went a couple rounds with you and won. It's another miracle."

He laughed. "Yeah, you did. Enjoy your victory. It's hard won, for sure."

Gabriel added, "I will. See you later."

"OK, sounds good." He turned back toward the water. Gabriel hadn't realized what he was asking. He couldn't describe the things the guards in Tora had done to him. His mind would probably never heal, and he knew for damn sure he'd never forget, but he wanted to go for an hour, maybe even a day or a week without reliving the ghastly pain and the awful helplessness of sitting alone in the cell, unable to defend himself.

He should have resisted. Shame overwhelmed him every time he thought about how he'd let them hurt him. His mind insisted he'd had no choice. But the man he was sneered and whispered, *you're such a fucking coward.* First Angelo, then Danielle, and now Gabriel wanted to know, wanted him to share his *experience,* and tell them what he'd endured. But he'd never tell a soul.

Mid-November
Houston, TX
McKenzie had grown accustomed to Houston, navigating his way around the city during the mornings and spending his afternoons on the patio overlooking the pool, jotting notes or working on his laptop. He'd logged a productive three weeks, making quiet inquiries and learning everything he could about the two police officers who'd been killed. Ed and Juan were not what he'd call upstanding representatives of the Houston Police Department, or at least he hoped not.

He lounged in his favorite chair and watched the pigeons waddling across the patio. He'd never seen so many pigeons in a city, and he'd been to a *lot* of cities. The damn things were everywhere. Getting back to DC would suit him, weather notwithstanding. He punched Leigh's contact on his phone. They'd talked weekly, which wasn't enough for him. He couldn't wait to see her.

"Hi Jack. How goes the investigation today?"

"Seems like our two dead cops crossed the line a few times while attempting to serve and protect the city of Houston."

"Hm. Breaking laws instead of upholding them?"

"You might say that. I've learned that the vaunted Houston Police Department has an effective inner machine that keeps a lot of things under the public radar. Their individual banking records have proven interesting, as well."

Berenger replied. "Are you watching your back? When you start digging, sometimes certain people don't like it."

"I'm careful, Leigh. You have to remember, I've been at this sort of thing for quite a while now."

"All right, but please keep that in mind. What about their banking records?"

"Back to that. During the month or so before Milani arrived in Houston, their accounts didn't receive any deposits other than their paychecks. However, during the previous two years, beginning shortly after they each had some kind of work-related, step-over-the-line problem, both of them started receiving substantial cash deposits on a somewhat sporadic basis."

"Now you're talking. It's as if someone saw them as exploitable."

"Exactly. Their bank accounts weren't hurting."

"But it sounds like none of this relates to Milani."

"That's just it. I can't find a connection. Cash deposits don't leave a trail. I've had to concede this as a dead end."

She replied. "What about Milani's surprise attorney?"

"That's another dead end, at least for now. I drove down to Austin. Beautiful city, by the way. Mr. Vincent Black is on vacation. Gone until the first of the year. His secretary was gracious and apologetic."

"Does that strike you as a bit odd?"

"A bit, perhaps. I am curious as to why he took it upon himself to represent Milani, and I'd still like to ask him."

"You're not thinking of staying in Texas until the first of the year, are you?"

He smiled at the misgivings in her tone. "Heavens, no. As a matter of fact, I'm ready to head back to DC after I reach out to Ms. Stratton. Which reminds me. I checked into ownership of the beach property in Key West where Milani stayed. I tracked it back to a Dubai corporation. The properties on either side are also owned by the same company."

She replied. "Milani could have rented the property from a firm representing that company."

"Indeed, he probably did. A trip to Key West to knock on the door is a definite possibility."

"That may prove interesting."

"I'll keep investigating here for a few more weeks and then see what I can turn up in Seattle. After that, I believe I'll be ready to head home."

He heard the smile in her voice. "I'm looking forward to that."

"Same here."

Key West, FL

Rowan made his way along the walkway, relishing the warmth of the gritty, crushed white shells on his bare feet. The water he loved rolled and foamed, leaving glistening bubbles on the hard-packed sand where he should be walking.

But his best friend, walking next to him wearing black leather loafers in what he figured must be size fourteen, along with gray dress pants and a white shirt was ready to leave for Chicago. He'd wanted a private conversation, so he'd dragged his friend to the beach. He stopped, raised his sunglasses to the top of his head and squinted up at Chad. "Thanks for making a quick trip down here. I appreciate you inspecting the security systems and protocols Mike and Roberto set up."

Chad gazed at the water for a moment before answering. "I didn't mind. I see why you love it here."

"Yeah, it's great. Look, I know you want to get going, so I'll make this quick. I need help only you can give me, and you're one of the few people I trust in this world."

"Of course. What do you need?"

"I need a plan to disappear. For good. I know you can make that happen."

Chad frowned. "You want to expand on your idea a bit?"

"I want out, OK? This whole deal of being Johnny's partner is *not* what I want to do. I've lost my appetite for the fight. I'm done. I want to sit on a beach on an island, someplace where people don't even think about jihad, or the Muslim Brotherhood, or me. I want to be a local at some off-the-wall bar and be left alone."

"Gotcha. You wanna take anybody with you?"

"You mean Danielle? No. I'm done being a selfish jerk. I can't ask her to make that kind of commitment to me. She has a great life ahead of her."

"You know Rowan, if you do this without at least giving her the option, you *are* being a selfish jerk. She's a smart woman who deserves the chance to make her own decisions about how she wants to live her life. Can't you see that?"

He watched a pelican skim across the water, not sure he could answer. The pain of letting Danielle go took his breath away every time his thoughts strayed to the hard truth. "I've hurt her more times than I can count. She deserves better, you know?"

"I know she loves you. I've seen firsthand how much you leaving hurt her. It wasn't pretty in Sioux Falls or Kauai. But if you do this the way you're thinking, you'll be hurting her worse than you ever did before."

"If she thinks I'm dead, *for good*, she'll get over it and keep going with her life. You'd have to tell her, and Bettina, and everyone."

Chad said, "Stop. I can't lie to Danielle and Bettina, or your parents. Damn it, Rowan. I can't be responsible for hurting all the people who love you."

"What am I supposed to do? There's *nothing* for me anymore. Don't you think I've thought about this? I don't see a way out, except to disappear."

"We can come up with something better than this *mess* you've concocted. I think you're drinking too much Jack while you're sitting down here by yourself."

"Yeah, well you're wrong. I ditched the booze. Dumped it. I haven't had a drink since the day after Danielle left Chicago."

"Seriously?"

"Hell yes, *seriously*. I'm telling you the truth. You're the one person I've never lied to, mostly because you're so smart, I always figured you'd be on to me."

Chad grinned. "That's the first smart thing you've said. And thank you. I've never lied to you, either, by the way, which is why we're standing out here on the beach arguing about your screwed-up plan."

The flippant words had hot anger roiling in his chest. He answered as neutrally as he could. "It's not screwed up. I don't know what else to do. Will you help me, or not?"

The grin faded from Chad's face. "Yes, I'll help you. But with something sane, where you don't have to lose even more. You've lost enough."

Seeing the compassion in Chad's eyes sent a sliver of guilt through his mind. He shoved it down, hard and deep into his subconscious and lied for the first time to his closest friend. "OK.

I know you're right. I'll forget about disappearing. We'll figure out something else."

Chad hesitated, then nodded. "There's a better way, brother. We'll make something work, don't worry."

He pulled his sunglasses down, covering his eyes so Chad couldn't see the duplicity he wasn't sure he could hide. He looked at the friend, the man he'd trusted with his life, and for the first time wondered if he still could. Or should. "Thanks. I appreciate your help." He'd have to figure out how to vacate his life on his own. Not for the first time, he wished he hadn't quit drinking.

Chad strode with Michael across the tarmac toward the sleek Lear 75, waiting with APU running. He'd only been in Key West for a couple days, and already understood, at least in part, why Rowan had chosen to return. The frigid temps and sooty gray, black and white of Chicago in late fall didn't quite compare with the turquoise water and humid warmth.

His talk with Rowan replayed in his mind. He'd seen the deceit in his friend's eyes. He grabbed Michael's arm and stopped walking. "Hang on a minute."

Michael pivoted sharply to face him. "Whoa, hey brother, what's up?"

"I need to tell you about a conversation I just had with Rowan."

"All right. I'm listening."

"I know he meant for me to keep it confidential, but I'm too worried about what he might do."

Michael replied. "I understand. Spill it."

"He told me he wants out. He doesn't want to be Johnny's partner or fight the Muslim Brotherhood. But get this. He wants me to help him fake his death. He wants me to lie to everyone, even Danielle."

"Damn. What did you tell him?"

"I told him I'd help him figure something out, but that I can't lie to everyone."

Michael said, "How'd that go over?"

"He gave in right away, and you know as well as I do, when Rowan does that he's thinking *fuck you, I'll make my own plans."*

"You're right. If he's hell-bent on disappearing, I'm not sure we can stop him."

Chad started walking again. "Call me right away if he seems like he's getting antsy, or acting more secretive than usual."

"We're all keeping a close eye on him. I don't think he'll try anything until his rehab is completed."

"That's reassuring. Thanks for looking out for him. The last thing any of us need is for him to go off on his own again. I don't think Bettina and I could take it."

They reached the air stairs and the roaring APU made conversation difficult. Michael shouted, "I'll stay in touch. Give my best to Bettina."

He yelled back. "Will do. Take care." He climbed the air stairs and took a final look at the palm trees and green grass. He couldn't wait to get back to Chicago.

The Next Day
Spokane, WA
Danielle woke slowly, reveling in the rare luxury of sleeping in. She peered at the thin strip of daylight trickling into her hotel room between the drapes and reached for her phone. A wave of nausea rolled through her stomach. She rolled to her back and stared wide-eyed at the ceiling, fully awake. Somehow, she knew. "I'm pregnant," she whispered.

Simple joy diminished the next wave of nausea, and she lay motionless, absorbing the revelation. She placed quivering hands on her abdomen. While she stared at the ceiling, she whispered again, "We're going to have a baby."

She shoved herself upright and spoke out loud into the quiet room. “We’re going to have a baby.” She’d never be the same person again. She grinned. Rowan would never be the same person either. He’d be a father, and she’d be a mother, a *mommy*. She giggled at the thought of his reaction to a toddler calling him *daddy*.

She fumbled for her phone, wanting to share the news with him. But the training meetings she’d traveled to company headquarters to attend started in an hour in one of the hotel’s conference rooms. A stronger wave of nausea drove her to the bathroom. She hoped she could make it through the day.

Hours later, she swiped her key card and let herself back into her room. She dumped her notebook and training manual on the desk and flung herself down on the bed. She tugged off her shoes and wiggled her toes. The rest of her body felt too tired to move. Conversations from the day swirled through her mind. She’d given automatic answers, expressing the appropriate enthusiasm for her new position, saying the kind of things she knew the company execs wanted to hear.

Sometime during the endless day, she’d made up her mind. Rowan, their baby, and a life together meant more to her than achieving any company’s goals. From that moment on, she couldn’t wait to call him. She changed into one of his t-shirts she’d brought back from Chicago, propped herself up in bed and grabbed her phone.

He answered after a few rings. “Hey, Danielle. What’s up?”

Sudden reticence gripped her and she didn’t know what to say. “Um, hey.”

“Are you OK? Anything wrong?”

She smiled through silly tears. He always worried about her. “I’m fine. I just wanted to hear your voice.” She hadn’t realized how talking to him would affect her after the long, draining day. And she couldn’t understand why she hadn’t shared their life changing news.

"Oh good. How's your new job going?" His voice sounded muffled, like he was outside on a windy day.

She sniffed and hoped he couldn't tell she was crying. "Everything's fine. I'm in Spokane at a training session. We just finished up for the day, and I wanted to talk to you. What are you doing right now?"

"I just got done with a rehab session, and Gabriel always makes me take a walk afterward."

"How's the rehab going? Are you feeling better?"

He sounded tired, discouraged even. "I don't know. Gabriel says it's going great. It must be, because it hurts like hell. Gotta keep it up though, so I can get my body back in shape and start hunting those bastards again."

What had she been thinking? She couldn't tell him. His lifestyle didn't have room for her or a baby, of all things. "I'm a *dope,"* she murmured.

"What did you say? I'm sorry, the wind is blowing like crazy here."

"Nothing. I mean, it's been a long day. Sometimes it's just nice to hear your voice."

"Same here. Hey, I need to get going right now, but I can call you later. Sound good?"

She wiped at the tears running down her cheeks and tried to keep her voice steady. "How about if we talk after I get back to Seattle? This training is making me crazy tired, and the days are long."

"OK. Call me when you get home. That way I'll know you made it back. Have a good night. I love you."

"I love you too. Bye for now." She scrunched down and pulled the covers to her chin. Apprehension replaced her earlier, carefree happiness. Why hadn't she thought about birth control when they were in Chicago? Rowan would be furious with her. He'd use it as one more reason to keep her far away and safe.

And what about *her* life? She'd been fooling herself, thinking she could leave her career and have a family with Rowan. But how could she raise a child and work full-time to support both of them?

"I'm going to be a single parent." She clutched the covers with one hand, the other covering her abdomen, protecting the new life they'd created. "We're on our own, little one. But it's all right. We'll make it, somehow."

The Next Day
Key West, FL
Rowan hunkered down in the deck chair and propped his left foot on his right knee. He watched gulls swooping down toward the water and heard them squawking. He took deep breaths of the salty, fishy ocean air and felt restless.

He dusted sand from his foot and wiggled his toes. His left foot had never been the same after CIA agent Hancock stomped on it over a year and a half ago. But then, no part of his life had been the same since Hancock and Talbot had conducted their early morning takedown.

They'd left him hanging by his cuffed wrists in a deserted warehouse, planning to return and force a confession from him. He swallowed hard and wished he could forget. But he could still hear the door close and the dead bolt turn while he hung there in the pitch dark, covered in his own sweat and blood, knowing he wouldn't make it. He'd *never* forget the shimmering golden light, the unfathomable kindness, and the elusive voice. *Rowan, come with me.* Utter peace had enveloped him as he'd lost consciousness.

And then, Sal Capello had pulled out all the stops in Quantico's brig. He rubbed his side, thinking about the horrific five days. The bastard had humiliated him, strung him up, cracked two of his ribs, and then water boarded him. He'd passed out and woke up in the infirmary. Of course, he didn't rate pain medication, and he'd lain there in agony, knowing he was finished.

That's when it happened again. The shimmering golden light surrounded him, and his pain disappeared. He heard the tantalizing voice whisper through his mind. *If you'll only ask me, Rowan, I will help you. Ask me to rescue you.* In utter despair, he'd begged for help.

Rescue had come, the very next morning, in the form of Michael and Gabriel. "I'll be damned," he muttered and tipped his head up, staring at the cloudless sky. Every time, the crazy experiences had slipped into his subconscious mind, forgotten until the last time, in Tora. But he didn't want to think about that. Not yet.

He'd never forget the conversation he'd had with Angelo on the anniversary of 9/11 a year ago. Hiding out at the Kauai estate, he'd watched a special on one of the networks, describing him as America's most-wanted home-grown terrorist. He tugged the coin Danielle had given him from the pocket of his cutoffs and held it in the palm of his hand.

The Twin Towers glowed in the sunlight. He'd lost everything on 9/11 and done his damnedest to prevent another attack. He closed his fist around the coin. His anger had driven him to Angelo. The shrink always delved into forbidden territory in his mind and hadn't wasted any time that afternoon. He stuffed the coin back in his pocket.

Angelo hadn't known what he'd lost. No one did, because he'd never told anyone about Michelle's pregnancy until that day. He'd felt a *presence*, while sitting in the study with the canny shrink, and heard the voice, whispering through his mind. *Don't be afraid, Rowan. Let me help you.*

He'd left Angelo for the one refuge that soothed his mind and stumbled along the beach, grieving like he'd never been able to before. And again, in the midst of his anguish, he heard the comforting words and felt the inexplicable kindness. *I held them in my arms, Rowan... they were never alone.*

He blinked back tears. How the hell did these things happen to him, and why? He was finally ready to talk about what had happened in Tora, mostly because he couldn't get it out of his mind. The previous night, he'd had another vivid dream about the man who'd come to his cell. He needed answers, and Angelo was the only one who knew about this kind of stuff.

He heard the shuffling sound of flip-flops and pushed himself up in the chair. Angelo came around the corner. The psychiatrist had left him alone since the move to Key West, simply telling him he'd always be available. "Hey Doc. Thanks for taking the time."

The shrink plopped down in the adjacent chair. "I have to confess, this is probably the most beautiful place I have ever had the privilege to live, other than Kauai. Thank you for the opportunity."

"You're welcome. I'm glad you like it here."

Angelo shoved his wire-rimmed glasses up his nose. "What would you like to talk about today?"

He decided he might as well dive right in. "Do you remember when we were talking, and you said, *redemption is yours, if you choose it?"*

"I do. Your reaction led me to believe I had touched a nerve. I regretted saying something that caused you pain."

"My reaction wasn't your fault. Something happened in Tora. I don't want to talk about it, but I can't get away from it. I have dreams about it, all the time."

"I see. Tell me more."

He gripped the arms of the wooden chair, took a deep breath and let it out slowly. "This is hard for me, you know?"

Angelo nodded. "I know, Rowan. Take your time."

"That won't make it any easier, but OK. See, one day I was lying on the floor of my cell in Tora and knew it was over. I couldn't take much more. I heard footsteps and thought it was the guards coming again."

"Terrifying, I am sure."

"Oh yeah. Anyway, it wasn't the guards, it was a man, and he appeared in my cell, without opening the door. He wore a robe of some kind. It seemed like it was white, but it was strange, it had different colors I couldn't recognize."

Angelo sat up straight. "Interesting. Please continue."

"The man knelt beside me. Somehow, in my mind, I saw him smile. He touched my face, and the pain went away. And then he said, '*redemption is yours, if you choose it.*'"

Angelo gazed at him for a long moment, tapping his fingers on the arms of the chair. "No wonder you reacted the way you did. I had no idea."

"I know, Doc. I couldn't handle it that day. I've tried to tell myself it was a delusion. You know, my mind's desperate attempt to get help in a tough situation."

"But you no longer believe that?"

"I don't know what to believe. I need to figure it out before I lose my mind."

Angelo's lips formed a sober line. "Are you sure you want to know my thoughts?"

"I'm sure, else we wouldn't be sitting here."

"All right. First of all, I believe only you can determine whether what you experienced was merely, as you said, your mind's concoction, or an actual presence, a man."

He scowled. "You're not helping me much. You can't tell me you don't have *some* theory about this kind of thing."

Angelo replied. "It is true, you are not the first person to experience this type of phenomenon. However, it is difficult; actually impossible, for me to know whether its origin is within your mind or not."

"Where else could it be from, if not my mind? I don't know why I do this. You always manage to turn things inside out."

"Rowan, answer one question, please."

The psychiatrist's unflappable nature never failed to aggravate him. "What?"

"If you are convinced the man who appeared to you was nothing more than a figment of your desperate mind, why did you seek my counsel about it?"

"Because I want to be sure. And because it seems related."

"Related to what?"

"To the other times."

"What other times?"

"This is too goddamned hard. You know, the other times when I've I felt a presence of some kind."

Angelo replied. "Rowan, you have never shared any of this with me."

"No? Are you sure?" He glared at the psychiatrist, nonplussed. "Oh hell, you're right. My mind is so fucked up. I remember now. I told Danielle last year, on September 11th, after you and I talked. She had some strange idea that it might be God."

"What do you think?"

"I don't know what to think. That's why I'm sitting here, talking to you."

Angelo gave him a patient smile. "As I said before, you are the only one, in the end, who can determine the source of your experiences."

"Yeah? What if I'm just crazy, because of, well, because of everything that's happened?"

"Rowan, we both know you have exhibited behavior consistent with post-traumatic stress, but that is to be expected after what you were subjected to in Tora, as well as prior to that."

He couldn't explain the lump forming in his throat or the stinging, unwanted tears flooding his eyes. "OK. Help me, would you? How do I figure out where this man, or whatever, comes from?" He wiped his eyes and hoped Angelo hadn't noticed.

"Why don't you try reaching out to this presence, or man you encountered in Tora?"

"And how would I do that?"

Angelo continued. "Sometime when you're walking on the beach, ask this presence, or man, to reveal himself to you in a way you can understand, or relate to."

He didn't bother to hide his derision. "I'm not sure how that helps me figure out whether I'm suffering from a delusion. But it ranks right up there with color psychology and the character of palm trees."

Angelo said, "You may be surprised. At the very least, it engages your mind in the process and that, possibly more than anything, will help you determine the source of your experience."

He pushed himself up and out of the deck chair. "You know, I'm starting to think talking about this was a mistake. Forget I brought it up."

Angelo clambered to his feet and faced him. "Do not be afraid to include your heart in your search for the truth, Rowan."

He met Angelo's compassionate gaze and smirked. "If I remember correctly, and that's up for debate, I believe I told you I don't have a heart."

Angelo sighed. "Perhaps this is not the time for self-deprecation."

"Whatever you say, Doc. I'll see you later." He trudged along the walkway, cursing the limp he'd always have, and then headed across the deep sand until he reached the smooth footing at the water's edge. He waded in, ankle deep. The waves rushed in and rolled back, sucking sand from beneath his feet as they receded, leaving him unsteady on his feet.

Why did he feel so empty? What was he looking for? Or *who?* He couldn't forget the voice whispering through his mind and the unfathomable kindness he'd felt, in the worst possible circumstances. His longing for something or *someone* to fill the emptiness inside would never go away. Somehow, he'd learn to live with it, the same way he'd learned to live with a lot of other things in what his life had become. Angelo didn't have the answers he needed after all.

CHAPTER TWENTY-THREE

Two Weeks Later
Seattle, WA

Tom gave Danielle a quick glance, noting the dark circles under her eyes, and wondered if she'd tell him what was really bugging her. It had to be about Milani, much as that ticked him off. What had the guy done to her in Chicago, to affect her weeks after she'd seen him? Sometimes he wanted to shake her and say, *hey, forget about him and let me love you.* But he always held back, afraid he'd push too hard. He'd told her how he felt, and it was up to her to respond, or not.

He'd cajoled her into taking off a few hours after the busyness of Thanksgiving Day and the weekend after. A fifty-degree, sunny day shouldn't be wasted, especially since a front headed their way promised snow. The sun felt good, and the crisp air invigorated him as they walked the trail crisscrossing the park. Leo chased a tennis ball and busily explored, nose to the ground, covering the entire area.

He touched her shoulder. "How are things going? You seem a bit distracted. Work got you down?"

Her eyes brimmed with tears and she stopped walking. "Oh, I don't know, maybe. I've been second-guessing a few things lately, and I'm not sure what I'm doing. Or what I should be doing."

Surprised she'd blurted her thoughts and concerned with her tears, he tread carefully. "You can tell me about it if you want. I don't mind being a sounding board."

The tears slid down her cheeks. "I'm sorry to be such a crybaby. I don't know how to explain."

Leo rushed up, and he bent down to scratch behind the Rottie's ears, giving her time to regroup. When Leo woofed and bounded off after a squirrel, he said, "It's all right, you don't have to explain anything. I just want you to be happy. I hate seeing you cry."

She sniffed. "I don't know where to start or even if you want to hear this stuff."

"Dani, if I wasn't interested in hearing what's going on, I wouldn't have asked."

She twisted Leo's leash in her hands. "I needed to see Rowan, you know? And he, I mean, he's suffered so much. It made me sad."

"I can imagine. It's hard to see someone you care about go through a hard time."

"He won't let me help him, or be with him. Because of, because of a few things that have, uh, happened, I've decided to move on for good."

He'd never understand how Milani could keep throwing her away. "Is that what he wants you to do?"

"Yes, he wants me to keep going with my career, and as he put it, live my life."

For a moment, he forgot to be cautious. "How generous of him."

Her voice took on an edge. "He told me I should settle down with someone who could give me a wonderful, normal life. I know he meant you."

Milani's arrogance amazed him. "How could he mean me? We've never even met. I could be a total creep, for all he knows."

"Oh please, stop with the sarcasm. I know you don't like him, but you don't have any idea… I mentioned our friendship, and he picked up on a few things, right away."

"I'm sorry, Dani. It's impossible for me to understand how he could walk away from you."

Tears slid down her cheeks again. "He doesn't have a choice about what he has to do. Please don't judge him, Tom. He only wants what's best for me."

Her words cheered him. If he stayed patient and kept loving her, someday he'd be thanking Milani. He put an arm around her shoulder and drew her closer. "I don't mean to get down on him, but it bothers me a heck of a lot to see you so sad."

"I'll be fine, eventually."

His hopes were buoyed when she didn't pull away. "I know you will, Dani. I'm here, always. I'll help you any way I can. You know that, right?"

"I know," she whispered. "Thank you." She clutched her stomach and bent over. "Oh no, I don't feel good." She put a hand over her mouth.

He held onto her arm. "We better get you home. I'll make you some chicken soup. That fixes everything, or at least that's what my mom keeps telling me."

She kept a hand over her mouth, nodded and thrust Leo's leash toward him.

An hour later, they sat at the breakfast nook in her cheery kitchen. She'd nibbled on a few crackers and insisted he didn't need to go buy chicken soup. "Are you sure you don't need anything? I'll go fetch whatever you want."

She rubbed her arms. "No, I'll be all right. I'm going to lie down and try to take a nap. Thanks for everything."

He'd give anything to cuddle her close and keep her warm. "Call me if you need anything. I'll be at home working on a project that's got to be done by Christmas."

She managed a smile. "You better get at it then. I don't want to be responsible for you missing my first Orcas Island Christmas."

He stood up. "No chance of *that* happening. See you later. I'll lock the door on my way out."

Danielle cradled her head in her arms on the table after Tom left. Why hadn't she said no when he asked her to bring Leo to the park? The wretched nausea hit without warning, she had training manuals to work on, and lack of sleep left her continually exhausted. She woke up multiple times every night and lay staring at the ceiling while the mantra played constantly in her thoughts. *You're going to be a single mother. How could you do this? What will you do? You can't tell Rowan. You have to tell Rowan.*

She thought about the pregnancy test she'd picked up at Walgreens and shoved into her medicine cabinet. She saw it every time she retrieved her toothbrush, but she couldn't bring herself to do the test, because that would make it official and then she'd *have* to tell Rowan. Keeping it from him wasn't fair, but she wanted to tell him at the right time. After she knew she could handle the baby on her own; when his rejection wouldn't devastate her, she'd let him know.

The contrast between Rowan and Tom hit her again. Rowan's persistence that she face the truth and move on contrasted with Tom's gentle and, at times, almost suffocating kindness. At the moment, she wanted nothing to do with either one of them. God, she was sick of crying over everything, too. She raised her head. If she tried to take a nap, she wouldn't be able to sleep. The bistro's ID chimed on her phone, and she grabbed it. "This is Dani. Hi Steph." She frowned. "All right, tell him I'll be there in half an hour. Give him a free coffee. Thanks for calling."

She punched END and wondered why a FOX News investigative reporter wanted to talk to her. Had *insisted* on talking to her. His name was familiar, but— she gasped. *Jack McKenzie* had broken the news about Rowan's return. "Oh no. I shouldn't talk to him," she murmured. How would she get rid of him? If he knew about her job, he probably knew where she lived. She sat up and heaved an irritated sigh. She'd talk to him, but she wouldn't tell him *anything.* And she'd ask him to never contact her again.

Danielle surveyed the crowded bistro. A bald-headed man standing near the door with a mug of coffee smiled and waved before making his way toward her. Leo followed her as she stepped forward to greet him. "Hello, Mr. McKenzie. I'm Danielle Stratton. What can I help you with?"

He grinned and stuck out his hand. "Call me Jack, and thank you for agreeing to meet with me. Do you have a quiet spot anywhere in here where we might have a chat?"

His undisguised enthusiasm only amplified her exhaustion. She ignored his outstretched hand and said, "My office. Follow me. Come, Leo." She turned on her heel and marched down the hallway without waiting for him to respond. She led him into her peaceful domain and gestured at the chairs in front of her desk. "Have a seat." She slid into her chair and faced him. "What do you want, Mr. McKenzie?"

He leaned forward, and if anything, his intensity increased. "More than anything, I want the world to know the truth about what happened to Rowan Milani."

"Oh. Why would you think I could help you with that?"

"My investigation has uncovered some remarkable information, but I need to talk to Rowan himself."

Leo sat panting beside her, and she scratched his head while formulating her response. "I don't have any idea where Rowan is staying."

"But I'm certain you've been in touch."

She forced a chuckle. "Where did you get that idea? Rowan and I ended our relationship almost a year ago."

"You haven't been in touch with him since his release?"

"No, and I don't expect to hear from him. As I said, we agreed to end that chapter of our lives. I've got an amazing career and a wonderful new boyfriend. I wish Rowan the very best, but I have no interest in reconnecting with him."

He frowned, and she could tell he doubted her. "That's interesting, because the transcripts of FBI interrogations, which I've been privileged to read, reveal a man who cares deeply for you."

She willed the stupid tears not to form, but his words expanded the crater of sadness inside. She shrugged. "Rowan is a difficult man. He may care for me, but I don't miss the hassle of being with him. I've moved on with my life, and I hope Rowan can do the same, wherever he is."

McKenzie raised a forefinger. "Speaking of location, my research into Rowan's movements before his capture in Houston led me to Key West. Does that ring any bells?"

She remembered his words, *I'm heading for a beach house…* "No, Rowan never mentioned Key West while we were together."

"Who's your new boyfriend, Ms. Stratton?"

She replied without hesitation. "Tom Hanford. He's an engineer at Boeing. How does that information help the world know the truth about Rowan, if you don't mind my asking?"

"It's the reporter in me. I crave information."

She wanted to tell him he was full of crap and that she knew he'd hoped to trip her up. "Do you have any other questions for me? I'm not feeling well today, and I'd like to head back home."

"Oh, I am sorry if I've disturbed you." He pulled a business card from his shirt pocket. "If you happen to hear anything from Rowan or one of his associates, would you mind passing along my request?"

She took the card. "None of Rowan's associates have contacted me since we broke things off, and I don't expect them to. Have you tried contacting any of them?"

He stood up and held out his hand. "My investigation is just getting started. Thank you again for chatting with me."

She didn't bother to stand, but shook hands with him. "You're welcome. If you don't mind, I would appreciate it if you would leave me out of your investigation. I'd rather not be reminded of that period of my life."

He nodded. "I fully understand, Ms. Stratton. Take care. I will see myself out."

She leaned back after he left and closed her eyes. A headache had started while they talked. Rowan needed to know about the nosy reporter and his plans. She caught a whiff of coffee, felt the telltale nausea and opened her eyes. "I need to go home."

Key West, FL

Rowan trudged up the stairs to the master bedroom. He closed the wooden blinds on the windows and double doors leading to the private deck, shutting out the pink, blue, and blazing gold of the sunset. He sat on the bed and glared at the two pain pills lying in the palm of his hand. Gabriel had insisted he take them after his latest rehab session, before adding, *a shot of whiskey wouldn't hurt you, either.*

Angelo would blow a gasket if he heard that, but his shrink didn't have to worry. Much as he craved the whiskey, for some reason he could no longer bear the darkness that came with it. He hated taking the pain pills too, because he didn't want to depend on them the way he had on the booze. They didn't bring on the darkness the way the whiskey did, but they left his brain foggy and his thoughts halfway incoherent.

But hell, what difference did it make, whether he could think or not? His keepers, from Key West to Chicago, would make sure he didn't take a single, fucking *step* in the wrong direction. He couldn't control either them or the pain that dogged his every move. The enormous damage done to his body enraged him, and the tedious, agonizing rehab left him exhausted and discouraged. He couldn't change any of it, so he gave up and tossed back the pills with a swallow of water from the bottle Gabriel had thrust into his other hand.

He stuffed a pillow behind his head and tried to stretch out. In a while, the pain would dull and maybe he'd get some sleep, while everyone else sat around the fire pit. They seemed to enjoy spending evenings there, and he was sure it gave them a chance to discuss him. He hoped they had a damn good time at it. He closed his eyes and took a couple deep breaths. As the pain relinquished its hold, his tensed muscles relaxed, and he drifted toward sleep.

His phone vibrated, and he groped for it, pulling it from his shirt pocket, cursing under his breath. He squinted at the phone, saw the ID, and punched talk. "Hey Danielle. What's up?"

"Rowan. You won't believe this. I had to call you right away."

He yawned and rubbed his eyes, trying to wake up. She sounded mad, but he couldn't think it through. He hadn't done anything, had he? "What happened? You OK?"

"A FOX News reporter showed up at the bistro today, fishing for information on you."

He stared at the ceiling while her words sank into his befuddled mind. "What?" He somehow willed his body upright and sat swaying on the edge of the bed, the tiled floor cold on his bare feet.

"I didn't tell him anything. He wanted to know if I'd heard from you or knew where you were. I told him we broke up, and I hadn't heard anything."

Dizziness came and went. "Huh. OK, good. What was his name?"

"Jack McKenzie. He said something about thinking you were in Key West."

"What else did he say?"

"He told me he wants the world to know the truth about what happened to you. He said he wants to meet you and mentioned reading FBI transcripts of you talking to agents."

"Oh great." He needed to talk to Chad, or maybe Ralph, or Johnny. He frowned, couldn't decide.

Danielle sniffed and her voice wavered. "I tried not to tell him anything."

"Are you OK?" He wondered if she'd been crying.

"I'm all right, just not feeling good."

"Don't worry about this guy, Danielle. I'll take care of it."

"Um, fine. Guess I'll let you go."

God, he hated being away from her. "Are you sure everything is all right? I'll call you back later, and we can talk more, OK?"

"I'd like that." She whispered and he could barely hear her. "I love you."

"I love you, too, and I'll call you in a couple hours. Bye, Danielle."

"Goodbye Rowan."

He ended the call, stared bleary-eyed at his phone, and chose Chad's contact.

His friend answered right away. "Hi Rowan. How's everything in Key West? We're looking at six inches of snow, plus thirty miles-per-hour wind gusts in Chicago. It's twenty degrees."

"Nice. I just got a call from Danielle. A FOX News reporter came to her coffee shop and asked a bunch of questions about me. He mentioned Key West. What do we need to do?"

"Damn it. Did she tell you his name?"

He frowned and rubbed his forehead, willing his drugged mind to cooperate. "Yeah, she did. But I can't think of it right now."

Chad intervened. "When Harandi showed up and talked to Ralph and the Boss, he called a FOX News guy. He's a long-time media contact of Ralph's, Jack McKenzie. Does that sound right? You knew about him, didn't you?"

"That's him, and the answer is no, because nobody tells me anything."

"I'm sorry about that, brother. Guess it's hard to cover all the bases between Key West and Chicago. Plus, we all want you to de-stress and not worry about anything besides getting healthy."

"Oh yeah, thanks for that. Meanwhile this guy has been reading transcripts of my FBI interrogations, which means he's involved with what's-her-name, you know, the new power-tripping Bureau director. Goddamn it, I can't think."

Chad replied. "I guess that's one more thing you didn't know. During that same conversation, McKenzie talked about working with Director Berenger to clear your name. Harandi was involved in their investigation as well."

The ongoing revelations of everything he'd been left out of wound their way through the fog enveloping his mind. "What else have you all *not* told me?"

"Take it easy. No one is leaving you out of anything on purpose. It's like I said, we all want…"

"OK, whatever. I gotta go." He punched END before Chad could answer. When he woke up, he'd talk to somebody, or do something. He lay down and turned on his side, facing the wall. As he faded away, he remembered his promise to call Danielle. "Sorry, Danielle. Later, I promise," he mumbled.

Chicago, IL

Chad laid his phone in his lap. For only the second time in the years he'd known Rowan, his friend had hung up on him. He stared at the fire place, watching the flames overtake the logs he'd arranged earlier and wondered if he should call Michael. Rowan had sounded both belligerent and out of it, a strange combination for his friend. First though, he needed to talk to Harandi, much as he loathed the idea. Johnny allowed Harandi to stay in the opposite wing of the enormous home, which he'd vehemently disagreed with, to no avail. Even Ralph had sided with the Don.

But Ralph had never sat cuffed and shackled in an interrogation room in Quantico and then County, trying over and over to get Harandi to listen to him. And Ralph had never seen the woman he loved walk away and been helpless to do anything about it. He shuddered and grabbed his phone. He'd agreed with Rowan about turning Harandi over to either Whitman or Shemal. But his new boss, *the* Boss, had hired him instead. He hit Harandi's contact and waited.

"Hello. This is David."

"This is Chad. Unfortunately, I need to talk to you."

"I'm glad to help. What do you need?"

"In your room, five minutes." He ended the call and left the soothing comfort of his and Bettina's bedroom. The trek to Harandi's room took him through the living, dining, and kitchen areas of the home to the service elevator. Exiting the elevator on the lower level, he walked across the deserted, underground ballroom, his footsteps echoing in the semi-darkness. He made his way along a hallway with doors marked *Storage,* to the end of the hall and the last door. He resisted the urge to barge in and knocked instead.

Harandi opened the door wide. "Come in, please."

He brushed past Harandi and swung around. "Tell me exactly what McKenzie and Berenger are up to."

Harandi replied. "I can only comment on what happened before I took off from DC. Berenger and I decided to work together, and I talked her into allowing McKenzie to join us. He's a valuable asset for many reasons."

"I know about your joint investigation."

"Then I don't know what else I can tell you."

"I repeat, what are McKenzie and Berenger up to?"

Harandi pulled a chair away from a rectangular wooden table in the tiny kitchen and sat down. "At our last meeting, we agreed that McKenzie would investigate on the down low and find out if

Abramson and Shemal had connections. From the get-go McKenzie wanted to create a FOX News special, showcasing Rowan, to show the world he's innocent."

He sat down across the table from Harandi. "And Berenger went along with that?"

"Berenger is a strict law-and-order type. She never conceded that Rowan had a valid reason for committing seven murders in Houston."

"Rowan called me a few minutes ago. Sounds like McKenzie is hot on his trail."

"Rowan doesn't have anything to fear from Jack. If anything, he's overzealous about getting at the truth."

"Pity you never exhibited that trait. What I need is for you to reach out to either McKenzie or Berenger or both of them, and find out where they're going with this."

Harandi ignored his jab. "I'll gladly talk to either one of them."

"Call McKenzie now and put it on speaker."

Harandi plucked his phone from his shirt pocket. "All right, let's do it."

"I'm waiting."

Harandi laid his phone on the table. "You know, I'm not interested in screwing you or Rowan. I wish you'd both figure that out."

"Just make the call."

"Fine." Harandi tapped out a phone number and hit the speaker button.

The phone rang three times. "McKenzie here. Who's this?"

"Hello Jack. Thought it was time I got back to you."

"David. Where the heck are you? Why'd you take off? Leigh was distraught after you left."

"I needed a hiatus from every obligation, including Whitman and Berenger. I'm refreshed now and anxious to learn how our investigation is progressing."

McKenzie said, “The investigation into Abramson and Shemal has revealed an interesting connection, but we’re tabling that for now and digging into what happened in Houston.”

Harandi frowned and glanced at him. “Houston? I thought that was a done deal once the DA asked for dismissal of the charges and Milani was released.”

McKenzie replied. “Leigh talked to the DA, and I’ve chatted with your detective buddy down there. Matthews has an interesting theory of Mafia involvement. He also swears up and down you both saw the evidence which somehow didn’t exist later.”

Harandi scoffed. “Matthews showed me evidence he supposedly collected. Besides, why would the Mafia give two shits whether Milani lived or died?”

Chad stared in surprise at Harandi’s breezy dissembling. Rowan had more in common with Harandi than he’d realized. For some reason that bothered him.

McKenzie continued. “Leigh and I agree with your assessment, and we both believe the circumstances of Milani’s release are fishy. I want to interview Milani and get the story from him.”

“Wait a minute, Jack. Have you read any of the FBI transcripts of Rowan’s interrogations?”

“Yes, but that’s not the only reason I’m so keen to talk to him in person.”

Harandi pressed. “What more is there? If you’ve read the transcripts, you know Milani told the same story every time, to Capello, me, Foster, and Berenger.”

McKenzie protested. “True, but I want to find out who got him out of jail. That has become a huge piece of his story, in addition to everything else. It’s exciting stuff, my friend. I wish you’d come back and join us.”

Harandi replied. "You never know what might happen, Jack. I'll think about it."

McKenzie gushed. "You'd make my day. We need your expertise in Houston. I can't wait to tell Leigh."

Harandi's forefinger hovered over the phone. "I'll call you again soon. You can let me know what she says. Take care, Jack." Harandi ended the call and heaved a sigh. "Berenger is damn clever, but I never would have taken Jack for a dupe."

He scowled. "What do you mean?"

"Think about this for a minute. Berenger is using McKenzie's quest to prove Rowan's innocence for her own ends. She's never accepted Milani's assertion that he was only doing his job in Houston."

"That figures. She'd probably use her own mother to advance the Bureau's agenda."

Harandi replied. "The only reason Berenger is investigating in Houston is to make Rowan accountable for those killings and put the screws to whoever she deems responsible for his release."

A sliver of panic had his hands sweating. "Johnny needs to know what's going on."

Harandi agreed. "Yes, and the sooner the better."

He shoved away from the table and stood up. "Let's go."

An hour later, he sat in the Don's well-appointed study in a leather chair with Harandi seated beside him. Johnny and Ralph faced them across a polished mahogany table.

Johnny addressed Harandi. "You believe we've got something to worry about in Houston? Again?"

Harandi replied. "Berenger has taken the time to talk to the DA and send McKenzie down there to poke around. It's only a matter of time before agents are dispatched."

Ralph jumped in. "Damn it, I'd have to agree. Even as an agent, she was known for getting to the bottom of things. We should have realized this from the beginning."

Chad spoke up. "Rowan called me earlier. McKenzie found Danielle and talked to her, asked her if Rowan was in Key West. We've got to find a way to get an inside track."

Johnny said, "My contact in Houston assured me that we had no need for concern. I trust my man. When Roberto had concerns about his crew, he took care of it."

Harandi replied. "An obvious concern, to me, is the superior hacking skill it took to accomplish the complete erasure of the chain of evidence. What if Berenger starts looking for hackers? If it's occurred to me, you can bet she's thought of it, too. What if she gets a wild hair and launches an in-depth Bureau investigation of the Texas legal system?"

Ralph said, "God almighty, he's right."

Chad couldn't escape his sense of urgency. "I haven't intercepted any emails, which tells me Berenger has gotten smart. She probably assumes I'm tracking Bureau communications."

Ralph replied. "You got any bright ideas?"

Harandi smacked his fist on the table. "Send me in. McKenzie trusts me, and I can make sure he doesn't find a damn thing. And if I'm on the inside, we can stay a step ahead of Berenger."

Johnny stabbed a forefinger at Harandi. "I thought you were in Whitman's cross-hairs. Isn't that why you're hiding out in my basement?"

Chad added, "You've said Whitman figured out somehow that you were involved in Rowan's release. Berenger's just going to put you in custody if you show up again."

Harandi replied. "Berenger asked me to meet with her about joining McKenzie in Houston. I thought she wanted to get me in her office for questioning and possibly to detain me, on Whitman's orders."

Ralph replied. "How do we know you won't sell us out if things go south?"

Johnny said, "We may not have a choice. I need to protect my interests in Houston. Mr. Harandi, are you sure you can persuade Berenger to keep you out of Whitman's hands? Because if you end up in the pokey, I won't be coming to your rescue, but I will make damn sure your mouth stays shut."

Chad swallowed hard. He knew what the Don was capable of, but hearing the words and seeing the intent in the cold brown eyes gave him insight into Rowan's desire to get out of the powerful man's orbit.

Harandi responded. "I can read Berenger pretty well. I'll call and offer a mea culpa or two. If I get the sense she wants to turn me over to Whitman, I'll stay away. Another option is for me to head for Houston on my own."

Ralph said, "I'm still not a complete believer in you, Harandi. You could have planned this all along, in cohoots with Berenger."

Johnny stepped in. "In this instance, I think we're gonna have to give Mr. Harandi a chance. If he's thinking of shafting us, he'll be dealt with."

Chad brought up one more contingency. "What about Rowan? We need to get him out of Key West before McKenzie shows up."

Harandi replied. "No, let McKenzie find him. If Rowan pretends to be surprised to see him, McKenzie and Berenger won't be able to make a connection to Ms. Stratton or any of us."

Chad had to concede. "You're right, much as I hate to say it. But what's to stop Berenger from sending agents with McKenzie?"

Ralph replied. "For now, she's on a fishing expedition. But we need to keep close tabs on this. Johnny, I'm beginning to see things your way. I don't think we have a choice but to send Harandi in, *if* he can convince Berenger."

Johnny wrapped it up. "All right people. We've all made our points. We're gonna move on this." He turned to Harandi. "When are you calling Berenger? I want the three of us to sit in on that call."

Harandi gave them thumbs-up. "You got it. I thought I'd give it a few days, so McKenzie could tell her I'm interested in coming back."

Johnny nodded. "All right, we'll meet back here in three days to make that call."

The Next Day
Key West, FL

Rowan stared at the flames hissing and popping in the fire pit, courtesy of Gabriel, who'd hiked along the beach collecting driftwood and seaweed that afternoon. Sparks sailed into the night sky, and he half-listened while Mike, Gabriel, Roberto, and Gino exchanged stories, drank beer, and puffed on their fat cigars. He wouldn't be telling any of his stories around the fire, for damn sure. He stayed on the periphery of the group, like he always did, drawn instead to the solitude of the beach.

His phone vibrated, and he scrolled through a text from Bettina. She'd sent half a dozen pictures of his small nephew. He couldn't miss the uncomplicated joy on Chad and Bettina's faces while they took turns cuddling the chubby baby, but the images left him restless and sad.

He couldn't take another story, or more cigar smoke burning in his sinuses. When he stood up, the conversation died away. He raised a brow. "Carry on. I'm going for a walk on the beach. I might even take a swim to get the stink off."

Gabriel chided him. "Amigo, you could try joining in once in a while."

He stuffed his hands deep in his jacket pockets. "I couldn't get a word in if I tried. I'll see you all tomorrow morning, or maybe in the afternoon, the way this party's going."

Roberto said, "Don't worry Rowan, we've got your back."

"Well, all right then. See ya later."

Mike raised his beer. "Later."

Gino added, "Be careful, boss."

No doubt they'd alert Johnny's crews stationed in the houses on either side to keep an eye on him. He turned and followed the lighted pathway, toward the comforting sound of the waves. When he hit the beach, he stopped to take in the view. The full moon, extra-large and radiant, created a surreal, almost daylight scene. Its replica shimmered across the water and even the sand glowed in its light.

He trudged along, hands still stuffed in his pockets. He wished Bettina and Chad would quit sending him the pictures. They reminded him of the life he'd embraced, thought was his, too many years ago. The path he'd been forced to choose ensured he'd always be alone, and no matter how hard he tried, he couldn't seem to get past that simple fact.

He thought about Angelo and his kind words, meant to encourage, but instead leaving him even more confused and angry. How could he reach out to something or someone, to God or whatever? An errant thought whispered through his mind, there and gone. *Why don't you try?*

"This is ridiculous," he muttered. He walked further along the beach, but the thought kept coming back. "OK, what the hell." He stopped and pulled his hands from his pockets. He spread his arms as wide as he could and looked up, at the oversized moon and the blue-black night beyond. "Here I am. Whoever you are, if you're real, help me out. Give me what I'm looking for, what I know I can't have."

The light breeze had turned cool after sunset and he pulled his jacket close. The endless rush of the waves punctuated the stillness. "I'm a fool." The emptiness stayed with him. Nothing had changed, and he knew nothing would.

Two Days Later
Woodley Park, Washington, DC

Berenger relaxed in what she'd come to think of as her corner, on the sofa in McKenzie's comfortable family room. He'd fixed dinner, again, and she felt spoiled. She'd missed him, more than she realized. He'd invited her for the weekend, and in hesitant anticipation of saying yes, she'd driven herself. Before long, he'd head off to Key West, and she wanted to spend some time with him. But she hadn't decided for sure if she could commit to staying even one night, let alone the entire weekend.

McKenzie plopped down next to her. "This beats phone conversations, by a long shot. For once, it feels good to be back home."

"Are you saying you prefer being on assignment? You've got a beautiful home."

McKenzie shrugged. "Ever since Anne died, coming back to the silence and the emptiness has been difficult. Thank you for making it easier."

His words touched her. "Oh Jack, I'm sorry. But I'm glad my being here helps."

"More than you know, Leigh." He patted his mid-section. "Plus, this way I don't eat the entire meal when I cook. You're helping keep me in shape."

She laughed. "You're welcome. I loved your version of a post-Thanksgiving dinner." Her phone rang, and she plucked it from the low table in front of the sofa. "Who would call me from a blocked ID?"

McKenzie said, "Maybe it's David. He called me from a blocked number several days ago. Said he'd be in touch before long. He wants to rejoin our investigation."

"Oh my, let's find out." She tapped the phone. "This is Berenger. Who is this?"

Harandi answered. "Hello, Director Berenger. How are you?"

She didn't bother to hide the irritation his blithe response engendered. "Mr. Harandi, what form of underhanded clandestine activity are you indulging in this time?"

McKenzie frowned and opened his mouth to speak. She put a forefinger on her lips, and he nodded.

Harandi replied. "Nothing underhanded, Director, I can assure you."

"I see. Perhaps you'd care to explain why you didn't make your meeting at my office, let's see, a couple days short of two months ago?"

"I need to apologize for that. Whitman called me after you did, and I got the distinct impression he wanted to detain me."

She chuckled. "Your CIA paranoia is showing. Whitman did want to question you, but not for the reason you think. He and I both wanted to pick your brain for what kind of connections Milani could possibly have that may have facilitated his release."

"You may be right about my paranoia. What would you say to my rejoining our investigation?"

"Hmm, I'd have to give that some thought. Why did you seek out Ralph Johnston? And why did you call Jack and ask for him to vouch for you to Johnston?"

Harandi said, "You know how determined I've been to make things right with Rowan. I wanted Johnston to tell me where he was, so I could reach out to him one last time. I confess, I also wanted to ask him how the hell he got out of jail in Houston. That seemed like a done deal to me."

She continued. "Were you able to connect with Milani?"

"No, unfortunately. Johnston claimed he didn't know where he was. I didn't necessarily believe him, but he was adamant about Milani taking off to parts unknown."

"Jack said someone else was with Johnston. Who was that?"

Harandi didn't miss a beat. "That was Chad Cantor's father, Clifton. He and Johnston met with me."

"How interesting. Where have you been for the past two months?"

"I met with Johnston in LA and headed up the coast to Carpinteria. I spent summers there as a kid, and I felt kind of adrift, because I don't have a family anymore. I'm sorry for being incognito, Director. This thing with Milani got to me, in a big way, and I needed time to work through the fact that he's out of reach, probably for good."

She silently cursed his skill. He made her want to trust him, every time. She wouldn't make that mistake again, but he didn't need to know. "I understand. Whitman is finished with the Milani affair. He has other domestic and foreign issues to deal with."

Harandi said, "Of course. What do you think, Director? Any chance of my rejoining you and Jack? Even though I can no longer reach out to Milani, I'm interested in bringing Shemal to justice. Abramson, too, if he's involved. Not to mention the two CIA agents who murdered my uncle Sa-id."

She'd enjoy reeling him in, for a change. "You know, I'm sitting here with Jack, and he's practically jumping out of his skin with enthusiasm. I think we'd both welcome your input again." She tipped her forefinger at McKenzie.

McKenzie grinned. "She's right, David. Welcome back. How soon can you be in DC?"

"I'll fly out tomorrow. I'm looking forward to getting back up to speed."

She'd make sure he didn't call the shots this time. "Let me know when you're back, and we'll schedule a meeting. Thank you for calling, David. See you soon." She tapped her phone and ended the call.

Chicago, IL

Harandi slouched in his chair and gazed from Ralph to Chad and then met Johnny's hard stare. "Well, what do you think?"

Johnny replied. "I'd watch my back if I were you. Seems to me she's a fool-me-once kind of woman."

Ralph said, "You're too damn slick Harandi. For a minute, I even started to believe you. Johnny's right though, you better be careful."

Chad added his two cents. "I'll never trust you, but I think Berenger at least halfway bought it. Quick thinking to mention my dad."

He surveyed each man again and wished once more that he'd told Hennessey to stick it all those month ago when she'd asked him to find Rowan and bring him in. His ex-friend wasn't the only one whose life had been destroyed. He didn't have a friend left, and depending on how he played this next venture, he might find himself wanted by both the FBI and Johnny Giacopino. He knew which entity he feared more.

He addressed Johnny. "I'd like to stay on your payroll, in a matter of speaking, in this operation. I'll keep whomever you want informed of everything Berenger has in the works."

Johnny replied. "You still work for me, Harandi, so you answer to me. Keep the lines of communication open. I want to hear from you daily. Capisce?"

He gave the Don a sharp nod. "You got it, sir."

Johnny returned the nod. "Good. Now go. Get your gear and head back to the District."

Harandi retreated to his tiny basement dwelling to prepare to rejoin Berenger and McKenzie. The new, dual role he'd play would take every bit of his skill and focus. He still held onto the ragged hope that somehow, one day, Rowan might appreciate his efforts.

CHAPTER TWENTY-FOUR

Three Days Later
Key West, FL
Michael waited on the deck of the home he shared with Asal and Gabriel, situated down a short stretch of beach from Rowan's abode. He tapped impatient fingers on the wooden railing and watched a trio of pelicans swooping low over the glistening waves. He turned at the sound of voices and clumping footsteps. Gabriel and Roberto tromped up the steps to the deck. A pang of guilty sadness hit him. He and Gabriel should be meeting with Rowan, the way they always had. Instead, they had to keep their friend in the dark, until they could agree on how to handle him.

He gestured toward the lounge chairs. "All right boys, have a seat. We need to put a plan together."

Gabriel slid into the chair next to his. "Harandi said the gringo reporter will be here in a couple days, right?"

Roberto slouched into the other chair, facing them, and cracked thick knuckles. "I got a bad feeling about this. My gut tells me we should clear out and head back to Chicago before the reporter gets here."

He considered. "Your idea has merit. I could get on board, but getting Rowan to budge is a whole other deal. What say you, Gabriel?"

Gabriel eyed Roberto. "I knew I liked you. That's the best idea I've heard yet. The gringo needs to find an empty house. We could even get Harandi to plant the idea of Rowan being in San Francisco."

Roberto said, "Harandi's got some sort of fixation on Rowan. It ain't healthy, and I don't know why the Boss wants to keep him around."

Michael replied. "I agree. Look, I'm all for telling Rowan we're heading back to Chicago for a few days until this fucking reporter goes away." His phone rang, and he tugged it from the front pocket of his shorts. "Hi Angelo, whatcha need? *Right now? Damn it.* We're on our way." He stood up and stuffed his phone back in his pocket.

Gabriel shot out of the chair. "What the hell happened?"

He waved an arm. "That reporter is here, *now*, at the gate, and he's not leaving. Angelo said he's looking for a way under the fence. *Son of a bitch.* Somebody dropped the ball."

Roberto lurched to his feet. "I'm tellin' ya, that damned Harandi can't be trusted. I'll grab Gino and meet you there."

Gabriel stared, wide eyed. "Holy mother of God, we've got to get there before Rowan shoots him."

He muttered a reply while they headed down the steps. "I'd like to shoot the guy myself. And then go after Harandi."

Gabriel added, "I'll spot for you."

Five endless minutes later, he wiped sweat from his forehead and peered with Gabriel from behind a huge bougainvillea bush that sported a profusion of dark pink blooms and served as the perfect cover. Roberto and Gino crept up behind them. A bald-headed man strolled back and forth in front of the gated and fenced property. While they observed, he picked up the phone mounted on a gate post.

"Fuck me. Rowan's gonna go ballistic if he keeps calling." He pointed at Roberto and Gino. You two wait here and make sure we don't have company in the form of Bureau agents poking around. Gabriel and I will get rid of this jerk."

Roberto nodded and muttered. "You got it. We'll keep a sharp eye."

He drew his .45. "All right amigo, let's go."

Gabriel drew his .357. "I'm ready."

He crept toward the gate, keeping his pistol close to his side. "Excuse me. Can I help you with something?"

The man spun around, the phone still at his ear. "Thank you, Mr. Milani."

How in the hell had the reporter gotten Rowan on the phone? "I said, can I help you with something?"

The man hung up the phone. "Jack McKenzie here, with FOX News. I've just spoken to Mr. Milani about interviewing him. He agreed. You must be his friends."

He replied. "Who we are is none of your business, and there is no way Rowan agreed to be interviewed."

McKenzie feigned surprise. "Oh, so Mr. Milani *is* here. That's great news. I've been wanting to speak with him ever since Ralph Johnston first told me about his dilemma."

He stared in momentary shock. The reporter had tricked him with ease. He raised his pistol. "Whether Rowan is here or not is immaterial, because you're leaving, right now."

Gabriel stepped up beside him, Sig at the ready. "What did you say to this bastardo? Did you tell him Rowan is here?"

"Shut up. I didn't tell him anything."

McKenzie faced them with his hands raised. "Listen, guys, I'd really like to talk to Mr. Milani. I honestly don't think you're going to shoot me, and I'm not inclined to leave."

He couldn't believe McKenzie's balls, or his brazen attitude. The bad thing was, the reporter was right, they *couldn't* shoot him out in the open, next to the road meandering along the beach properties. "Maybe we won't shoot you, but we are sure as hell going to escort you from this property."

McKenzie shrugged. "I guess you could, but wouldn't you rather I air my special on FOX without giving Mr. Milani's location to the rest of the world? And I think it'd be best if it contained the truth in his own words, don't you?"

He glared at McKenzie. They'd been had. Rowan would have their asses, but the reporter would get his way. "All right. You'll have your interview. If Rowan shoots you, it's your problem."

Gabriel erupted. "No, no, no, amigo. What are you thinking? Rowan will shoot *us."*

"You heard him. We don't have a choice."

Gabriel muttered and cursed, holstered his Sig and grabbed McKenzie by the arm. "Stinkin' gringo. It's your funeral."

He grabbed McKenzie's other arm and picked up the phone. When Angelo answered, he said, "Open the gate. Tell Rowan to meet us on the patio, *now.*" He slammed the phone down before the shrink could respond.

The gate slid open, and they escorted McKenzie down the drive, through the stillness of the house and onto the patio off the kitchen. Rowan waited, hands on hips, looking like the old Rowan, the one who'd vanished after Tora. The sight of his unshaven friend, eyes black with rage, would have cheered him under different circumstances.

He jerked the reporter to a stop. "Here he is, McKenzie. Start talking."

Rowan's gaze shifted from McKenzie to him. "Let go of him and get out."

He scowled, and Gabriel resumed cussing in Spanish. "What the hell? We're not leaving you alone with him."

Rowan tapped his left side. "I'm not worried about it."

"All right, whatever you say." He let go of McKenzie. "We'll wait outside."

Rowan glowered at McKenzie. "You managed to fuck around with those two and get in here. So what the hell do you want from me?"

McKenzie replied. "Can we sit down and have a conversation? I've looked forward to this moment for a long time, Mr. Milani. I want the world to know you're innocent. You deserve to have your story told, and that's what I intend to do."

He took two steps, clenched his jaws in anticipation of the pain, and grasped McKenzie's shirt collar. "You know, they really shouldn't have left you alone with me." He twisted the collar tight. "Did it ever occur to you that I don't want or need *my story* told?"

McKenzie swallowed hard against his fist and took a step back. His voice croaked. "No, can't say the thought ever crossed my mind."

He let go of the shirt and worked at controlling his breathing and the rage. But it felt goddamned invigorating, and besides, he'd rather choke the reporter than talk to him. He pointed at the door before he chose to indulge himself. "Now you know. Get your ass back to DC or New York and find another story."

McKenzie coughed. "No, you don't understand. I have the utmost respect for you, and I've done my research. Your story *needs* telling. The country ought to know what you've done, what you've sacrificed."

Why couldn't the dumb bastard get it? "I said, *I don't want my story told.*"

"Look Mr. Milani, I discovered the original intelligence community connection to Shemal. I've identified the man who ran the scam on you from behind the scenes. The country needs to know about that, too."

He glared at McKenzie and tried to hold onto the rage. "Who?"

The reporter gestured at the deck chairs. "Please, can we sit, just for a few minutes?"

He took a deep breath and heaved a sigh. "Sure. Why not. Have a seat. Let's *chat.*"

McKenzie sat down. "Thank you."

He slouched into the adjacent chair. "OK. Your few minutes are running. Start talking."

"The man behind the curtain, pulling levers from the beginning, is CIA Director Oscar Abramson."

He gazed at the dark clouds piling up in the southeast, stirring a breeze and bringing the scent of rain. "Abramson? How did you figure that out?"

"I dug deep, found out he's known Shemal for thirty years or so. He's a closet Muslim convert and attends mosques that preach the subjugation of the country to Islam."

"Yeah, the Brotherhood's enduring wet dream. Good luck convincing anyone else."

"You may be surprised to know FBI Director Berenger has this information as well."

He sneered. "I've found a huge disparity between Berenger having information and acting on it. As in, she doesn't."

"She works within the framework of the law, which is something you seem to have a tough time with of late. Who got you out of jail in Houston?"

He didn't intend to answer for his actions, but the reporter had guts, he'd give him that. "I don't know. Wish I did though, so I could say thanks."

McKenzie twirled a forefinger. "How can you afford a place like this?"

He raised a brow. "I thought you said you'd done your research. Guess you'll have to keep digging."

"How did you come across Vincent Black as your attorney?"

"He showed up and said he wanted to represent me. I wasn't going to refuse."

"Detective Matthews swears the Mafia helped you."

He laughed and shook his head. "Matthews is bat-shit crazy."

Mckenzie said, "Maybe it has something to do with the concussion you gave him."

He shrugged. "You never know."

"I know you confessed to those killings in Houston; to Agent Foster, Director Berenger, and Detective Matthews. Yet you walked out of Harris County Jail a free man."

“Weird shit happens to me all the time. Like waking up one day and hearing that I’m the country’s most-wanted home-grown terrorist. Or being labeled an enemy combatant and getting renditioned to Tora, courtesy of my own government.”

“But you did kill those seven people.”

“And I’m sure you know, I told every single interrogator that I was doing the job two Presidents hired me to do.”

“You know, I spoke to Ms. Stratton.”

“How is the dramatic redhead getting along?”

“She seems to be doing quite well. But you probably already know that.”

“Nope. I ditched her when I left Kauai.”

But Mr. Milani, your initial stay in Quantico’s brig came about because you surrendered on her behalf. Obviously you had feelings for her.”

“Biggest mistake I ever made.”

“Love of a woman can make a man do things he wouldn’t normally consider.”

“You don’t know the half of it.”

“If it’s any consolation, Ms. Stratton appears to share your dearth of feelings. She told me you were a difficult man, and she has a new boyfriend.”

“Your minutes are running out. What’s the point of this conversation?”

McKenzie fiddled with a flag pin on his shirt pocket. “Years ago, you had a problem with speed, on a Harley, if my research is worth anything. Lost your driver’s license eventually, didn’t you? Rumors floated around about your affinity for whiskey. Specifically, single barrel Jack Daniel’s, correct?”

The reporter had done his homework too well. “None of this is any of your fucking business, and not anything the world needs to know about me.”

McKenzie kept pushing. “First you lost everything on 9/11. It’s happened to you again. Tell me, how does a man like you adjust to losing everything?”

He searched for another flippant answer, but nothing came to him. “We’re done talking. You need to get out. Now.”

McKenzie kept going. “Losing everything the way you did, that’s gotta be hard on a guy like you. Maybe your ego is what’s driven your pursuit of so-called justice.”

He pushed himself out of the chair. “You can think what you like, but we’re finished.”

McKenzie stood up and held out his hand. “Thank you for talking with me, Mr. Milani.”

He ignored the hand and instead ripped the flag pin from McKenzie’s shirt pocket. “You need to leave before I decide to wreck more than your little video camera.”

McKenzie stumbled and grasped at his pocket. “You don’t miss a trick, do you?”

“Get out. Don’t come back.”

McKenzie nodded. “Goodbye, Mr. Milani. I do appreciate your time.”

He didn’t answer, just watched the reporter pull open the patio door and enter the house. Michael appeared, gave him thumbs-up, and closed the door. He turned away and headed for the beach.

Two Days Later
FBI Headquarters, Washington, DC
Berenger placed her hands on her desktop, folded them together, and gazed at McKenzie and Harandi, seated across from her. “Jack, I am not sure how to address the foolhardiness of your approach to Milani.”

McKenzie frowned. “Sometimes the direct approach is most effective. Besides, I was never in any real danger, either from Milani or his colleagues.”

Harandi spoke up. "Director Berenger is correct, Jack. Did you forget about Milani killing Rodney Ainsley? Or how Patricia Hennessey died? He did a number on me at ADX Florence and if he hadn't been so weak, I don't know what might have happened."

McKenzie retorted. "I am a fairly good judge of character, and neither of Milani's colleagues were interested in harming me. They were infinitely more concerned about how my presence would upset Milani."

Berenger stepped in. "We can argue the wisdom of your choices all day. More importantly, were you able to gain anything from your interview? I have to ask, since we don't have access to the video recording you attempted."

McKenzie replied. "I gained valuable insight into his psyche. He simply doesn't give up *any* information and in addition to that, he has a wonderfully dry sense of humor."

Harandi chuckled. "Either of us could have confirmed that and saved you a lot of time and effort. Except, your analysis is erroneous in one regard. I don't think Milani possesses anything remotely resembling a sense of humor."

Berenger said, "Enough, you two. In essence, you didn't get anywhere. Would you agree, Jack?"

McKenzie argued. "I wouldn't say that. I quite enjoyed sparring with him, until near the end of our conversation. He deeply resents any intrusion into his past. I regret my final statements. Next time, I'll utilize more subtle tactics."

Harandi snorted, and Berenger shot him a quick glare before she addressed McKenzie. "There will not be a *next time.* You're fortunate to return without injury, and probably damn lucky you returned at all."

McKenzie replied. "For heaven's sake, Leigh. How many times must I remind you that I've been doing this kind of work for a long time? I think the man I spoke with is different than the one either of you encountered."

She couldn't understand his strange naiveté. "Trust me, Milani hasn't changed. You've been fooled by his ability to deceive."

Harandi said, "I have to concur. Milani is a dangerous adversary. I've tried over and over to get through to him based on our shared history and finally had to accept that he's beyond any kind of redemption."

McKenzie arched a brow at Harandi. "Yes, of course, Milani is a one-of-a-kind warrior, and I guess you could say he's a deeply flawed human being. But beyond redemption? He made it clear to me, in so many words, that what he wants is actually very simple."

Berenger forced her hands to relax and staved off her frustration. "What does Milani want, Jack? Make it quick, because I have work to do."

McKenzie replied. "Milani wants to be left alone. Period. End of story." He shrugged. "Maybe it's the end of my story with him. Guess I have to think about that, but I believe his wishes should be honored. He's suffered plenty, in my book."

She'd heard more than enough about what Milani needed. "If that's what he wanted, he could have chosen a different course. But that's a topic for another time."

Harandi said, "What's next, Director? Want me to take a crack at Milani again?"

She had other plans, but no way would she share them with Harandi. He'd play hell getting her to trust him again. "No, I'd like you and Jack to return to Houston. Milani's attorney is scheduled to return after Christmas. I still believe he may have played a part in Milani's release."

Harandi replied. "I'll hunt him down for an interview. What about the police department? For evidence to disappear, or become non-existent, someone on the inside had to cooperate."

Berenger said, "True. When you were in Houston pursuing Milani, were you able to establish a rapport with anyone besides Matthews?"

Harandi stroked his goatee. "Now that you mention it, I spent an evening at dinner with Matthews and his captain, Shirley Lavoe. Dinner was her way of apologizing for my encounter with the PD's SWAT team."

Berenger replied. "Perhaps you could touch base with her. She must have some kind of handle on what goes on and might direct you to places and or people we wouldn't connect with otherwise."

McKenzie added, "David, this is a great idea. You may be able to reach out to Matthews again as well, and explore some of his claims."

Harandi replied. "I'm open to whatever needs doing."

Berenger eyed Harandi, pretending to consider. "Do you have plans for Christmas?"

Sadness flitted across Harandi's face. "I've got no plans."

"Excellent. I'd like you to remain in Houston indefinitely. Unraveling the subterfuge that allowed Milani to walk away is going to require some serious covert investigation. I trust your skills in that department, Mr. Harandi."

Harandi shoved back his chair and stood up. "I'm looking forward to the challenge." He held out his hand. "Thank you for allowing me to rejoin the investigation. I appreciate it."

She gripped his hand in a firm shake. "Welcome back, Mr. Harandi. I'm looking forward to making some real progress in several areas of our joint venture."

"I am as well, Director. I'll stay in touch."

McKenzie stood and clapped Harandi on the back. "I'm glad you're back, David. We make a great team."

Berenger ushered them both to the door, regretting that she couldn't kiss McKenzie in front of Harandi. "Goodbye, Jack. Mr. Harandi, we'll talk again soon." She waited until they'd left her office before allowing herself a satisfied smile. While McKenzie's so-called interview with Milani had proven fruitless, his surprise encounter with Milani's colleagues was pure gold.

She checked her calendar. Christmas was barely two weeks away, giving her just enough time to organize her strategy. At some opportune moment, she'd thank Harandi for insisting she bring McKenzie into their investigation. Who'd have guessed how that singular act would change so many things for her, both personally and professionally?

Christmas Eve
Key West, FL
Rowan heard Danielle's ringtone and felt his phone vibrating before he woke up. He winced when he stretched, groaned as he turned, and fumbled for the phone lying somewhere close to him. He opened one eye. Weak light glowed behind the wooden blinds, so he guessed it must be close to sunrise. He squinted at his phone and answered as panic set in. Something must be wrong. "Hey Danielle, are you OK?"

"Hi Rowan. I'm all right. I had to call, though. We need to talk."

He lay flat on his back and blinked at the ceiling. His phone put the time at 6:15 a.m., which qualified as the middle of the night in Seattle. "OK, sure, we can talk." He yawned. "What's going on? Have you been to bed yet?"

"No, I can't sleep, I keep thinking about… about certain things. Rowan, we need to talk, in person. I can't, um, I'll explain when I see you."

She sounded damn near desperate, but why? The possibilities flooding his half-awake mind filled him with dread. "Hey, don't worry. I can fly to Seattle today."

She sniffed, and he wondered if she'd started crying. "I'm sorry. I don't mean to bother you, especially today. You probably have plans for Christmas. It's just, *I have to see you.* It's important."

"You're not bothering me. I'll be there this afternoon. I'm not sure what time, but I'll call when I'm close. Take it easy, OK? Try to get some sleep, and I'll talk to you in a few hours."

Hysteria edged her voice. "Wait, don't hang up. You need my address, and directions."

"Danielle, it's me, remember? I've got your address, and I know how to get to your townhouse. Promise me you'll call if you need to, OK?"

"I'll be all right. Thank you, for coming today. I love you. Bye," she whispered.

"I love you, and I'll see you in a while." He ended the call and yawned again. What the hell did she need to tell him that couldn't wait? He stared at the ceiling, unable to shake a sick feeling of dread, settling in his gut like a lead weight.

He clenched his jaws, forced himself upright, and sat on the edge of the bed. He'd better get moving and tell Angelo he'd be gone for at least the day. Gino and Roberto had headed to Chicago to spend Christmas with family a couple days earlier. Mike and Asal and Gabriel were going to spend Christmas with everyone in Chicago, and Johnny had sent the jet back for them. And now he'd fuck everything up.

He found Angelo where the shrink spent every morning, on the patio with coffee and a notebook and pen. "Good morning, Doc."

Angelo gazed at him from beneath furrowed brows. "Good morning, Rowan. Heading for a walk on the beach? I made fresh coffee, if you want to take a cup with you."

"Nah, I don't have time for a walk. Danielle called. I'm flying to Seattle and just wanted to let you know. I'm not sure when I'll be back. Probably tomorrow."

Angelo raised his coffee cup. "Then I will wish you both a Merry Christmas now. Take good care and enjoy the holiday with Danielle. I am quite content here on my own."

"Thanks, Doc, and same to you. Merry Christmas, or whatever. I'll see you in a day or two." He left Angelo slurping coffee and headed back into the house. Christmas hadn't meant anything to him in a long time. He heaved a sigh and shoved his bitter thoughts aside.

He needed to call Mike and tell him about the change in plans. Maybe Mike and Asal and Gabriel would make the trip with him. On the way back, they could stop in Chicago. That way his friends wouldn't miss celebrating Christmas, and he could be alone on the jet for a while. Depending on what Danielle wanted to talk about, he might appreciate that.

Two hours later, he stared out the window of the Lear 75 and wished he could fall asleep. Hell, even cuffed and shackled, flying from ADX Florence to Houston, he couldn't stay awake. This time, though, every time he closed his eyes, their brief conversation played over and over in his mind.

She'd sounded unhappy, or desperate, or *something* he couldn't quite put his finger on. Maybe she'd made up her mind about being with her engineer friend and wanted to tell him in person. After all, he'd as much as told her to go for it. If that was her choice, he'd walk away, and hate himself for the rest of his worthless, empty life. A light touch on his shoulder startled him. He realized his fists were clenched, and he was breathing hard. He turned and looked up. "What?"

Michael gave him a grim stare. "I just got a call from one of Johnny's crew. We've got a problem."

"Great. What's going on?"

Michael sat down in the seat facing his. "You aren't going to believe this. About an hour ago, a shitload of FBI agents swarmed your house. They marched Angelo out in cuffs and took off with him."

He stared back at Mike. "What the hell. Why would Berenger come after me now?"

"I don't know, brother. You think Harandi ratted on you somehow? Or maybe that damned reporter found something in Houston?"

He tried to sort it out. "Harandi might have decided to save his own ass and give up Johnny to Berenger. We need to call Chad."

"I'll get on that right away. You think Angelo might slip up, or give Berenger's goons any idea where you are?"

"No, Angelo's solid. He'll psychoanalyze every agent and talk them in all kinds of circles. I'd almost like to be a fly on the wall for that. Besides, they won't hold onto him. Why would they?"

Michael shrugged. "Who the hell knows? You wanna keep going to Seattle? Berenger will probably send agents there next."

He tamped down the panic churning through his mind. "Yeah, I have to get to Seattle. But you're right. When we get there, you and Asal scope out the coffee shop where Danielle works. Gabriel and I will check out her townhouse. I need to see her, at least for a few minutes, then we've got to get out of the country."

Michael spoke quietly. "You want to head for Dubai?"

"I don't think we have a choice. You talk to Gabriel and Asal, and put things in motion with Chad. I'm calling Harandi. If he fucked us over, he's going to pay." Michael nodded his assent and headed back down the aisle of the aircraft.

He took a deep breath, blew it out in a gusty sigh, and willed his heart rate to slow before pulling his phone from his shirt pocket and punching the contact he'd never, *ever* planned to use.

Harandi answered right away. "Rowan, I'm glad you called. Merry Christmas."

"What the hell did you do? This time, *I'd* like an explanation. And no CIA double-speak, goddamn it. Just the truth."

"What are you talking about? I'm in Houston, doing my best to slow down Berenger and McKenzie's investigation, on orders from your partner. I thought you knew."

"I don't believe you."

"Rowan, please. Tell me what you're talking about. I'm in the dark here."

"This morning, after I left Key West, a bunch of my *former colleagues* arrived. No one was home except Angelo, and they took him into custody. So now I'm asking you one more time, *what did you do?"*

Harandi persisted. "Listen, Rowan, I didn't do anything. I had no idea Berenger was setting up anything like that. McKenzie hasn't said a word, and I don't think he'd be in favor of her pulling some kind of raid to drag you back into custody."

"Berenger has no reason to come after me unless *you* gave her one."

"For crying out loud, you just don't listen, do you? I haven't told Berenger squat, and I won't. But you might want to think about the fact that McKenzie saw your two buddies, Michael and Gabriel, when he paid you a visit."

He gripped the arm of the seat as stunned realization hit him. "By God, for the first time, I don't think you're lying."

"Oh come on, Rowan. Of course I'm not lying. Berenger didn't take me into her confidence about this. I'm sorry. If she had, you'd have known. I'm glad you weren't there."

"You and me both," he muttered. "Find a reason to call Berenger. Let me know what she's planning next, if you can find out."

"I'll do my best. Stay safe, wherever you are. I'll be in touch."

"Yeah, I'll stay safe, don't you worry."

Mid-Afternoon
Seattle, WA
Tom swung his Outback into Danielle's driveway and shoved the gearshift into Park with extra satisfaction. He'd spent until noon tying up numerous loose ends on the project he'd been under the gun to finish for the previous six weeks. A voice mail from Danielle had prompted him to rush home, load the car with presents, and head out. She'd sounded stressed and upset. *I'm not sure I can make the trip to Orcas with you. I'm sorry.* He needed to see her and find out what had happened.

He hoped Milani hadn't done something stupid to ruin the holiday. He'd looked forward to this Christmas more than practically any other, and he was sick of Milani wrecking things for both of them. He stared at Danielle's townhouse. He'd still like to meet the guy, just once, and give him a piece of his mind. He shoved aside his misgivings and decided that no matter what, he'd convince her to come with him.

He had everything worked out. In a few hours, he'd be introducing her to his family. They'd all pile into a couple of vehicles for a tour of lights and come back home for eggnog and homemade Christmas cookies. He was pumped about making Danielle's entire holiday memorable and happy. And for the first time in five long years, he wouldn't feel like the odd man out.

He heard Leo's excited woofing when he rang the bell. Danielle opened the door. "Tom, hi. Come in. Did you get my message?"

"Hi Dani. Hey Leo, my buddy." He knelt to rough up the Rottie and turned his cheek for a couple swipes from the dog's tongue. He looked up at Danielle. "I got your message. Are you all right? Ready for your first Orcas Island Christmas?"

Her eyes went wide and she wrung her hands. "Oh Tom, I'm so sorry. I just don't know if I can go with you."

He stood up. “Hey, come on. Let’s head out. You can explain what’s going on while we drive. You need a break and some time to relax.”

The doorbell chimed and she gasped. “Oh no. You shouldn’t be here.”

“Wait a second…”

She interrupted him and grabbed his arm. “Don’t, um, just don’t provoke him. Oh my God, this wasn’t supposed to happen.”

Her genuine fear alarmed him. “Don’t provoke who? Dani, what’s going on?”

The doorbell chimed again, and she pushed him away. “Please, sit down. Hang onto Leo for me.”

He took a seat on one of the overstuffed chairs he’d helped her pick out at a flea market and took a firm hold on Leo’s collar when the big dog woofed. “Leo, sit. Stay. Let’s see what the heck is going on.” Danielle opened the door, and his heart sank as he watched her step into the arms of the man he’d despised since the first time he read about him.

Milani, in a black leather bomber jacket and black jeans, folded Danielle protectively against him while his gaze swept the room. When Milani’s dark eyes focused on him, the hair rose on his arms, and his heart rate ticked up. Milani didn’t look away, and he couldn’t either. He opened his mouth, remembered Danielle’s admonition, and closed it. The man terrified him, made him want to be anywhere else, and they hadn’t exchanged a single word.

When Milani’s gaze shifted to Danielle, he stared, transfixed, as the ferocious demeanor mellowed. Danielle cupped the frightening man’s face in her hands and whispered something. Milani smiled and then kissed her. He watched, sick inside, as they embraced. They fit together in the intimate, familiar way of lovers who knew each other’s bodies.

She’d never clung to him like that. He should be the one reveling in the feel of her breasts and hips against his body. He’d been patient and kind, there for her whenever she needed someone to talk to or simply be with. He loved her and deserved a chance to give her a good life. A happy, secure life, filled with family and friends.

He'd dreamed about making her part of his family; about making a family with her. He'd planned carefully and taken things slowly, hoping she'd figure out that he'd meant it when he told her he loved her. But instead, for reasons he'd never understand, she remained committed to the man who'd thrown her away, again and again.

Milani deepened the kiss and caressed her body, claiming her. Danielle responded, pressing closer. The passion between them lit the room. He felt the heat and couldn't drag his eyes away. That's when he knew for sure. He'd been fooling himself, hoping for something that was never going to happen. How could he have been so stupid? The sweet love he had for Danielle flickered like a candle next to the wildfire burning in the man holding her.

Danielle ended the kiss and laid her head on Milani's chest. He couldn't deny the truth of what he'd been forced to witness. Leo whined and growled. He patted the broad head. The Rottie had figured it out too.

Rowan stepped further into Danielle's living room, keeping one arm around her shoulders. He gazed at the man hunched on a chair, clutching the collar of the huge Rottweiler sitting beside him.

Danielle said, "Rowan, this is my friend, Tom Hanford. Tom, this is Rowan Milani."

Hanford stood up and stuck out his hand. "Nice to meet you."

Rowan tried and failed to keep the impatience, the urgency to get the hell out of the country, to himself. "Yeah, right. I'm sure." While they shook hands, he couldn't resist assessing her friend. They were the same height and shared a similar build, although

Hanford had him by a few pounds. He didn't think Hanford liked him, which made their feelings similar, too.

Danielle squeezed his hand so hard it hurt. "Rowan, please."

He glanced at her, raised a brow, and sighed before turning back to Hanford. "Nice to meet you."

Danielle murmured, "Thank you," and snapped her fingers. "Leo, come." The dog leaped to her side. "Good boy. Sit. Say hello to Rowan."

The Rottweiler sat squarely in front of him, barked once, and lifted a paw. He took the paw, then scratched the dog's head. "This is one hell of a mutt, Danielle. But hey, we need to…"

Gabriel burst through the door and slid past him, blustering. "You gonna stand here all day? Mike and Asal are finishing up their security checks at the coffee shop. Everything's cool here."

Danielle pulled away from him. "Gabriel, it's so good to see you." She hugged his burly friend and pecked his cheek. "I hope your family is doing well."

Gabriel hugged Danielle. "Merry Christmas sweetheart. My family is fine. You look fantastic. Seattle agrees with you, no?"

Danielle replied. "It's been nice."

Rowan had heard enough. "Hey, Danielle, I'm ready to talk, but we don't have much time. Something's come up and I can't stay long."

Her face paled, highlighting the dark hollows beneath her eyes. "Oh, OK." She took his hand and led him through the living room, down a carpeted hallway to her bedroom. She sat on the edge of the bed and patted the blue and yellow comforter. "Sit beside me, please."

He sat next to her, on edge, sweating, expecting to hear boots clumping through the house, and agents shouting orders to surrender. "OK. Let's talk."

Tears glimmered in her eyes and slid down her cheeks. Her lips quivered. "I wanted, um, I couldn't tell you on the phone. I needed to see you."

He wished she'd get it over with, so he could leave knowing she'd be all right. He'd deal with his pain later, alone, the way he always did. "I'm here, and I'm listening. Please tell me what's going on."

She gave him a shy smile. "I'm sorry. It seems like I cry all the time now, because I'm pregnant. We're going to have a baby."

Shock burned and buzzed from the top of his head through his entire body. He took a shallow breath and whispered, "Are you sure?"

She nodded. "Yes. I sort of knew a month ago. I bought a pregnancy test, but I waited until yesterday to check. I couldn't sleep, thinking about it." She smiled again, but more tears spilled down her cheeks. "I can't button my pants, and I'm exhausted all the time."

He'd forgotten how it felt; the crazy, dopey joy rolling through his mind and bursting in his heart. More than a decade ago, he'd been delirious with it. "Let me see, it's been how long since we, uh?"

"It's been just over two months since we were together in Chicago."

"That's right," he muttered. A fierce instinct to protect her overwhelmed him. He drew her into his arms and held her tight.

She wrapped her arms around him, and he felt her trembling. "I've been so worried, all this time. I didn't know what to do."

He stroked her hair while their new reality settled deep into his heart and mind. "Shh, hush, it's all right. You don't have to worry. You don't have to do anything."

She melted against him. "I hope you're not angry with me."

He drew away, frowning. "Angry with you? No. Why would you think that?"

She picked at the comforter and didn't look at him. "Because now you'll feel obligated to take care of me. I'll be in your way or keep you from doing what you need to for Mr. Giacopino. Especially now, since you have to leave."

He tipped her chin up and saw the uncertainty in her eyes. *"Obligated?* For God's sake, Danielle, I *want* to take care of you. You and our baby mean everything to me." He crushed her close again. "We're a family. You're *my* family."

"I'm so glad," she whispered, then pushed him away. "I know you need to get going. Thanks for coming all this way, especially right before Christmas. I couldn't tell you on the phone, and I just couldn't wait any longer."

He met her red-rimmed eyes. "Nothing and *no one* is going to keep us apart anymore. When I leave, you're coming with me."

She leaned against him and he heard the relief in her voice. "I've wanted to be with you for so long." She hesitated. "But it wouldn't be right for me to leave without giving Small-Batch a thirty-day notice. Later, I can meet you wherever you want."

He smoothed the remnants of her tears away with gentle fingers and tried to shake the vision of Berenger and her agents closing in. "I'm sorry, there's no time for that. For some reason the FBI wants to detain Gabriel and Mike. Maybe me, too. I'll explain as much as I know, I promise. But we need to leave, right now."

She sat up straight and nodded. "All right. I keep a carryon bag packed, so I'm good. Tom can take Leo, for a while." She touched his cheek. "You know I don't care where we go. I just want to be with you."

He shoved off the bed and grasped her hand. She stood up and faced him. The trust in her eyes scared the hell out of him. He hung onto her hand and smiled. "OK, Danielle. We're out of here." They left her bedroom and headed down the hallway, her hand firmly in his. He didn't know how they'd handle their new future, or even the next few hours. But he did know one thing. No one could take away his family. Not this time. He'd make damn sure of that.

THE END

The Rowan Milani Chronicles continue…

About Mary Yungeberg

Mary has been an avid writer all her life. After graduating from Iowa State University with a B.S. in Animal Science and almost a minor in English, she pursued several careers that included selling hybrid swine breeding stock, professional resume writing, and the airline industry. Along the way, she wrote numerous freelance articles, raised two rambunctious sons, and showed her National Show Horses and Arabians. In 2008, on an Alaska cruise, relaxing for the first time in decades, she made the decision to pursue the career she'd always dreamed of: writing thrillers.

CONSUMMATE BETRAYAL introduces readers to the world of Rowan Milani, decorated FBI agent and secret, presidential assassin. UNHOLY RETRIBUTION explores the dark side of Rowan's character and the catastrophic consequences of his choices. A DIFFERENT MAN chronicles Rowan's determination to change course. TERMINAL REDEMPTION follows Rowan on a globe-hopping journey toward his destiny. THE MAN BEHIND THE SHADOWS is the most recent title of the series. All of Mary's books are available in print and digital formats.

Mary shot a pistol for the first time while researching Consummate Betrayal. The experience changed her life. She is an active member of the DC Project, a nonpartisan group of diverse women from every walk of life educating and advocating for the Second Amendment on a national and state level. She is passionate about empowering women to defend themselves, and you'll often find her at the shooting range encouraging others as they develop their skills.

Mary lives in the great state of South Dakota with her husband Ernie and Lucy, an intemperate Rat Terrier who runs their household. When she's not working on the next installment of the Rowan Milani Chronicles, you may see her tearing up the pavement in her black Mustang convertible attempting the fine art of autocross, enjoying a glass of wine with friends, or busy with her family.

Mary Yungeberg

Photo by A. Miller, USMC

For more information about the Rowan Milani Chronicles,
visit Mary's website: MaryYungeberg.com

Made in the USA
Monee, IL
20 March 2023

29950004R00304